LUCID

BOOK 2

NEW YORK TIMES BESTSELLING AUTHOR

P.T. MICHELLE

LUCID

COPYRIGHT

2012 BY P.T. MICHELLE

Print ISBN-10: 11939672112
Print ISBN-13: 9781939672117

To stay informed when the next **P.T. Michelle** book will be released, join P.T.'s free newsletter http://bit.ly/11tqAQN

SERIES READING ORDER

Brightest Kind of Darkness Series

ETHAN *
BRIGHTEST KIND OF DARKNESS
LUCID
DESTINY
DESIRE
AWAKEN

*ETHAN is a prequel that delves deeper into Ethan's background. It's best read **after** BRIGHTEST KIND OF DARKNESS.

The Brightest Kind of Darkness series is best suited for readers 16+.

CHAPTER 1

"*D*id you just plug your flat iron in my car charger?" I rolled my eyes at Lainey brushing rose blush across her cheeks in fast swipes while holding the iron in her other hand. "Only you would multitask like this. No wonder you're always late for school."

She tore an exasperated glance from her image in the sun visor's lighted mirror and jabbed the iron in the air like a fencer's foil. "I wouldn't be doing this in the car if you hadn't tried to wake the whole neighborhood with your horn."

Lainey might be my best friend, but this was why we'd never shared rides to school, even though our neighborhoods were only five miles apart. I owned my *own* lateness, not someone else's.

I turned my attention back to the steady stream of bustling traffic on Highway 29 and shrugged. "I wouldn't have had to do it if you'd come out of your house on time."

Lainey clamped the flat iron around a hank of wavy auburn hair, then slowly slid it to the end before grabbing another wavy chunk. "And here I thought having you take me to school would be less stressful than my dad."

"Why? Does your dad's patrol car cramp your style?" I snickered and pressed on my brake to slow for the line of stopped cars when my attention snagged on a red sports car doing the same a couple of lanes over. Only, instead of slowing, the car's front end jerked, then lifted up, as if something big had pushed it out of the way.

"Did you see that?" I whispered just as the red car's front end landed partway in another lane. A silver car slammed into the red car's back fender. Tires squealed…metal crunched. The red car spun until its front end crashed into the front of the silver car in a shower of headlight glass. More tires screeched, and oncoming cars veered to avoid the collision.

But my attention wasn't on the accident or the cars slowing down to rubberneck. My gaze was locked on the huge spinning image that had catapulted from the bulging space in the air not more than twenty feet above the red car. A yellow, gray, black, and skin-colored "blur" barreled toward the red car in a tumble of vicious fists, bunched muscles, feathers, claws, and scales… and blood. Lots of blood. Surrounded by puffs of fog, the two massive beings' velocity would flatten the red car's roof like a piece of tinfoil.

My heart lodged in my throat and I jammed my finger on the window button. I ignored the biting December wind and clasped my steering wheel in a death grip to lean out the window and scream, "Get out of your car!"

I mentally braced and winced, waiting for the fighting duo to hit. When the strange beings and their cloud of haze slammed into the red car, they disintegrated in a poof of nothingness. I blinked rapidly, staring at the unmarred roof. Jerking my gaze to the airspace above the car, I shook my head. No bubble or distortions warped the fluffy white clouds and clear blue sky beyond. Had I imagined all of it? A horn blared behind me at the same time Lainey yanked at my arm.

"Nara!" Lainey's pitch elevated as she shook me harder. "I've called nine-one-one to report the accident, but you need to move. People are getting pissed at the rubberneckers."

My hands trembled. I slowly pushed on the gas pedal. "Did you see if the people were okay?"

"They looked like they were fine," Lainey said in a shaky voice. She'd unplugged her flat iron, and since I'd glanced her way had yanked hard at her seatbelt at least three times to make sure it caught properly. She was probably reliving her own car accident from a few weeks ago. "Why did you yell for them to get out of their car? With all that traffic around, they could've been killed if they had."

I kept glancing in my rearview mirror at the red car, then back to the road. "Didn't you see that?"

"See what? I saw the red car spin around and hit the silver car, if that's what you're talking about." Lainey's brow furrowed. "You okay, Nara? You're acting like you've never seen a car accident before."

My gaze snapped to the rearview mirror once more. *Not an accident I wasn't expecting. Or that crazy hallucination.*

∼

LATER THAT DAY, I got a text I *was* expecting.

Adam [Omni Admin] – 3:45 p.m. ∼ The feather message doesn't exist. You must be mistaken.

Even though I'd seen these same words in my dream last night, I ignored the swell of people bolting out of school around me as I shuddered against the cold wind. The message board owner's snappy reply had made me grind my teeth in my dream. Seeing it in real time today was like coarse salt scrubbed into a festering wound. I punched the keys, cutting and pasting the response I'd typed in my phone the moment I woke this morning, then hit Send.

*Me – 3:46 p.m. ∼ There was **definitely** a post on your message board from two years ago. I ran across it a few weeks back. The poster asked if anyone had experienced a feather tattoo suddenly appearing on their shoulder. Here's the link to the cached info from the Internet. I'm not asking you to provide an email address. I'd just like to be able to private message the original poster.*

"Nara," Lainey said.

Instead of hitting Send like I'd done in my dream, I preempted the response the owner would eventually send back to me late in the day.

3

Me – 3:46 p.m. ~ And before you tell me "The person deleted their profile, so there's no way you can provide that info" —

"Nara! We're freezing our asses off out here for a reason," Lainey hissed in a low tone. "Quit Ethan-texting and pay attention."

My fingers paused over the keyboard. "Huh? This isn't Ethan—" I began, but then Lainey jerked her head in stiff-neck fashion at a couple who'd passed, telling me to look. I followed her line of sight to Jared, her ex, who was snuggling a platinum blonde, apparently to keep her warm against the cold wind.

The girl was pretty in a plastic-y kind of way. I folded my frozen fingers into a fist to warm them and shrugged. "She's not all that."

"Her hand," Lainey huffed. She wiggled her gloved fingers. "Did you see her left hand? Was she wearing his class ring?"

I returned my attention to my phone and waved absently, saying as I finished typing my text message, "It's not. It's some ring she picked up in an antique shop."

Me – 3:47 p.m. ~ I'm sure you have a way to get to the history through your administrative panel. PLEASE. This is pretty important.

At the same time I hit Send, Lainey grabbed my arm in a grip worthy of a Blue Ridge wrestler. "Antique store?" Auburn eyebrows raised, hope flickered through her brown eyes. "What makes you say that?"

Every muscle inside me tensed. I'd been so distracted with the message board guy that I hadn't thought to make up something other than the truth to squelch Lainey's angsting. I wouldn't learn the truth from Lainey about the ring until the end of the day, when she called me at nine tonight with the news.

Swallowing past the sudden knot in my throat, I made a goofy face. "Uh, 'cause I dreamed it?"

Lainey dropped her hand and scowled. "Don't make up crap on my account. If you didn't want to help, you could've just said so. You didn't even look as they passed."

While part of me heaved a silent sigh of relief that Lainey thought I was joking, another part of me wished I could tell her.

I really did dream it, Lainey, because I have this gift. I dream my entire next day every night when I go to sleep. That's why I was freaked by the accident this morning. I hadn't dreamed about it. Nothing surprises me. Ever. Well, until I recently had a deadly run-in with Fate over my meddling in people's lives in order to save them from strange accidents—including your *life, by-the way. You're welcome!* I met Lainey's frustrated gaze and simply said, "Sorry, Lainey. I was just distracted by this project I'm working on."

"Project? You weren't texting Ethan?"

By the squeak in her voice, I had just made another *major* best friend faux pas. Even though the crowd had thinned, I stepped close and gripped her hand. "What I meant to say was, I think you're going about getting over Jared all wrong. You need to find something else to focus on, not stress over a guy who's proven he's not worth your time."

Tears filled her eyes and she quickly brushed them away. "Just because I dumped Jared for cheating with Sophia doesn't mean I can just cut off how I feel about him, Nara. I've tried, but—" She paused and waved in the direction Jared and his new girlfriend had headed. "Look how fast he replaced me. The thought he might've given her his ring after only a few days with her when I never even got to see the damn thing after several weeks of dating...it just hurts."

I nodded as she sniffed. "I get it, but that's just another reason to move on. He's a jerk. Can you at least try to put him out of your mind?" It didn't help that soccer season was over and we were in the weird in-between hiatus before indoor season began. It gave Lainey too much free time to get worked up about Jared-related stuff.

If Ethan were here, I'd enlist his help. My boyfriend also has a unique power, though neither one of us knows why he has the ability to absorb the negative energy in people's lives whenever he's around them. Just by touching you, he can make all your worries fade away. I could really use his ability to keep Lainey from angsting about Jared every five seconds. In the meantime, I needed a distraction *right now.*

Glancing past her shoulder to a guy with ash-blond hair tossing a basketball into the back of a dark blue Jeep, I nodded

in his direction. "I remember seeing that basketball player with
the new girl Jared's dating. I'm pretty sure they were a couple
before. He didn't even look at them. Seems like he's taking their
breakup okay."

Lainey cast her gaze over her shoulder and I continued in a
softer tone, "He moved on, Lainey. You can too—*aouff.*" Air
whooshed past my lips with Lainey's sudden bear hug.

"You're brilliant!" Pulling back, she glanced at the guy
again, then at me, eyes shining. "I'm going to go talk to him."

"Wait. That wasn't—" I tried to grab her arm, but Lainey
backed away before my fingers could connect.

"This is *just* what I need. Thanks, Nara."

"—what I meant..." I trailed off as she made a beeline
straight for the guy. Lainey was always so impulsive. The
whole breakup with Jared wasn't going to change that aspect of
her DNA. If anything, it seemed to intensify it.

As she lifted her hand to tap the basketball player on the
shoulder, I held my breath, unsure of what would happen next.
This part wasn't in my dream. Once I'd slipped up in front of
her, I'd improvised, which sometimes changed how events
unfolded for the rest of my day.

"You're on your own, Lainey," I whispered just as my phone
pinged with a new text. I quickly glanced at the screen,
surprised that the message board owner had gotten back with
me so soon.

Ethan – 3:45 p.m. ~ Hey, Sunshine. How are you?

Excitement spread through me. That was another unique
aspect about my boyfriend. Unlike everyone else in my life, he
never starred in my dreams. Even conversations I had with
Lainey about him didn't show up in them. Nothing with him
was a do-over. I'd missed hearing from him. He wasn't big
about talking on the phone, but ever since he got his phone,
he'd been great about texting. Recently though, his texts had
slowed to just a couple over the last few days.

*Me – 3:45 p.m. ~ I'm doing good! You've been kind of quiet. How
are things with your parents?*

*Ethan – 3:46 p.m. ~ Been working through some stuff. Headed in
the right direction at least.*

Me – 3:46 p.m. ~ That's fantastic! I'm so glad to hear it. How—

Another text from Ethan came through before I could send the question singeing a hole in my thoughts.

Ethan – 3:47 p.m. ~ I wanted to let you know. Looks like I'll be here a little longer. I know that's not what you want to hear.

My anticipation of his impending return deflated. I resisted the urge to text back the next thoughts spiraling through my head. *How much longer? I miss you so much. Did you know there's a winter dance coming soon? I'd love to go together.* My fingers hovered above the keys, shaking from more than the cold. I didn't want to make Ethan feel guilty about being gone. He needed to work things out with his parents.

They didn't know about his ability, just like my mom didn't know about mine, nor did she know that my "deserter" father had the same ability and had passed it on to me. Ethan had built-up resentment toward his mom and dad because of their inability to support him while his manifesting powers turned his life into a full-blown nightmare. His parents clung to the belief that he was highly emotional and was just acting out. I didn't want to interrupt the mending he was trying to accomplish now that he'd figured out how to deal with his ability.

Me – 3:48 p.m. ~ What matters is that you're making progress so you can be on good terms with your parents before you come back to Virginia.

Ethan – 3:49 p.m. ~ Are you sure you're okay? Is Fate leaving you alone?

My heart swelled that he still worried for me, even while he was dealing with his own personal stuff. I started to respond when Lainey came running up, bursting with excitement.

"Matt is great!"

"Matt, is it?" I teased as she tugged me into step beside her. I'd driven Lainey home yesterday, because she'd needed someone to talk to once she'd seen Jared openly pawing his new girlfriend.

"Matt agrees with me that it's awfully convenient Tarra dumped him and got together with Jared right before the winter dance."

I watched Matt drive off in his Jeep. "Convenient? I don't understand—"

"Don't you get it?" Lainey grabbed my shoulders. Wide-eyed, she shook me like she was trying to rattle the answer from my brain.

I shook my head and shrugged, waiting for her to fill me in.

"Haven't you been paying attention to the morning announcements?"

"Not really."

She rolled her eyes. "Jared and Tarra currently have the highest votes to be Ice King and Ice Queen of the winter dance."

"Is there an 'Ice Couple' award this year?" I snorted at my own joke, but quickly adopted a serious expression when Lainey narrowed her gaze. "Um, what difference does that make?"

Lainey heaved a sigh, then kicked a pebble before she continued walking. "It means, that maybe the reason Jared is suddenly so hot and heavy with Tarra is because he wants to make sure he's got the Ice King vote locked in."

I had to rush to keep up with her. The more worked-up she became, the faster she walked. "You think he's using her?"

When Lainey nodded, I gave up trying to talk logically with her about Jared. "Maybe she's using him too."

Lainey tugged her Fossil purse higher on her shoulder, then adjusted her backpack strap on the other one. "That's what Matt thinks. I'm going to his house this afternoon so we can discuss it. Did you know he lives on the far side of your neigh-borhood, near the second entrance?"

"Really?" *That's probably why I'd never seen his car before. I never took that entrance.* "Er, you're going over there?" *To discuss it?* What she really meant was...strategize. At this rate, she'd never get over Jared. "Why don't you come to CVAS with me instead? Volunteering is good for the soul. Plus, you said you wanted to see why I spend so much time there. You'll get to play with kittens and puppies," I cajoled with a winning smile, hoping to entice her. Helping out at the Central Virginia Animal

Shelter would be a perfect distraction for her until soccer started back up.

We'd stopped next to her car and she shuddered as she dug into her purse for her keys. "*And* clean up their poop. Thanks, but I'll pass. Anyway, you can't stop by the shelter today. You're coming with me."

"What?" I frowned. "Why do I have to come?"

Lainey pursed her lips. "'Cause it'll feel weird going over there by myself, silly."

And here I thought you wanted me there for a logical reason—like, to stop you from doing something you might regret later! Who was I kidding? When it came to Jared, Lainey's logic was like a circular reference in an Excel spreadsheet—permanently stuck on "no resolution." I suddenly regretted not volunteering at CVAS this afternoon. Then I'd have a valid I-have-to-work excuse. "Why can't you just be thrilled Jared and Sophia didn't end up together and let this Tarra thing go? It's not like you want to get back with him, right?" I really needed to derail her from this new—and possibly even crazier—path.

"Of course not." Lainey pointed at me with a jingle of her car keys. "And you're going!" As she unlocked her car, she glanced at my phone. "Think of your sacrifice as payment due for all the times you ignored me during your Ethan text-fests these last couple of weeks." A thoughtful expression crossed her face. "How's he liking cyber school?"

Ethan! I glanced down at my phone to see he'd sent another text. It was hard to resist looking at it, but I managed. Her question made me realize I hadn't asked him how his online schoolwork was going. Lainey didn't know his issues. Just that he was spending some needed time with family. "It's fine." Ethan was naturally smart. I was sure he'd aced all his tests.

"I'd be bored out of my mind," she said, then wrinkled her nose as she gestured toward the three ravens hanging out on top of my car. "It's like they've adopted you since Ethan left."

"They're just birds." Lainey eyed them warily and started to say something else, but I cut in, "Fine, I'll go with you. See you in an hour."

I waited until she drove off before I grabbed some kibble

from a baggie in my backpack—the last thing Lainey needed to see was me feeding them—then scattered the hard bits on my car's roof to occupy the birds. Once they began to chow down, I leaned against my door and read Ethan's text.

Ethan – 3:50 p.m. ~ You there? Don't leave me hanging here, Sunshine. I need to know you're okay.

Me – 4:00 p.m. ~ Sorry! Lainey was in a chatty mood. Fate hasn't shown up. Really, I'm good.

Of course, I hadn't had to butt into anyone's life these past couple of weeks, either. Just because I'd outsmarted Fate to keep him from killing me in my dreams didn't guarantee that he'd leave me alone while I was awake if I started interfering in people's lives again. Thankfully things had settled into uneventful normalcy.

I considered mentioning the oddness that had happened this morning since Ethan understood what it felt like to see things he couldn't explain, but decided not to. It would be too hard to explain via text, and I hadn't felt threatened in any way. I'd tell him about it once he got back.

Ethan's text came through at the same time the most dominant raven, Patch (I'd named him that because of the patch of white feathers around his right eye), walked right up behind me to lean around my shoulder, looking over it.

"This is private," I said, shooing him away before I opened Ethan's message.

Ethan – 4:01 p.m. ~ Glad to hear it. I've got to go for now. TTTWFO.

The meaning behind that very special sign-off made me tingle all over. He rarely used it, but when he did, it felt as if the sun was rising inside me. Smiling, I texted back.

Me – 4:02 p.m. ~ Cross my heart.

While I drove home, I sighed with wistful longing as I recalled the first time Ethan had used that acronym.

CHAPTER 2

 *wo weeks ago*

"ARE YOU KIDNAPPING ME?" I loved the fact I had no idea where Ethan was taking us. All I knew was we'd left our hometown of Blue Ridge behind and were heading north.

His dark blue eyes slid my way as he laid his hand casually across the steering wheel. "It's a surprise."

Instead of excitement, his gaze held something else. He'd looked at me the same way the last fifty times he'd stolen a glance—like he wanted to stamp my features in his memory.

My chest tightened and I reached over to clasp his free hand. "What kind of surprise?" I asked, my voice sounding scratchy.

He pointed our locked fingers toward the window, indicating the sunshine streaming across the dash. "It's a beautiful day. I just want to spend it alone with you." His smile was genuine, but his expression still seemed pensive.

Twenty minutes later, the rumbling Mustang took a hairpin turn, gravel pinging the car's fenders as we took what appeared to be a back access road. Sunlight dappled through the thick canopy of firs lining our path, warming the car's interior to the point I'd cracked open the window. Somewhere far off in the distance, a grill billowed a delicious mesquite aroma. Looked like others were enjoying this rare warm November day too. When I turned my nose toward the window and inhaled, my stomach suddenly growled like a bear waking up from a long winter's nap.

Releasing my hand, Ethan laughed and patted my noisy belly. "Don't worry. We're going to eat."

The easy way he laughed set my questions about his mood aside, making me smile.

I was pretty sure we were on Montpelier land, because I'd seen the "Home of James Madison" signs as we drove near the area. Montpelier was a historic landmark and private land, so I was surprised we were able to just drive in without being stopped by someone. "Um, don't we need to like ask permission to be here?"

He gave a sly half smile. "We're not actually on Montpelier property, just near it, but if anyone asks, this is when having a brother with government connections comes in handy."

"Samson got permission? Wow, that was nice of him. What's the catch?"

"Catch?"

"Yeah. Why'd he do this? Your birthday is already past and mine's not for a few weeks. Seems like a lot of trouble..."

Ethan shrugged. "I asked and he found us a way in."

I squinted in suspicion. "Just because?"

With a resigned sigh, Ethan slowed his car until we rolled to a stop in the middle of the road. "You're not going to let me surprise you, are you?"

His steady gaze made me squirm. All it took was that look to remind me I still had a hard time *not* knowing every step of my life before it happened.

I gave a sheepish smile and laced our fingers together once more, setting our hands on my thigh. "Surprise away."

Relief rolled through his features and his grip on my hand relaxed. Why was he so tense? I wondered, but then brushed aside my anxious musing. Today was about spending quality time alone. Ethan and I really hadn't had much of that since I'd faced off with Fate a couple of weeks before. As soon as my mom got home from her trip and found out about Lainey's car accident, she'd taken me on two back-to-back girls' weekend trips.

I was glad Mom and I were finally starting to reconnect, but the trips had eaten into my time with Ethan. I was definitely ready for some alone time.

I tensed when Ethan turned off the dirt road, driving straight through a narrow pathway between a group of trees. It looked so overgrown, I wondered if we were going into uncharted territory and would unknowingly plunge into a ravine. Before I had a chance to ask, the Mustang emerged from the thicket into a clearing.

A patchwork blanket of fall-colored leaves completely covered the secluded quarter acre of land surrounding a gorgeous pond. Several geese quietly maneuvered around maple leaves the size of dinner plates, while the sun sparkled off the rippling water. The idyllic scenery could have been plucked right out of a Kinkade painting.

"It's gorgeous!" I whipped out my phone, but after a couple of attempts, I frowned that my phone couldn't come close to capturing the breathtaking colors. "Cheap camera," I grumbled and tucked my phone away.

While Ethan carried the basket he'd hidden in the trunk of his car, I grabbed the huge blanket he'd brought along. The noon sun shined, making me giddy as it warmed me from cheek to toe. As soon as I laid the blanket out, I slipped out of my jacket and shoes, then plopped onto the middle of the blanket, throwing myself back to stare into the crystal blue sky. If I didn't *know* it was November, I would have sworn it was early September, where only the mornings were brisk and cool.

"You couldn't have picked a more perfect day for this." I sighed happily, resisting the urge to make a "snow angel" against the blanket's soft lamb's-wool lining.

Ethan nudged my foot with his black army boot. "Scooch over and give me some room, blanket hogger."

I snickered and rolled onto my belly. "What's in the basket?"

"Something I slaved over." Ethan set the basket down with anticipation lighting his eyes.

"Ooh, you cooked?" I sat up, reaching for the basket to see what kind of meal he'd put together.

Ethan swatted my hand away. "A fine meal like this should be savored."

I waited with barely controlled patience as he made a show of first pulling plastic plates, cups, and napkins from the basket. My mouth watered when he finally reached in. What would it be? BBQ chicken? Grilled steaks? When he pulled out a cracker and cheese tray, a small fruit tray, then a couple of candy bars—all courtesy of our local grocery store—we both laughed.

I shook my head and smiled. "Slaved over, huh?"

Ethan shot me a cheeky grin as he opened the food containers. "It's the thought that counts."

Leaning over, I kissed him on the jaw and whispered, "It counts for a lot. And so does bringing me here."

Before I could pull away, Ethan pressed his mouth to mine. I smiled against his lips and kissed him back. When he cupped my face to pull me closer, tiny shivers rippled through me. I melted into him, wanting to drown in the closeness we'd both missed lately. While I'd been out of town with my mom for a long weekend, Ethan had been working on a home project with Samson. If Ethan spent time away from me, his power's effect on me faded and he no longer continued to absorb my dreams. They'd returned to me last night, but since Ethan never appeared in my dreams, I'd only dreamed that I spent this afternoon reading at home.

Dates like this—surrounded by nature and Ethan's own heady smell of outdoors and spicy deodorant—oh, yeah, I was already addicted. Ethan's warm fingers slid under my shirt, splaying wide across my bare skin. He pressed me to him as if he couldn't get close enough. My heart thumped and I started to tug him back onto the blanket when my stomach had the nerve to growl, ruining the moment.

As I murmured my embarrassment, Ethan kissed my chin and then my nose. "Guess we'd better eat before your stomach gives away our super-secret location to anyone within a ten-mile radius."

While we made ourselves plates, Ethan asked, "Have you heard from your dad yet?"

"Aunt Sage hasn't heard anything new beyond what his office said when she called. Guess he's still out of the country on 'extended' business. You'd think he would have an international phone that worked, but apparently not," I said, frustrated. Popping a cheese square in my mouth, I glanced at the slight sunburn across his nose. "How's the deck coming?"

Ethan exhaled a sigh, then launched into the woes of his deck-building project with Samson. "I came pretty close to punching him yesterday."

I snickered. "I can see it now...you two scuffling in your backyard."

He snorted. "It would've turned into a brawl. We'd gotten on each other's last nerve."

"Ah, but you would eventually have to forgive each other. I wish I knew what a sibling bond felt like." In my mind, Samson was extra special. Not all older brothers would raise their younger siblings.

"Yeah, well...yesterday I'd have traded places with you for some peace and quiet." He crunched on a cracker and tilted his head. "Speaking of family keeping us busy, has your mom planned any more weekend trips?"

"None that I'm aware of," I said, biting into a strawberry. "At least until after Christmas. When we got home last night, I was so happy to crawl into my own bed after the awful hotel beds in Williamsburg."

"Your bed *is* pretty comfy." A wicked smile crooked his lips as he ran his finger along my lower lip, swiping away strawberry juice before I could lick it. I stared in mesmerized fascination when he sucked the sweet liquid off his finger, murmuring in a deep rumble, "Mmmm, Strawberry Nara."

While hundreds of butterflies exploded inside my belly, Ethan glanced down and lifted a half loaf of stale bread from the basket. "Want to feed the geese? It'll probably involve fast reflexes if we want to keep our fingers, but we've never shied from danger, have we?" he finished with an ironic chuckle.

I grinned. "Let's see how far we can make them swim for it."

We took turns tossing the hard bits of bread to the group of geese in the pond. After our food was gone, and I'd tossed the last of the bread into the water, a quiet settled between us. At first it was nice, but then the silence thickened, like there was a sudden edge in the air. I glanced sideways at Ethan, but he seemed to be intently watching the geese.

Shaking off the feeling that Ethan was too quiet, I tried to focus on the peacefulness of nature all around us, but apparently, the geese had other plans. I guess they weren't happy we'd stopped being their food source, because a couple of them paddled up to the embankment, then began to waddle closer, honking in obnoxious bursts that sounded strangely close to *moremoremoremoremore*.

As soon as the biggest goose moved within five feet of us, something dark swooped down in my peripheral vision, landing with a light thump in the crunchy leaves to my right.

A raven, sporting a white patch around one of his eyes, let out a deep, throaty, *kaugh, kaugh, kaugh*. He hissed at the approaching birds and raised his wings, stalking toward them as he rocked back and forth.

Ethan snorted, amusement sparking in his eyes. "Look at that crazy bird. He's trying to make himself look just as big as these fat geese."

The moment the lead goose charged after the black bird, honking in his direction, three more ravens landed beside their buddy, hopping around and flapping their wings. They made all kinds of racket as they dove toward the goose, snapping their thick, hard beaks.

Ethan and I exchanged surprised glances before he tossed the last few grapes toward the ravens, saying in a calm tone, "It's okay. We're fine."

The other birds instantly calmed at his voice. Once they swooped up the grapes, they flew back to their perches in the trees. The first raven remained, eyeing the geese with an unwavering, wary stare. I snickered. "He looks like he's ready to take them out if they so much as fluff a wing."

"I don't doubt it." Ethan leaned over my lap to shoo the bird away. "I said, 'Go,' bird!"

With what sounded like a huff of anger, the raven instantly took flight. Unlike the other three birds, he landed on the driver's side mirror of Ethan's car, then began to preen his feathers, as if we'd been a waste of his time.

"Temperamental bird," Ethan muttered.

I'd leaned back to give him access to the bird, and as I moved to sit up, that's when I saw a black feather had landed near my hand. I smiled and picked up the feather, turning to hand it to Ethan. "He left you a present."

Ethan pulled away without taking it, his expression shuttered. I set the feather on the blanket and studied his profile. He looked uncomfortable and tense. "What's wrong? Don't you think it's a good idea to learn as much as you can about ravens? They helped tell me when Fate was coming after me, then they showed up in my dream when I confronted Fate, and not only were you *in* my dream, but you seemed to know why the ravens interfered when he attacked me."

Ethan shook his head, frustration pulling his brow down. "Go figure, the one dream of yours I finally star in, and I don't remember any of it."

I waved to the birds observing us from afar. "Obviously they have some connection or attachment to you *beyond* the raven sword tattoo across your back." Ethan hadn't said much about the mysterious raven's feather tattoo that had magically appeared on his shoulder. Later the tattoo morphed into a sword featuring a raven yin-yang symbol near the hilt with the original raven's feather decorating the sword's blade. That change in his tattoo had happened after Ethan had helped me face Fate in my dreams.

The way he'd just acted about the feather made me believe he hadn't been researching raven tattoos like he'd told me he planned to. Still, I had a hard time believing he'd accepted a full-length sword tattoo slicing across his back from shoulder to hip like some kind of ancient gladiator gear. He'd been pretty upset that morning in my room when he woke up with it on his back. "Are you okay with the tattoo now?"

Ethan's lips thinned as he stared across the pond's smooth surface. When he glanced back at me, his eyes finally reflected the turbulence I'd been sensing. He reached up and slid his fingers down my ponytail. "I have to make my life whole, Nara."

My stomach dipped that he'd avoided answering my question. I scooted closer until our thighs touched. "I'm here for you. You know that."

Ethan folded his elbow around my thigh, locking our legs together as he set his chin on my bent knee to stare at me. "It's like, my engine revs, ready to move forward, but all I hear is the rattle."

By the look in his eyes, he wasn't talking about the tattoo any more. Ice seized my lungs, and this time it wasn't due to Fate's interference. Nor did I feel a single spark of static electricity like I always had when Fate lurked. This was all me, reacting to Ethan's somber mood. I tried hard not to let him see the panic in my eyes. "I—I don't understand. What are you saying?"

He straightened and tilted my chin so the sun's warm rays shined across my face. "Even in bright sunlight, your eyes are crystal clear. There isn't a flicker of uncertainty. You know who you are and never apologize for it. I want clarity too."

Turbulent blue eyes sought my understanding. It's not like I didn't feel uncertainty. I was still waiting to hear from my dad so I could learn more about my powers. *Why hadn't my dad called my aunt now that she'd let him know I was finally ready to talk to him?* The wait was driving me nuts. I gave a self-deprecating snort. "I have my murky moments too."

A smirk of amusement tilted his lips before resolution tightened his jaw. "You mean everything to me. That's why I have to do this."

"Do what?" I gripped his arm, my muscles a bundle of knots.

Fierce determination reflected back at me. "I'm going home."

"You're leaving?" I couldn't help the crack in my voice as fear set in.

Ethan winced, then rubbed his hand over mine, where my nails had dug into his forearm. "Just until I can set things straight with my parents. I'm leaving first thing tomorrow morning. I hope to be back after Thanksgiving break."

I was speechless. I wanted to scream "No!" and do something extreme like slash his tires so he couldn't leave. Yet another part of me wanted to hug him for trying to reconcile with his parents. Samson had wanted to tell their parents that Ethan had gotten his act together a while back, but Ethan had been too resentful to let him. Ethan's brother would support Ethan's decision to speak to his parents alone and in person. And now I knew why Samson had helped get Ethan access to this private land today. I swallowed, wanting to say the right thing, but my heart and mind had shifted way beyond torn; they were in full-on, down-and-dirty combat.

"And look…" Ethan's gaze never left mine as he reached into his jeans back pocket. "I even got this so we can keep in touch."

He'd gotten a cell phone, which *so* wasn't Ethan. He didn't carry one because he'd said, "I don't like being that easy to find," yet he'd made the sacrifice for me. It wasn't a smart-phone, so we couldn't have face-to–face chats, but at least we could text. I *should* feel special, but all I could think was…*he's leaving*. My heart folded inward.

Ethan ran his knuckles along my jaw, deep furrows etched around his mouth. "Say something, Sunshine."

I closed my eyes against the bright light shining down. *Sunshine*. I'd never be able to hear that word or feel the warm sun kissing my face without thinking of Ethan and the way he made me feel: Unique. Special. Needed. *Wanted*.

"Nara?" Ethan slid his fingers along my scalp, slipping the red ribbon and elastic band from it.

When he ran his fingers through my hair, then cupped the back of my neck, I felt the tension in his hold. I told my heart and mind to cease fire and opened my eyes. "Just…promise you'll come back," I managed to whisper.

Relief flooded his features, and he gave that brilliant smile that never failed to melt me all the way to my toes. Running his thumb in a caress along my throat, he said, "Never doubt it."

I forced a smile. "It's just...I'll miss you."

Ethan glanced down and swept the raven feather from the blanket, then pushed me onto my back, a mischievous look in his eyes. "I just thought of a great use for this feather," he began as he leaned over me.

"Oh, yeah? What's that?" I asked in a breathy voice. Tingling shot through me as he ran the feather from my chin to my neck. My heart tripped when he continued along my chest, then trailed it down the buttons of my shirt until he reached my exposed belly where the cotton material had ridden up.

"Sending a message." Eyebrow raised, he said in a serious tone. "If you start to question us..." He paused and ever so slowly traced the feather in a horizontal line across my belly button, then joined that line with a perpendicular one that stopped at the top of my jeans.

He'd created a *T*.

"Always remember..." he continued, this time writing two more of the same letter.

"This..." he finished with three more letters. A *W*, an *F*, and an *O*.

Dark blue eyes locked with mine right before he lowered his head. I let out a gasp of excitement as his warm lips touched my skin, imprinting his message on me. Clasping my waist in a firm grip, Ethan then pressed a longer, lingering kiss on my belly button. As goose bumps skittered along my body, I bit my lip and slid my fingers into his long dark bangs and thick hair, encouraging his exploration.

Ethan looked at me, his eyes swirling with primal intensity. Promises reflected in his gaze as he shifted higher, then tucked the feather into the top opening of my shirt, sliding the entire soft vane past the lacy edge of my bra. When he settled over me, his chest crushed the feather between us, and my breath hitched.

Without words, he'd shown me where he wanted to kiss me next. I burned everywhere, blistering hot. God, I was ready now, but I finally understood. When he came back, we would both be ready to move forward.

Lowering his hard body fully on me, Ethan finished his message in a husky tone, "Forever and always, Nara."

The intimacy of his actions, and the feel of his weight pressing me into the soft blanket, his legs entwined with mine, played havoc with my pulse. Picturing the letters he'd written in my mind's eye, I forced myself to focus.

TTTWFO.

Then the meaning dawned. It was the promise I'd made him after he discovered his tattoo had changed into a sword. He was confused and freaked out by the change. I'd told him that I loved him, and I'd promised I'd be there for him, that we'd be *together 'til the wheels fall off.*

Tears prickled the corners of my eyes, and I dug my fingers into his broad, muscular shoulders, pulling him even closer. While he settled things with his parents, I planned to learn everything I could about ravens and his tattoo. I'd be ready when he came home to help him resolve that aspect of his life, or, at the very least, acknowledge it. Clarity was about *full* acceptance. Nothing was going to stop us from moving forward.

"Cross my heart—" I started to whisper, but Ethan cut me off, pressing his lips to mine with a fierceness that sent fire shooting through my veins. I tugged him even closer, loving that his heady kiss sealed our promise better than words ever could.

CHAPTER 3

*H*onk, honk...honk, honk, honk, hooooooonk! "I'm coming," I hollered out my bedroom window, then grabbed my purse and keys while my laptop powered down.

"You're early," I huffed as I slid into Lainey's car. I was out of breath from rushing down the stairs at breakneck speed. She'd torn me away from a fascinating website I'd just discovered that mentioned ravens. The forum administrator had finally gotten back to me, saying he couldn't provide any contact info, but he sent me the last link the original poster had followed from a thread on his message board. And the best part was, the info on this forum was all in Latin. He probably thought he was sending me on a wild goose chase, but the Latin made it a double win. I couldn't believe my luck. I was salivating to translate it. "What's with the crazy horn honking? I heard you the first time."

"Payback, plus...change of plans. Matt's coming over to my house. He had an errand to run first," Lainey said, checking her lip gloss in the mirror.

"That's great! Now you won't feel awkward about it." I put my hand on the door handle. "So, guess you don't need me then."

"Oh no, you don't. You're not getting out of this." Before I could bolt from the car, Lainey backed out of the driveway, then cut a suspicious gaze my way. "Also, you have some 'splaining to do about Tarra's ring."

"About what?" By her tone, I could tell my earlier slipup had come back to bite me. I looked down at my short fingernails, then rubbed absently at the ink smudging my thumb. I'd just started to translate the first few sentences on that website when Lainey pulled up.

"How did you know it came from an antique store? That was just *way* weird that you knew that. When I got home I had a text from Janet, telling me the deets she'd overheard Tarra saying. And don't give me some craptastic answer that you dreamed it." She paused, adopting a thoughtful look. "That's strange, not counting this morning, I suddenly feel like we've talked about you dreaming things before..."

Oh, God! I'd completely forgotten that I'd confessed to Lainey about my ability to see the future via my dreams while she lay in a coma after her car accident a few weeks ago. She must've heard what I'd said on some subconscious level.

I'd known Lainey since we were in middle school. She couldn't handle the truth. First, there'd be denial. Anger would follow that I hadn't told her. Then, she'd move to, "Tell me my entire day." Which I'd hear... Every. Single. Day.

"I'm sorry, Lainey. I was just trying to get you off the subject. Earlier in the day, while I was in a stall in the bathroom, I overheard Tarra tell one of the cheerleaders about shopping for the ring."

"Why didn't you just tell me?" Lainey took a right at the light, gripping the steering wheel tighter.

"Because I didn't want you to dwell on the fact that Jared was with her when she picked out the ring."

"What?" Lainey's gaze jerked to mine briefly as her foot pressed harder on the pedal. "He *never* went shopping with me! Said he didn't have the patience for it." Gritting her teeth, she seethed. "The Jared *I* dated wouldn't be caught dead in an antique store!"

Lainey hadn't learned that part? *Crap.* Guess she hadn't drilled our soccer teammate, Janet (who'd *actually* been the one to overhear this conversation in the bathroom) as much today as she had in my dream scenario. Maybe she hadn't asked as many questions because she'd been distracted by meeting Matt? *Argh, I was royally screwing this up.*

We took the left into her neighborhood on a whiny squeal. I gripped the dashboard as my stomach bottomed out. "Lainey, slow down—"

Lainey let off the gas and exhaled a frustrated huff.

I put my hand on her arm. "Maybe Jared really is trying to suck up to Tarra. That kind of makes sense with this complete one-eighty he's taken." Great, now I was letting myself get sucked into her conspiracy theory.

She narrowed her eyes. "I want to drive by his house right now. See if he's washing her laundry by hand."

I snorted at the absurd image of Jared scrubbing a pair of designer jeans up and down an old-time washboard in a tub full of soapsuds, then pointed toward her driveway ahead. "Matt's coming, remember?"

Lainey perked up. "You're right. Matt'll be here in a few minutes."

We'd just walked in the door and shrugged out of our coats when Lainey rubbed her hands on her arms. "Why is it so cold in here?" Glancing around the living room, she continued, "Where's Lochlan? Loch, where are you, boy?"

"Maybe he's upstairs?" I said.

"Oh, no...the door!" Her eyes went wide and she took off toward the back of the house.

By the time I reached her side, Lainey was standing at the open back door in her kitchen, calling, "Lochlan, Lochlan!" in a high-pitched, frantic voice.

I quickly retrieved the box of dog biscuits from the pantry and handed them to her. "What happened?"

Lainey shook the box hard and called the dog's name once more, then whistled several times. "I took him out when I got home. I must not have latched the door all the way and the wind blew it open." Worry creased her forehead as her fingers tightened on the box. "My dad will kill me if something happens to him. Sometimes I think he loves that dog more than me."

You didn't see your dad the night you had that car wreck. "Trust me, he loves you, Lainey. Grab Loch's leash. We'll find him."

When Lainey picked up the leash from the rug at the back-door and the collar was still attached, dog tags jingling, I gave her an are-you-kidding-me look. She raised her shoulders, looking sheepish. "Loch hates his collar, so we only make him wear it when he's outside."

We'd just put our coats back on when the doorbell rang. Lainey finished pulling her wavy red hair out of her coat collar. "Oh, God. I forgot about Matt," she whispered.

"No better time than the present to find out if he's really a 'team player,'" I said, then opened the door. "Hi, Matt. Hope you don't mind helping us out..." But the rest died on my lips. A guy with light brown hair shot with blond streaks stood behind him. "Um, hi."

"Hey, you're Nara, right?" Matt said from his position at the door. Running his hand through his short hair, he turned and glanced at his friend standing on the sidewalk, his hands shoved in his jeans pockets. "Lainey, Nara, welcome Drystan Maddox, an exchange student all the way from Wales. He caught an earlier flight and got here a few hours sooner than we expected. Thought I'd bring him along so he could get to know some peeps."

Drystan nodded. "Nice to meet you both. Just call me Maddox."

I smiled. "Welcome to Virginia, Maddox. What made you choose the US—"

"Hi, Maddox," Lainey spoke over me, then hissed in my ear, "We have to find Lochlan!"

My gaze darted between the guys. "Do you two mind helping us find Lainey's dog? He's roaming around here somewhere."

Maddox pulled his hands from his jeans pockets and grinned. "I don't mind. I'm pretty good at finding things." He stepped onto the porch and glanced at the leash in Lainey's hand. "Is that your dog's?"

As Lainey nodded, I met her gaze. "When Loch's gotten loose before, what direction does he usually go?"

Lainey grimaced and skimmed her gaze over the whole neighborhood. "The woods. Remember, he hunts with my dad."

I frowned. Her entire neighborhood was one big wooded playground for a hunting dog.

"I think we'll cover more ground if we split up." I looked at Matt and pointed to the thick grove of trees across the street from Lainey's house. "Why don't you and Lainey head in that direction. Maddox and I will check out the woods behind Lainey's house."

"Do you have another leash, Lainey?" I asked Lainey.

Maddox shot his gaze to the cloudy sky, then quickly unhooked Lochlan's leather collar from the leash in Lainey's hand. "Looks like it'll be dark soon. Let's not waste time. This should do."

"Thank you for helping, guys." Lainey's hazel gaze pinged with appreciation between Matt and Maddox.

Matt smiled and turned his collar up against the cold wind. "No problem. We'd better get going."

Before we left, Lainey shoved a pair of tan gloves in my hands. "Wear these. Lochlan's wily. This might take a while."

After I'd tugged on the soft leather gloves, I was surprised Maddox held onto the collar instead of handing it to me, but I didn't say anything. Instead, I fell into step beside him as we made our way around the house and through the backyard.

"What's the dog's name?" he asked once we'd entered the woods.

His accent had a pleasant, sing-song rhythm that made me smile. "Lochlan," I said before I cupped my gloved hands around my mouth. "Lochlan! Come here, boy!"

Maddox turned in the opposite direction and yelled out for the dog. Then we began walking forward, diagonally away from each other and deeper into the woods, calling in unison.

Off in the distance I heard Lainey's higher-pitched call, then

Matt's deeper voice echoing our calls for the dog. The trees whipped with wind, full of chimney smoke and forest smells. The gusts stripped colorful leaves, leaving behind gnarled limbs creaking with the currents' constant tug and pull.

After hollering once more, Maddox and I stopped to listen.

A group of black birds passed overhead, squawking and beating their wings. I watched their flight, then slid my attention to Maddox, who'd made his way back over. "Why don't you go by Drystan?"

He stiffened then scanned the woods. "Maddox's the name my dad always called me."

I raised my eyebrows. "Your dad doesn't call you by your first name?"

He cut a sharp glance my way, his lips thinning. "No, he *didn't* call me by my first name. My dad is dead."

"Oh, I'm sorry. I didn't know," I mumbled, glancing away.

He lifted his shoulders, then let them fall. "No big deal."

By his reaction, it was a big deal. I needed to lighten the mood. "I like the name Drystan better than Maddox. Like Tristan with a D, it just rolls off the tongue better. You're in a new country...how about a new name? I'm going to call you Drystan."

He laughed, his green eyes crinkling. "Well 'tis my name. Is Nara your actual name or is it a nickname?"

"It's Inara." I smiled. "Lainey gave me the nickname 'Nara.'"

We both turned and walked farther into the woods. After we'd called the dog's name several times, I asked the question I'd started to earlier. "What made you decide to come to the US?"

He slid the buckled leather collar in a continuous circle between his fingers as his gaze met mine. "My mum thought it'd be good for me. Said it would make a good transition before we officially moved to England."

"Are you excited about moving to England?" I asked, then called Lochlan's name once more.

"It's not Wales," he said, pride in his tone. "But sometimes you need to travel away to appreciate your home."

"Is that why you're here? To appreciate your homeland more?"

"I'm here to broaden my scope."

Broaden my scope? The way he said it sounded like someone else's words. Guess this exchange trip wasn't his idea. I pulled a glove off and put my hand on his. "You've got friends now, Drystan. We'll make sure you have fun while you're here."

Drystan blinked, then quickly glanced down at the collar in his hand. "So weird," he mumbled.

Did he think what I said was lame? I pulled my hand away and took a step back. "I was just trying to make you feel better."

Drystan glanced at me, his brow furrowed. "No, I was just thinking that Lochlan's an odd name for a smallish dog." He pointed to the name stamped on the collar's gold nameplate. "But I suppose it probably suits a Jack."

It seemed like we weren't making any progress and the sky was getting darker by the second. I was about to suggest we head in opposite directions, when he held up a finger. "Listen."

"Do you hear something?"

"Shhh." He closed his eyes and tilted his head as if tuning in. "Do you hear that?"

After a couple of seconds, the distinct sound of water running across rocks floated to my ears. "It's rushing water. I forgot there's a creek back here. Lochlan might've gone this way." I took off toward the sound with Drystan's heavier footfalls close behind.

I'd just started down the incline toward the creek when he grabbed my arm and pulled me to a halt. "Careful." His gaze slid up and down the creek bed below, then he released me. "Take it slow."

It was just a creek. Nothing down there could hurt anyone, but the caution in his tone slowed my pace, especially since this entire afternoon was all new to me. I really needed to *not* improvise my dreams. "I'll be careful." I moved with caution down the hill's slippery leaves toward the flowing water.

I'd just gotten to the bottom of the hill and was about to step closer to the creek bed, when Drystan gripped my elbow in a vise hold. "Stay out of the underbrush along the edge."

Maybe he was worried about snakes. They weren't even out this time of year. *Wait? Did they even have snakes in Wales?* I glanced back at him, getting ready to ask, when he released me with a nod, telling me to move on.

I stepped over the leaves and onto the pebbles near the creek. "Lochlan!" I called a couple more times, peering up and down the long winding creek.

No paw prints were visible in the mud to prove the dog had come this way, but my gut told me the creek was our best shot.

"Which way should we take?" I said. A couple of seconds later, a cacophony of cawing echoed above me before another set of black birds took flight from a tree. I watched them circle, then head to my right. *Were they telling me which direction to go?*

Casting a surreptitious gaze toward Drystan, I started to suggest we follow the creek bed around the bend to the right, when I saw his gaze was completely focused on his thumbs sliding along the collar's soft leather.

Drystan's head snapped up as if he felt the weight of my stare. Setting his mouth in a determined slant, he took off ahead of me to the right. "Let's go this way."

After we rounded the bend, we'd walked another thirty feet or so when a low sound, an animal's yelp of pain, came in loud and clear. The babbling water and tall embankment had muffled the sound earlier. Drystan rushed ahead. Once I reached him, he was squatted beside Lochlan, talking in a soothing tone.

A muscular bundle of white fur with black floppy ears, black eyebrows, and a stripe of black down his nose, Lochlan lay on his side on a bed of leaves next to the creek. Exhausted and terrified, the Jack Russell's rib cage sawed up and down. He whimpered his recognition as I squatted next to him. Blood coated his left front paw, which was clamped inside some kind of poacher's trap. By the blood staining his snout and along the underside of his right paw, poor Lochlan must've tried several times to free himself.

"It's going to be okay, Lochlan," I crooned, then stripped off the other glove to run my warm hands along his soft coat. Lochlan turned frantic brown eyes my way, but he was too tired to lift his head. My cheeks flooded with anger that anyone would lay traps like this. This kind had to be illegal. And all for what? Fur? Whoever this poacher was, he'd encroached on the wrong man's land. Lainey's father was a Central Virginia police officer, and he would make it his personal mission to hunt the poacher down for his illegal trap setting.

Shoving the gloves into my jean jacket pockets, I glanced at Drystan with unshed tears burning my eyes. "Can you try to find a stick that'll be strong enough to spring the trap? I'll distract Lochlan when you're ready."

LAINEY FREAKED the moment she saw Drystan carrying Lochlan. Tears streamed down her cheeks and she gathered his muscular body in her arms, saying in a soft voice, "Oh, Locky, what happened to you?" My heart ached to see her normally hyperactive dog in such a sad state. Blood coated his white fur and his left leg hung a little too loosely as Lainey scooped him even closer to her chest. I really hoped his leg was just bruised and not broken.

Matt drove Lainey and Lochlan in her car to the vet, and I called her father and asked him to meet her there.

After I hung up, Drystan gave a rueful smile. "Well, that was an adventure. I'm glad we found Lochlan. Jacks are usually pretty tough. He'll make it through. Though he'll probably avoid the creek if he ever gets loose again." Pulling a set of keys from his coat pocket, he said, "Ready for me to take you home?"

I eyed the keys with doubt. "Which side of the road do you drive on in Wales?"

He gave a cocky grin. "The right one."

I narrowed my gaze at his superior tone. "Maybe I

should've asked a different question. Have you ever driven in the US before? I'd like to make it home in one piece."

Drystan smirked and twirled the key ring around his finger, catching the keys in his palm. "Always keep your bum on the yellow line and you're safe. Good enough for you?"

Laughing, I nodded. "Guess that'll have to do."

CHAPTER 4

ok-tok-tok. Tok-tok-tok.

I came wide awake with a wheezing gasp. Fear prickled my sweat-soaked skin as I glanced at my bedroom door, looking for the source of the creepy sound that had followed me from my dream.

Tok-tok-tok. Tok-tok-tok.

The sound came from my right. Jerking my attention to my window, I let out a sigh of relief when I saw Patch pushing his thick black beak under the one-inch opening, trying his best to wedge it up.

"Why can't you just stick with one sound?" I lifted the window for him to enter.

Patch hopped onto the back of the reading chair next to the window. Scrunching his neck, he fluffed his throat feathers and let out a rapid-fire *groak-groak-groak-groak,* which sounded suspiciously like laughter.

"Could you at least learn to say, 'Good morning, Nara'?" I smirked and tossed him a piece of kibble from the glass cookie jar on my dresser. It had become our routine over the past couple of weeks. Ever since that day by the pond, the raven had shown up at my window each morning, tapping to be let in.

Had he followed me home from the pond? I really didn't

care. Having him there was strangely comforting. His presence reminded me of that special day with Ethan.

The first day he'd shown up at my window, I'd let Patch in and he'd trashed my room. Flying here and there, he'd picked up every shiny object he could fit in his beak. He shredded paper, broke pencils in half, got his beak caught in one of my spiral notebooks, then turned over a glass of water, but after that, we'd settled into a strange, if not comfortable, routine.

Once he'd snarfed down the kibble, I peeled off a sticky note from the paper cube on my nightstand, then handed it to him so he could fly over to settle on my desk.

While Patch shredded the paper into tiny bits, I normally worked on transferring notes or scraps of information to the expensive brown leather-bound journal I'd bought specifically for this project. Anything new or potentially useful about ravens, specialized tattoos, or swords with feather designs from the prior night's Internet research made it into the book.

I usually did this before I left for school, but not this morning. I ran my hand over the soft leather, then opened it to the page I'd marked with the feather Ethan had left behind as an intimate reminder of his promise to return. For a little over a week, I'd kept the feather with me at all times, but I was worried I'd lose it, so the journal became its new home.

I'd stayed up late last night, doing my best to translate the Latin information on the website the message board owner had given me. I'd never run across this particular resource before, because I'd always run a search on "raven". This website was entitled, *Corvus Corax*, which was the Latin term for raven.

The *Corvus Corax* site had some interesting information, particularly about the mythology and how each culture either held the raven in high esteem—a savior/creator of the world, a spirit and even as a divination source—or under dark scrutiny as an evil entity whose very presence signaled death and destruction. The views spanned the opposite ends of the spectrum, but they were never ambivalent.

The duality of different societies' perception of ravens intrigued me, especially after I'd translated a story claiming that at one time all ravens were stark white like the dove. That is, until a raven committed an unforgivable crime against a god. As punishment, the angry god turned all ravens as black as a starless night.

The very last story of a raven being light, then turning dark made me think of the black and silver raven yin-yang symbol on Ethan's sword tattoo. Yet I couldn't find *any* reference to the symbol itself on the Internet, nor could I find any mention of a sword tattoo with that symbol and a raven's feather etched along the blade.

Over the last two weeks, I'd hunted for anything remotely similar. I'd stalked the London Tower information page on ravens and superstition, New Age message boards, raven enthusiasts' forums, and tattoo blogs and websites. Everywhere I could, I left cryptic messages with enough information to draw out someone who knew anything, without giving too much information away. Never once did I fully describe Ethan's tattoo.

The more I looked, the more information I collected for Ethan, which helped muffle the ache in my heart from his absence. So long as I focused on the research, I felt like a small part of him was still with me. The journal would be my welcome home gift to Ethan when he came back.

Before I'd gone to bed, I'd clicked on another link on the *Corvus Corax* website that led me to a reference about an old newspaper article from thirty years ago: "Crows and ravens all over the world fall out of the sky: Biologists Speculate." No other information was given, just the title. I'd written down the title, the newspaper name, and year and month of the article. I planned to head over to Central University Library's microfiche archive as soon as school let out the next day.

But in my dream last night, I'd felt like I was being watched while I stood at the card case in the library looking up the microfiche call number associated with the article.

My fingers grip the index card tightly as I pull it from the card case, then slowly scan the quiet library, past the black-and-white checkerboard floor. Students are scattered among the long mahogany desks. Warm, glowing desk lamps halo their heads as they bend over open textbooks. No one is looking my way, so I shrug off the sensation and assume it's my imagination.

Later, the creepy feeling follows me, trailing just beyond the dim light's reach as I walk down the deserted hall at the back of the library toward the stack elevators. I force myself to keep moving forward, to not constantly glance over my shoulder. As I lift my finger to push the elevator button, my hand trembles. The last time I was in the stacks — where all archived resources are housed—Ethan and I were almost crushed by falling bookshelves. That had been Fate's doing.

The air in the hall is still and warm, but not as stifling as the air in the elevator will be. I run my hand over my hair, feeling for flyaways that indicate static, which has been present whenever Fate was lurking in the past. My hair feels smooth. You're just being silly. Fate's not here, Nara. He's *not* here. Yet I can't bring myself to push the elevator button either.

I only need to go to the fourth floor. My gaze locks on the glowing stairwell sign at the same time another creepy feeling slides up the back of my neck. I tense and look behind me. The hall isn't lit all the way down. The shadows framing the hall send apprehension zipping along my spine. Anything could be lurking just beyond my line of sight.

I step toward the stairwell and open the door, then quickly slip inside.

I'd just jogged up the second set of stairs, when I think I hear the stairwell door open. I pause and grip the railing, my heart thumping against my chest.

Eerie silence.

God, I'm imagining all kinds of things. As soon as I set my foot on the next step, a slow shhhTok------shhhTok------shhhTok rings out, like the sound heavy shoes—boots? —make while climbing cement stairs.

Swallowing several times, I grip the metal railing as I lean over to peek through the open stairwell. My head rams against the railing while I peer down through the fluorescent-lit opening. I don't see anything, but the tapping sound gets stronger and faster, as if the person is increasing their pace up the stairs.

I take off running, but instead of leaving the sound behind, the *running noise grows louder and closer, changing pitch. I grab the fourth floor's door handle, then yank open the door...*

And jerked awake to Patch's morning window-tapping antics.

Glancing over at Patch, I smiled. He was trying to stand on my soccer ball. Again. If watching a huge black bird hissing at a rolling ball weren't so fruitless, I'd let him attempt this for hours.

I chuckled. "Trying to conquer your fears?"

"Nara! You need to get going or you'll be late for school," Mom called from downstairs. "Am I going to have to come up and get you?"

"Shoo, Patch. You have to go now—" I herded the bird toward the window.

Patch flapped his wings, then landed on my nightstand, tilting his head with an expectant look. "I don't have time—" I began, then realized he wasn't going until he got what he'd come to expect.

"Be downstairs in a minute," I called back and grabbed a nickel from my drawer to set it on the nightstand for him. Patch turned his head and eyed the coin up close, then looked at me with a flap of his wings. *Was that a "meh, I'm unimpressed" shrug?*

I grunted and changed the nickel for a dime, swiftly sliding the coin across the smooth surface toward him. Patch backed up with my hurried movements, his obsidian gaze wary. When I moved my hand away, he quietly squawked, but didn't attempt to touch the dime.

Mom's footfalls had started up the stairs.

"You. Have. To. Go!" I quickly replaced the dime with a quarter, giving the bigger coin a swift spin.

The quarter had barely made three rotations when Patch snatched it up in his beak, then took off out the open window with two strong *whoops* of his powerful wings.

I shut the window after him, grumbling, "For a bird that doesn't care what he eats, you sure have expensive taste," just as my mom opened my bedroom door.

"Who were you just talking to?" she asked, looking confused.

"Myself." I sighed for effect. "It happens close to exam time."

"Okaaaayy." Mom pushed her blonde bangs out of her eyes. "Since you'll be running out the door to get to school, I didn't want to miss telling you that I'll be late tonight. David is taking me to dinner."

I forced a smile past the sudden gulp in my throat. I'd encouraged Mom to take Business Spanish lessons from my Spanish teacher in hopes that another twelve years wouldn't pass with her letting work absorb her life. It was time for her to move on from a husband who'd left without a word.

So why was it so hard to hear my mom talk about going out on a date with Mr. Dixon? Maybe because I knew my dad would be getting in touch with me soon, and a tiny part of me hoped his leaving us was just a giant mistake.

Then again, maybe this wasn't a *date* date. "Is Mr. Dixon taking you to an authentic Mexican restaurant so you can work on your Spanish?"

"Of course not, silly." Mom laughed as she fluffed the newly-cut angled ends of her chic bob. I'd noticed she'd been fiddling with her hair a lot more lately. She'd also been choosing salad instead of bread as a side during dinner. "We're going to that lovely new Italian place downtown."

She started to leave, then poked her head back into my room. "Oh, by the way, our new neighbor down the road, Mr. Wicklow, borrowed the leaf blower to clean up the leaves in his yard."

Yay! That meant I wouldn't have to clean up the leaves any time soon. No blower, no leaf bagging.

Mom must've read the look on my face, because she grinned. "Don't worry. He said he'll return it right away."

I gave her a "greeeeeaaaat thanks!" look. "I didn't realize there was a house for sale on our street. When did he move in?"

Mom shook her head. "Mr. Wicklow is a visiting professor at Central. He's just renting for a couple of months from the Goldsteins while they winter in Florida." Mom waved as she backed out of my room. "Got to get to work. I won't be home too late."

"Better not be," I mumbled under my breath.

As I drove to school, I chewed my lip and tried to figure out what to do about the library. I really wanted to find that article. What if I was just being paranoid in my dream? Maybe I'd imagined that I'd heard the door opening? Had the noise Patch was making entered my dream and my mind translated the auditory sound to fit my environment...like the sound of someone coming up the stairs?

Which had never happened before! I snorted my frustration. One thing I knew for sure: I was going to the library this afternoon, but I was *not* going alone.

CHAPTER 5

*K*nowing things were going to progress in a not-so-good direction without a clue as to how to stop it gnawed at my insides every time I saw Lainey and Matt together at school.

This morning, I'd seen the two of them chatting at her locker. After lunch, they'd walked together down the hall. A little too close. This afternoon on my way to study hall, I fell into step behind them while Matt walked Lainey to class. As I passed by Jared on my way to an empty table in study hall, I saw him do a double take and narrow his gaze on Lainey and Matt talking together outside the door.

When Lainey entered study hall, I waved her over, intending to talk to her about Matt, but then a girl with straight black hair and fair skin set a pile of books down on the table beside me. "Do you mind if I sit here?" she asked, blinking her brown, mascara-free eyes at a rapid pace.

"Um, sure." I slid my books over to give her room. "Are you new here?"

Wearing a starched button-down shirt tucked into a pair of pressed khaki pants, she pushed her hair behind her ear and smiled. "I'm new to the school but not the area. I'm Harper, by the way."

Lainey walked up right when I started to introduce myself.

Waving to indicate Lainey, I said, "This is Lainey," then pointed to myself, "and I'm Nara. Nice to meet you." I caught Lainey's eye and continued, "This is Harper. She's new."

With a half smile, Lainey surveyed the girl from head to toe. "I gathered that."

Harper pressed her lips together. Was she annoyed or embarrassed? I couldn't tell. I sighed at Lainey and leaned across my books to ask, "Where did you go to school before?"

Harper pulled out a pencil from her three-ring binder, then lined it up beside her math book. She didn't look up until she was satisfied it was perfectly parallel to the spine. "I didn't. I was homeschooled."

Lainey cocked her head. "That explains a lot." She cleared her throat at my cut-it-out look, then said in a brighter tone, "I mean, public school must be a bit of a culture shock."

Harper looked directly at Lainey for the first time, a slight smile on her pale oval face. "Yeah, it's a big change, but I've taken classes at private schools here and there, so I'm used to a structured school system."

"Well, private and public schools are two entirely different animals." Lainey made sure the teacher wasn't looking, then flipped open her phone and settled back in her seat. She held Harper's gaze as she typed on her slide-out keyboard. "You might want to ditch the prep school clothes. You look like you're going to church or something."

Harper's lips twisted. "Thanks for the advice. I'll keep it in mind."

"No problem," Lainey said, then glanced down at her text screen.

She completely missed Harper's sarcasm, but I didn't. Inwardly snickering, I smiled at Harper, then said to Lainey, "You didn't text me when you got home last night. How'd it go at the vet's yesterday with Lochlan?"

"Loch's going to be fine. He did have to get a cast, though." Sitting up, she pinched her thumb and forefinger together. "You should see his tiny wittle cast, Nara. I made them put a manly dark green one on him. Of course, Dad went ballistic when he got to the vet's office and saw Lochlan. He spent a half hour talking to the vet until he was assured his 'little guy' would make a full recovery. Dad took today off and stayed home to keep an eye on him." She sighed. "Told you he loved that dog more than me."

"You could always offer to go hunting with your dad." When she rolled her eyes, I smirked. "What'd your dad say about the trap we found?"

Lainey leaned closer, eyes wide. "You should've seen him out there last night with his police flashlight. He tromped around in those woods for hours, pulling up every single trap he could find. He's already got someone at the office tracing the numbers stamped on them." Her voice filled with pride. "This poacher doesn't stand a chance."

"Poacher?" Harper jerked a concerned gaze from Lainey to me. "Sorry for interrupting, but I'm hoping to become a vet. I hate hearing stuff like this."

"Ugh, the horrific condition we see some animals come into CVAS..." I pressed my lips together and shook my head. "Makes me want the government to establish an eye-for-an-eye law."

"You work at CVAS?" Harper shifted forward in her seat, brown eyes lit with interest.

I nodded. "I volunteer."

"I've been thinking about doing an internship there. Do you think they'd want more help?"

"Always." I grinned. "Just call and ask for Sally. She'll get you an application."

Harper jotted Sally's name on a piece of paper. "Thanks, Nara." Peering up through her hair, she asked in a less-confident voice, "Do you think you could meet me there after school today and introduce me to her?"

I shook my head. "Sorry. I can't today. I'm heading over to Central's library after school." She looked so disappointed, that I added, "But I'll be happy to call and give her a heads-up that you're coming."

As Harper beamed her thanks, Lainey sent me a text.

Lainey – 2:20 p.m. ~ I have the BEST idea. Meet me by my car after school.

Once Harper went back to studying, I texted Lainey.

Me – 2:25 p.m. ~ Will do.

I already knew what she planned to tell me, and I wasn't sure how, but I was going to do everything I could to talk her out of it.

~

THE MOMENT I exited through the double doors at the end of the school day and saw Lainey leaning against Matt's Jeep, chatting with him, I realized how I was going to solve my library dilemma, *and* stop my best friend from hatching some kind of crazy scheme.

In my dream, Lainey told me she had the "best idea evah to deal with Jared" but she refused to elaborate, other than to say her idea involved Matt, before she drove off. When I pointed Matt out to her yesterday, I'd hoped that seeing him moving on with his life would help her get over Jared. I didn't expect her to *use* him to deal with her "Jared issues" or worse, to get back at Jared. Neither scenario was fair to Matt.

"Hi, guys," I said.

Lainey's eyes widened. While Matt's attention was on me, she jerked her head toward her car, telling me to "go wait over there." I ignored her signal. "Thanks for offering to go to the library with me, Lainey."

Lainey frowned. "What are you talking—"

"Don't you remember?" I met her irritated gaze. "Since I helped you with that *project* yesterday, you promised to help with mine today."

"'ello, everyone," Drystan said, strolling up beside me.

I nodded to acknowledge him, surprised I hadn't seen him at all today. Guess we were on opposite class schedules. "Hi Drystan, what did you think of your first day at an American school?"

"Drystan? What happened to Maddox?" Lainey tossed a knowing look my way.

"New country, new name. Right, *Inara*?" Drystan winked,

then yanked his leather jacket's collar up around his neck to ward off the brisk wind. "American schools aren't much different than schools at home. "Well,"—he paused, grinning —"other than the ladies can't seem to get enough of my accent."

Despite his cocky comment, the way he said "enough," like "e'nuff" and dropped the h off hello would totally attract the girls.

Lainey snickered. "This is perfect. Since I need to chat with Matt about something, *Drystan* can go with you to the library and charm all the college girls while you research."

Drystan glanced at me, eyebrows raised. "I can?"

"Lainey," I began, reaching for her. The second my hand touched hers, a bolt of electricity shot between us.

"Ow!" Lainey jerked her hand away and frowned at me as if I'd done it on purpose.

I'd yanked my hand back too, rubbing my throbbing fingers. That really hurt. Like, all the way to my teeth kind of hurt. "Sorry," I mumbled.

"Damn! I even heard that one." Drystan gave a confident laugh as he intentionally hooked his arm in mine. "I'm not afraid. Come on, *Inara*. Take me to Central's library. I've been meaning to head in that direction anyway. I hope they'll have some old videos I've been looking for."

Static sparked through my sweater, underneath my jacket, as Drystan pulled me away from Lainey and Matt. I glanced back at Lainey, whose head was already bent toward Matt's in conspiracy fashion. I'd lost my chance. Apparently, Fate had adjusted his tactics to keep me from interfering...in a very painful way. Just how high of a voltage could the human body take? Did Fate have the ability to amp it to a deadly level? I really didn't want to find out.

～

As I PULLED into the library's parking lot, Drystan glanced around, his green eyes scanning the bold white columns framing the main library's entrance. "I can see why it's such a popular college. It's visually appealing."

"'Jeffersonian' is the quickest way to describe the architecture." I swept my hand to encompass the column-infused, sprawling campus.

We mounted the stairs toward the library entrance and he mumbled, "It'll be ironic if I run into my uncle while I'm on campus."

I paused on a stair. "Your uncle's a student?"

Drystan gave a half smile. "No, he's a guest, visiting at the request of the history department."

"How funny that you're both here at the same time," I said, continuing my climb.

"Yeah, it's right funny, but I don't plan to see him while I'm here. He's paying for my expenses, so I'll honor his request that I get back into football while I'm here."

"I'm assuming you don't mean American football. Now you're talking my language. Well, we call it soccer here."

His eyebrows shot up. "You play?"

"What? I don't look like I'd play soccer?"

Drystan shook his head, clucking his tongue. "The girls who play football back home don't look like you."

We'd reached the entrance, and I laughed, ignoring my warmed cheeks as I pulled the door open. I hadn't expected his indirect compliment. "I take it you aren't close to your uncle?"

"How can you be close to someone you've never met?" Drystan held the door for me to proceed him inside.

"You've never met him?"

"I didn't even know he existed until after my dad died. He started calling, trying to convince us to move to England." He lifted his shoulder, then let it drop. "I'm only moving for my mum. I couldn't care less about getting to know my uncle, even if he's supposedly 'taking us under his wing'."

Drystan wore his resentment like an invisible cloak of protection. I started to ask him if his uncle and mom also called him Maddox, but his gaze was already locked on the media room in the back corner of the library. "While you're researching, I'm going to talk to them."

46

Before he walked off, I asked, "What kind of video are you hoping to find?"

His lips tugged upward. "An old-school one."

After he strolled away, I straightened my shoulders and headed for the card catalog. I already felt better having someone with me. Once I turned off my phone—per the instructions in ALL CAPS plastered every five feet in the library —I pulled out Ethan's journal and turned to the feather-marked page. I jotted down the name of the article, the title of the newspaper, and the date on a scrap piece of paper before closing the book to rifle through the cards for the library's call number location for the article.

At one point, my neck tingled as if someone were watching me, but the intensity in my dream had been much stronger than the low vibe I felt right now. I scanned the entire library, then let out a sigh of relief that no one was looking up from their books. Every single student on the main floor had his or her head down, studying.

"What are you looking for?" Drystan whispered in my ear, making me jump. With a triumphant smile, I showed him the card I'd just found, then jotted down its stack location on a scrap of paper. "It's an article I discovered while surfing. Since it was from thirty years ago, I could only find a snippet about it on the Internet. I want to read the entire article." As I slipped the card back into place in the catalog, I asked, "Did they have your video?"

Drystan rocked on his heels. "Yep, they're copying it onto a flash drive for me." He held up his phone. "Said they'll call me when it's done."

"Uh, we're supposed to turn our phones off. How come you get to keep yours on?"

A dimple displayed in his right cheek. "I got special permission."

"Let me guess..." My gaze narrowed. "The girl working the counter swooned over your accent."

He flashed an unrepentant grin, then nodded toward the paper in my hand. "You ready to find your article?"

The long hall toward the stack elevators didn't feel nearly as ominous with Drystan by my side. It was still shadowy, but I could ignore that when I had someone to distract me. "So, tell me what's on this video."

Drystan walked beside me at a leisurely pace. "I'm looking for new techniques."

"New techniques? On an old video?"

He smirked. "Old techniques I can adapt in new ways."

"I'm almost afraid to ask," I snickered. "But if the library is letting you check out a copy, it can't be too risqué."

Drystan's light brown eyebrows lifted up and down with his grin. "This technique requires loads of stamina, acute depth perception, the ability to think several steps ahead, and guts. It involves your entire body and mind. It isn't for the faint of heart."

We'd reached the elevator where a sign had been taped over the button. OUT OF ORDER.

"Great. Out of order." I sighed, then glanced at Drystan. "Now I'm totally curious…what kind of *technique* requires all those things?"

"Parkour." Turning to our left, Drystan pulled open the stairwell door and held it for me.

"Parkour?" I used my foot to push the metal chair that blocked the way to the stairs off to the side.

"Yeah. You've never heard of it?"

I shook my head and continued climbing the steps.

"Parkour is like a form of exercise, except it's so much more than that. I guess you could consider it a form of training."

"Training for what?" I reached for the fourth floor door.

"Combat," Drystan answered in a clipped, matter-of-fact tone.

I paused as I pulled the door open. "Combat? Who do you plan on fighting?"

Drystan's serious expression melted away. "Nobody, I hope. It's meant to be defensive more than offensive." He shrugged. "Parkour came in handy from time to time back home."

"For exercise?"

"Among other things," he said dryly.

Drystan was an open book with hidden passages. "I'd like

to see this parkour." My tense shoulders relaxed the moment we walked into the room and the motion sensor lights popped on, illuminating the dark room.

He tilted his head, contemplating. "It'd be much easier to show you than try to explain it." Drystan grabbed my hand and squinted at the scribbled note clutched in my fingers. Releasing his hold, he pointed to a MICFICH sign hanging down from the ceiling at the back of the thirty-by-thirty room filled with tall bookshelves. "Guess that's the section you want back there." His brow puckered. "Do you know how to work the machine?"

"I've used one before."

After I'd spent twenty minutes riffling through the microfiche bin for the article I was looking for, I sat back in my chair and huffed my frustration. "I can't believe it's not here. The microfiche with the one article I want seems to be missing."

Drystan's head popped around the edge of the bookcase. "You couldn't find it?" He'd been wandering around the stack, humming various Welsh songs I didn't recognize while I searched through the entire year of articles.

"No."

He squatted down beside my chair and held out his hand. "Let me see where it's located."

"I've looked through the entire section." I pointed to the paper with the article's supposed location lying on the desk.

Drystan picked up the piece of paper, then rubbed his thumb across the numbers several times, his gaze focused on my chicken scrawl.

I snickered. "It's not going to grant you three wishes."

His green eyes flashed amusement as he grabbed the bin from my lap. Flipping past the section I'd looked through twice, he skipped to an entirely different year, then pulled out a handful of microfiche. He quickly fanned through the stack before pulling out a thin square of plastic with a triumphant smile. "Here it is. This whole section had been filed in the wrong year."

I gaped at him. "Um, thanks." As I took the microfiche from his hand, I saw that the plastic edge was labeled with the year I'd been looking for. "How in the world did you know it would be there?" *Even more amazing, how did you know that this partic-ular microfiche held the article I sought?* There were at least ten other misfiled microfiche he could've chosen from. Only a machine could read the microscopic print.

Maybe he was just guessing, I told myself as I slid the microfiche under the lighted viewer, then began to scroll through the articles. When I slowed to a stop at the article I wanted, Drystan peered over my shoulder, reading out loud in his lilting accent, "'Crows and Ravens All Over the World Fall Out of the Sky: Biologists Speculate.'" A pause. "That's a right strange subject. What's it for?"

I tensed, not planning to share the reason behind my research. I cast a suspicious sideways look his way. "Not any stranger than you finding it without x-ray vision. Seriously, how'd you do that?"

"Talent." Just as Drystan gave a confident grin, a song began to play. I smiled when I recognized his ring tone as one of the Welsh songs he'd been humming.

He grabbed his phone from his back pocket. "'ello? That's brilliant! I'll pick it up on my way out—Oh? Okay, then. Be right down."

Hanging up, he started to walk backward. "The media room closes in five minutes. I'm gonna run and grab my flash drive. Be right back."

Glad for some brief privacy, I waved him on, then turned back to read the article. After I'd scanned the article twice, I took notes on the basic gist in the leather journal.

* *Thirty years ago, crows and ravens inexplicably dropped from the sky at the exact same time all over the world.*

* *Two-thirds recovered after a few minutes and flew away, but one-third of the Corvid birds in the Corvus genus died across the world that day.*

* *After studying their bodies, scientists speculated something stunned them and that their drop from the sky had caused their hearts to stop.*

* *No one could point to any worldwide phenomenon that could've caused the birds to react the way they did. No weather event, no*

atmospheric event, no environmental event...nothing correlated
across the entire world at the exact same time.

I'd just jotted down the last note when the lights popped off, sending the windowless room into darkness. The only light came from the machine in front of me. Apparently, I'd been so focused on the article I'd barely moved. I stood on tiptoe and waved my arms above the tall bookshelves to activate the motion sensor in the lighting.

Nothing.

I sat back down with a sigh, then quickly put the microfiche back. Once I'd shut down the machine, the stairwell door click closed. I snorted, wondering why Drystan bothered to be quiet when he came back. On his way out, he'd let the heavy metal door slam like a garbage truck on trash day.

"Hey," I called out. "Do me a favor and move around back there so the lights will come back on."

I was surprised he didn't respond. Maybe he'd tried and it didn't work, so he was just waiting on me by the door where the exit sign's red glow gave off extra light. Hugging the leather journal to my chest, I tugged my backpack up on my shoulder. My eyes had started to adjust to the darkness, and I realized I could make out my hands and stuff, so light was coming from somewhere. At least it was enough for me to make my way back to the stairwell.

As I walked out of the back section, I saw a thin dark-haired college-aged guy not much taller than me standing in the middle of the aisle. Dim track lighting from the ceiling reflected shadows across the smug look on his face.

My steps slowed to a halt and my stomach knotted as the feeling of being watched from my dream came back to me. "Um, hey." I thumbed back toward the microfiche machine and gave a nervous laugh. "If you're looking for the microfiche section, the machine's all yours. Hopefully you won't have as much trouble finding what you're looking for as I did."

The guy tilted his head and looked me up and down, then snorted. "You're not much to look at. Such a tiny bird."

I stiffened. "Not that I was asking for an opinion, but since you're handing insults out like candy, I wouldn't even notice you if I passed you on the street."

He folded his arms against his birdcage chest. "Oh, really? You wouldn't give me a second look?"

Arrogant much? This had to be the oddest conversation I'd ever had with a stranger. Where the heck had Drystan gone? To the moon? I squared my shoulders. We were practically the same size. If he tried to lay a hand on me, I could take him. "Nope. Now that we've shared our mutual disinterest, I'm out of here," I said before I turned down a bookcase aisle that led to the stairwell.

I'd made it halfway down the aisle when the guy suddenly appeared at the other end. He leaned against the bookcase, dark eyebrows elevated. *"This* is going to be fun."

His speed had surprised me, but it was the depth of his laugh that sent a chill rippling through me. As it resonated in the small space, the baritone seemed at odds with his size, like the laugh of a giant coming from an ant. I stopped, clutching the leather journal to my chest. "What do you want?" I'd tried for confident, but my voice shook a little.

He pushed off the bookcase, a lazy smile spreading across his face. "A good fight."

CHAPTER 6

*H*ad I been dropped into another person's life, someone who'd really pissed this guy off? When he took a step forward, my insides quivered. I spun around, then bolted in the opposite direction. As soon as I rounded the bookcase and turned back into the main aisle, he was there, blocking my path.

I screamed, trying to backtrack, but he grabbed my shoulders and slammed me against the end of the bookcase. Sheer delight danced in his dark eyes.

His bony hands were heavier than they looked, biting like claws into my skin through my jacket's jean material. "Come on. Give me your best shot, my little tweet. You're not making this *any* fun."

I tried to twist free from his grip, but his hold was surprisingly strong. His thin arms didn't budge against my struggles. "You must think I'm someone else. I don't want to fight you."

His narrow face creased in confusion. "You're just going to *let* me kill you? Without a fight?" he said, shaking me so hard I lost my grip on the leather book.

When the journal hit the floor, he glanced down and hissed as if his eyes burned. He shut his eyes for a second, then drilled his dark gaze into mine. Wild excitement had replaced his annoyed confusion. He yanked my backpack off my shoulder and held it out, demanding, "Put that book inside your backpack and zip it closed."

Anger boiled inside me, puffing my chest in defiance. He wanted my journal? *No way was I giving up my only connection to Ethan.* I jerked my head back and forth and gritted, "Do it yourself!" I didn't know why he wanted my journal, but he'd have to release me to retrieve it. When he bent to pick it up, I'd knee him in the head, then grab my journal and make a break for the door.

He sounded like a dragon about to expel fire as he shoved me to my knees, ruining my plans for escape. Yanking my jacket, he pressed my face close to the opened journal on the floor. "I said, 'Pick it up, bitch!'"

"Screw you!" I screamed at the same time I purposefully fell to my side, kicking my legs toward his ankles. I hooked his feet then jerked forward. When his legs went out from underneath him and he went down, I started to crawl to get away, but he recovered quickly, yanking at my ankle with a vise grip.

As soon as I rolled over, he was already standing above me. He lifted me off the ground by my jacket's collar, then gripped my throat and slammed me against the bookcase once more. My throat burned and terror clogged my chest as he effortlessly slid me up the wood surface until my feet dangled several inches off the ground.

When I clawed at his wrist to relieve some of the pressure on my throat, I expected to see fury in his eyes. Instead, grudging respect flickered in their dark depths.

"Not bad for a fledgling." His lip twisted in a derisive smile as I struggled to breathe. Just before I lost consciousness, he adjusted his hold upward to my jawbone, giving relief to my airway. Tears filled my eyes from the pressure of my weight on my jaw, but at least I could breathe.

Determination filtered into his expression. "Do as I say and I'll make sure your death is quick."

I tried to shake my head, but he growled, "Yes, you will!" His voice had altered with his impatience. It sounded like ground-up glass grating across asphalt. Hundreds of tiny needles pounded against my eardrums. I winced and yanked at the hand holding me with the strength of a WWF wrestler, then rammed my boot into his groin, hard.

He barely flinched, but he let out a vicious growl and shifted his hold back to my throat. As my vision began to spot and then fade, I couldn't believe I was going to die. Not like this. Tightening my grip on his wrist, I gathered all the strength I could and used the bookcase as leverage to quickly tuck my knees toward my chin on either side of his arm.

With a grunt of anger, I jammed my feet into his chest. My attacker flew backward and I fell too, landing hard on my back. Pain exploded along my spine, making me gasp for air as I rolled to my side and into a crouched position.

I stumbled to my feet and wheezed. My head buzzed, but I didn't stop. I grabbed the journal, then pressed it close to my chest as I took off as fast as my legs would carry me. A horrific snarl raised the tiny hairs on my arms and the floor shook as the guy's feet pounded in fast pursuit. When the elevator pinged right before the doors began to slide open, I veered toward them, screaming. "Help me!" *Please let someone be there. Someone big and intimidating.*

Drystan looked shocked as I flew into him, my momentum drilling us both into the elevator's back wall.

"Nara? What the 'ell? What's wrong?" He wrapped his arms around me to keep us from falling to the grimy elevator floor.

I glanced over my shoulder and half-turned, pointing to my pursuer as he pivoted and headed for the exit. "He—he attacked me!"

Drystan quickly set me aside, and I barely had time to register the flash of anger in his green eyes before he took off after the guy.

"Wait!" I screamed, running after him, but Drystan was already through the exit door.

Yanking the door open, I screamed, "He's stronger than he looks" as Drystan ran down the stairs toward the next level. I'd barely made it to the third floor landing when I saw Drystan grab hold of the metal railing just below me, then vault into the air. Curling up and over the stairwell turn, he shot like a bullet down to the second floor, skipping an entire flight of stairs with his pivoting move.

Astonished, I glanced through the stairwell to see him land in a smooth crouch, as if he'd landed exactly where and how he'd planned. With furious determination hardening his face, he took off from the second floor toward the first floor in a similar fashion. Partway into his swing around the turn in the stairwell, he spread his legs and caught himself against the opposite wall in a fast halt.

I blinked at the show of upper-body strength he'd displayed, hanging for a split second above the stairs, before he pushed off the wall with this other leg. In a backward curling motion worthy of a seasoned gymnast, he swung his body back around, grabbing on to the bend of the stairwell's railing like parallel bars.

He'd just landed in a cat-like crouch atop the railing's shoulder-wide turn as the metal chair from the bottom floor clanged up the second floor's stairwell to slam against the landing's back wall.

When the chair clattered to the floor in the wake of the heavy metal door banging shut below, Drystan jumped to the landing, his face full of fury.

He gripped the railing and tensed, ready to continue his pursuit, but I called from my position a floor above, "Don't leave, Drystan. Please!"

With a grunt of frustration, Drystan vaulted back up the stairs, reaching me just as my trembling legs gave out and my butt hit the third floor's top step hard.

"Ow. That hurt." My voice shook as I began to button my jean jacket, starting at my waist.

Drystan wrapped an arm around my shoulder, pulling me against his side. He rubbed his hand up and down my jacket sleeve. "I'm here, Nara."

His hand covered mine, halting my movements. I glanced down at my fingers curled around the buttons halfway back down my jacket. I hadn't realized I was hyper-obsessing until he stopped me. "Breathe. Just...breathe," he said in a calming voice. As I took several breaths, he released his hold, yet continued to rub his other hand along my jacket sleeve.

As I met his concerned gaze, my cheeks flooded with heat. With my ability, unexpected events and I rarely collided. Yet hanging with Ethan, whose power literally shifted my dreams to him the moment we touched, I thought I'd gotten better about dealing with not knowing events before they happened. Then again, Ethan made sure to keep me safe from things he saw coming via my dreams. *I wish you were here, Ethan.*

When I exhaled a deep breath and blinked, his hand stopped moving. "In case I forgot to tell you earlier, you officially have the best timing ever." My voice rasped as I rubbed my fingers along my sore neck. "Five minutes sooner would've been even better." I paused. "I thought the elevator was broken."

He lifted my chin and stared at my throat. "Jesus, Nara! I can see red marks." Pained regret filled his gaze. "I'm so sorry I wasn't back sooner. I tried to return through the stairwell door, but even though the knob turned, I couldn't get the door to budge." He nodded toward the chair in the stairwell. "The bastard must've used that to block the door."

A shudder rippled through me. That meant my attacker knew there was someone in the stack to torment.

Drystan's hand on my arm tightened. "Since I couldn't get in, I decided to try the elevator. I was surprised when I pushed the button and it pinged to life right away."

My eyes widened. "You think it was working the whole time?"

He glared at the stairwell. "I do now. What happened? Did you know him? What did he say to you?"

I rubbed my fingers across my eyes and sighed. "I've never seen him before, but the things he said to me...it was like he knew who I was, or thought he knew."

Drystan released me and rested his forearms on his knees, his brows pulling together. "What exactly did he say?"

I closed my eyes, trying to recall. "He said that he wanted a fight, like he expected me to fight him. He seemed shocked when I said I didn't want to fight. Isn't that crazy?"

"He sounds bloody mad." When I nodded slowly, Drystan frowned. "That's all the bastard said to you? That he wanted to fight? He didn't say anything else?"

I considered telling him about the guy's strange interest in my journal, but he'd wanted to fight me *before* he'd seen it, so his motive for coming after me was for some other unknown reason. I curled my fingers around the journal against my chest and shook my head. Several seconds of silence passed and my nerves had started to settle. I eyed him, tilting my head. "You were right, by the way."

He frowned. "Right about what?"

"Parkour needs to be seen to be appreciated. I'm assuming that's what I just witnessed in the stairwell. Some of those moves seemed impossible."

Drystan flicked his hand with a snort. "Not if you do it all the time. I was in total chase mode. Didn't even think about it."

I raised an eyebrow. "Is that something you do all the time? Chasing?"

When his open gaze instantly shuttered, I bit my lip to keep my questions to myself. *Hidden passages. Where's a good decoder ring when I need one?* I smiled. "It was pretty impressive."

"Wait 'til I really try to impress you," he said, flashing a cocky smile. "Are you okay to stand now? I'm assuming they have campus security here?"

I nodded and he grabbed my hand, pulling me to my feet. "Come on then. Let's go report this bloke and tell them what happened."

AFTER MY INTERVIEW with campus police, I was exhausted, but didn't want to go home to an empty house. Mom was on her *date* with Mr. Dixon. Dang that sounded weird.

I desperately wanted to call Ethan and tell him what

happened, but I didn't want him to leave Michigan until he was ready. I knew he would the moment he thought I was in danger. I was sore and bruised, but otherwise fine.

I called Aunt Sage. "Inara! I was just getting ready to call you." A pause. "Oh, I guess you knew that already," she said, amused.

"Contrary to popular belief, I don't *always* know everything," I said, exhaling a tired sigh.

"What's wrong, hon?" My aunt instantly sobered. "The only time you don't know what's going to happen is if you've changed something."

I tensed. My aunt just recently discovered that I had her brother's gift. She's into all the New Agey stuff and is *all* about preserving the balance of nature, so I'd gotten an earful about not interfering in people's lives from her already. *Ugh!*

"I didn't change anything," I began, then trailed off, too tired to defend myself. As far as I knew, the only person's path I'd changed was mine, by bringing Drystan with me to the library. "I just wanted to spend some time with you and the boys."

"Of course, sweetie," she said in a breathy voice. "Why don't you come for coffee now. I'll see you in a few."

What? No dinner? Before I could tease her, she hung up, leaving me staring at the phone. It wasn't like my aunt to be so abrupt. Something was up. Tucking my phone into my backpack, I shoved the worries as to why I'd been that guy's target at the library to the back of my mind, then pushed harder on the gas pedal, heading to my aunt's house in Barboursville.

When my aunt's dogs, Bo, Luke, and Duke, didn't immediately come flying out the dog door to greet me the moment I drove up, I knew something was off. I quickly turned my car off, then dashed to my aunt's lighted porch, knocking with more force than I meant to. "Aunt Sage!" I called in a high-pitched voice.

She jerked open her door and she looked at me with wide-eyed worry. "Inara? What's wrong?" she asked, tugging me into a tight embrace.

I gripped her elbows and leaned into her tall, willowy

frame. After a couple of seconds, I realized the material felt wrong. I stared down at the cream cable knit sweater under my fingers. *Cable-knit sweater? Where were the loose, silky bohemian dresses she usually wore?* I leaned back to take in her entire outfit: sweater, fitted jeans and tall shiny brown boots. I glanced into her concerned gaze and gave a half smile. "You ah, look wonderful. You should wear skinny jeans more often. They suit you. What's the occasion?"

My compliment softened her expression before she cupped my cheeks, her hazel eyes searching my face. "What is it, Inara? I won't leave if you need me here."

Was my anxiety that obvious? I gulped. "You're leaving?" I didn't mean for my question to come out as a squeak, but Aunt Sage pulled me through the door and into the living room, her brow creasing.

It was strangely quiet without the dogs. The absence of pastries and incense smells jarred my senses into full alert. Not one of her New Age books sat on the coffee table by the couch. There was usually at least a couple. Instead they were all neatly stacked on her bookshelf. Her usually tidy house was even tidier than normal, and the dogs' beds were missing. My heart began to pound. "Where are the boys?" I looked around, panic starting to roll through me all over again.

"They're at—"

"Where are you going?" I asked as my roving gaze landed on a roller bag sitting near the kitchen doorway. Only one bag. She would've packed more if she were leaving for good. A switch inside me released and the dam opened, flooding my tight shoulders with relaxing relief.

"That's why I was calling." She nodded, her curly auburn hair bouncing. "I wanted to tell you I'd be gone for a few days. And don't worry, the boys are with a neighbor down the road."

Other than an occasional expo in the surrounding counties she attended every so often to gain exposure for her home-based jewelry business, she didn't venture far. She never stayed overnight. I frowned, confused. "But you never take trips." As far as I knew my aunt hadn't taken a trip out of town—I realized with sudden shock—since my dad left twelve years ago.

"Where would I go?" she used to say when I'd ask why she didn't travel. "Virginia has everything I want right here." And she'd always looked at me with loving, dedicated eyes.

What could possibly drag her away? "Where are you going?" I repeated, then quickly followed with, "How long will you be gone?" What I really wanted to say was, "Please don't leave. Not right now!" I couldn't have two important people disappear from my life. I missed Ethan so much. Not her too!

My aunt gave a secret smile. "Wow, you weren't kidding about not knowing. Guess my last-minute decision to ask you here tonight when you called *can* make a difference in what you foresee."

When I scowled at her, she snickered, then hooked her arm in mine. "Let's have some coffee."

The familiar routine we'd shared since I was old enough to sit still—sipping coffee and chatting at her kitchen table—eased some of my anxiety. I let her pull me into the inviting kitchen decorated in bright reds, deep teals, and warm yellows. Her kitchen had always felt warm and welcoming.

As Aunt Sage moved around the room making coffee, I watched her efficient movements with a clenched jaw and growing confusion. My normally talkative aunt stayed focused on her task, not looking up once. She was way too quiet. By the time she set my mug on the table, then slid into her seat across from me and cupped her hands around the warm mug, my teeth hurt. When her hazel gaze met mine, I suddenly understood. "It's about Dad, isn't it?"

She slowly nodded. "Even without your ability to see your next day, you've always read people well. I like to think you got that from me." A brief smile flitted between us. "I don't like the answers I've gotten from Jonathan's secretary. She claims he's out of the country on business." My aunt snorted, then expelled a frustrated sigh. "I want to look this tight-lipped woman in the eye when I talk to her. I'll get a better read if I can study her face."

I took a big sip of my coffee. It burned, but I gulped it down anyway. "What does your gut tell you?" I asked, my voice barely above a whisper.

My aunt pursed her lips. I'd only seen her do that once when I was almost seven. Lured by the creek sounds in the woods behind her house, I'd disobeyed her rules and left the yard to explore. She'd been so angry when she finally found me turning over rocks looking for crawdads. In one breath she was furious, then in the next she was crying and pulling me into a tight hug.

"I don't think I'm being told everything," she finally said, drawing me out of my reverie.

Despite the coffee warming my body, chill bumps scattered across my skin and my stomach tumbled. Whenever my aunt had said that to me, her penetrating eyes drilling hard, she'd always been right. I just hadn't always fessed up to my crimes. "Are you also going to his apartment, um, house…er, wherever he lives?"

"That'd be the first place I would go." Aunt Sage lifted her shoulders, then let them fall with an exasperated exhale. "If I knew where he lived."

My jaw dropped. I knew my aunt had kept a cool distance from my dad after he'd left us when I was little, but I'd assumed she knew where he lived all these years. All I knew was that he lived in the D.C. area. "How can you *not* know that? What about the monthly check you give us? Doesn't he mail them to you? There has to be a return address."

She shook her head. "The return address has always been his office address." A sly, confident gleam flitted across her face. "How do you think I know exactly where to go to hunt down his secretary?"

I rubbed my forehead, worried. "What are you going to do? March into his office and demand to know where he is?" I frowned when a second realization occurred. "What kind of work does he do, anyway?"

My aunt waved her hand. "Some government job." She took a sip of her coffee, her gaze hardening. "And yes, that's exactly what I'm going to do. No appointments. I don't want his secretary to know I'm coming. I'll come back with answers."

The hitch in her voice concerned me. I ignored the knot that had formed in my stomach and reached across the table to grip her hand. "I know I've asked to know more about my powers and only Dad can provide those answers, but right now..." I paused and had to work hard to keep my hand from trembling. "I—I just want to make sure *you* come back."

"Please, please don't act on things you dream about, Inara."

The pleading in my aunt's voice distracted me. "I'm not," I answered in a dry tone, even as I mentally finished, ...*going to be able to without a painful punishment.*

Aunt Sage visibly relaxed. Turning her hand over beneath mine, she squeezed my fingers, her eyes full of warmth. "And don't worry. Didn't you know you're stuck with me forever?"

Tears threatened and I willed them away, giving her a trembling smile. She smiled back, then quickly stood. "Come, I have something for you."

I followed her into the living room and for the first time noticed the wide black box with a gold lid sitting on the ottoman. Normally that was Bo's hangout spot.

Aunt Sage grabbed the box and her eyes lit with excitement as she handed it to me. "Happy early birthday, Inara."

I blinked my surprise. "But my birthday's not for a couple more weeks."

Aunt Sage touched my jean jacket's worn collar. "I think you could use this now. Go ahead, open it."

I lifted the lid, then pulled back the white tissue paper. "It's so soft," I said in surprise, running my fingers over the supple black leather jacket nestled in the paper. I fiddled with the silver zipper pull, then turned my gaze to my aunt. "You didn't have to buy such an expensive gift, but thank you. I love it!"

My aunt clapped her hands together, her eyes sparkling. "I'm so glad you love it, sweetie." She tugged on my jean jacket sleeve, pulling it over my hand. "Now try it on and let's make sure it fits."

Once I slipped into my new jacket, my aunt zipped it up, then smoothed the collar into place. "It's a perfect fit," she said, her voice full of pleased warmth. "And it's my absolute pleasure, Inara. You know I think of you as more than my niece."

Tears prickled and I smiled through them as I threw my

arms around my aunt, giving her a tight bear hug for the first time. Ever.

Aunt Sage froze for all of a second before I heard her let out a breath. She quickly wrapped her arms around me, then kissed my hair, murmuring, "I feel like it's my birthday too. Don't worry, I'll be back with answers for both of us."

I hugged her tighter. "Don't be gone too long."

CHAPTER 7

The house was quiet and dark as I entered. I glanced at the clock on the microwave. Six. Mom wouldn't be home for a few hours. I locked the door, then trudged upstairs to my bathroom.

After I inspected my throat in the mirror, I was glad to see only slight bruising. No one would notice it unless they stared at my neck under bright sunlight. I didn't want to have to explain what happened to anyone. God, I didn't even understand why it had happened.

Setting my backpack on my desk, I clicked the switch on my desk lamp. As soon as the light illuminated the desk, I stared at my partially opened laptop. The light in the back glowed blue, indicating the machine was on.

I *never* left my laptop on. I always completely closed it once it'd powered down. My stomach tensed and I quickly scanned my gaze around the room. My pulse rushed in my ears. Had someone been in here, looking at my laptop? Maybe I'd spaced out for once and forgot to turn my laptop off? Yeah, that had to be it.

I opened my laptop and my heart nearly stopped when the screen came to life. Someone had clicked on my computer's search history. They must've forgotten to close out of it. Or had my arrival interrupted them before they'd been able to close the history?

I dropped to my knees to look under the bed. Nothing. My focus slid to my open closet as my heart slammed against my chest wall, pounding in an erratic, fearful beat. I could easily see beyond my clothes. No one was hiding behind them.

The window! My eyes skittered to the window I hadn't bothered to lock for the last couple of weeks. That's probably how someone got in. Angry with myself, I crossed my room in three long strides, then slid the locking mechanism into place with a determined flick of my wrist, murmuring, "Sorry, Patch."

Now that I felt somewhat safer, I slid into my desk chair and put my hand on my laptop. It felt warm to the touch, which meant I *had* just missed whoever had been here. Were they thieves? I picked up my phone, intending to call the police, then scanned my room once more. Why hadn't they taken my iPod, my small TV, or the laptop itself? Had my arrival scared them away before they'd been able to haul the stuff out of the house? What kind of thief takes the time to look through someone's laptop history?

My pulse raced. Or could that person still be here in the house? My room was untouched, and even though it was shadowy downstairs, nothing had appeared missing or out of place. The police would think I was ridiculous for calling in a break-in if nothing was stolen. I forced myself to take even, calming breaths.

The doorbell rang, making me jump. I gasped and quickly shut my laptop. *Who could be at my door?*

I shuffled down the stairs in the dark, then peered through the living room curtains to see who was on the front porch. The back end of our leaf blower hung in the air, held by someone. I breathed a sigh of relief and moved to flip on the front porch light.

"Hello." A gray-haired man with dark brown eyes and a salt and pepper goatee smiled as I opened the front door. Holding the blower toward me, he continued, "Your mother was kind enough to lend this to me. I told her I'd return it as soon as I was done."

Taking the blower from him, I held its bulk awkwardly and smiled, liking his crisp English accent. He sounded so formal. "Thanks."

He slid his hands into his corduroy pants pockets and rocked on his heels, dark eyes gleaming. "According to your mother, my request saved you from leaf duty. I'm Mr. Wicklow, by the way."

"I'm Nara." I held the leaf blower back toward him. "You're welcome to keep it all week if you'd like. There's still a few more leaves on the trees."

He chuckled, tilting his head to the side. "Much as I'd like to, I think your mother might think I've absconded with it if I kept it that long." With a slight bow of his head, he said, "Please tell Mrs. Collins thank you for me."

"I will," I called after him. Once I'd locked the front door, I hauled the leaf blower back into the garage, then ran upstairs to make sure nothing else had been done to my laptop.

After I'd searched the "Today" tab to see if any new files had been opened or any software had been downloaded to my computer, I was thankful no spyware popped up. Returning to the search history page someone had pulled up, I scanned through it. Tons of raven websites, sword websites, tattoo websites, the *Corvus Corax* website. A tremor rippled through me when my gaze landed on my last search. It was the CVU library, where I'd looked to see if they had that article from thirty years ago. I'd also left a sticky note on my laptop about researching there today.

Was I followed based on that note? But then who was just in my room? I wondered as I unzipped my backpack to pull Ethan's journal out. The leather book slipped from my fingers, falling open on my desk.

As my gaze landed on the huge raven yin-yang symbol I'd drawn that covered the entire first page, my hands began to shake. This was exactly how my journal had opened on the floor in the library. It was the page the guy had shoved my face toward, demanding that I pick up the book.

If he'd wanted it so bad, why hadn't he picked it up himself? Why insist—no, command—that I do it?

I glanced at my locked window once more and a tremor rippled through me. I needed to hear Ethan's voice. He would calm me.

I dug into my backpack for my phone, then turned it on. When it powered up, I saw Lainey had left a message and there were several from Ethan. Excitement zipped along my body. I looked at the time of his texts. He'd sent the first one while I was filling out paperwork with the campus police.

Ethan – 5:00 p.m. ~ You there, Sunshine? Something just doesn't feel right. Tell me you're okay?

Ethan – 7:00 p.m. ~ Where are you? I'm worried!

Ethan – 8:30 p.m. ~ Nara, PLEASE text me back. I need to know that you're okay!

Then a voice mail thirty minutes ago. *A voice mail!* My first one since he'd left.

"I'm going out of my mind with worry. I swear to God, Inara, if I don't hear from you before the end of the day, I'M COMING HOME!"

The vehemence in his voice, the near desperate violence in it —I didn't want him to worry—but I couldn't help but feel thrilled at how very loved it made me feel. My fingers raced over the buttons to call him back.

He answered on the second ring, rock music blaring in the background. "Nara?"

"Hi, I'm okay—"

"Thank God!" he interrupted in a deep growl. "Hold a sec. Let me get where I can hear you."

When the screeching noise dwindled to a dull roar in the background, Ethan said, "Why didn't you text me back?"

"Where are you?" I asked, briefly closing my eyes to absorb the resonance of his deep voice. I'd missed that bone-melting sound.

"My dad dragged me to a concert," he said, sounding slightly disgruntled before shifting direction. "It's so good to hear your voice. I was freaking out—" he paused, surprise edging his words. "So you're really okay? Nothing's happened?"

I clenched my teeth and pressed my lips together. *Plenty has happened. I desperately want to spill my guts.* But he was at a concert *with his dad.* That was a good thing. It meant they were getting along. I didn't want to do anything to disturb their reconnection. It was vital to Ethan's overall peace. "No, nothing exciting here," I lied, doing my best to keep apprehension out of my voice.

"Are you sure?"

Ethan sounded suspicious, unconvinced. I could just picture him sliding a hand through his thick hair, then fisting his fingers in his bangs as he paced. I chewed the inside of my cheek, jealous. I wanted to run my fingers through the dark mass, smell his shampoo and spicy deodorant mixed with his own unique smell. "Yes, I'm fine. I'm sorry you were worried. I was at the library researching. I forgot to turn my phone back on."

Ethan blew out a harsh breath. "For once I'm glad my 'something is off' vibe was wrong."

I bit my lip to keep from saying, "Oh, Ethan, always trust your gut!" Instead, I said quietly, "I've missed you."

"I've missed you too," he said, tenderness softening the tension in his voice.

Tears gathered in my eyes and I clutched my phone tighter. Blinking rapidly to hold them back, I rushed on, "There's a winter dance at school, not this Saturday, but the next. Will you be back in time for it?"

When he didn't answer right away, I wondered if he'd heard what I said. There was still a lot of noise in the background. "Did you hear me?" I asked, my stomach tensing.

"I'm sorry, Nara, but I don't think I'll be back before then. There are still things I need to—" He cut himself off, but not before I felt the frustration and something else—regret?—lacing his tone. "I'll try my best to make it up to you when I get back. I promise. Okay?"

He had no idea when he was returning? The uncertainty made my heart ache. "I understand," I said, then pressed my lips together to keep from sobbing my disappointment. "You'd better go find your dad."

Ethan expelled a deep breath. "Yeah, I need to get back in there. Please keep your phone on, Nara. I can't think straight if I'm worried about you. And right now, thinking straight is pretty damned important," he finished with a harsh snort.

Guess his dad wasn't making it as easy for him as I'd first thought, but his confession of his feelings unraveled my tightly held restraint. Silent tears streamed down my cheeks. "I'm sorry I worried you. I'll keep my phone on. Come home soon. Now go enjoy the concert."

"I can't wait to come home to you," he said, his voice slipping into a silky purr.

Home. To me. That sounded absolutely wonderful. I rubbed the tears from my cheeks, smiling like crazy. "I can't wait either," I whispered.

"Good night, Nara. Dream of me."

I bit back a bittersweet whimper. He sounded like he was *willing* it to happen. *How I wish I could, Ethan!* "It would be so much easier to fall asleep and dream of you if you were holding me," I shot back.

"You're *killing* me," he gritted out, but I felt his smile too. "Go to bed, Sunshine."

A thrill zipped through me. I'd never get tired of that sweet nickname. Ethan sounded a bit different, the way he spoke more confident. This trip had been good for him, despite his annoyance with his dad. I could suffer through. "Goodnight," I said in a breathy voice before hanging up, my aching heart seesawing with sad-happiness.

THE NEXT MORNING, I was woken early by a text ping from my mom.

Mom – 6:45 a.m. ~ I see the leaf blower is back. Hmmm, wonder what that means? ;) Just wanted to let you know that I had a six a.m. conference call this morning with the international team.

*Ugh, I'm dragging. I'll see you tonight, sweetie! Italian
sound good?*

Mom wasn't usually so long-winded. Normally her texts
were to the point.

Had a six a.m. meeting. I'm bringing home Italian tonight.

She'd gotten home after I fell asleep. I wasn't sure how I felt
about the whole "dating" thing. *Discombobulated* came to mind,
a big word with all kinds of confused emotions attached.

As soon as I walked into the school's main atrium, Lainey
slammed into me in a tight hug and a cloud of spicy chic
perfume. She'd hit me so hard she knocked my red pageboy
hat off.

"What was that for?" I asked, grasping her elbows for
balance. Was something else going on with her *other* than the
scary scenario that would happen this afternoon? I could only
handle one emergency at a time. As far as I was concerned, Fate
could hop off. Nothing was going to happen to my best friend.

Unshed tears glistened in her eyes as she pulled back and
squeezed my shoulders. "Why didn't you call me back last
night?" A frown quickly replaced the worry. "And why did I
have to find out what happened at CVU's library through
Matt?"

Heat suffused my face. My call with Ethan had completely
eclipsed my scary library experience. *What was it with me and
libraries?* "I'm sorry, Lainey. I got distracted. First, I went to my
aunt's, and then I talked to Ethan for the first time since
he left."

Her auburn eyebrows shot up as she released me to scoop
up my hat. She adopted a cheeky grin as she plopped it on her
own head. "Ooh, finally! What's his deal with not talking on
the phone?" Before I could reply, she rambled on, "So, is he
coming back soon?"

I tucked a strand of hair behind my ear, trying not to look
too disappointed. "No, not yet."

When Lainey folded her arms and grunted her annoyance, I
met her gaze. "His relationship with his parents was pretty
messed up. That takes time to unravel."

Sympathy filtered into Lainey's eyes and she touched my

shoulder once more. "Seriously, Nara, are you okay...about yesterday? Especially since Ethan's not here, I can't help but feel guilty I didn't go with you."

Guilty? My eyes widened. If she had gone instead of Drystan, things could've turned out very differently for me and possibly her. Deadly different. I'd never been so glad for Lainey's bullheadedness as I was at that moment.

"Don't you dare blame yourself. Things worked out for the best." I smiled to let her know I was fine. "Talking to Ethan helped." As much as I liked talking about Ethan, my focus wasn't on me today. It was on her. "How about I come over this afternoon so we can hang?"

"That would be great." Her lips pursed into a pout. "I'm stuck with dog-sitting duty right after school."

She sounded so put out, my lips twitched. "Guess your dad decided to volunteer you for some quality pet-time anyway." The first bell rang and I had to yell over the sudden noise of students milling toward their lockers. "By the way, I want to talk to you about Matt."

Just then, I saw Matt moving at a fast clip through the hall. He looked like he was going to pass us by, but he quickly stopped beside Lainey to lift the end of her French braid peeking under the edge of the hat. Twirling the braid slowly around his finger, he winked at her before heading off down the hall without a word.

As she laughed after Matt's retreating back, then cut her gaze in another direction with a triumphant smile, I followed her line of sight. Jared stared at her with a hooded gaze over his girlfriend's shoulder. I swiveled a narrowed gaze back to her. "What scheme are you cooking up, Lainey O'Neal?"

Her attention yanked back to me, pleased victory dying in her eyes. "What are you talking about?"

I jerked my chin in the direction Matt took, glad I didn't have to touch her when I laid it on the line. *Ha, take that Fate!* "He seems like a good guy. Don't hurt him."

Lainey sighed and stepped close to hook her hand in the crook of my arm. Pulling me toward the lockers, she adopted a breezy tone. "Don't worry. Matt's a big boy."

That wasn't exactly an answer. I wanted to know her plan. I could see the wheels spinning in her head as she gazed at Jared. "Lainey..." I began, then let it go. The hall was too loud and crowded for a conversation. It would have to wait until study hall.

∾

THE MOMENT I walked into study hall, all plans of a deep conversation with Lainey about Matt evaporated. Harper sat across from Lainey at our table, waving me toward her, an excited smile splitting her face.

As I approached them, the smirk on Lainey's face radiated like a beacon all the way across the room. She knew my intention to grill her had been derailed. When I set my backpack beside hers on the table, I whispered, "I'll have your rapt and undivided attention this afternoon at *your* house."

I snickered at the sudden downturn of Lainey's lips, but Harper tugged on my jacket sleeve, distracting me. "Nara, thank you so much for talking to Sally for me!"

I sat down and turned to Harper. "Did you work yesterday?"

She nodded, her ponytail swishing, brown eyes lit with excitement. "I love CVAS! I don't know why I didn't do this sooner."

"It's a fun place to volunteer," I said, cutting an I-told-you-so gaze to Lainey, who snorted, then pulled out her phone to tap on the keys in rapid precision.

Ignoring her, I turned back to Harper. Today Harper had on dark blue trouser jeans and a bright green sweater over a pressed madras shirt in the same shade of green and various shades of pink. Still preppy, but at least she wore jeans, I thought with a smile. Hopefully she changed out of her designer clothes into casual stuff for the shelter. I could tell Harper was brimming to talk about her experience. "What was your favorite part?"

"The puppies and kittens, of course." Harper bubbled.

When I heard Lainey mumble, "I thought for sure it'd be pooper-scooper duty," I stepped on Lainey's foot under the table. *What was her problem?*

Harper ignored Lainey completely. "When are you coming to the shelter? I'd love to work with you, so I can learn the tricks of the trade from a good friend."

"I'm not sure what my schedule will be this week..." I said, then swallowed the rest of my sentence. I'd planned to visit my great aunt Corda tomorrow afternoon, since I hadn't seen her in a while. I also still had the leaves to contend with. When I felt Lainey's foot settle on top of mine under the table, I glanced her way. An auburn eyebrow was raised high. *Good friend?* I read the irritated look on her face.

I was a bit surprised by Harper's comment, but she was new and probably hadn't made many friends yet. Harper's hand landed on my arm and just as I turned my attention back to her, Lainey said, "Don't forget, we're going shopping for dresses tomorrow."

I cut my gaze to Lainey. "I'm not going to the dance."

"Yes, you are." Stubborn determination had settled on her face. "I'm going with Matt. You can go with Drystan."

My jaw dropped. *This was her plan? To go to the dance with Matt?* I wanted to lay into her, but I wasn't going to go off in front of Harper. "My *boyfriend* would be pissed. I'm not going with Drystan," I said, breathing heavily through my nose.

Lainey flipped her hand, batting away my argument. "That's why Drystan will make the perfect date. You'll just go as friends, just like Matt and me."

I opened my mouth to argue, but Harper's hand squeezed my arm. "Since tomorrow's no good, how about another day this week?" When I glanced at her, she continued, "Please come, Nara. I can't help feeling a little lost." Her pleading brown eyes blinked so fast, I literally felt the anxiety radiating off her.

"I'll be happy to come by the shelter tomorrow after I visit with a relative," I said in an accommodating tone. I completely ignored Lainey's annoyed "uh" directed at the back of my head.

74

Harper's eyes darted between Lainey and me. "Are you sure? It can be any day this week. I don't want to keep you from—"

"Tomorrow works for me."

"Wow, your schedule's filling up, Nara. I'm so glad you're coming to my house this afternoon," Lainey said in a sugary-sweet voice.

Her words came from above my head. I slanted my gaze over my shoulder to see her standing, books clutched to her chest, her lips pinched. "I've got some research to do in the library."

She'd never used our school library for research. "Lainey—"

See you later," she said, forcing a smile on her face.

As she walked off, her back ramrod straight, I heaved an inward sigh, knowing I was going to get an earful the moment I walked into her house.

"She's really not a very good friend, Nara," Harper said quietly beside me.

In the rapid-fire battle of wills between Lainey and myself, I'd pushed Harper to the back of my mind. I glanced her way. "What are you talking about?"

She shrugged a delicate shoulder. "Why would she try to get you to go to the dance with another guy if you have a boyfriend? I'm assuming, for whatever reason, your boyfriend can't or doesn't want to go…"

As she trailed off, I murmured, "He's not able to go."

Harper's eyebrow shot up. "Did Lainey conveniently forget you have a boyfriend then?"

"No, she didn't forget." *At least I'm pretty sure she didn't.* A fissure of annoyance splintered my thoughts. Harper hadn't known Lainey as long as I had. Sure she came across self-centered and only aware of her own sphere, but Lainey…well, she was Lainey. She was hard to explain. "Lainey's complicated."

Harper curled her upper lip, then muttered, "Seems pretty simple to me."

CHAPTER 8

"*N*ice jacket," Lainey said as she closed her front door.

Sheer annoyance fringed her compliment, effectively canceling it. She was really ticked. When I heard the deadbolt slide into place, I tensed, ready for a battle. I turned to her and murmured, "Thanks. It was an early birthday present from my aunt Sage."

Lainey's arms were folded across her chest, a scowl creasing her face. "What's your problem, Nara? I was trying to get you out of having to say 'yes' to Harper, yet you threw my help in my face."

"You mean you *didn't* want to go dress shopping?"

"Of course I do." Lainey rolled her eyes. Sighing, she walked past me into the living room. "But I hadn't decided what day I was going to go." Bewildered, she looked at me, spreading her hands wide. "I was just trying to be a friend. You know, look out for you like a *real* friend would do."

And I'm here because I'm doing something a real friend would do too, despite what Fate may do to me for going against him! I wanted to yell at her, but I couldn't. Instead I focused on something I *could* talk about.

"I'm sorry if I screwed up your bail-Nara-out plan, Lainey, but I was pissed at you about Matt. I saw the way you looked at

Jared after Matt left your side today. Was *this* that 'best idea ever' you were talking about yesterday; to go with Matt to the dance as payback to Jared? That's really low, Lainey!"

Lainey's cheeks flushed bright red. "The dance was Matt's idea," she hissed. "He asked me, Nara!"

I blinked rapidly and sputtered, "Wh—what? You're not trying to make Jared jealous? But I saw the way you looked at him this morning after Matt walked away. You had a he's-wrapped-around-my-little-finger look if I ever saw one."

Lainey's eyes fluttered. "Really? That's how I looked at him?"

I pressed my lips together, nodding. "It was a very 'triumphant' look."

Lainey's hand fluttered over her hair, a pleased grin spreading up her face. "Well, making Jared and Tarra jealous was definitely high on our list. That part is true."

"Our? What?" I shook my head, running my hand through my hair. "I'm confused."

"It was my idea to just flirt and hang out a lot at school." Her eyes narrowed briefly. "I want Jared to see he's not the only one who can move on. And Matt, well he wanted Tarra to feel that way too, so we agreed to put on a show for their benefit."

I spread my hands wide, at a loss. "So you were serious when you said you and Matt are going to the dance as friends?"

She nodded. "Of course. Matt thought it would make our flirtation seem more realistic."

I rubbed my temples to clear my original thoughts. *Matt was a part of this craziness?* Peering at Lainey, I couldn't help but trust my gut. "I don't know, Lainey. Either Matt's a great actor, or I think he might really be into you."

Lainey's eyes widened, and then she began to laugh so hard she bent over and curled her arms around her stomach.

"What's so funny?" I grumbled.

Tears trickled down Lainey's cheeks when she looked up at me. "Wow, maybe I should enroll in acting classes too if we've got *you* convinced. Matt really can act."

"You didn't see the way he looked at you today," I said,

straightening my spine. "Lainey, the look in his eyes was...he likes you. I mean, *really* likes you."

Lainey flicked her hand, snickering. "Matt's fun. We've had some great laughs while plotting together, but he doesn't like me that way, Nara. He's still stuck on Tarra."

I opened my mouth to say something else, then clamped it shut. She didn't believe me. She was so blind. "Whatever," I huffed. Throwing my hands up, I flopped onto the couch.

Lainey joined me, sliding across the soft brown leather to face me. Her eyes brimmed with excitement. "Since you're *busy* tomorrow after school, you're going to come dress shopping with me on Thursday then, right?"

"I've got a lot to do this week," I hedged. Dress shopping might be fun for Lainey, but since I wasn't attending the dance, I saw no point in going. Lainey started to frown, so I changed the subject. "You don't like Harper very much, do you?" I said with a half laugh.

Lainey stiffened. "She's not your *good* friend." A scowl creased her brow. "No, I don't like her. At all."

I shook my head. "Why? She hasn't done anything to you."

"Pretending like she's known you forever..." Lainey screwed her lips into a sour pucker, then slit her gaze. "I don't trust the starched-shirt prissy."

She thinks she has you pegged too. I knew I wasn't getting anywhere with Lainey about Harper, so I slid my hand into my jacket pocket and retrieved the lone tan leather glove. Rubbing my thumbs across the soft material a couple of times, I held it out to her with an apologetic look. "Last night, I went to pull your mom's gloves out of my jean jacket pockets to give them back to you when I saw you today, but there was only one."

Blood drained from Lainey's face and panic crept into her eyes. "Oh no!" she whispered as she took the single glove from my hand, crushing the soft leather between her fingers. "Dad is going to freak out. Those were a Christmas present for Mom he'd ordered from a specialty store in Ireland."

Even though I'd already heard this same reaction from Lainey in my dream last night, I wasn't prepared for it. My nerves were wound so tight, my shoulders ached. In my dream world, I'd called Lainey to tell her about the lost glove. I wasn't at her house, which is how she ended up going to look for the missing glove in the woods by herself. Apparently, she'd taken the wrong path, going in the opposite direction than Drystan and I had the day we'd found Loch.

That's when she got shot in the arm. They'd found her bleeding and unconscious not that far from her house. She was still wearing my red pageboy hat she'd swiped from my head earlier in the day at school. Had the poacher been lurking in the woods and decided it was payback time for his traps being taken? Or was the shooting some random accident no one wanted to confess to?

"I'm so sorry, Lainey," I said, coming back to the present. "I stuffed the gloves in my pockets so I could comfort Lochlan with warm hands. He was so pitiful, his little leg caught in that trap. I guess I didn't tuck in the gloves as well as I thought. One must've fallen out on our way back to your house."

Lainey took calming breaths, then stood and headed for the coat rack by the front door, calling behind her, "You stay here with Loch. I'm going to go look for it."

I was beside her in an instant, tugging her black wool coat from her hands. "No, I'll go."

Lainey pried the coat out of my grip, determination in her gaze. "I should never have grabbed Mom's gloves. She calls them her 'lucky' pair since they're from Ireland. I was just in a panic over Loch. Getting the glove back is my responsibility." When she shrugged one arm into her jacket, panic gripped me.

"Listen to me!" I squeezed my eyes shut as I reached for her hand, expecting a bone-jarring shock. When my fingers connected, but nothing happened, my eyes flew open and I exhaled a breath of relief. "You're *not* going."

The same stubborn look I'd seen on her face during study hall resurfaced. She started to speak, but I cut her off. "I'll go shopping with you on Thursday if you let me go look for the glove, Lane."

Lainey clamped her mouth shut. She knew when I called her "Lane" I was speaking from the deepest part of our friendship, which meant she needed to listen. Excitement suddenly flickered in her gaze. "You'll go?"

I nodded. "Now put your coat back. You don't know the path Drystan and I took. You'll be wandering around out there forever. I can retrace our steps and be back here in minutes," I said, tipping the scale in my favor.

Lainey sighed and nodded her agreement. She grabbed my red pageboy from the rack, then jammed it on my head. "Here's your hat back. The temperature's dropped." As I buttoned my jacket, she glanced at my hands with an exasperated look. "*Really*, Nara? Where are your gloves?"

I smirked. "Why does this sound familiar?"

"You nut," she murmured, then commanded, "Stay here."

I frowned after her, but waited, wondering what she was up to.

She came back swinging a bright red gift bag. I stared at it, confused. "What's that?"

"Happy early birthday!" she said with bright eyes. "I wasn't going to give this to you yet, but…" She paused and skimmed her gaze over my jacket. "It seems your aunt and I were on the same wavelength."

As I took the bag from her, I said for the second time in as many days, "But my birthday's not for another couple of weeks."

Lainey smirked. "Sometimes you just have to go with the flow. Open it."

Setting the bag down, I pulled out the white tissue paper and unwrapped a beautiful bright red cashmere scarf. "Oh, it's gorgeous! Thank you, Lainey." I wrapped the scarf around my neck.

When I looked up at Lainey and spread my hands wide in a "ta-da!" stance, she was holding a smaller tissue-wrapped package out to me. "You had two presents in the bag. Here's the second one."

When I unrolled the white paper and a pair of black finger-less gloves fell into my hands, Lainey said, "I thought about getting you the capacitive ones for your touch screen, but they're bulky. These are sleek, bad-ass, and totally go with your leather jacket and lace-up boots."

That was Lainey, ever the fashion conscious. Once I slipped the gloves on, she gripped my fingertips on my right hand, her hazel eyes glimmering. "Now you can text with Ethan anytime, anywhere. No more stiff fingers."

Lainey had put a lot of thought into my gift. And the fact she hadn't forgotten about Ethan was an added bonus that effectively ripped Harper's assumptions about her to shreds. Oh, how she'd gloat if she knew the truth. Either that, or she'd bitch slap Harper. Probably both, I thought with an inward snort.

As I stared at Lainey's fingers gripping mine, gratitude and emotion tightened my throat. I was so thankful for my ability to see my next day. I would keep her safe. Pulling her into a tight hug, I sniffled. "Thank you so much, Lainey. Your gift is perfect in every way."

When I leaned back and we locked eyes, her lips were set in a determined line. "I should go with you."

"You can't leave Lochlan." I glanced at her dog, who was snoozing in his bed by the fireplace. "He'll try to walk on that cast if you go outside too."

She heaved a grunt of frustration, then walked beside me into the kitchen where she opened the back door.

While I jogged down the deck stairs, she called after me from the doorway, "Hurry, Nara. I don't like this at all!"

The moment I crested the small hill just outside the entrance of the woods, I knew I was cut off from Lainey's line of sight. I jerked the red hat from my head and just as I started to tuck in into my jacket pocket, I remembered that hunters wear bright colors so they *are* seen. Then again, Lainey was wearing my bright red hat when she got shot. As the next thought, *Isn't the center of a bull's-eye red?* flitted through my mind, I quickly pulled off the red scarf, then shoved it in the other pocket.

My breath plumed in puffs of frost as I jogged deeper into the woods. Lainey wasn't kidding about the temperature, I thought wryly and shoved my hands into my overstuffed jacket pockets to keep my fingertips warm.

Pine and the smell of moist underbrush assaulted my senses as I walked in the direction of the creek, scanning the ground for the missing glove. Sunlight shined through the canopy of leaves above me, briefly brightening the fall colors that had faded to duller yellows, reds and oranges. The leaf coverage wasn't near as thick now. Winter's harsh bite would soon strip them all from the trees, shriveling them to brown husks.

Leaves crunched under my boots as I scanned the under-brush on the forest floor. It didn't help that the dead leaves were the same color as the glove I was trying to find. Why couldn't *it* have been bright red? I sighed and kept scanning.

The crack of a branch echoed in the woods in the direction I'd come. My feet locked in place. Heart racing, I jerked around, looking for the source in the stand of trees behind me. Was someone lurking behind one of them? My eyes skipped from tree to tree within my periphery, touching on any one that was wide enough to hide a person.

Nothing.

I tried to slow my breathing, to focus my hearing, but all I heard was the rustle of leaves in the trees. Blood rushed in my ears as I quickly spun in a full circle, checking each trunk for the edge of a shoulder, the bend of a knee or the straight line of a leg. *Anything* that was out of place.

When a group of birds took flight from a tree to my left, my attention shifted to the trees below them to see a shadowy blur zip away from the trunk. It was so fast that I blinked, wondering if I'd actually seen anything or if it was just my imagination.

Kaun, kaun, kaun, kaun a raven squawked somewhere in the trees, but to me it sounded like *run, run, run, run.* I didn't need any more prompting. I took off toward the creek. If the glove was anywhere, that's where I'd find it. Digging my boots' thick soles into the moist ground, I pushed toward the hill that led to the creek. I thought I saw a shadow to my right, so I veered to my left, still heading toward the hill that led to the creek. I'd come out farther down and would have to follow the creek bed to make my way back to the area we'd found Lochlan, but at least I'd moved away from the shadow.

My feet scattered the crunchy leaves and underbrush, making it impossible to hear if anyone was behind me. I desperately wanted to check over my shoulder, but doing so would slow me down. I'd check once I reached the hill.

At the top of the hill, I halted and glanced over my shoulder, doing a quick scan of the woods. A hundred feet away, a couple of deer had stopped grazing. They stared at me with wide-eyed apprehension, as if they were debating if they should abandon their feeding area for safer ground.

I waited while my breathing quietly sawed in and out. The deer would hear any type of disturbance in the woods far sooner than me. I'd take my cue from them.

When they began to amble in an unconcerned fashion down the hill toward the creek, I breathed a heavy sigh and followed at a much slower and quieter pace. My dream had spooked me into imagining all kinds of scary intent-to-kill scenarios. Lainey getting shot was probably an accident. Plus, I wasn't anywhere near where Lainey had been found.

After that pep talk, I gathered my courage and made my way to the spot we'd found Lochlan by the creek. Sure enough, lying on the bed of leaves still indented in Loch's form, I found the other glove.

I picked up the glove, and as I shoved it deep into my pocket past my hat, I mumbled, "If you have any good luck in you, please make sure I get back to the house in one piece."

Taking a deep breath, I took off running up the hill, the deer scattering with my sudden burst of movement.

I exited the woods, and as I approached the small hill, I slowed from a fast run to a brisk walk, my thudding heart stuttering and slowing down to a rapid thump with my relief. *I'd made it out.*

Just as I started up the slight incline, Drystan came running over the hill in full-on speed right in my path. He looked so intense, I froze. At the same time he yelled something, a loud boom detonated, ringing my ears.

CHAPTER 9

*D*isoriented from the deafening sound, I tried to dodge out of his way, but my body moved as if I'd been dropped into a vat of molasses.

Drystan launched toward me, grabbing me by the waist. As we flew toward the ground, he curled inward, taking the brunt of our fall before we tumbled down the rest of the incline in a fast spin of flailing limbs.

We rolled to a stop with Drystan on top, his weight whooshing the air out of my lungs. Wheezing, I panicked and tried to push him off. Drystan gripped my arms and held me down, hissing, "Stay down, Nara. Just stay the 'ell down."

It seemed like we lay there forever, Drystan breathing heavily in my ear while my ponytail dug into the back of my head. Just as my breathing shifted from frantic pants to stuttering breaths, a siren sounded in the distance. Tension eased from Drystan's hard frame and he released his death grip on my wrists, rolling off me. "Thank God! The police are here."

"I almost got shot, didn't I?" I said quietly.

Drystan sat up and pulled me to a seated position too. In our current position, the hill still blocked us from the house's view. "You knew you were going to get shot?" Shock registered in his green eyes.

I gulped. I hadn't meant to say it like that. I'd blurted my thoughts before I had a chance to think of the right way to say it. "Um, I meant…did you just save me from getting shot? How did you know?" Drystan opened his mouth to speak, but two police officers, a man and a woman, came running over the hill, guns drawn.

"Let's get you both inside and under cover," the stocky red-headed woman said in a gruff voice. While the blond officer stared off into the woods, scanning for the shooter, the female officer escorted us into the house.

As soon as we walked inside, a babbling, hysterical Lainey immediately folded me in a hug so tight, I could barely breathe.

"I'm okay, Lainey," I rasped. While I stroked her French braid to calm her, I saw the worried look in Matt's gaze as he stood behind her. Fists clenched by his sides, torture reflected in his eyes when they flicked to Lainey, then back to me. I saw what he was thinking, *It could've easily been Lainey.*

You have no idea, Matt.

"I'm glad you're okay, Nara. Drystan insisted we call the police. He thought he heard gunshots that sounded way too close," Matt said, sounding shaken.

"Yes, thank goodness he was there just when I needed him," I murmured. My gaze locked with Drystan's over Matt's shoulder, but he broke eye contact when the redheaded police officer asked him to give her a play-by-play of exactly what happened.

MOM FREAKED the moment I walked in the door. She grabbed my shoulders and yanked me into a tight hug, breathing hard against my hair. "I was so scared when I got the call from Lainey's dad. I let him have an earful that he didn't call me until you'd left to come home. I would've picked you up."

"I was fine to drive myself, Mom," I mumbled into her shoulder, but that didn't stop me from hugging her back just as tightly. I'd waited almost twelve years for my mom to show strong emotion and hug me with such intensity. I wasn't passing this opportunity up for anything in the world.

Mom pulled back to look at me and mistook my tears of joy for fear. "It's okay. Everything's okay. You're safe now." Yanking me back into a quick hug, she huffed, "You're not allowed to go back over to Lainey's until they arrest this psychopath poacher."

The unknown poacher was the only logical explanation the police could come up with for the shooting. I'd shivered when I heard Drystan tell the officer he'd heard the bullet whiz past, barely missing us. They'd scoured Lainey's yard and house as well as the surrounding yards and houses, looking for the bullet, but didn't find anything.

"Understand, Inara?" Mom said, bringing me back to the present as she tightened her hold.

I nodded against her shoulder, basking in the warm, protective mama bear hug. The frantic fierceness, the I'll-kill-anyone-who-tries-to-hurt-my-baby tension in her hold…there really wasn't anything quite like it. I wished I could bottle it to save for potential future reassurance needs.

Mom and I had a great dinner, where I finally got to hear how her date with Mr. Dixon went. Listening to her talk about Mr. Dixon didn't bother me as much as I thought it would. Maybe it was because I was distracted, but she seemed less stressed than she usually was, even a bit giddy. I knew she rambled for my sake, but her happiness helped me to forget about the close call I'd had today.

After we finished dinner and were gathering the takeout containers, Mom brought up the shooting while spooning left-overs into a plastic storage bowl. "I tried to call your aunt to let her know you were okay—just in case she heard about it on the news—but I got her voice mail." Mid-scoop, her brow furrowed. "That was hours ago and I still haven't heard from her. I hope she's okay."

I paused loading my glass into the dishwasher, my happiness for my mom taking a bittersweet turn with her inadvertent reminder that my aunt had left on a mission to find out what was up with her brother. Mom didn't know Sage had kept in touch with him or that I'd requested a talk with my dad to learn more about my powers. After he'd left us with no explanation when I was five, it took Mom years to stop wearing her wedding ring. And it was just in the past couple of months that she'd started to show emotion around me like she used to when I was little. For now, it was for the best she didn't know anything. "Oh, Aunt Sage flew to Florida for vacation yesterday," I said.

Mom blinked, looking a bit hurt. "Really? I know Sage and I don't talk often, but she usually tells me if she's going to be gone."

"She asked me to let you know. Sorry, it slipped my mind with everything that happened."

Mom's tense expression relaxed as she swept the crumbs off our placemats into the trash. "Well, good for her. It's about time she went on vacation. She hasn't had one in years."

As I loaded Mom's silverware into the dishwasher, I nodded my agreement, while mentally reminding myself to warn my aunt *where* I'd said she'd been while she was away.

An hour later, after a long hot shower, I crawled into bed. I was completely exhausted. It had been a very long, emotionally draining day. After I'd pulled my covers to my chin, I realized that I'd been so distracted by everything, I hadn't checked my phone for hours.

Crawling out of bed, I grabbed my phone from my back-pack, then dove back under the covers. When I saw I had a few texts, I bit my lip and scrolled through, expecting them to be from Ethan. He was probably freaking out again.

There weren't any from Ethan. I was a bit surprised and slightly disappointed, but also relieved. He didn't need to worry about me when he was so far away. Everything turned out fine...and for that I was very thankful.

There were three texts from Lainey and one from Drystan. *Drystan?* How'd he get my number? Lainey, of course. I sighed as I opened Lainey's texts.

Lainey – 6:22 p.m. ~ Police protection?! Ack! I don't want my dad's buddies following me around everywhere. Can you imagine the crap they'd report back to him?

Lainey – 8:05 p.m. ~ Good news! They found the poacher who'd buried those illegal traps on our land. He's in custody now. He had an unregistered gun that had been recently fired. I'm SO relieved!

Lainey – 8:18 p.m. ~ Dang! Dad said the protection stands. At least until they confirm if the poacher has an alibi for this afternoon, yada yada. Grrrr.

*Me – 9:50 p.m. ~ Thanks for the update. Guess you'll have to be on your best behavior. Am SO glad I'm busy tomorrow. *snickers**

Lainey – 9:53 p.m. ~ Just for that last comment, you're also trying on dresses, not just watching me!

I grimaced at her last text, then opened Drystan's.

Drystan – 8:45 p.m. ~ Just wanted to check if you're okay?

Me – 9:57 p.m. ~ That was pretty close, but I'm fine. You?

Drystan – 10:04 p.m. ~ I wasn't the one being shot at!

Me – 10:05 p.m. ~ Thank you for saving me! You ah, realize you're going to have to tell me how you knew, right?

I expected a response back right away. After five minutes of silence, I set my phone down, frustration knotting my stomach. Guess I wasn't getting one.

Drystan – 10:15 p.m. ~ Only if you tell me how I was able to see myself saving you from getting shot in the chest; that's where the bullet probably would've hit you if I hadn't gotten to you first.

Way to sugarcoat it, Drystan! I blinked at his message, my heart racing. Obviously I hadn't seen myself get shot, so did he have some kind of ability too? I blinked at his message several times, processing as my mind raced between surprise over his revelation and the idea I'd almost been shot. God, I'd almost been shot! The knot in my stomach turned to nausea.

How was me getting shot possible? Lainey was the one who was shot in my dream. Yes, I'd prevented the shooting and therefore changed how the rest of my day would unfold. I'd been surprised Fate didn't shock me when I tried to stop Lainey, but Drystan's comment sent a chill of dread slamming through me. Was I the intended target the whole time? Lainey *had* been wearing my red hat while traipsing through the woods. She also had on her black wool pea coat and her hair was in a braid, making it hard to tell it was red from a distance. She could've been mistaken for me. Was that why Fate let me stop her, because I was supposed to get shot? *Twisted bastard!*

But wait...in the chest? That meant that whomever had shot at me wasn't in the woods at all, but had been located either beside Lainey's house, or possibly in the woods across the street from Lainey's house. Was Lainey the target or me?

Drystan – 10:18 p.m. ~ You there?

I stared at my text screen. I *knew* Drystan had some kind of ability. At least my subconscious knew. He'd found that misfiled microfiche in no time, as if he'd known exactly where to look. He was also the one who'd found Lochlan. We could've been in those woods for hours looking for the poor little Jack. *Jack!* Drystan's comment from that day in the woods came back to me.

"I was just thinking that Lochlan's an interesting name for a smallish dog...but I suppose it probably suits a Jack."

How had Drystan known that Lainey's dog was a Jack Russell? Neither Lainey nor I had told him, and he hadn't been in Lainey's house to see pictures of her dad hunting with his dog on the fridge.

Even though I wanted to know how his ability worked, I wasn't sure if I wanted to share mine with him.

Me – 10:20 p.m. ~ I'm here. Not sure what you're talking about with your earlier text. That's freaky, which reminds me...how did you know Lainey's dog was a Jack that day we went looking for him? We never told you what kind of dog he was.

*Drystan – 10:23 p.m. ~ Distraction? That's your answer? The only way I knew he was a Jack was because I saw myself laying him in Lainey's arms! Seeing **myself...in the future**, those are both new to me. The only common factor in both cases (the shooting and Loch) was YOU.*

I bit my lip, dying of curiosity to know what his ability was. And why did being around me change his? When I didn't respond right away, Drystan sent another text.

Drystan – 10:26 p.m. ~ I'll share if you do. In person. Otherwise, according to my uncle, I'm brilliant at denial. See you tomorrow.

CHAPTER 10

My planned visit with my great aunt Corda, whom
I'd always called Gran, made a great excuse to
avoid seeing Drystan in the parking lot at the end of the day.
Drystan might be "brilliant at denial," but he'd soon learn that I
was "phenomenal at avoidance." Lainey was too distracted by
her new bodyguards and her ongoing flirtation with Matt to
give me a hard time about leaving early.

On the way to Westminster's Retirement Community, I
stopped by Mocha Java's and grabbed a very large latte. Last
night, I'd been so keyed up from everything that had happened
and then Drystan's revelation, I didn't fall asleep until three in
the morning. I'd only slept for a couple of hours before Patch's
morning window pecking woke me.

After I took a drawing gulp of my coffee, I mumbled,
"Here's to the adventure at Gran's. I hope she's having a sharp
day." I had no idea how she'd react to my surprise visit. I
usually let her know when I was coming. At seventy-eight,
Gran had memory lapses and moments of non-clarity, but she
could also be so sharply keen, where nothing got past her.
Guess we were both in for surprises today, since I'd only
dreamed as far as school ending before Patch woke me.

Twenty minutes later, I knocked on Gran's apartment door.
"Be there in a minute," Gran called out, but when she didn't

answer within a couple of minutes, and I heard sounds of heavy shuffling behind the closed door, I jostled the doorknob.

"Gran! It's Inara. Are you okay?"

"Yeah—" More shuffling, then a sliding sound. "Just... give...me...a...sec." She'd heaved out the last word right before she opened the door, green eyes full of excitement. Several tall boxes surrounded my great-aunt, making her petite cardigan-framed body look even frailer. "What a lovely surprise! Ooh, I like your new jacket. And the red scarf is so smart with it," she said, kissing me on the cheek before pulling me inside to stand in her box-scattered entryway.

Gran smelled like caramel. I'd bet ten dollars she had a few pieces of candy sitting in her light green cardigan's pocket. To say my great-aunt had a sweet tooth would be an understatement. Maybe that meant she'd given up on gummy worms as a fertilizer source for her plants, I thought with a wry smile. "Thanks Gran. Aunt Sage gave me the jacket and Lainey gave me the scarf for early birthday presents."

"Ah, yes, your birthday's in a couple of weeks. The big seventeen." She closed the door behind me, singing, "Sexy and Seventeen."

I coughed past my embarrassment and turned to the boxes, counting five in the hall and three in the living room. "What's with all the boxes?" Gran had been at Westminster for years. I had no idea where these boxes came from.

"It's Storage Wars!" Gran declared, wiry gray eyebrows raised in glee.

"Storage wars?" I weaved around the opened boxes and wrapping paper strewn across her living room floor, following Gran into the kitchen, where she reached into a smaller box she'd set on her table.

"Clara and I have gotten hooked on that show." She pulled out a package wrapped in newspaper and began to unravel it. "And since we both had storage units, we decided to have a little storage war of our own."

Oh no! Clara again. I really hoped Gran found something that would trump whatever her neighbor found among her storage stuff. Gran and Clara had an ongoing who's-the-best rivalry, and I'd gotten pulled into it the last time. I gestured to the boxes. "And how will you and Clara determine who has a better haul?"

Gran's lips tilted in amusement. "This time it's not about winning. It's about remembering. When you get my age, Inara, unpacking stuff you haven't seen in eons is like seeing it for the first time. Except memories eventually come flooding back. That makes it even better." A pause. "Well, usually." Shaking her head as if to clear it, she continued, "Clara and I plan to take trips down memory lane and share our stories."

She glanced at the item in her hand and finished unwrapping it. It was a hand-painted Williamsburg blue pitcher with small pink flowers. "This was from an art class I took with Margaret fourteen years ago." A smirk formed on her lips as she turned the pitcher around in her gnarled hands. "Not my best work, but the class wasn't really about that."

My grandparents on my dad's side had passed away several years before I was born. I didn't remember my mom's parents —Margaret was Gran's sister—because they'd died in a car accident when I was little. Taking a sip of my coffee, I nodded to the pitcher. "Not about art? What was it about then?"

Sadness crept into Gran's eyes, her shaky hands spreading around the pitcher. "Margaret and I had started taking classes together a couple of times a year at CVU so we could do something fun, like we used to when we lived in the same house as kids. This was the last class I took with my little sister before that stupid drunk driver cut her life short." She ran her fingers over the flowers, her bitter tone turning wistful. "The last memories I have are of her laughing at my silly pitcher."

I ran my fingertip over one of the flowers. So what if they weren't all perfectly even? "Silly? It's practical. You can use it for water or as a vase and fill it with sunflowers."

"A vase?" Gran's eyes brightened. "That's a wonderful idea. When sunflowers are in season, I'll do that. The bright yellow and blue combination will be striking, a perfect reminder of Margaret."

I tilted my head. "And what did my grandmother make that she felt she could tease you about your pitcher?"

"Oh, Margaret was very talented. Her project ripped mine right out of the volcano."

Gran's mangled sayings resembled a pair of mismatched socks...in polka dots and argyle. Still, they always made me smile.

"Here, I'll show you—" Gran shuffled over to another small box that sat on her couch. As she riffled through it, the label on the side read: Margaret's Stuff.

I blinked when she held out a package that had been carefully bundled in bubble wrap. "You do the honors, Inara. I want to watch your face when you see *just* how talented your grandmother was."

As I started to take it, she pulled back slightly, eyes narrowed in suspicion. "Wait, you've already seen this, haven't you?"

I shook my head and snorted. Gran and my aunt Sage were the only two family members who knew about my gift. "I didn't sleep well last night and was woken before I saw my whole day, so I never saw this visit with you."

"Good." Smugness filled her gaze as she pushed the package my way, eyes twinkling with pride. "Go on, open it."

I broke the tape and began to unwrap the "masterpiece," expecting to see an intricately painted coffee mug. When a black raven statue with piercing eyes rolled out of the packaging into my hand, I stared at it in surprise.

"It looks so real it takes your breath away, doesn't it?" Gran said, running her fingers along the bird's back. My grandmother had carved each feather in painstaking detail, even giving the bird personality in the way she formed its head, tilting it just slightly as if the bird were looking right at you.

"Yes, it does," I whispered. "Why did she choose a raven?"

Gran chuckled. "I blame an earlier classmate from our watercolor class for that. Freddie had painted a stunning raven and my sister was so impressed, she got to know him better, asking how he could draw with such amazing clarity." She rubbed her nose, then sneezed. "Turns out he raised them."

I tore my gaze from the raven statue. "Raised them? I didn't think you could keep ravens in captivity. Aren't they protected by law?" I'd researched ravens enough to know that little bit about them.

Gran shrugged. "I remember him saying he had a license to study ravens for research, since he was going to write a book about them."

My eyes widened and my fingers tightened around the bird. "He was from Virginia?" When Gran nodded, I said, "I...um, am studying ravens for a school project. I would love to interview him. What's his last name?"

Gran gave a blank stare, then frowned. "I don't know his last name. I can't remember if it even came up in conversation."

Tension zipped along my spine. "Did he publish his book?" I should be able to find a way to contact him through the book or his website if he had one. Was he in his seventies as well? Maybe he was retired.

Gran shook her head. "I don't know. Margaret and I lost touch with him after that class was over."

I glanced down at the raven in my hand. I couldn't believe my grandmother had molded and painted the bird. Gran was right, she was incredibly talented. But what blew my mind was that my grandmother had chosen a raven. What were the odds? Or was I only seeing a connection due to my own current raven fixation? "I wish I'd gotten to know her," I said wistfully.

"I wish you could've known her too—oh, I knew there was another reason I pulled these boxes out." Gran's eyes flashed and her gaze bounced between three tall boxes, before she dove into the one closest to the door. "Your upcoming birthday reminded me..." she began, sounding muffled as she half-hung inside the box. While she flung wrapping paper over her shoulder, I edged closer to the droopy potted plant beside her couch.

Three gummy worms hung halfway out of the potting soil. Gran believed even plants needed sugar. With a silent chuckle, I pulled the worms out, then dumped the baggie of coffee grounds the Java place kindly donated onto the soil. After I'd quickly mixed the coffee in with my finger, I zipped the gummy worms into the baggie.

I'd just slipped the baggie into my pocket when Gran

surfaced, her gray hair all mussed. "Well, pooh, I can't find it." She shook a finger at me. "But I will."

"Find what?" I casually took a sip of my now lukewarm coffee.

"Never you mind, young lady. You'll see." Planting her hands on her hips, she eyed the other boxes with a determined stare.

I drained the last of my coffee, then tossed the empty cup into the trashcan under the sink. Gran was already elbow-deep into the next box when I came out of the kitchen. "I promised I'd stop by CVAS tonight, Gran, so I'm going to have to go."

When Gran came up for air, I picked a piece of wrapping paper off her shoulder. "Thanks for sharing some memories with me."

"Thank you for coming for a visit." She rose on her toes to kiss my cheek. When she sat back on her heels, her nose was wrinkled. "Whew, you really smell like coffee. Got an extra strong one today, didn't you, dear?"

I snickered. "Well, you smell like caramel. Got any in your pocket?"

Gran gave me a sheepish smile as she pulled a piece of wrapped candy out of her cardigan. "Only a couple left." She pushed it toward me. "Want one?"

"No thanks, you have it." As I turned to leave, Gran said, "Wait!" She quickly gathered the raven back into its bubble wrap then set it in my hands. "Here, take this for inspiration."

Tears prickled my eyes as I grasped the statue. "Are you sure?"

Gran swallowed as if she were choked up too. "She'd want you to have it, especially since you've got that project you're working on."

I hugged the package close and smiled. "Thank you, Gran. This means a lot."

~

I INHALED DEEPLY as I walked past the front desk and into the back of the Central Virginia's Animal Shelter. Animal smells mixed with sounds of dogs panting, cats playing and volunteers talking coalesced into a comforting montage I would never tire of.

I waved to Harper, who was in the process of feeding the dogs. "I'll be back," I said, keeping my pace brisk. I was determined to catch Sally before she went back up front. Jane had told me she was in the bathing section showing a new volunteer how we bathe the animals.

"Okay," Harper called back as I poked my head around the open doorway that led to the bathing area. Someone had propped open one of the heavy swinging doors. I was thankful, since it was either steam-bath hot or teeth-chattering cold in that room. The one constant was the moisture in the air. I smirked, thinking Lainey and her wavy hair would totally declare this space off-limits so she could avoid the dreaded "frizz hair."

Sally was in the process of showing a freckle-faced guy how to spray down a dog that had the face and floppy ears of a Lab with the solid body of a Rhodesian Ridgeback. "Like this Scott, smooth, even strokes. Got it?"

Scott nodded and followed her hand movement. He'd just taken the sprayer out of her hand when I said, "Hey, Sally. Harper asked me to stop by, but I did have a quick question for you."

Sally blew her frizzy blonde curls out of her eyes. Several pieces had come out of the fast ponytail she'd put up, sticking to her round face in the moist room. "Ask away," she said, while she watched Scott spray down the dog.

"Do you know of a local author who has published a book about ravens? A Freddie something?"

She quickly shook her head. "No, I haven't heard of him. Why?"

"My great-aunt mentioned a guy that she took art classes with over fifteen years ago. She said he raised ravens to study and write about them. Unfortunately she can't remember his last name. I'd like to contact him so I can interview him for a school project."

She rubbed a wet hand on her chin. "I've only been with CVAS for eight years, so that was before my time." Pausing, her eyes lit up. "But if you can't find him, you could check with the Wildlife Preserve facility. I know that they've fostered ravens in the past. I'll give you their number before you leave."

When Scott lifted his hand off the dog's coat in order to spray its legs, Sally quickly turned to put her hand on the wet fur. "Always keep your hand cupped on the back of the dog's head. He'll be less likely to shake, soaking you," she gently reminded.

"Thanks for the tip, Sally. I'll check it out—"

My jacket and shirt were yanked hard, cutting me off. I fell backward with the force, choking as I slammed into a slight frame.

At the same time a blast of cool, moist air blew toward my face, warm breath slid down the back of my neck and a feminine voice said, "Whew, that was close!"

Harper.

My heart pounded and my throat burned from being clotheslined by my own shirt. I blinked in confusion for a second until I saw the bathing room door swinging to a stop against the other closed door. The wedge must have slipped out, sending the heavy door flying toward my head and shoulders.

"Ugh, that *was* close." I ran my hand down my hair, feeling for flyaways. No sparks or electricity of any kind. It wasn't Fate. The door must've slipped on its own. I turned to Harper. "That wouldn't have felt good. Thanks!"

She beamed and her cheeks bloomed with pleased color. "My pleasure," she said, tugging her black hoodie's zipper toward her neck as if she needed to make sure it was completely closed. "By the way, I did an internship with the Wildlife Preserve that Sally mentioned."

Even in a casual hoodie, the way she had it zipped all the way to her throat like that made her look stiff and preppy...and young. "You did?"

Nodding, she continued, "Yep. Sally's right, they used to have ravens, but they haven't had them for a couple of years. I interned there first semester last year. We sheltered and rehabilitated all kinds of wild animals, but no ravens."

I sighed inwardly. *One step forward, two steps back.* "Thanks. Maybe I'll give them a call and see if they've heard of this raven guy."

She nodded, her ponytail swishing. "It can't hurt."

I glanced down at the fur caking every surface of her black hoodie and smiled as I unzipped it a few inches for her. "Now that I'm here, CVAS tip number one - dark colored clothes and fur...not a good combo. Also, I keep one of the lint roller things in my car."

Harper clapped her hands and grinned. "I'm so glad you're here."

I ended up staying until CVAS closed. Harper had so many questions, she followed me around like a puppy, yipping away. Ironically she left before me, since her boyfriend picked her up in an old clunker pickup truck.

When he got out of the truck to open the stuck passenger side door for her, I paused in the process of inventorying the dog food cart in the storage room to peer through the window curtain. A prep school, floppy-haired blond boy was the kind of guy I expected to see her with, not a tall, shaved-head, wiry-framed guy wearing a leather jacket, combat boots, and a chain hanging out of the back pocket of his ragged jeans. My eyebrows shot up at the Anarchy sign on his t-shirt as he walked back around to the driver's side. When he leaned across the seat to kiss her before patting her on the head, I shook my head, stunned by the unexpected pairing.

Once they drove off, I smiled and resumed my work. *Sweet, shy Harper has a rebel boyfriend. Never make assumptions, Lainey!*

Before I left, I was almost knocked over by a tawny-colored dog rushing past, bolting for freedom. Scott stood at the end of the hall, leash dangling, shocked embarrassment stamped on his face.

"Stop!" I called in a commanding voice. The runaway dog

tensed and tried to stop, but his paws skidded across the slick tile. I winced as he slammed into the door that led to the front of CVAS. I hurried to his side as he scrambled to his feet. Brown eyes wild with fear, he panted in fierce, gusty dog breath.

I put my hand on his head and pulled him close to my thigh, speaking in calming tones. Scott approached with trepidation, his wary gaze on the dog. I held my hand out for the leash. "He's just a little freaked out. He'll adjust."

"How did you get him to calm down like that?" Scott asked, respect reflected in his gaze.

I smiled and slipped the leash around the dog's neck. "I learned a trick or two from a friend who works here. You'll get to meet him at some point."

Awe filled Scott's eyes. "You're talking about Ethan, right? I heard he's like a magician with all the animals."

"Yeah, he's wonderful with them." Nodding, I patted the dog's head. "And he'd have you wrapped around his little finger, boy," I crooned at the dog who turned calm brown eyes my way.

Scott laughed. "Looks like you've made a fan. It's Nara, right? I'm Scott."

"Yep, I'm Nara. It's nice to meet you." I rubbed the dog's jowls, then gently scrubbed behind his ear. "You ready to go with Scott like a good boy?"

While Scott walked the dog back to the kennels, Sally spoke from behind me. "We're so full right now. I would love for someone to foster that one until we have more space in the bigger kennels."

I glanced her way with an apologetic look. "You know I would if my mom weren't allergic, Sally."

Sally wrapped her arm around my shoulder and pulled me to her side for a quick hug. "I know you would in a heartbeat, Nara. We'll figure it out."

CHAPTER 11

$\mathcal{T}$he next morning, I woke feeling groggy. A muffled hammering ricocheted in my head. Sunlight streaked through my room, blinding me as I tried to focus my gaze and decipher the noise.

A flash of something black in my periphery drew my attention to the window. It was Patch flying off. I rushed over to unlock it, then lifted the pane as fast as I could, but the moody raven was gone. He'd often shown his displeasure if I didn't open the window fast enough by demanding more than his requisite two sheets of shredding paper before he'd settle. I slid my gaze to the clock and blinked in surprise. It was thirty minutes later than I usually got up. *Why hadn't my alarm woken me?*

"Sorry, buddy," I muttered, then shook my head to clear it as I lowered the window back down. Why was my mind so muddled? It literally felt like someone had stuffed oversized cotton balls in every nook and cranny inside my skull.

Last night when I got home, my head was pounding so hard from the lack of sleep from the night before, I quickly glanced through my texts for anything from Ethan. I was disappointed when I didn't see one, but then maybe that was because things were going well between he and his parents. I did have a text from Lainey complaining about her babysitting detail. I also had a text from Drystan.

Drystan – 8:00 p.m. ~ Am I officially in denial mode now?

I didn't know how to respond to that. Instead, I closed his text, then tried to surf the Internet for information on Freddie, the raven guy. After a half hour of fruitless searches and increasing needle-shooting pain in my head, I'd taken some headache medicine, then gone straight to bed, where I had strange, psychedelic dreams.

Everything was a long-tail blur and completely out of focus, like a photographer showing off all his camera's special settings, one picture frame zipping by after another. All flash. No substance. The medicine sped me through my entire day on super-high, fast-forward mode. In other words, my dream from last night was totally useless.

With a frown, I grabbed the medicine bottle from my night-stand to see if I should have only taken one pill instead of two. As I read the instructions, my eyes widened and I quickly turned it to the label on the front. *Headache PM? Crap!* I'd taken a sleep aid medicine by accident. Produced by the same manufacturer, the headache medicine and sleep aid bottles were identical in size and shape. The only difference was that the sleep aid medicine's front label had a dark purple background with PM marked in bright red. I would have seen all that if I'd bothered to read the front!

I closed my eyes and sighed, thankful I didn't have anything more extreme planned today than shopping for dresses with Lainey. *Then again...*

I marched into the hall to riffle through the closet's medicine bin. This time I retrieved the headache pill bottle and tossed it into my backpack, murmuring, "An ounce of prevention..."

"Still have Central Virginia's finest watching over you, huh?" I whispered to Lainey as I cut my gaze to the two police officers dressed in regular clothes (like they thought they blended in, ha!) sitting in their car a few spaces down from hers in the parking lot. They'd rolled up their window against the brisk air, but they were watching us as if they could read lips.

Lainey put her back to them, shoved her hands in her jacket pockets, and rolled her eyes. "Ugh, I am not letting them ruin my mood today. Yesterday they informed my dad of every move I made from the time I left school. I mean, does he really need to know that I went shopping at Seraphine's Closet?"

I coughed into my gloved hand. "What happened to you and Matt going to the dance together as friends?"

"Not you, too?" Lainey hunched her shoulders and frowned. "You do realize Seraphine's also has pajamas, right? You know, the long pants and long-sleeved shirt kind? That's what I was buying, but of course my dad assumed I'd gotten lingerie. I thought for sure he was going to have a heart attack. I had to show him the receipt so he'd calm down. I was ready for World War III if he'd tried to forbid me from going to the dance with Matt."

"What's this about the 'dance with Matt?'" Matt draped his arm around Lainey's shoulders, then pressed a kiss to her temple.

Lainey placed her hand on his chest and fluttered her eyelashes. "Oh nothing. Nara and I were just discussing dress shopping. That's where we're headed, so I can't stick around and chat long."

Running a hand through his short blond hair, Matt heaved a relieved sigh. "Ah, dress shopping. Is it a good thing or a bad thing that the winter dance requires ice colors?"

"Totally sucks." Lainey pursed her lips ruefully. "There are only so many dresses in white or silver, which means chances are I'll see my same dress at least once if not more than once at the dance."

Matt thumbed toward his chest. "Makes it easy for us. All white tux with a silver or gray tie and vest. In and out of the tux place in five."

"Don't forget the mask," I chimed in. "Since it's a *masked* event."

Matt rolled his eyes. "Great. One more thing."

When Lainey snorted and shook her head, he laughed. "What? Guys like things simple. We like minimal fuss, our instructions short and clear, and our women easy."

"What!" Lainey's eyes bulged and she punched his arm, making him laugh harder. When she moved to smack him again, he held his hands up in submission. "I meant *easy* to get along with, Lainey," he said, eyes twinkling.

"Now who's making assumptions," I teased her.

"I'll take *honest* over uncomplicated any day," Drystan said in a dry tone.

As he moved to my left, I glanced at him, unsure what to say, but Drystan ignored me completely, addressing Lainey. "Any news on the poacher? Was he the one who took that shot?"

Lainey started to speak when the undercover guys started their car, then waved to her and drove off. She watched them leave, a surprised look on her face. A couple of seconds later, her phone pinged with a text. "It's from my dad," she began as she scrolled through the note. "He says they don't have any evidence to prove the poacher was the one who shot at Nara. He's still going to be held on various charges from hunting violations to possession of an illegal substance, so they've called off the security detail. Thank God!" she breathed out, lowering her phone to her side.

"I don't know if getting rid of your protection so soon was a good idea. That shot could've come from anyone or anywhere," Drystan said.

I cast my wide-eyed gaze his way. *Would he tell her what he "saw"?*

Lainey shrugged as she dropped her phone into her purse. "Yeah, but if your theory is right, that would make the shooting sheer randomness, not a case of 'that poacher's pissed at me for pulling up his traps, so he's going after my family.' The poacher's locked up for now, hence the cancellation of my ever-present bodyguards. The last thing I want is to have to worry about security every day of my life."

Drystan's lips set in a grim line and I held my breath. *Please don't say anything. Please. Don't. Say. Anything.*

"What do you think..." Drystan's green eyes swung my way, full of bristling challenge. "Nara?"

Everyone turned to me. Who would want to have to always look over their shoulder? To keep themselves under constant lock and key? I wondered. *Lock? Oh crap, did I lock my window this morning?* I frowned, trying to remember.

"Nara? You okay?" Lainey drew my attention.

"Sorry, all this talk about security made me wonder if I'd locked my house this morning. I don't remember doing it." I started to walk backward. "I need to run home to check before we go shopping. How about I'll meet you at the mall?"

Lainey waved me on. "Gives me some time to hang with Matt then. See you there at four."

"I'll walk you." Drystan glided into step beside me as I turned toward the back parking lot.

I tensed and gripped my backpack strap tighter. "Okay," I said grudgingly.

As soon as we were out of Lainey and Matt's hearing range, Drystan said, "Lainey doesn't know, does she?"

I stopped and frowned. "Know what?"

He faced me, tension in his expression. "About your—" he gestured toward me as he finished, "—ability...whatever it is."

I cut my gaze back to Lainey. She and Matt were watching us with interest.

Forcing a smile, I hooked my arm in Drystan's and made him walk with me. "No, she doesn't," I said in a low, snappy tone. "No one does."

As soon as we rounded a corner where a patch of trees obscured the main parking lot's view, I let go of Drystan and put a couple of feet between us. "And I would like to keep it that way."

Drystan shoved his hands in his jeans pockets and clenched his jaw. "What if Lainey gets shot at this time?"

I counted to five. "As long as Lainey hangs with me, she'll be fine. Trust me."

My answer seemed to suffice and we'd walked a few more

steps before he glanced my way, hurt reflected in his voice. "Aren't you curious at all?"

I met his frustrated gaze. "Yes, I'm curious how your powers work, but not at the expense of sharing. I'd rather stay blissfully unaware."

"Why?" His penetrating eyes demanded an answer.

"You're not going to let this go, are you?" I glanced around to make sure no one was watching us. Everyone must've had stuff to do after school today. Thankfully, the lot was empty.

He slowly shook his head. "I want to get this sorted in my head. I've run across a couple of people here and there who've had some psychic ability, but I've never met anyone whose powers played off mine. It's a strange experience."

"Are you going to say anything to Lainey if I don't tell you?"

He looked insulted, then shrugged. "Lainey probably wouldn't believe me anyway. I don't go around advertising my...special skills. Matt doesn't know. You're the only person, outside my mum, I've felt comfortable enough to tell."

He felt comfortable telling me? Why did I feel this internal struggle, like I was being pulled in two directions? Was it because I'd kept my secret locked away for so long? Gran had known about my gift since I was thirteen, but Aunt Sage had just recently learned about my powers. Of course Ethan knew, but ours was a special connection.

Is that why I couldn't tell Drystan? Because I didn't want to mess up my bond with Ethan by sharing with someone else? Would my ability to connect with Ethan be severed if I shared with Drystan? I was pretty sure once he learned what my powers were, Drystan would want to combine our powers again—to experiment for curiosity's sake.

Neither Ethan nor I knew why my powers flowed to him whenever we spent time together. My dreams helped him cope with the constant darkness of his own dreams, which made me feel extra special and needed in his life. Ethan and I thought it was some kind of psychic connection. Is that what happened with Drystan? A psychic connection? What if my bond with Ethan no longer happened when he came back because I'd worked with Drystan? My heart twisted at the thought. I shook my head. "I'm sorry, Drystan. I just...can't."

Drystan tensed and surprise reflected on his face. "You don't trust me."

"No, that's not it." I stepped closer, but he pulled back, his jaw working.

"I saved your life. Twice." His gaze narrowed. "And my uncle says *I* have trust issues," he ground out before abruptly walking away.

"Drystan!" I called after him, but he refused to stop or look back. I felt like the lowest of low. He had every right to be pissed. He'd saved my life, more than earning my trust. But how could I explain my reluctance to share without exposing Ethan's secret?

I'd woven a web of lies and half truths and now I was flailing around in its convoluted stickiness. Guilt knotted my stomach as I headed for my car.

CHAPTER 12

J'd beeped my car and had just reached for my car door handle when something swooped down in front of me, landing on the roof of my car.

"Patch! I'm sorry about this morning, boy," I said as I dropped my keys back inside my backpack to retrieve a piece of kibble. I dropped it on the roof and continued, "That's what happens when I take the wrong medicine."

Patch ignored the kibble and spread his wings, squawking at me. When I stared at him in surprise, he stepped closer, then began to sway back and forth, making the same long, low warning sound. It reminded me of that day by the lake when he'd tried to intimidate that goose into leaving us alone.

I started to reach for the kibble, but he pecked toward my hand, causing me to jerk back. "What the…what's wrong with you?"

As my car re-locked itself (since I'd taken so long to open the door), Patch flew off. I called after him, "If you didn't want it, you could've just flown away without snapping at me." Shaking my head, I fished my keys back out of my backpack and beeped the car again. Just as I touched the door handle, Patch swooped down between the door and me, making a loud *raaaak* sound.

As his wingspread batted me back, I gasped, "Patch!" and

watched him make a wide, arching swoop in the air. *God, he must really be mad about this morning.* I started to reach for the handle once more, but he dove in again. This time his wings smacked at my head and I thought I felt his talons grab a few strands of hair.

"Ow!" I yelped, patting the top of my head to make sure I didn't have a bald spot. As Patch arced in the air once more, I glared. "*What* is your problem?" I yelled at him, shaking my fist in the air.

When he made a deep *gronk, gronk, gronk* noise and dipped down again as if he was preparing to dive bomb me, I beeped my car to lock it and backed away, hands held up in surrender. "I'll come back when you've gone to hunt!" I grumbled.

As soon as I walked away, Patch flew off toward the trees. Pleased that he fell for my ploy, I turned back toward my car and lifted my key fob to beep it. Patch came out of nowhere, making high-pitched *kaugh, kaugh, kaugh* sounds.

"Fine!" I stomped off in the direction of the main parking lot and tapped out a text to Lainey.

Me – 3:45 p.m. ~ Are you still here? Decided to skip going home. It'd be more fun to ride together.

Once I sent the text, I snorted my annoyance when I realized Patch was still watching me from a nearby tree. What was wrong with him? Was he really that mad at me for not opening my window this morning?

Lainey – 3:46 p.m. ~ I was just getting ready to leave. I'll drive back and get you.

THE MOMENT we strolled into the department store's formal dress section, Lainey squealed in delight and quickly grabbed an emerald-green sequined gown off the rack at the front of the store. Holding it against her chest next to a full-length mirror, she beamed. "Isn't it gorgeous?"

It really did go well with her auburn hair, but I tugged it

from her tight grip, then slipped it back on the rack. "Silver or white, remember?"

"Ugh!" Lainey heaved an annoyed grunt. "I'm going to look like a washed-out vintage photo. I really don't like that they wouldn't at least consider letting us wear blue," she said wistfully as she brushed her fingers along a gown in electric-blue satin.

Clasping her hand, I steered her toward the center of the store. "Um, yeah, 'cause electric blue is one of the colors you see in ice." When she tensed, I met her gaze and squeezed her hand. "But what you do see are shades of very pale blue," I said, tilting my head toward a rack of blue dresses in every spectrum.

Lainey's eyes lit up like it was Christmas. She made a little hop, then shot over to the dresses, calling over her shoulder, "This is why I made you come. I knew you'd help me find something that would look right on fair Irish skin."

As she grabbed several dresses in shades of light blue to try on, she nodded. "You too, Nara."

I folded my arms. "I'm not going to the dance, so there's no point in trying anything on."

Arms full of dresses, Lainey approached. "What if Drystan wants to go just so he can experience his first American school dance?"

Was she really trying to play the sympathy card? "I've seen the way the girls get all swoon-goofy whenever they hear him talk. Trust me, he won't have trouble finding a date." Then I remembered how Drystan probably hated me now. "Anyway, you're not going to have to worry about Drystan's feelings. I'm the last person he would ask."

Lainey's gaze slit in suspicion. "What's going on, Nara? I saw you two talking. Then I saw him walk away. Well, more like stalk away."

"He was mad at me that I didn't back him up about you keeping your security. I happen to agree with you. I think you're safe." I shrugged. "Drystan didn't see it that way."

"Awww." Lainey smiled. "Isn't that sweet that he's so worried? Matt was the same way. He wasn't happy about the police protection being called off either, but I trust my dad's instincts. Drystan really is a good guy, Nara. If he asks you, you should say 'yes.' He would only ask you to go as a friend. He knows you have a boyfriend."

"He does?" I stared at her, some of the tension easing out of my shoulders. How did he know? The subject had never come up between us. For all I knew he had a girlfriend back home in Wales.

Lainey shifted the heavy stack of dresses in her arms. "I told him you weren't going to the dance because your boyfriend couldn't make it. He thought that was a lame-arsed reason to stay home."

My eyebrow shot up.

"His words, not mine," she said, lifting her shoulders.

I really didn't want to talk about Drystan anymore. With Lainey, distraction always worked, so I grabbed the first two dresses in my size from a silver-and-white themed dress rack. "Okay, we're here to try on dresses. Let's do this!"

An hour and a half later, I was completely exhausted, but enjoying myself. For every dress Lainey tried on, she insisted that I do the same. After about the thirtieth dress, she finally found a gorgeous floor-length dress in satin with a sequined halter-style bodice. The color was so pale blue it looked gray, and best of all it complemented her fair complexion.

I was in the process of slipping out of a silver-sequined gown when Lainey's arm came over the top of the dressing room door, holding a white and silver dress. "Here. One more."

"But you found your dress..."

Lainey shook the dress. "Please, Nara! It was hidden on a back rack and I'll bet it'll be gorgeous on you. Dresses like this only look good on tall people."

"Five eight isn't *that* tall," I said in a disgruntled tone, taking the dress from her.

"You know what I mean. Quit pouting and put it on. I want to see it on you."

I slipped the soft satin and thin tulle over my head, then quickly zipped up the back. When I turned around to look at myself in the mirror, I was shocked. Holy cow, it was amazing the difference a fitted, strapless bodice could make. I had some awesome cleavage. Though if I wore it like this, I'd feel naked underneath. I'd still wear a strapless bra.

Tiny silver beadwork created a two-inch band across my chest, then the beadwork crisscrossed over the white tulle bodice, enhancing my breasts. Right above the silver band that encircled my waist, diamond cutouts revealed even more skin on my left and right side. Below the fitted waist, a flowing skirt of fine white tulle overlaid a soft satin underlayer that touched my toes. With every movement I made, the skirt flowed in and out of my legs beautifully.

"Well? Let me see!" Lainey insisted. I could literally hear her hopping from foot to foot outside the door.

I stepped out to let her see. "It's very pretty."

"Look at your boobs!" Lainey squealed in glee, then quickly lowered her voice when several people in the store turned toward the dressing room section.

My face flamed and I started to cover my chest when she grabbed my hands. "Oh no, you don't. This dress is stunning on you!" As she looked me over from head to toe, Lainey whispered, "This is exactly how I picture Athena, all Grecian and gorgeous!" Letting go of my hands, she turned me toward the full-length mirror and held my hair up, piling it on top of my head. "Can't you just see it, Nara? With curls tumbling around your face."

I smiled. Lainey's excitement was infectious. "Thanks for making me come. This was fun."

"You have to get it. It was made for you."

Maybe for a future event. I glanced at the tag and my heart nearly stopped. Two hundred and fifty dollars! I thought Lainey's hundred and seventy-five dollar dress was too much for a one-night event. "Oh, my God, Lainey!" I hiss-whispered. "Why'd you pick the most expensive dress in the store? That's like offering a dieter chocolate."

"Because I knew you would do it justice," she snapped, peering at me in the mirror. "Not many girls could pull off this dress." She slid her hands across my shoulders. "You have just the right build. Broad shoulders, athletic…" Pulling me back, so

I had to bend down to her five-four height, she finished with a wicked grin, "and with fantastic knockers."

Her last comment made me snicker. As I straightened to my full height, I smiled sadly. "Thanks, but this dress is way out of my league."

Lainey frowned. "You're such a party pooper. Go take it off and I'll put it back."

While I got dressed, Lainey paid for her dress and bought a pair of matching shoes.

"Want to get some coffee?" she asked as we walked out of the department store into the mall.

I grinned. "Yeah, but let's get it to go. I need to get my car and go home. If I don't get the leaves up, Mom's going to kill me."

As soon as I got home, I tried to start the leaf blower, but it just sputtered and immediately cut off. "Lovely," I murmured as I glanced at the gas reservoir. It was almost empty. Mom was the one who mixed the oil/gas mixture. I didn't know the ratio, so I'd have to wait for her to do that before I could take care of the leaves. I taped a note on the blower. *Needs fuel.*

Snickering at my reprieve from leaf-blowing duty, I started to head for the stairs when my gaze landed on the glowing light on the dishwasher. The green light mocked me as I tried to walk past it, so I stopped and took the time to put the clean dishes away.

Once I slid the last dish into place on the shelf, I closed the dishwasher, then trotted upstairs with a spring in my step. *Mom might not be happy about the leaves, but she'll be shocked that I emptied the dishwasher without being asked.*

I'd just turned into my room, when I gasped and froze, my heart jerking. Someone was lying on the floor next to my desk.

CHAPTER 13

*A*s the woman pushed herself up with one hand, while holding her head with the other, realization dawned. "Ohmygod, Gran!" I cried out, rushing to her side to help her sit up. "What happened?"

"Apparently, I fell," Gran said in a surly voice.

"I know, but...what..." I paused and helped her to her feet. I was afraid to let go of her frail arm. "Can you stand?"

Gran put her hand to her head once more and mumbled, "Maybe I should sit down."

As soon as I helped her sit on my bed, I fell to my knees again and pushed her gray hair back to see the slight lump on her forehead. "You've got a nasty bump. I'm going to get you some ice."

I was back in less than a minute, pressing a cold compress I'd wrapped in a hand towel gently against her forehead. "Here, hold this on for a few minutes."

As Gran held the compress on her head, I stared into her bright green eyes. "I'll take you to a doctor. You might have a concussion."

Gran waved me off.

I held up two fingers. "How many, Gran?"

"Two," she grunted.

"Recite 'Peter Piper.'"

"What?" She scrunched her nose.

"Recite the nursery rhyme, Gran," I said in a stern voice. "The whole thing."

She sighed her frustration, then did as I asked.

"Now do this," I moved my fingers up and down each other like a spider climbing a web, "while saying the 'Itsy, Bitsy Spider.'"

After she recited the rhyme while performing the hand movements, slowly but flawlessly, she put the compress back on her head. "If you'll stop giving me concussion tests, I promise to have the doctor at Westminster check me out when you take me back."

"I guess that'll have to do." I frowned, shaking my head at the whole scenario. "How'd you get here? Are you AWOL again?"

"I took a cab." Gran snickered and pointed to my window. "And I came in through your window. You know, even though you're on the second floor, you really shouldn't leave it open. If an old woman like me can get in here..." she began in a lecturing tone.

I was about to speak when my phone rang, Dokken's "Alone Again." "Hi, Mom."

"Your Gran's gone missing again. I've been in a meeting and just got the voicemail the Westminster administrator left."

Gran was miming in the background, slicing her hand across her neck. I pressed my lips together and shook my head. "She's right here."

"She's with you at home? Is she okay?"

"Yeah, I'm at home. Gran's bumped her head, but she's fine—"

"Oh God. I'll be right home!" Before I could say anything else, Mom hung up.

"Now look what you've done," Gran grumbled. "She's going to come in here, freak out and insist I go to the hospital."

"You probably should. I can't believe you climbed up here into my room—"

"I've climbed far taller trees and much harder obstacles in my day. What was I supposed to do? It's not like I had a key."

I cracked a smile. Gran's off-center logic might sound crazy to others, but it was totally Gran. She sounded fine to me. I would back her up about having the doctor at Westminster check her out if Mom tried to insist on the Emergency Room. I cupped her cheek. "If you're going to keep sneaking out, I'll give you my spare key so we don't have to worry about you freezing to death or breaking your neck."

"A key is good." Gran's eyes suddenly snapped with fire. "I'm here on a mission. Since your Mom's on her way home, I don't have much time," she began, then pointed to a black purse with a long strap lying on the floor.

I grabbed her purse and handed it to her, mumbling, "How did you climb while holding onto a purse?"

Gran pushed the strap out of the way, then unzipped her purse. "I hung it on my neck, of course," she said matter-of-factly as she retrieved a half-inch thick, paperback-sized journal in a black paisley design with silver-edged pages from her purse. She held it out to me with a big smile. "Happy birthday, Inara."

As she put her compress back on her forehead, I took the journal from her gnarled hand and shook my head in disbelief. "You went to all this trouble to bring me a birthday present? You really shouldn't have, Gran. I could've gotten it from you the next time I visited."

"It's not just *any* journal." Gran nodded to the book, eyes brimming with excitement. "Open it."

I slid off the black elastic strap holding the book closed. I expected to hear new pages crackling, but the journal opened with a whisper of well-used pages instead. I gasped at the beautiful flowing script. Pages and pages of notes, doodles; it was a diary of sorts.

"You said you wanted to know your grandmother. Did you know she wanted you to call her, 'Nana'?"

When I shook my head, totally speechless, Gran smiled. "This was in Margaret's belongings in storage. She asked me to pass this on to you when you turned seventeen if she wasn't around to do it herself. And since you never really got to know your grandmother, I think this is a wonderful way for you to connect with her. My sister was always so smart, thinking way ahead."

I smiled. "I think I would've liked her a lot."

Gran touched the journal and gave me a stern look. "It's probably best that your mother *not* read this, since it's her mother's personal scribblings. Margaret filled the journal with her random thoughts, life experiences, and events of importance to her. There's stuff about your mother and you in here as well. Even though we were close, I didn't read it—that'd feel like an invasion of privacy—but I did flip through, looking to see if she mentioned Freddie. Luckily, she did! She even wrote down his surname. I marked that page with the ribbon bookmark for you."

A thrill jolted through me, and I gripped my grandmother's journal to my chest, itching to delve into it. "Thank you so much for this, Gran. It means the world to me."

She smiled, then winced as she lowered the compress from her forehead. "Does the lump look better?"

I pushed her hair out of the way. "It's just a red spot now." Perplexed, I asked, "After climbing inside my window like a geriatric ninja, how did you manage to fall and bump your head once you made it inside my room?"

Gran grimaced, her face crinkling as if she were trying to remember. "I don't know. I was tired after climbing, so I thought I'd take a nap on your bed while I waited for you to get home from school. I remember bending over your desk to write you a birthday note, and then all of a sudden my knees buckled. I must've hit my head on the desk as I went down."

"Please don't ever do that again!" I said, squeezing her hand. I tried to picture Gran climbing up the side of our house. My mind boggled. She must've been a wild child when she was young. Her climb could've ended in a horrible, life-threatening fall. I rubbed my temples, trying to push away the thought. "How did you know my window would be unlocked?"

"I heard the black birds cawing on the back side of the house, so I walked around to investigate. That's when I saw them circling above your window. I thought it rather odd, but since the window was open I climbed my way in."

"But my window wasn't open—"

The front door slammed, cutting off my comment.

"I'm here!" Mom said as she rushed into my room, looking disheveled with wide eyes and windblown hair.

When she went straight to Gran and hugged her tight, rambling about how worried she was, I stepped back and blinked in shock. Mom had avoided spending time with Gran ever since I could remember. She'd always kept up with how Gran was doing through me. I knew she didn't visit her aunt because it was too painful for her to look at her without thinking of the mom she'd lost, but it had always bothered me that she avoided such a fun, special woman as Gran. Giving Gran a thumbs-up over Mom's shoulder, I said, "Hey Mom, Gran wants to stay over tonight."

Gran hugged Mom tight and breathed in next to her hair. "If that's okay with you, Elizabeth. I'd love to stay for an evening."

"Yes, yes. Of course. You're more than welcome." Sitting back on her knees in her charcoal-gray pencil skirt and heels, Mom grasped Gran's hands and peered into her eyes. "Nara said you fell. Did you hit your head? We should take you to the Emergency Room and have you checked out."

Gran's eyes jerked to mine, a knowing smirk on her lips. "I did bump my head, but I feel fine. Nara has asked me several 'concussion' questions, and since I'll be here tonight, you can keep an eye on me."

When my mom gazed at me, an uncertain frown on her brow, I said, "Remember I took that sports medicine first aid class last year? Don't worry, I'll take Gran home in the morning where she promised to have the doctor at Westminster look her over."

Mom nodded her agreement and asked Gran in a calmer tone, "Why didn't you call and let us know you were coming?"

Gran rolled her eyes. "How would it be a surprise then?"

"Surprise?" Mom glanced at me, clearly confused.

"I brought Inara her birthday present."

"Present?" When Mom returned her gaze to Gran, I tensed. Gran had said she didn't want Mom to know about my present, so why did she mention it?

"Yeah," Gran turned and pointed to the black raven statue sitting on my nightstand next to my jewelry box. "Did you know your mother made that?"

I exhaled a breath of relief and quickly tucked the journal inside my desk drawer while Mom's attention was on the statue.

And how did you know I hadn't already shown Mom, Gran? I hadn't, of course. Thank goodness.

AFTER A WONDERFUL DINNER, where Gran insisted on making a homemade birthday cake ("*My* birthday present to you, Inara," she'd whispered in my ear while stirring the batter), she and my mom sat around the table laughing and crying over stories about my grandmother for a couple of hours. I smiled through the entire evening. It was wonderful to see Mom enjoying time with her aunt.

I made sure Gran was settled in the guest bedroom and then headed back to my room, anxious to learn the raven man's name. I'd felt stalled with my research lately, so I was looking forward to jumpstarting it again.

But first things first. I pulled out my phone and checked to see if I had any messages. I had one from my aunt, responding to the text I'd sent right before dinner.

Me – 6:00 p.m. ~ Gran is having dinner with us. Yes, mom and me! Shocker! How are things going? Did you find out anything? By the way, I told Mom you were on vacation in Florida.

Aunt Sage – 7:45 p.m. ~ Oh, that makes me so happy, Inara! I'm glad your mom is starting to open up some. There's some big event going on here in D.C. with tighter security. It has been hard to get in to see his secretary. I'll think of something. In the meantime, I discovered a gem show will be here at the beginning of next week. Might as well stay and buy some stones to beef up my jewelry selection. Okay, Florida it is.

Me – 9:50 p.m. ~ You'll be home sometime next week then? What has your tarot told you? You brought your cards, right?

Aunt Sage – 9:57 p.m. ~ Yes, I'll be back at the end of next week. Oh, you are such a smart girl. You just gave me the best idea for how to get in. Will update you when I have something. Love you!

Me – 9:58 p.m. ~ Don't know what I did, but yay for unintentional inspiration. Keep me updated and stay SAFE. Love you too!

I also had a text from Lainey. It was probably about her new dress. I kept staring at my text message screen, surprised Lainey's was the only other message. The hopeful part of me wanted to believe that no messages from Ethan meant that his week was going well, but another part of me felt left behind... or somehow forgotten. My heart ached at the sad, fleeting thought, so I sent Ethan a text. I was tempted to write, TTTWFO? But instead I opted for a less freaked-out version.

Me – 10:00 p.m. ~ How are you doing? Haven't heard from you lately...

Ten minutes passed. Nothing. I couldn't help the worry that swept through me.

Me – 10:10 p.m. ~ I'm allowed to worry about you too, you know. Let me know you're okay.

When another ten minutes passed without a response, my stomach started to knot. All kinds of scenarios began to flit through my mind. He was back in his old bedroom with all those negative memories; the room where he'd been so freaked out by the darkness trying to consume him he'd tried to take his own life. And now that he didn't have my dreams helping him cope, he was spiraling. I didn't even know his parents' address or phone number in Michigan. It's not like I could call and ask to speak with him. I fired off one more text.

Me – 10:20 p.m. ~ If I don't hear from you by tomorrow night, I'm calling your brother!

Breathing rapidly, I tried to calm my raging imagination. I needed a distraction so I opened the text from Lainey.

Lainey – 7:20 p.m. ~ What happened between you and Drystan? He's being a total ass. You need to smooth things over with him, or I swear he and Matt are going to beat the crap out of each other. I had to jump on his back to pull him off Matt earlier. Damn, it wasn't easy either. He's like one big muscle!

Ugh! I felt horrible. How many people had treated Drystan

so horribly that he'd gotten so angry over what he felt was my distrust? He deserved an answer. If there was a way for me to tell him about my ability without him insisting we figure out how our powers had combined in the past, I would, but I hadn't figured out how to do that. For now, he at least deserved an apology.

Me – 10:30 p.m. ~ I'm sorry, Drystan! Please don't be angry. I don't want to lose our friendship over this.

Then I sent Lainey a text.

Me – 10:31 p.m. ~ I tried. Hopefully he'll calm down. Tell Matt I'm sorry.

Lainey – 10:33 p.m. ~ Thanks! See you tomorrow.

When ten minutes passed without a reply from Drystan, I figured that was my response. He was done with me. My spirits sank a little as I set my phone on my nightstand. I was being honest. I appreciated his friendship and didn't want it to disappear.

I retrieved my grandmother's journal from my desk drawer, then lay back in bed and flipped to the page Gran had marked with the ribbon.

Corda and I had lunch with one of our classmates today, Erik Holtzman. I'd been in awe of the watercolor he'd painted of a raven in our class, and when I asked him how he'd painted it so vividly, he invited us to lunch so he could tell us all about it. I've never seen someone as dedicated to his work as Freddie is. He insisted we call him Freddie, saying that's what all his friends call him. We learned that the reason he could draw with such detail was because he raises ravens for research. So fascinating! He's even publishing a book about them.

Erik Holtzman? No wonder I couldn't find any publications when I scoured the Internet with search terms "author name Freddie and ravens". Freddie and Erik? Hmmm, maybe it was a pen name. Then a thought occurred and I felt like smacking my forehead. I'd been so focused on the name Freddie in my searches, I didn't think about it being a nickname. The use of Erik for his author name made total sense now. Freddie was derived from Frederick. Holding the journal, I walked over to my desk, then pulled open the bottom drawer I'd tucked Ethan's journal in, while I continued to read. I planned to add Freddie's author name and information to Ethan's book.

But to listen to Erik talk, the passion in his voice, the ravens are more like family—

When my fingers didn't connect with the cloth bag I expected, but paperwork instead, I immediately glanced down, my heart thumping.

Ethan's book was gone!

I quickly set my grandmother's journal on the desk. My hands shook as I squatted to search under the paperwork for Ethan's book. Nothing.

Frantic, my gaze jerked around the room. I knew it wasn't in my backpack. After the attack in the library, I'd kept it in my room, hidden inside a dark green drawstring bag that had come with my laptop to protect it. Had I unknowingly set it somewhere else? I tore through my room, looking in places I might have set it: the top of my chest of drawers, inside each of the drawers, inside my nightstand drawer, on top of books on my bookshelf, under my desk, underneath my bed.

My breathing turned rampant as I yanked open my foldable closet doors to scan the wire shelves inside. Nothing but neatly folded sweaters and jeans.

Falling to my hands and knees, I slid my palms along the carpet under my hanging clothes just in case I'd dropped it and it had somehow gotten pushed beneath the clothes. I was just getting ready to stand when a roughness on the carpet right in front of my hanging clothes snagged across my palms.

I frowned at the dim light in my closet, then moved to grab the tiny flashlight from my desk drawer. I returned to the closet to shine the bright penlight on the carpet.

My throat closed when I made out a muddy footprint on the beige surface. It faced toward my bedroom, as if someone had been standing just inside my closet, looking through the closed doors. With a sick feeling in my stomach, I turned and put the toe of my shoe inside the shoeprint to compare size. It was huge, at least four sizes larger than my own.

I gripped the tiny flashlight and sank to the floor, my trembling legs refusing to support my weight.

Gran had been adamant that my window was open, and now I believed her.

Someone had been in my room. Oh God, while Gran was in here! I closed my eyes and blew out a breath, thankful nothing worse had happened to Gran.

The footprint had to be at least a size twelve. I shook my head. It couldn't have been the guy from the library. His feet weren't that big. They would have stuck out like clown shoes on such a small guy. Who had been in my room then? And why did he take Ethan's journal?

The realization that someone had been in my house and in my room freaked me out. I jumped up and ran downstairs to grab the carpet cleaner and scrub brush. I quickly sprayed the remover onto the stain on my carpet. While I scrubbed, I tried to focus, but my thoughts pinged all over the place.

All that work gone. The loss of Ethan's journal, combined with the fact I hadn't heard anything from him, even after several texts, left me feeling lost. *It's like he's slipping through my fingers, disappearing from my life. More like he's being yanked out of my life!* The spot was already gone but I continued to scrub until my fingers began to ache. I fisted my hands on my knees to stop myself before I wore a hole in the carpet. I wanted to scream my frustration, but instead I locked my jaw and ground my teeth. When my breathing began to slow, another thought occurred: what if Gran had interrupted the person's search? Would he come back?

I walked on shaky legs to my desk and picked up my phone. My hands trembled as I dialed the CVAS voice mail. "Hey Sally, it's Nara," I began, trying my best to sound calm. "If you're still looking for someone to foster that dog, I can take him on a temporary basis. Let me know and I'll swing by to pick him up tomorrow afternoon if that's okay with you." After my close call with almost getting shot, I didn't think Mom would give me a hard time about the dog, so long as I kept him off the furniture while he was with us.

Once I set my phone down, I pressed my lips in a thin line. Even if I'd dreamed last night, I probably wouldn't have seen this, since Ethan's journal didn't show up in my dreams. When

I first started working on the book, it was part of my dreams, but then it just stopped one day. The fact I couldn't see myself working on it was part of the allure of this project. I loved the first-time experience while at the same time creating a special present for Ethan.

I jerked my gaze around my room, scrutinizing it. If my room had been in pristine condition, it wouldn't have taken me this long to figure out someone *had* been searching through it. With a burst of speed, I began a frenzied organization of every nook and cranny.

Three hours later, I inspected my super-organized room and desk with a critical eye so I'd know exactly how to reorganize it after Patch's morning visits. Drawers, books, music CDs, pencil and paper holders, stapler, paperclip tray—everything was stacked or placed in such a way that I'd know if they'd been moved even a millimeter. After I triple-checked that my window was locked, I tucked my grandmother's diary into my backpack to keep it close, then fell into bed, letting sheer exhaustion override my racing mind.

CHAPTER 14

School dragged by in a foggy blur. Because I'd gone to bed so late, I'd only dreamed the first few hours of my day before the alarm clock rudely jerked me awake. I didn't wake to a text from Ethan and even Patch seemed to have deserted me. I missed the bird's crazy antics as I got dressed this morning. After the way Patch acted yesterday, dive-bombing me the way he did, I didn't know if I'd ever see him or the other birds again.

The only highlight of my day was that I successfully found Erik Holtzman's website and contact information using the library computer. Before the bell rang, ending study hall, I sent Mr. Holtzman an email asking if I could interview him for a school project.

As the end of school neared, my nerves wound tighter and tighter. I kept checking my phone, waiting for Ethan to respond, but I'd only received a voice mail from Sally confirming that she was thrilled I'd be fostering the dog, whom, she said, "I've affectionately named Houdini for his uncanny ability to slip his leash. He's a wily one, Nara, just so you're warned."

When the final bell rang for the day, I walked out to the parking lot in the afternoon at a clipped pace. While I slid on the peach-colored sunglasses Ethan gave me—I needed the connection after hearing nothing from Ethan all day—I left a voice mail for Sally to let her know I'd be late picking up Houdini. I'd told Ethan in my text that he had until the end of the day today. As far as I was concerned, the day ended at six thirty. When Samson drove into his driveway from work, I'd be there to ask him if he'd heard from Ethan.

My phone rang just as I hung up from leaving Sally a message.

I stopped in the middle of the parking lot and immediately answered, my stomach fluttering. "Ethan!" I breathed out as people streamed past.

"Hello? No, this is Frederick Holtzman. Is this Inara Collins?"

Disappointment flitted through me, but I kept my voice upbeat. "Oh, hi, Mr. Holtzman. Yes, this is Inara. Thank you so much for getting back with me."

"It has been a dozen years since I published my book on ravens," he said, sounding pleased. "But I'm always happy to hear from a raven fan. Did you find my book in your library?"

I smiled, warming to the kindness in his raspy voice. "Actually, I heard about you from Gran...I mean, my great-aunt Corda. She and her sister, Margaret—my grandmother—met you while taking an art class at the university. Gran said you were in the process of writing your book at the time."

"Ah, Margaret." His rasp softened when he said her name. "She was a pleasure to talk to. I remember her sister, Corda, being a bundle of energy. How are your grandmother and your great-aunt doing?"

"Gran's doing well. Unfortunately my grandmother passed away when I was a baby."

"I'm sorry to hear about your grandmother," he replied in a subdued tone. "I'd planned to do a phone interview with you, but I would be honored to show Margaret's granddaughter around my raven sanctuary and discuss the beautiful Corvus corax with you for your school project. Would you like to see it?"

"I'd love to see your raven sanctuary!" Excitement flitted through me, temporarily overshadowing the sense of helplessness I'd felt over losing Ethan's book. "Is this afternoon too soon?"

Low laughter rumbled across the line. "I see you have your grandmother's enthusiasm. This afternoon works for me." A car beeped at me as Mr. Holtzman finished giving me directions to his house, which turned out to be thirty minutes southeast of Blue Ridge. I moved to the side and told Mr. Holtzman I'd see him in an hour.

As soon as I hung up, I started walking again, when someone gripped my arm and yanked me to the side. As I fell against Drystan's chest, he hissed in my ear, "Are you trying to get yourself killed?"

A black sports car zoomed past a couple of seconds later. I quickly pushed myself off Drystan and glanced his way. "Thanks, but honestly, the car had time to stop."

When his gaze narrowed, I gave a brilliant smile. "I'm glad you're talking to me though."

Drystan scrubbed his hand through his messy hair and shook his head, his jaw tight. "You're the most stubborn—" Cutting himself off, he blew out a breath, then continued, "I'm here to make a deal."

"A deal?" My voice squeaked. I glanced away and saw Lainey and Matt watching us from across the parking lot. Lainey smiled and gave an encouraging nod, while Matt looked like he wanted to choke me if I so much as looked crossways at Drystan. Great. Just what I needed.

Drystan followed my line of sight and sighed. He nodded toward the back parking lot. "Come on, I'll walk you to your car."

Since he'd already turned and walked away, I had no choice but to follow. He shoved his hands into his jeans pockets and slowed his steps to match mine. "No matter what you say, I feel like you don't trust me, so I'm going to earn your trust."

My stomach churned with guilt. "That's not it, Drystan—"

He held his hand up, his expression hard. "Don't talk, Nara. Let me finish."

Oh, boy. He was still angry. I nodded and clamped my lips shut.

Once we'd reached my car, Drystan leaned against my car door and shoved his hands in his jeans once more. He stared at his black boots for so long the entire back lot was almost empty of cars. After the last car pulled out of the gravel lot, I jingled my keys to let him know I was waiting, and that he was blocking my way into my car.

His green gaze snapped to mine. "I'm going to share, but only if you promise me something in return."

"I didn't ask you, Drystan—"

"I'm not asking to know what your power is, though I hope you'll tell me eventually. Instead, I just want your promise you'll cooperate."

"Cooperate?"

He nodded, squinting against the afternoon sun. "Yeah. It has nothing to do with your ability."

Relief flitted through me, yet I couldn't help but squirm at his open-ended request. What did he want me to cooperate about? At least he wasn't insisting I tell him about my power. I straightened my shoulders. "Okay."

Drystan gave a curt nod. "My ability is psychometry."

"I've never heard the term," I said, shaking my head.

"Remember when I found Lochlan, as you put it, 'pretty easily'?"

I nodded.

He set his mouth in a thin line. "And you asked how I knew exactly where to look for that lost microfiche you were looking for?"

I kept quiet, waiting for him to tell me the rest.

Drystan held his hand out, palm up. "When I touch something, either worn by or related to what I'm looking for, I can locate what I'm seeking."

I remembered him rubbing Lochlan's collar intently with his thumbs. "So that's what you were doing when you held Loch's collar? You were trying to locate him by touching something of his?"

Drystan nodded. "It's easier with living things like people and animals. They leave residual energy behind, which I'm able to zero in on when I hold a personal item. With inanimate objects, if I concentrate hard enough I can find them too. I just have to have something that directly ties them together, something I can focus on. Like I did with the call number you'd written on that piece of paper. If it's specifically related to the object I'm looking for, it can act like a radar, giving off a kind of low grade vibe that will allow me to find its location."

"Wow! That power's amazing," I said as I set my heavy backpack down on the ground, then leaned against my car beside him.

Drystan gave a self-deprecating smile. "Yeah, an odd, but handy ability from time to time."

Turning toward me, he rested his elbow on the roof. "Now for your promise."

"Promise?" I gulped.

He nodded. "Give me one month. I'd like more time, but regardless, the sooner we start the better."

"Start?"

A wolfish smile tilted his lips. "Your training."

"Training for what?" I asked, stiffening.

"I'm going to train you to defend yourself, with the added benefit of you learning how to get the 'ell away in case you're outmatched."

"I don't have time to train," I began, spreading my arms wide. "Soccer will be starting up soon, and I volunteer at CVAS. Why do you want to train me anyway?"

Drystan folded his arms and set his mouth at a stubborn slant. "You were attacked in the library, and I'm pretty sure that bullet was meant for you, not Lainey. One event I can ignore as random, but two?" He paused and shook his head. "Since you won't tell me what's going on with you, you've just promised to let me teach you how to protect yourself."

He tricked me! I started to shake my head, but before I could utter a word, Drystan moved with lightning speed and wrapped his arm around my neck. Hauling me back against his chest, he clamped his other arm around my stomach in a vise hold. "Go ahead, Nara," he breathed in my ear, his accent heavy with his anger. "Get out of this choke hold and I'll let you out of our deal."

Somewhere I heard ravens making *raaaaack* sounds in the trees, but they weren't anywhere in sight. Where were their dive-bombing efforts when I needed them? *Fickle birds!*

"Let me go!" I bit out and pulled against his muscular arm. I did everything I could to shrug out of his hold, but he didn't move. At all. God, Lainey was right, he felt like one big muscle.

His arm held me in such a way that my jaw was locked tight, my neck craned back. I could barely open my mouth, let alone get a good bite in. When I tried to stomp his toe, he moved his foot out of the way. "I can do this all day," he murmured in my ear.

"Let me go now, Drystan!" I hissed through my teeth.

The world spun and I was facing him once more as if he'd never touched me. Determination lined his face. "We'll start tomorrow morning. Meet me at Stonehaven Park at nine."

I gaped. "It'll be freezing that early."

"Better dress in layers then," he said with a shrug. "On weekend days we'll meet early."

"This is crazy. I didn't agree to this," I mumbled.

"A deal's a deal, Nara. During the week, we'll meet right after school. Once soccer starts up, we'll meet after practice is over."

"Wait? You want to train every day? No way." What would Ethan think? He was definitely protective, but was he the jealous type? He probably wouldn't be happy, but then he wouldn't want me *not* to be able to protect myself while he's not here either. Ethan always cared about my safety. "How about two days a week?"

Drystan set his jaw. "Five."

"Three."

"Four." He turned and walked away, calling over his shoulder, "Nine a.m. sharp. Don't be late."

As I watched him stroll away like our exchange had never happened, I curled my hands into fists, my heart thumping at a rapid rate. *Why was he doing this?*

Once he was out of sight, a flapping sound distracted me as Patch and a couple of his buddies flew in, landing on the roof of my car. I rolled my eyes, grumbling, "Now you show up? Traitors!"

Patch stepped forward and made a deep *grooooock* sound, the other birds following suit. I shook my finger at them. "After the way you acted yesterday, and then your desertion while Drystan was giving me a hard time—I heard you in the trees!—no kibble for any of you."

The other birds seemed to understand my scolding, because they immediately took off, flying back to their perches in the trees.

But not Patch. He just made another *groooooock* sound and continued to walk around on my car, nonplussed. Tilting his head, he eyed me for a second, then bobbed his head up and down. Yesterday he was pecking at me, and today he's comical. "Moody bird," I mumbled just as my phone pinged with a text.

I unzipped my backpack pocket with swift movements, then pulled out my phone and glanced at the screen. It was from Ethan. Thank God!

I leaned against my car once more and opened his text.

Ethan – 3:55 p.m. ~ I'm sorry to make you worry. I'm fine. Was out all day yesterday and most of today in a location without cell coverage. My Dad and I went snowmobiling. I never want you to worry about me. All I could do was think of you while I was gone. Wish I could hold you close this very second.

As I sighed with happiness, Patch hopped onto my shoulder. He was surprisingly heavy. I froze, afraid to make any sudden moves. He'd never done this before. When he leaned over and pressed his long beak against my cheek, then tilted his head and ran the soft feathers on the top of his head along my jawline, my throat worked with emotion. It was as if Ethan were right there with me, pressing his face against mine, giving me his touch.

Just as I started to lean into Patch, the bird took off into the air with powerful wing flaps. Soaring high, he did an aerial drop-spin, then glided gracefully out of sight into the tree line.

"Show-off!" I called after him even as a wide grin split my face. Ethan was safe...and our connection was still there, stronger than ever.

I texted Ethan back.

Me – 3:57 p.m. ~ I'm so relieved you're okay. I miss you too, so much. You won't believe what just happened! Hmmm, I think you'd have to see it to believe it. I'm late for an appointment, but I'll tell you more later.

I couldn't wait to share this with Ethan. Even though I probably never would have experienced what I did with Patch while Ethan was with me, I hated him being gone. I didn't like worrying about him or wondering when he would return. Training with Drystan would be good for more than just learning self-defense. It would help make the time go by faster until Ethan came home.

CHAPTER 15

*M*r. Holtzman's place was buried deep in the Afton Mountain area. The drive out was gorgeous. With the crystal blue sky and the afternoon sun shining in my car, I could almost believe it was warm outside, instead of forty degrees. As I drove down the long dirt drive to get to his house, late afternoon sunlight dappled through the mixture of oaks, maples firs and pine trees.

There was a note taped on the front door when I walked up the steps to the ranch-style house.

Inara,

Had to go into the woods to check on a couple of nesting ravens. I'll be back shortly. If you want to check out the sanctuary while you wait, it's around the back side of my house. Just take the path and it'll take you right to it.

~ F

I pulled the pen from the spiral binding on the pad I'd brought to take notes and jotted my response under his signature.

I'm here. Am going to check out the sanctuary as you suggested. See you soon.

~ N

Mr. Holtzman's secluded property was on acres of woods. He kept a small lawn mowed in the front and back of his house, but other than that it literally looked like he'd built his home in the middle of the mountainside.

I only had about a half hour of daylight left, so I rounded the side of the small house with swift movements and easily found the well-worn footpath at the edge of his backyard. Following the slight incline about thirty yards into the woods, I spotted his ravens' sanctuary—an aviary—in a clearing another ten yards ahead.

The ravens began to make all kinds of interesting sounds when I got within five yards of the enclosure. Mr. Holtzman had cleared space for his bird sanctuary well. Cut out of the dense woods, only six trees filled the cleared space, including a massive oak in the middle. Strong chicken wire surrounded the group of trees, and a roof had been constructed using the same chicken wire on one side and roofing material and plywood on the other half to complete the structure. One opening had been left in the chicken wire, creating a doorway that went all the way up to the thirty-foot high roof.

When I walked inside, the birds' cacophony grew louder. I turned inside the enclosure, taking a few pictures with my phone camera. Wooden boxes had been sporadically built in the V of some trees, I assumed to encourage nesting. Long black trays lined the forest floor near the chicken wire walls. Remnants of a small animal carcass lay in one of the trays. *Ah, they were like food troughs for the ravens.*

A round bench painted in a deep forest green had been built in the center of the sanctuary around the oak tree. *I'm surprised it's not completely covered in bird poop,* I thought with a half smile as I settled on the bench to take the amazing place in. Wow, it truly was something.

As I sat there, a couple of ravens flew out of the sanctuary, but then a few minutes later, they swooped back in, followed by a whole slew of new birds. I lost track once I'd counted thirty. *Did Mr. Holtzman really study this many birds at once?* I only counted about five boxes in the trees. Did the rest nest outside? How did he keep track of them all?

The ravens had grown so loud, I could barely think. While the birds inside the enclosure settled on the tree branches and let out deep, reverberating *groaks* and *raack* noises, more and more ravens flooded in until every tree branch space was covered.

I stared at them, watching them watching me. And they *were* watching me. It was unnerving, yet comforting too when I thought about Patch's actions earlier. What would Patch think of this huge "unkindness"? I didn't particularity like the official term that described a group of ravens. Considering Patch's antics, "unpredictable" would be more appropriate, I thought with a smirk.

I'd never seen so many birds at once. Except for in my dream where I'd seen them swirling around Ethan in a rushing tornado of black wings while I confronted Fate.

A few ravens flew down from their perches, landing ten feet away. When I didn't move, another group fluttered down to settle near the first set. Then another set and another set. I wanted to take a picture, because I didn't think anyone would believe me if I told them of the strange phenomenon happening right before my eyes.

Instead, I gripped my phone and stared at the forest floor covered in a sea of black-feathered birds. Would they scatter if I stood? There was only one way to find out. Slowly and with as little movement as possible, I stood up.

The birds closest to me hopped back a little, but they didn't fly away as I expected they would. As I turned in a tight circle to take all the birds in, I realized that I wasn't hearing several sounds anymore...only one. All the ravens had synced into a croaking sound that came from deep within their throats.

My hand trembled as I dialed Ethan's number. *Please answer, Ethan!*

I exhaled a pent-up breath when he picked up on the second ring. "I was just thinking about you," he started to say, then paused, "Where are you? What's that noise?"

"Hold on a sec." I held up my hand in a fast motion, expecting the birds to scatter. Instead, they lowered their sounds several octaves. "Tell me how much you miss me," I said in an awed voice.

"Are you okay?" He sounded tense. "Do you need me to come home?"

I closed my eyes, picturing his face in my mind's eye. Brackets would be around his mouth right now. "Do this for me, please."

"I ache everywhere when I think of you." His voice sounded deeper as if he'd pressed the phone closer to his mouth. "It's not right that you make me feel so much," he continued, sounding almost embarrassed to admit the second part.

My throat knotted until all I could do was rasp, "Oh, Ethan..."

"I miss holding you close and smelling your sunshine," he continued.

The ravens had gone completely silent, the absence of noise deafening. I stared at them, then gripped my phone tighter. "If you want to share with me, close your eyes," I whispered.

"What?"

"Just close your eyes."

A husky sigh sounded across the line. "Closed."

I exhaled a steadying breath. "Pretend you're standing right here with me. Now, pull me close. Don't speak...just imagine and feel."

When I finished speaking, I closed my eyes and imagined Ethan standing right in front of me, his broad shoulders blocking out the light as he skimmed his fingers along my cheek.

Air brushed my cheek and I heard the whoosh of wings. Ethan's warmth enveloped my arms and back as if he'd just wrapped his arms around me and pulled me close. Giddy, I kept my eyes closed tight, not wanting to break the spell. "What do you feel?" I asked.

He inhaled deeply. "I smell...sun after a spring rain and shampoo. I smell you, Sunshine," he murmured in disbelief. "How is this possible?"

Soft wings brushed my arms, my face, my back. Ever so slowly, I lifted my hand and let the passing wings bat against it.

Ethan sucked in his breath. "Did you just touch me?"

I smiled, tears of happiness trickling down my cheeks. "In my own way."

"How are you doing this, Nara?" he asked, astonishment roughening his tone.

"I'm not. You are."

When Ethan snorted and said, "I'm not doing this," I opened my eyes to see the tornado of ravens who'd been flying around me begin to disperse, a few birds at a time.

I sighed, sad to lose the intimate connection. "I'm at a raven sanctuary. When you thought of me just now, they encircled me just like they did you in my dream when I faced off with Fate."

"I had no idea..." Ethan seemed surprised, but not shocked like I expected him to be. "Why are you there, Nara?"

"I'm researching." I watched a mass exodus of ravens leave the enclosure, while only a dozen or so returned to the trees. Once they'd settled on their perches above me, the ravens reverted to their random *groooaks* and *raaack* sounds. I smiled, invigorated by the fantastical experience and spoke quietly into my receiver, "You believe me now, don't you? About your connection to ravens?"

"I had no idea it went so deep." He sounded mystified. I pictured him jamming his hand through his hair while he tried to process what had just happened. "Nara," he began, then paused for a second. "You need to let me do this on my own."

I wasn't sure how to take his comment. I didn't think he was trying to discount what had just happened between us, but it felt worse in a way, like he was shutting me out. Ethan had no idea how much time I'd put into his raven journal. How much all the research I had done had helped me stay connected to him during his absence. And now it was gone.

Just as I bit my trembling lip, I glanced up and my gaze

locked on a thin old man with a stock of white hair and a neatly trimmed white beard standing at the sanctuary's entrance.

Wearing a flannel-lined jean jacket, worn jeans, and construction boots with climbing spikes strapped to the soles, he gripped the frame around the doorway in a tight hold and stared at me with amazement in his blue eyes. "In fifty years of studying ravens I've never seen anything like that!"

Oh boy, I didn't realize he'd seen it. Then again, the enclosure's "walls" were chicken wire. "Hi, Mr. Holtzman," I spoke in a cheerful voice, then said to Ethan in a rush of words, "Um, I need to go for now."

"Do you understand, Nara? I have to do this on my own—" Ethan began, urgency in his tone.

"I'll call you tonight," I interrupted, smiling apologetically at Mr. Holtzman. Keeping this surprise from Ethan was causing me more pain and heartache than I ever thought it would.

A grunt of frustration rushed in my ear. "My dad's packing the car now. We're going cross-country skiing through Wednesday or possibly Thursday night. I'll call you when I get back. Please, stay safe!"

I wanted to ask him when he was coming back to Virginia. We really needed some time together, but now wasn't the time. I'd ask him when he called. "I will. Talk to you then," I said, and hung up.

As soon as I tucked my phone away in my pocket, Mr. Holtzman held up a bony finger. "I have to show you something." Excitement lit his eyes and he started to turn away, then glanced back at me. "Come on!" he said, beckoning as if he expected me to vanish into thin air.

Relieved he didn't ask any questions about the raven cyclone he'd just witnessed, I started toward the entrance of the enclosure, holding up my notepad and pen. "I'm coming. I need to interview you."

"All in good time," he called over his shoulder as he scurried back down the hill.

I followed, leaving the ravens behind. Or at least I thought I had. When I looked up, several of them were flitting from treetop to treetop, tracing my path as I made my way down toward the house.

As soon as I exited the woods and stepped into the small backyard, the ravens stayed in the trees, squawking amongst themselves. I'd never heard such a wide range of sounds all at once. I shook my head and smiled as I took the couple of steps up onto the back deck, then followed Mr. Holtzman through his sliding glass door.

His house had a heartwarming smell that chased away the chill, a mixture of spicy chili powder and smoked wood.

"Sit by the fire and get warm," he insisted, brushing newspapers off the old couch near a stone fireplace.

I sat on the edge of the faded leather couch, and he turned to add a couple of new logs before he stoked the fire. Once the flames leapt to life and the wood began to crackle, he turned to me, rubbing his hands together. "Would you like some chili? I'm making some for dinner."

I smiled and shook my head. "It smells great, but no thank you. I'm eating dinner with my mom later. Her spaghetti dinners are pretty rare. You mentioned that you wanted to show me something?"

His bushy gray eyebrows pulled together as he nodded his understanding. "Yes, yes. Okay, let me find it," he said, clapping his hands as he walked toward the far wall opposite the couch.

Tall bookshelves had been built into the wall. They reached from the ceiling to the floor, the shelving packed with books and magazines. I could tell by the sticky notes peeking out of the tops of a lot of them, they were all research books.

Were they all on ravens? Fascinating!

While Mr. Holtzman began to shuffle through his books, I made my way over to the shelving. I scanned the titles: magazines on birds, books on crows, ravens and various other members of the same bird family filled the shelves.

"I've never seen such a collection," I said, my voice full of awe.

Book in hand, he glanced my way, his beard enhancing his

broad smile. "It's amazing what you can collect over an entire lifetime, Inara. What is your school project's focus?"

I smiled. "Call me Nara."

He nodded as he placed the book back, then pulled another one out. "Only if you call me Freddie."

"Deal. My project is just about the history of ravens. I figured that if I was going to study the raven, I should understand the bird itself a little better, which is why I wanted to interview you." I turned back to the books and my gaze caught on a title, *Statues From All Over the World*. "Do you have any books on swords?"

"Swords?"

He had a different book in his hand when I glanced at him. I pointed to the title straight in front of me. "You have a book about statues." I lifted my shoulders. "Why not swords?"

"I've seen ravens featured on shields, coat of arms, flags and such throughout history." He paused as if sifting through his memory, but shook his head. "But not on a sword. Come to think of it, considering ravens have been featured on all the other items I've mentioned, it's interesting that I've never seen one on a sword."

"Maybe because a bear, a lion, or a wolf seemed more intimidating?" I tried not to let my disappointment show as I slid a finger along the books' titles, studying them. "What about tattoos?"

He chuckled. "Thinking of getting a raven tattoo?"

I pulled down a book about raven mythology and flipped through it. "Ever seen a sword tattoo featuring a raven?" I asked casually as I kept my gaze locked on the pages.

"You're a lot like your grandmother, you know."

When I cut my gaze to him, he had a fond look in his bright blue eyes. "She had a knack for reading people, but kept her own pages very close to her chest."

His insight about my grandmother warmed my heart. "I heard she was a great judge of character."

He straightened his shoulders and tilted his chin up as he held a dark blue book against the buttons on his shirt. "And what do you see about my character?"

I said the first thought that came into my head. "You're incredibly dedicated."

He winked, then touched his nose, his eyes twinkling with delight. "Spot on! Come," he said, turning back toward his living room area.

He clutched the hardback book close and gestured for me to sit. As I sat down on the couch once more, he settled on an old military trunk that doubled as a coffee table across from me, then he carefully set the book in my hands. "As soon as I saw the ravens spinning around you, I knew. You're the one I'm supposed to give this to."

Taken by surprise by Freddie's revelation, I stared at the midnight blue book in my hands with its gold-edged pages and filigree brass book corners framing the front and back. It even had brass half moon-shaped end caps on the top and bottom of the spine. The author's name took up most of the spine in fancy gold lettering, with the exception of a Celtic trinity-style symbol stamped at the bottom of the spine. The gold-embossed title on the front of the book simply read *Ravens*.

By the reverent way he handled the book, it was obvious he treasured it. Why would he want to give it to me?

CHAPTER 16

"Unique cover," I murmured as I opened the inch-thick book and flipped through the pages. It was about ravens: the rearing, feeding, and general care of the *Corvus corax*. The book discussed ravens from birth to death, their culture, their quirks, their intelligence. It had been written by a man who, like Freddie, had studied the birds all his life. I found it interesting, but as I flipped through, I didn't see anything in it that I hadn't already seen in other works. Apparently the author's publisher thought it spectacular, considering the cover's fancy presentation, I thought with an inward smile.

When I shut the book, he said, "Well?"

I could tell he was expecting something monumental once I'd finished looking through the book, or at the very least, he was waiting for me to say something profound. I felt like a fraud. "Thank you for letting me look at it, but I don't under-stand..." I began as I held it out to him. "Why do you want to give it to me?"

He shook his head and folded my fingers around the book. "I've held onto this book, kept it with me for twenty-eight years...until I found the person to give it to."

I still didn't get his obvious reverence for the book. I opened it once more and pointed to the unused card inside the sleeve in the back. "It's never been checked out, but this says it's from a library in London. Is that where you got it?"

Freddie stiffened, clearly offended. "Certainly not! I would never *not* return a book to the library." He pointed to the book, a faraway look filtering in his eyes. "I'd just come up the stairs from the Tube, where I planned to spend the morning walking around London before my symposium speech in the afternoon, when a very tall man in an expensive gray suit approached me. 'This is for you, Frederick,' he said in a deep, booming voice. 'Keep it safe. When the time is right, you'll know when to pass it on.'"

"Did you know the man who gave you this?" I asked, glancing down at the book in my hands.

Freddie shook his head. "I'd never seen him before. He walked away without saying another word. I tried to follow him and ask more questions, but I lost track of his blond head in the crowd." Staring at the book fondly, he continued, "I liked the idea of being entrusted with something special that related to my passion, so I've kept this book all these years, waiting to pass it on."

Who was the stranger who'd given Freddie this book? And why had he given it to him? When Freddie lifted his blue eyes to mine, my heart sank that I would disappoint him. I shook my head and carefully set the book back in his hands. "I'm not the one you should be giving this book to."

"I don't understand." Freddie looked perplexed. "What I saw with the ravens—"

"It's hard to explain," I interrupted, not wanting to give anything away about Ethan without his permission. "Keep it safe, Freddie. I'll come see you again." Ethan should have the book. Not me. As soon as Ethan returned, I would bring him here, so Freddie could give it to the right person. I didn't understand the book's importance. Maybe Ethan would. Or together we could figure it out, but I didn't feel right taking it. The book wasn't meant for me.

"I was so sure," Freddie said with a dejected sigh. His shoulders drooped as he walked back over to his shelf and slid the book into place.

When he slowly lowered himself onto the trunk across from me, I reached out and squeezed his bony hand. "I'm coming back. I promise. Then you can hand the book over, okay?"

Freddie straightened, his face lighting up. The corner of his mouth lifted in a ghost of a smile. "When you come back, will you do it again? How *do* you get them to do that?"

He was talking about the ravens. I'd come here to learn all I could about ravens, yet a certified expert on these enigmatic birds was asking me about them? Like *I* could control them? I snorted inwardly. Could we make it happen if Ethan was standing right beside me? I had no idea. I shrugged. "I don't know how it works, but I'll try."

I'd experience something amazing today with Ethan's connection to the ravens, but there was still plenty I could learn from Freddie. I picked up my notepad from the trunk, then pointed my pen in his direction and smiled. "Are you ready to let me interview *you* now?"

I GOT to CVAS ten minutes before it closed. The strong smell of pine cleaner made my nose tingle as the glass front door swung shut.

"Hi, Nara," Harper said, looking up from mopping the tiled lobby area. She blew tendrils of black hair that had fallen from her ponytail away from her face. "I told Sally you were on your way. She's getting Houdini ready for you."

"Thanks for telling her for me." I wrinkled my nose as I glanced down at the bucket. "Not my favorite duty. At least *everyone* has to do it."

"Yeah, I can't really complain when Sally rotates through mop duty too." Harper leaned on the mop with a tired sigh, her heather-gray sweatshirt splotched with water and pine cleaner suds. "Hey, did you ever find that raven guy you were trying to locate for your school project? If not, I can try to find out if anyone at the Wildlife Preserve might have heard of him."

"No worries. I just talked with Freddie." I smiled, then rolled my eyes. "I can't believe I didn't think of Freddie being a nickname for Frederick. Turns out his published name was Erik Holtzman. I just finished talking with him and took a ton of notes."

She lifted the mop into the rolling bucket, then slid it closer to me, her brown eyes bright. "That's awesome. I'll bet he was interesting to talk to."

I nodded, grinning. "It was a total rush. He had an entire wall full of books about ravens. Some prized possessions for sure. It was pretty amazing. I'm so glad he asked me to come and see his raven sanctuary. The birds were beyond cool."

Her eyebrows shot up. "I thought it was just a phone call. That's awesome he asked you to do a face-to-face interview. Did you have to drive far?"

"I think he asked me because he knew my grandmother from years ago, so yeah I really lucked out. It was a hike out to his house in Afton, but so worth it."

"I'll bet—" she started to say when Sally came through the door that led to the back, her curly blonde hair bouncing around her face as she tugged on the dog's leash. "Whoa, Houdini!"

I approached the hyped-up dog, who was currently trying to wiggle out of his collar and gently gripped his scruff, then pulled him close, speaking into his ear in a strong tone, "Calm down, Houdini."

When he started to squirm once more, I began to say, "Do you want to—"

His brown eyes quickly jerked to mine and he immediately sat down, his body on rigid alert as he tilted his head to listen.

"—come home with me?" I finished while trying not to laugh. His reaction made it hard to keep an authoritative stance.

"If we'd only known 'asking' was the way to his heart." Sally snickered and handed me Houdini's leash. "How long do you think you can foster him?"

"I haven't asked my mom yet, but she shouldn't fuss too much about a week."

Sally's blonde eyebrows rose. "I'm pretty sure I have a family lined up to take the shepherd mix back there, so space will clear out. They can't take him for a couple of weeks, though. Houdini's been fed for the night, but here's some food and treats to get you started," she said, lifting a bag in her arms.

I looked down at Houdini. Big brown eyes stared at me, begging for me to take him. I gave Sally a confident smile and hoped like crazy I could convince my mom to let him stay for two weeks. "Okay, two weeks then." Grabbing the bag Sally held out for me, I glanced down at Houdini. "Are you ready to go—"

I'd barely gotten the words out before he was bolting toward the front door.

The last thing I expected to see was another car in our driveway when I got home. As I pulled into the garage bay and cut the engine, I wondered how Mom was going to react to me bringing Houdini home without telling her. If she gave me a hard time, I was totally going to play the "protection card" for all it was worth.

Houdini was so excited, he practically dragged me into the house. As he yanked me into the kitchen, I tugged on the leash and said, "Whoa, boy!"

Mom paused from pouring spaghetti into the strainer over the sink. Mr. Dixon, looked up as he set another plate on the table. "Hi, Nara. You're just in time for dinner," he said, a friendly smile on his face.

It was one thing to know my mom was dating Mr. Dixon, yet another thing entirely to walk in on him setting the dinner table at my house. *Awkward.*

"Um, hi, Mr. Dixon." I glanced at Mom, who was looking at Houdini with a stern expression. Her gaze met mine with a "why didn't you tell me you were bringing a dog home" look of disapproval. I raised my eyebrows, then cut a narrowed gaze to Mr. Dixon's tall, lanky form leaning across the table to lay a napkin beside one of the plates with a "why didn't you tell me you were bringing my Spanish teacher home for dinner?" look.

A brief apology flashed through her eyes before a battle of wills commenced in our intense stares. When my mom opened her mouth to speak, I quickly lifted Houdini's leash and pasted on a smile. "Mom, meet Houdini. I'm fostering him for a couple of weeks. He'll make a great guard dog, don't you think?"

My mom's gaze dropped to the big dog once more. On cue, Houdini sat and pressed himself against my leg. With his head held high, he puffed his broad chest out as if he knew he was being inspected for appropriate protector material.

I raised an eyebrow, challenging her to deny me. When she exhaled in defeat, then said, "You'll need to vacuum a couple of times a week while he's here," my smile turned genuine.

"I know. Let me get Houdini settled in my room, then I'll be down to help with dinner in a few minutes."

As I ran upstairs, I was never more thankful for Mr. Dixon's presence. Not because I wanted my mom dating my Spanish teacher—ugh—but because she wouldn't give me a hard time about Houdini in front of him. Her Southern manners were too deeply ingrained.

Leaving Houdini happily chewing a bone on a pallet I'd created for him on the floor next to my bed, I ran downstairs to push past the first-dinner-at-my-house awkwardness with Mr. Dixon.

Mr. Dixon actually turned out to be pretty funny. Throughout dinner, I caught glimpses of his dry sense of humor. Apparently he'd only shown a small slice of himself to our class. It made me wonder what the other teachers were like outside of school. When I thought of my mean English teacher, I could only picture her throwing rocks at squirrels in her back-yard. I pressed my lips together, shaking the disturbing image from my mind.

Mom was currently cutting slices of store-bought chocolate cake for each of us. I smiled when I saw the way Mr. Dixon watched her while she set the slices on plates and collected silverware. He looked at her like it didn't matter that spaghetti was the only thing she could cook. He really liked her. *Go Mom!*

"Be right back," Mom said in a lighthearted tone as she walked out of the kitchen.

As she ran upstairs, I furrowed my brow. *What was she doing?*

"So, Nara, your Mom tells me you volunteer at CVAS," Mr. Dixon said, after taking a sip of coffee. "I knew you played soccer, but I had no idea you did that. I think that's wonderful. Do you foster a lot?"

I shook my head. "No, this is the first time. I would do it all the time, but Mom has allergies."

Mr. Dixon raised his eyebrows and I could tell he was wondering why I'd done it now, but thankfully Mom walked in the room with two small white jewelry boxes, one bigger than the other, and a card in her hand.

"Happy early birthday, Inara!" she said, setting the boxes and card on the table in front of me.

"You too?" I laughed and lifted the card. "Everybody has given me presents early this year. My actual birthday is going to be a total letdown."

Mom wrinkled her nose and pointed to the box. "Don't be a spoilsport. Open the bigger box first, then the smaller one." She grabbed the dessert plates, then set one in front of Mr. Dixon, the next one in front of me, then the last one by her chair.

I raised my eyebrow, but set the card down to pick up the bigger box. Mom had always insisted I open the card first. The fact she insisted I open the gifts first must mean they were extra special.

As my fingers brushed the lid on the first box, Mom said, "Your Gran made me realize just how mature you were. I've been waiting a long time to give you this gift and, well, I was too excited to wait until your official seventeenth birthday."

Mom's comment made my stomach flutter. Once I lifted the lid, I gasped at the long intricate silver chain nestled in the cotton. Pulling the necklace out of the box, I stared at the interesting inch-wide charm hanging at the end of the chain. "It's gorgeous!"

Mr. Dixon leaned over and stopped the charm from spinning, eyeing the design. "I believe that's an updated version of a traditional triskele. What a nice gift."

Mom glanced at Mr. Dixon. "This gift is extra special. It's from my mom to Inara. She died when Nara was little." Lifting the scrolled trinity charm against her palm, she met my gaze.

"Your grandmother gave this to me a long time ago. She asked me to save it for you until you reached 'your age of maturity,'" Mom said with fond tears in her eyes.

I touched the charm and inwardly chuckled at my grandmother's way of telling Mom to hold on to the necklace until I was old enough not to break it. "Did she wear it a lot?"

Mom's blonde eyebrows drew together. "I never saw her wear it, but she must've loved it enough to want to pass it on to you. My mom wasn't very sentimental when it came to jewelry. As a matter of fact, the only thing I have of hers is her wedding band. Her will stipulated the rest be donated to her favorite charity," Mom finished, shaking her head.

Once I'd slipped the chain around my neck, Mom handed me the other box. "Now open this one."

As I pulled the pair of silver post earrings out of the cotton, I squealed, "Thank you, Mom. I love them!"

"I wasn't sure what I was going to get you for this birthday." Mom spread her hands wide, then smiled. "But once I saw you'd pierced your ears, I knew exactly what to get you. I had Sage make a smaller version of your charm."

I removed my plain ball earrings I'd worn since Lainey pierced my ears, then put my new earrings on, tilting my head to display them for Mom and Mr. Dixon's inspection.

"They're perfect," Mom declared while Mr. Dixon gave a thumbs-up.

After we'd cleaned the dishes, I could tell Mom and Mr. Dixon wanted to chat, so I hugged my mom, saying, "Thank you for my gifts. I love them. I'm heading upstairs to get ready for bed."

Mom's hands tightened around me as she whispered in my ear, "Do I want to know how Houdini got his name?"

"Probably not." I gave a nervous laugh, then turned to Mr. Dixon, who was settling on the sofa. "See you at school, Mr. Dixon."

"Call me David, Nara."

Too soon, too soon! Probably never, I mentally screamed. "Um, that would feel weird."

He chuckled. "Fair enough."

Thankfully, I escaped before my mother could act on the embarrassed look on her face and insist that I call him David right then and there.

I walked into my room to find Houdini sprawled across my bed, his head on my pillow, like it was his personal throne. I shooed him off and back to his pallet, saying in a stern tone, "We're going to have a serious talk about boundaries, boy!"

By the time I'd washed my face and brushed my teeth, Houdini was once again on my bed.

I shook my head at his stubborn nature, then crawled into bed with my grandmother's journal. Houdini was at least smart enough to jump off while I straightened the covers. As soon as I pulled them to my chin, he quickly hopped back up, but this time, instead of laying his head on my pillow, he pressed his body against mine and settled his chin on his paws facing the door.

I patted his broad back and tried to get him to turn around so I could scratch his ears, but he only turned to look at me, then resettled in the same position.

"Stubborn dog," I mumbled affectionately as I flipped through the opening pages. I learned Margaret had many interests from art to music to volunteering. Gran had been right. My grandmother didn't journal daily. She'd just written about events that happened in her life or memorable people she'd met that made an impact. Hence the reason she'd written about Freddie. Sprinkled throughout were anecdotes about family. She liked my dad but felt he was a hard read. She dearly loved her sister, Corda, was proud of her daughter, Elizabeth, and absolutely adored her grand daughter, Inara, which brought a huge smile to my face. I'd only made it halfway through her journal when my eyes began to droop as sheer exhaustion took over.

The moment my bedroom door opened, Houdini lifted his head and growled.

Mom's gaze snapped to the dog. "Hush, Houdini!" she said in an authoritative voice at the same time I tucked the journal under my covers. When he blew out a snort and lowered his head to his paws, Mom's eyebrows shot up. "Looks like I don't have to spend a few grand on a security system anytime soon."

I patted Houdini's back. "Told you."

A smirk tilted her lips. "I just wanted to say goodnight."

"Night, Mom. Thanks for the gifts."

"You're welcome." Mom started to walk out, then turned back. "I'd like you to work on calling him David, Nara. He'll be coming over here more, spending time with us. It'll feel very formal if you continue to call him Mr. Dixon."

I'm not ready! I wanted to scream. Instead, I pressed my lips together. "I'll try." *Which means, I'll just avoid calling him anything.*

Satisfied with my answer, Mom closed the door behind her.

After I yawned for the third time, I tucked the journal in my nightstand drawer and turned off my light. When the flashing light from my phone blinked, lighting up my ceiling in a strobe of red, I grabbed it from my nightstand.

Freddie had left me a voice mail. "Hi Nara. I just wanted to say what a pleasure it was meeting you. I hope you got plenty of information for your project, though I think you enlightened me more today." A low chuckle rasped. "I'll be waiting for you to claim your book. You *are* the rightful owner, little one. I know it in my heart. Take care and I hope you'll come back and visit me very soon."

Even though I felt a twinge of guilt that he still believed me to be "the one," I couldn't help but smile at his nice voice mail. I enjoyed my time with him very much. Visiting him was one of the first things I would do with Ethan when he got back.

CHAPTER 17

oof woof woof woof woof woof woof! I jerked awake, arms flailing, heart thudding in panic mode. Houdini's bark was so deep and alarming that I glanced around the room, expecting to see flames, a flood, the roof missing, or something equally catastrophic. Houdini snarl-barked again, this time throwing himself against my window. *Wow, and I thought his size was intimidating. His roaring bark would scare the pee out of just about anyone!*

"The roosters are barely up, Nara," Mom's sleepy voice floated down the hall. "Keep him quiet."

I rushed over and gripped his thick collar, hauling him back from the glass. "Hush, Houdini!"

Patch stood on the ledge on the other side of the window, tilting his head back and forth. He gave an unimpressed squawk, then pressed his eye close to the clear surface before hammer-pecking three times, like he always did when he wanted in.

Houdini gave a low rumbling growl deep in his throat. He literally vibrated with the need to defend. *Defend?* My gaze slid back to the glass as realization dawned. That's exactly what Patch had done the other day. The bird wasn't being mean or temperamental when he wouldn't let me get in my car. He was protecting me. If I'd come home at that time on that particular day, I would have encountered the intruder stealing Ethan's book from my house.

"No, Houdini," I said in a firm tone and released him to see how he'd react once freed. Instead of lunging at the glass, he turned brown eyes my way for direction.

Anxious to stop something I'd seen in my dream last night, I glanced at my clock. Six thirty. This afternoon, Gran would fall from a tree on the Westminster property and break her arm. She'd explained to me how it happened while they were putting on her cast. "Clara didn't believe I climbed into your window on the second floor, so I had to show her I was still quite capable."

I was really starting to not like this Clara person. I pressed my lips together as I stared at Patch, who was impatiently bobbing his head up and down, winding up to hammer on the window again.

It was too early to call Gran and tell her *not* to climb that tree (that was one benefit of Gran knowing about my gift. I didn't have to convince her that it *would* happen), so I approached the window and said under my breath, "I'm probably going to regret this, but I have to see if we're all going to get along."

I was impressed when Houdini didn't immediately attack Patch once he flew into the room. He watched the bird with wild, wary eyes and a snarling lift of his lip, but once he saw me set out a piece of kibble for Patch, he immediately whimpered and gave me puppy eyes.

I tossed him some pieces, which seemed to calm his raging beast.

Whereas Houdini kept one eye on Patch's movements at all times, the raven seemed to adopt an I'm-going-to-pretend-that-big-animal-isn't-here attitude. Patch focused on the raven statue on my nightstand, making low gurgling noises and bobbing his head up and down as if in deep conversation with the mute bird.

While I tossed a few more pieces of kibble to Houdini, Patch opened my jewelry box on my nightstand and had already removed several of my necklaces.

"Patch!" The bird let out a *crooooack* and flew over to my desk as I quickly moved to untangle the mess he'd made of my chains. I held up the necklace Aunt Sage had encouraged me to create to help me retrieve my dreams. Gripping the blue crystal hanging from it, I told Patch, "If it weren't for this necklace and Ethan's help, I never would've been able to tell Fate to back off from his 'Nara must die for interfering' vendetta. Shiny things might attract you, but claws off!"

I carefully set the necklace back in my jewelry box on top of the bangle cuff Aunt Sage had given me when I turned thirteen, then retrieved my grandmother's journal to get some more reading in before I had to take a shower.

When Houdini let out a light bark forty minutes later, I looked up to see Patch pulling the crystal necklace from its new drawer. "Patch..." I began with a sigh as I stood.

He glanced at me, then lifted the chain with his beak. He'd protected me the other day. It wouldn't hurt to humor him. I looped the chain several times around the raven statue's neck, resting the crystal on the bird's chest. "Now you can see it but can't take off with it. Happy?" In answer, Patch fluffed his wings and approached the raven, eyeing the chain with pleased guttural sounds.

Patch started to tug at the chain with his beak, then he turned around and made an annoyed *raaaack* sound at Houdini. Apparently, the dog was too close.

"Okay, boys! Enough tolerance testing for one day. Time for you to go, Patch. I need to get a shower." Once I'd opened my window, I spun a quarter and watched with amusement at Houdini's bark of alarm when Patch snatched up the coin like a desperate kid in an arcade.

As I made my way to the park to meet with Drystan, my whole body was one tense ball of nerves. I felt guilty that I was already fifteen minutes late, but it's not like I could call or text Drystan and let him know I was delayed. An hour and a half earlier, I'd been in Mocha Java's drive-through line, waiting for my coffee, when I tried to call Gran. Fate decided to zap my phone the moment I hit Send. I gave the guy at the drive-through window quite a show when I screamed and threw my phone into the floorboard of my car.

I'd had no choice but to drive to Westminster, which didn't open its main gates until eight. I got shocked when I pushed the button on the retirement community gates' entrance. Another shock when I picked up the pen at the main desk to sign in. Yet another shock when I had to pull open the door that led to the elevators. To keep from grinding my teeth to nubs while waiting for the next electrical jolt, I bumped the elevator button with my elbow and knocked on Gran's door with the toe of my shoe.

By the time she rustled herself out of bed, and then insisted on calling Clara over for me to tell her neighbor the story how Gran had most definitely climbed to the second story of our house, my hair was so full of electricity, the entire top layer floated around my head like a halo of gnats. I refused to touch either Gran or Clara for fear I'd give them cardiac arrest. I left as fast as I could, but it was already five after nine.

As I turned into the main entrance of the park, I tried to think of the best way to deal with Fate's twisted form of shock therapy. Had he totally fried my phone? I grabbed it from my backpack and hit the On button. Thankfully it powered back to life. I set my jaw as I slipped it back in my pack. Even though my phone was fine, I saw another showdown with Fate in my not-too-distant future.

Ethan had helped me make Fate back off in the past. Would we be able to make him leave me alone again? Ethan hadn't liked me interfering with others' lives before, and since my life wasn't in jeopardy this time, would he even agree to help if he thought that me facing off with Fate in my dreams was a bigger risk to my life than an occasional shock? I honestly wasn't sure what Ethan would say.

You need to let me do this on my own, Nara.

Ethan's comment when he'd learned I was at the raven sanctuary had really hurt. I'd tried not to think too hard about what he meant by it, but with Fate up to new tricks, I couldn't help but think about him.

Did Ethan think I was pushing him with the ravens? That wasn't my intent, but now that I'd had such an amazing emotional experience with him through the ravens at the sanctuary, I desperately wanted to record my thoughts about it in Ethan's journal. Not to mention, I wanted to jot down notes on the mysterious book Freddie had tried to give me. My heart ached that all the work I'd done…all the information I'd collected was lost.

Lost!

When the realization hit me, I felt like smacking my forehead against my steering wheel. Drystan had proven his ability to find lost things. Could he help me retrieve Ethan's journal? I missed my daily experience of working on it. Just like I missed my special time with Ethan.

Would Drystan be able to see it? Maybe his powers were different from mine and he wouldn't be blocked from seeing the leather book like I was. I chewed on the inside of my cheek, while I considered how I could possibly ask Drystan to help me locate Ethan's book yet still keep my ability and Ethan's a secret. Guilt made my shoulders ache as I gripped the steering wheel tighter.

As I turned into the park's entrance, I decided that if I asked for Drystan's help, it was only fair that I told him about my own ability in return. It's what he wanted to know. I could still keep Ethan's power to myself. But what if I shared with Drystan, only to discover that he couldn't "see" Ethan's book either? I'd be risking telling another person about my ability for nothing.

"You're late," Drystan said in a curt tone from his leaning position against Matt's Jeep.

I rolled up my cracked window, then stepped out of my car and held up my Mocha Java cup. "Sorry. The drive-through line was extra long this morning." Skimming my gaze past Drystan's bed-head hair (Why couldn't I roll out of bed and look that good? So not fair!) to his thin black zip-up jacket and track pants with three stripes down the sides, I shivered in my thick fleece, sweatshirt and sweatpants. "Aren't you cold?" I wished my coffee was still warm as I wrapped my fingerless-gloved hands around the cup.

Drystan's green gaze turned icy as he stared at my cup. "Does that have milk and sugar in it?"

"Of course." Just as I started to take another sip, he took the cup and dumped what was left. I scowled. He didn't say anything about my drink in my dream. "What was that for?"

Jaw set, he handed me the empty cup. "Black coffee only before sessions. Water is preferred. I was going to work on something else with you..." he began, then turned and opened the trunk of the Jeep, where he retrieved a foldable six-foot ladder.

As he walked off toward the park without another word, I glared after his retreating back and called out, "You owe me a latte!" If water had been so important, he'd have said something in my dream. *Why did I feel like I was being punished?*

When I realized he wasn't going to acknowledge my complaint, I put the empty cup in my car, grabbed my backpack, then ran after him, grumbling, "I'll tell you what's preferred."

Drystan had entered the woods on a footpath. I followed, but kept my less-than-happy thoughts to myself. In my dream last night, we'd gone running for a couple of miles, then we'd worked on some self-defense moves. Now that I'd shown up late and apparently pissed him off, Drystan had changed his plans. My training session was blind now. Ugh!

He's doing this to help you, I repeated to myself over and over, but I frowned as I followed him deeper into the woods, leaves crunching under my shoes. "Why are you doing this, Drystan?" I asked the back of his head. I needed to know he wasn't planning to leave me lost in the woods, expecting me to find my way back as some kind of twisted punishment.

"Because you need it," he shot back in a terse tone as he veered off the path into the thick woods.

I stumbled over a root, but managed to catch myself as I followed suit. "No, seriously. Why?"

Drystan stopped so abruptly that I ran into his back. I took a step back and met his serious gaze as he turned around and set the ladder down on the ground next to a tree.

"This is about trust, Nara. You obviously have trust issues. So we're going to work on those."

"What are you talk—"

"I can tell you were lying to me about why you were late," he cut in, his lips tight.

I stiffened and snapped my mouth shut. I didn't want to get into an argument. Instead I glanced at the woods all around us. We'd reached a slight clearing about fifty feet wide where only a few trees stood. "I thought this was about learning self-defense."

Drystan smirked, the first glimmer of amusement he'd shown. In his current mood, I wasn't sure that was a good thing.

"It is, but first we have to start with balance." He turned his gaze upward, then jumped up and pulled on a flat, inch-wide elastic line that had been strung about seven feet up between the tree next to him and another tree thirty feet away. As it bounced up and down, he said, "This is called a slackline. It's great for working on balance."

Drystan dug the ladder's legs into the ground against the tree. When he held his hand out as if he expected me to climb the rungs, I shook my head in fast jerks. "No way! There aren't any cushions under that—that piece of thread you've got stretched between two trees. There's no padding. No safety net. I'm not getting on there."

"It's flexible nylon and it's not going to snap on you."

I smacked his outstretched hand. "That doesn't change the fact there's nothing under it to catch me when, not if, *when* I fall."

His lips tilted in a confident smile. "That's what I'm here for."

He'd totally laid on the accent with that last statement. I folded my arms. "You're not charming me up on that line. I like my legs and neck just the way they are. *Unbroken.*"

Drystan lowered his hand and climbed the ladder. He gripped the tree branch near his head, ducked under it, then stepped onto the nylon. The flexible line dipped with his weight, proving my biggest fear; every movement was like walking on a thin trampoline.

My stomach took a dive as he scooched out farther from the tree. I found myself subconsciously moving with him. I even held my hand up for him to grab, which made no logical sense, considering his outstretched hands were a good four feet higher than the line's seven-foot height. Despite my apprehension, Drystan stayed perfectly balanced as if he were walking on a two-by-four.

"Don't use your legs to balance. Only use your upper body and hips, like this," he said, demonstrating as he moved forward toward the middle. "When you first get up here, stay close to the tree until you feel more comfortable. There's less movement of the line there. Once you start forward, be sure to bend your knees and keep your chest forward. That'll help you maintain balance."

After he made it to the middle of the line, he jumped up and down a couple of times, then twisted a hundred eighty degrees in the air. He landed on the line with a shock-absorbing give of his legs, facing the opposite direction. He bounced up and down, and reversed his position, facing me once more with a wide grin. "See, it's not so bad."

He made it look too easy, which I knew was a big fat lie. It was like a sniper telling me I could hit my target from a quarter mile away on a windy day with the sun in my eyes. No problem. My only response was to scowl at him.

"Nara..." Drystan gave a slight hop and dropped onto his butt on the thin piece of nylon, his legs dangling.

On instinct, I grabbed his legs to keep him from falling backward.

A smug smile tugged his lips even as he rolled his eyes. "How do you think I was able to push myself off that stairwell wall and land back on the railing without falling off?" he asked, his voice softer now.

"You have a retractable cord in your belly?" Irritated that I'd worried for nothing, I released him and took a step back. "Either that or you're part cat."

Drystan chuckled and bounced back to a standing position. With a big swooping jump, he tucked into a backward flip to land on the ground in a crouch. He quickly stood, then walked over to me.

"Show-off," I muttered.

He smirked. "Learning how to quickly regain balance in combat situations as well as how to land so that you won't get hurt are aspects you should learn along with self-defense techniques. I'm going to teach you how to defend yourself, but you should also know how to get away, Nara.

"Parkour is perceived as constant movement using natural motion. The technique is very physical, but it's a way of evaluating and perceiving your environment around you in a strategic way, where you don't let your mind or physical barriers stop you. Defensively, if you can think at least two steps ahead of your pursuer, then your chances of getting away are much greater."

He paused and glanced at the line. "It all starts with getting comfortable with balance. Are you ready to give it a go now?"

I followed his gaze while chewing my bottom lip. "Can we lower the line to a couple of feet above the ground?"

He shook his head and turned me toward the ladder. "You'll learn to balance much faster if you fear falling. Consider it incentive."

I'd already put my hands on the ladder, but I quickly glanced over my shoulder with a sarcastic tilt of my eyebrow. "I *do* fear falling. I was pretty clear on that. From my perspective, your logic is flawed."

He squeezed my shoulders, a shameless grin spreading across his face. "You're just going to have to *trust* me."

And that was the crux of it. If I couldn't trust Drystan to have my back with this, how could I possibly trust him with my secret, regardless of the outcome? I took a deep breath and began to climb the ladder.

"Use the tree limb to help you get balance on the line," he called out once I got to the top.

With a tight hold on the thick limb, I put one foot on the line, then ducked under the limb like I'd seen him do. As soon as my weight shifted, the line began to wobble, then swing wildly. Pulse thrumming, I tried to tighten my hold on the tree but my gloves slipped.

I screamed on the way down. Strong arms caught me mid-fall, wrapping around my body. Drystan's low chuckle vibrated against my shoulder. "I suggest ditching the gloves since it's warmed up a bit. They kept you from maintaining a tight grip."

My heart was still beating on high rev when he set me on my feet. I didn't want to climb the ladder again, but the challenging "you're not chicken, are you?" look in his eyes made me tilt my chin at a stubborn angle.

Without a word, I stripped off my gloves and tossed them to the ground. My heavy fleece followed. As I started toward the ladder on wobbly legs, he spoke in a low, determined voice behind me, "You're going to learn to trust me if it kills you."

CHAPTER 18

True to his word, Drystan caught me each time I fell, which didn't stop my heart from slamming into my throat whenever my feet slipped off the nylon line and I plummeted toward the hard ground. By the time I finally managed to stay on the line for more than a minute, my trust in him was completely solidified. It only took me two and a half hours to figure out how to balance with my legs and hips, not my arms. Um, yeah, *hearing* that advice and actually *learning* it were two very different things.

Drystan lay back in the leaves underneath the slackline and tucked his arms behind his head. "I think that's a good start for today. You might not feel it now, but you're going to be sore as 'ell tomorrow." He paused and cast an amused gaze my way. "And no, I'm not cutting you any slack just because you ache all over in the morning. Nine sharp. You'll just have to suck it up, Miss Collins."

"We agreed on four days. Every other day works best for me." I settled into a crossed-legged position beside him. A light breeze blew through the trees, tinged with the smell of moss and pine as it cooled the sweat coating my temples.

"Nope. I'm taking four in a row," he countered. "As the week goes on, Lainey's going to distract you with winter dance stuff."

I laughed at the distasteful look on his face and shrugged back into my fleece. "They don't have school dances in Wales? Or do you not know how to dance, Drystan? Which is it?"

He grinned and rolled onto his side. Sliding his hand through his sweat-dampened hair, he propped up on his elbow. "I know how to dance, right enough. Why don't you come to the dance with me? That way you can keep the adoring American girls at bay."

I stiffened. I hadn't expected the conversation to turn in this direction. "I have a boyfriend, Drystan. I thought Lainey told you that."

"So." He shrugged. "I'm not asking you on a date. I'd just like to go with someone I know. Plus, I was serious about batting away all the girls wanting a go at the new Welsh boy," he finished, giving a smug wink.

"Cocky much?" I said, smirking.

"Where is this invisible bloke of yours? Lainey said he's taking cyber school right now while he's out of town for a while. If I were your boyfriend, I'd make the trip home to take you to the dance."

I tensed and plucked a crunchy leaf from the ground, then shredded it between my fingers. "Ethan's relationship with his parents is complicated. He's trying to work it out."

A hard, unsympathetic look poured into Drystan's green gaze. "My dad refused to acknowledge my ability, even when I'd proven my accuracy several times. He looked me right in the eyes and told me to 'cut that bullshit out.'"

"That had to suck." I grimaced, surprised he'd shared something so personal.

Drystan snorted. "That's nothing compared to him refusing to acknowledge he was my father."

My gaze locked with his. "What do you mean? I thought he was a part of your life before he passed away. At least you made it sound that way."

His mouth turned downward. "He lived with and supported us, but he never married my mum or introduced me as his son. He even called me Maddox—my mother's maiden name—as a constant reminder he refused to give me his last name. The selfish bastard."

As much as I heard the hate in his words, I also sensed deeper emotions reflected in his hard stare: hurt, confusion and disillusionment.

Before I could say anything, he interrupted with a confident smile, shrugging away the past. "But even with all that parental shite going on in my head, I'd manage to put myself straight and take you to the dance."

Put myself straight? His literal-speak, spoken in that Welsh accent was so quaint. "I'm sorry about your dad, Drystan, and thanks for asking, but I won't be going to the dance without Ethan."

"Your loss." Shaking his head, Drystan picked up a handful of leaves and tossed it at me. "We're going to have a grand time."

I sputtered and batted the leaves off my face and clothes, then held up my hands when I saw he was sitting up with another handful ready to throw. "But I do have a favor to ask. If you're willing to help, then I'll share."

He immediately dropped the leaves, excited anticipation in his expression. "Share? As in you'll tell me your ability?"

I inhaled to bolster my confidence and nodded.

"Done!" He moved to sit beside me, bent his knees, then leaned back on his hands with an expectant look. "What do you want me to do?"

"Maybe you should hear me out first before you agree."

An eyebrow shot up and his lips quirked. "I'm already intrigued."

I bent my own knees and wrapped my arms around them, resting my chin on my knee. "I'm trying to find an important book—a journal—that's disappeared. It's for a project I've been working on."

"Is that all?" he snorted, sitting up. "No problem."

I pulled a water bottle from my backpack. "I wish it were that easy." I sighed and took a sip. "It was stolen from my house and I have no idea who stole it."

Drystan let out a low whistle. "Trouble follows you like the plague." He rubbed his hands together, then continued, "Stolen or misplaced, my ability focuses on the result, not the how or why of it. *Locating* is all that matters."

I gave a half smile. "This will be a true test of your ability then, because I can't even see it."

He tilted his head. "Really? Well then, how about sharing what your power is…"

"Every night I dream my entire next day," I blurted, then held my breath, waiting for his reaction.

"Wow!" Drystan's eyes widened and he shoved a hand through his hair with an astonished laugh. "Just…wow. Now that I know, seeing myself in the future makes an odd sort of sense."

I frowned. "I don't understand."

Drystan held his hand out, palm up. "Remember I said that holding things is how I use my power to find what I'm trying to find? I was holding Lochlan's collar that day, seeking his location. But you didn't know that's what I was doing, and when you touched my hand, that's when I saw myself giving Lochlan to Lainey. It's like when you touched me, my power combined with yours and let me see a glimpse of the future."

I furrowed my brow. "What doesn't make sense is that I dream my *next* day. You saw something that happened later the same day."

"Maybe when my power and yours merge, there's a shift in how yours works? I've never 'seen' myself finding the object either until that day you touched my hand. That's definitely a change in how my ability has worked in the past."

"But you didn't touch me that day you knew I was going to get shot. How did you see the 'future' then?"

Drystan shrugged. "Apparently you also leave residual energy that conveys your power on items you've worn. When Matt and I got to Lainey's, she told me you were looking for the other glove you'd dropped. She asked me to catch up with you, since I knew the path we'd taken to find Lochlan that day. I grabbed the glove you'd left behind, and that's when I saw myself saving you. I told them to call the police before I went to find you."

"That's one of the downsides of my dreams," I said with a wry look. "If I change something from my dream, then my entire day can change in turn. I never dreamed about getting shot. Lainey was the one who was shot and seriously injured. I changed her fate when I went looking for the glove myself. And as for finding Lochlan, that wasn't in my dream. I was only at her house that day because I'd inadvertently changed something else earlier in the day."

"Inadvertently?" An incredulous expression filtered across his features. "You don't change things on purpose?"

"Rarely. There are too many consequences and unknowns if I do." I so wasn't going to go into my issues with Fate.

Drystan snorted. "I'd be all over changing stuff I didn't like in my life."

I pressed my lips together. "Trust me. If you'd lived in my shoes, you wouldn't."

"Why do I get the feeling you're not telling me everything?" he said, eyeing me with a narrowed gaze.

Because everything is too personal, too freaky, and would change your entire perspective on what you thought you knew about life in general. I shrugged and spread my hands wide. "And now you know my secret."

Drystan looked away, his eyes clouding over. "If I'd only known my dad was going to die that day, I would've never let him leave the house."

My stomach lurched. This was the danger of others knowing my ability; they'd expect me to save their loved ones too. I couldn't control everything, couldn't save the entire world. The pressure would be crippling to take on the fate of millions.

"That's the limitation to my power, Drystan. I only see what's going to happen in *my* life, things that directly impact me."

Drystan rubbed his forehead. "Wait, I'm trying to get it sorted in my head how your ability works. If you see your whole day, then why didn't you know you were going to be attacked at the library? And why didn't you foresee that your journal would be stolen? You could've taken it with you to avoid that from happening. And what about this conversation? Didn't you dream you told me about your power?"

I grimaced. "Glitches happen. If I'm woken early, I don't see my entire day, which is what happened the day at the library. I hadn't dreamed that far yet." I ran my hand down my face, feeling suddenly tired. "The journal is a little different. When I first started working on it, I dreamed about it every night, but later," I paused and shrugged, "it faded from my dreams, which means I wouldn't have dreamed about it being stolen. As for me telling you about my ability, I didn't dream this conversation, because it's about the book. Nothing about it shows up in my dreams, even talking about it."

Drystan shook his head and blew out a breath. "How do you keep it all straight? How do you freakin' not give yourself away constantly?"

My lips quirked. "I've been like this since I was seven, Drystan. I've had almost a decade to perfect my poker face, though I'm not perfect either. I slip up from time to time."

"So, if I'm going to make a right arse of myself, would you tell me ahead of time?"

I laughed. "Believe it or not, people can surprise me every once in a while, like you did today when you changed your plans and brought me here to the slackline." I raised my eyebrow. "In answer to your question, would it make a difference if I told you that you were going to be a 'right arse'?"

The corner of his mouth tilted darkly. "Maybe, maybe not."

"That's what I thought," I said in a dry tone as I glanced up at the wind whipping through the trees.

"Thank you for trusting me with your secret, Nara."

Drystan had turned serious. I smiled. "Thank you for being so stubborn."

His green eyes flared. "It's my specialty." Holding out his hand, he continued, "I'll need to touch something related to the journal, something that was in constant contact with it, like you."

Was I ready to go there? I wasn't sure that I was. Plus, having him hold my hand might feel too intimate. He'd been able to use my residual energy that had embedded itself in

Lainey's mom's glove. I turned and pulled a purple pen from its slot in my backpack, then set it in his hand. "Try this pen. I've used it every time I worked on the book. It should help you trace its location."

He stared at the pen in his open palm, then pressed his lips together. "You're doing it again."

I tensed, surprised by his comment. "Doing what?"

The green in his eyes sparked with disappointment. "You don't trust me."

"It's complicated, Drystan," I hedged, glancing away from his penetrating stare.

"No, *you're* complicated," he shot back and folded his fingers around the pen, closing his eyes.

I held my breath as I watched him rub his fingers back and forth against the pen.

It seemed like minutes ticked by, but it was probably only seconds when his eyes flew open. "Is it in a drawstring bag? I can't tell the color because there's very poor light."

"Yes!" I nodded, a huge smile on my face. "I can't believe you can see it, but that's great." *Why could he see it when it had completely disappeared from my dreams?*

Drystan shrugged, his earlier excitement subdued.

I glanced at his hand. "Where is it?"

"In a locker."

"A locker where?"

Drystan handed me the pen. "You can't get to it, but I can."

I shook my head. "No, you've done enough. Just tell me where it is and I'll get it."

He folded his arms, a stubborn look on his face. "Unless you can change your gender, you won't be able to get it."

"My gender?"

"It's stashed in a men's locker room at a gym."

I snorted. "If it's at a school gym, I can find a way to sneak in."

"No, it won't be that easy to get to. It's a private, members-only gym."

I wasn't letting him risk getting in trouble for me. "I'll find a way into the facility, Drystan. You've done enough. Just tell me the name of the gym."

His gaze narrowed. "Do you know how to pick a lock?"

When I shook my head, he adopted an arrogant smile and stood. "I do. I'll get the book for you. End of discussion."

I stood beside him. "This could be dangerous. I don't want you to risk getting hurt."

"I told you I'd get it and I will."

This time I narrowed my gaze. "What did you see, Drystan? It sounds like you just saw the drawstring bag. Are you saying you didn't see yourself there?"

Drystan shook his head. "Apparently your psychic energy can embed itself on natural fabric like the leather glove, but not on an inorganic item like a plastic pen. I was able to make the connection for the location using my powers only."

"But you didn't see yourself retrieving it. Is that what you're saying?"

As he slowly nodded, guilt and panic battled inside me. I couldn't let him try to recover Ethan's book without some assurance that he could retrieve it safely. Someone broke into my house to retrieve it. Who knew what they'd do to keep it. I'd never forgive myself if something happened to Drystan.

Ethan and I had shared that moment with the ravens *after* Drystan and my powers had combined over finding Lochlan, so I didn't need to worry that doing so again would break the special bond I had with Ethan.

"Then I need to know you'll be able to retrieve it without getting hurt." I took a step close to Drystan and I reached for his hand.

His broad smile returned as he slid his fingers against mine. With a swift move, he folded our locked hands against his chest, yanking me close. "Close your eyes and focus," he whispered in my ear.

I tried to keep my breathing steady and even, to stay focused like Drystan asked. After a full minute, he took a step back and released my hand, his expression hard. "I saw myself handing you a dark green drawstring bag. I need to steal it back tonight before whoever stole it moves it to another location."

I released a sigh of relief. "Thank you, Drystan. Okay, tonight it is. Let's make a plan."

When he started to shake his head, I held up my hand. "I *will* help you do this." *Also, while I'm there as your backup, you won't have a chance to read it.*

Drystan exhaled a frustrated breath. "Fine. It'll be easier to keep this re-stealing adventure between us if I don't have to borrow Matt's car. You can drive, but you'll stay in the car."

"I'm way too far away. I can't see detail." I peered around Drystan sitting in my passenger seat, and past the trees and sculpted landscape of the business parking lot to the three-story, members-only gym in the shopping center across the street.

On each level of the facility, people were working out on various pieces of equipment from treadmills to free weights behind the floor-to-ceiling glass windows. The building had an odd L shape of a two-story building connected to a three-story building with glass windows on all three levels; old mixed with new. The one positive aspect was that since we'd waited until dark, with the place lit up on every floor, it was easy to get a general layout of the taller building from the outside. Well, except for the locker rooms and business offices, they were either in the two-story building or on the back side of the three story.

"That's the whole point," Drystan said as he scanned the two buildings like he was sizing up possible entry and escape routes. "Up here, in this parking lot surrounded by trees, you're too far away for anyone to know you're here with me."

I snorted. "But that also means I'll be too far away for *you* to get to if you end up being chased." I started the engine. "I'm going to move closer."

Drystan reached over and turned off my car. "Oh no, you don't. I'm fast. I can get to you." He thrust something he'd pulled from his backpack into my hands. "Use these if you want a bird's-eye view. I borrowed them from Matt's dad's office, so don't go breaking them."

I glanced down at the binoculars and nodded. "What excuse did you give Matt as to where you were going tonight?"

He grinned. "Didn't have to. He's out helping Lainey pick up the decorations for the dance. She volunteered before she realized just how big they were."

That explained why she didn't call me for help. She needed muscle. "What do you think about this whole Matt and Lainey 'getting back at their exes' scheme?"

Drystan snorted. "That might've been his initial intent, but I think Matt has redirected his attention."

"To Lainey, right?" I said, throwing my hands up.

Drystan chuckled. "He hasn't admitted it, but I see it."

"Me too. Lainey thinks I'm nuts."

When Drystan's attention shifted back to the building, I asked, "How are you going to get in?"

He pulled a lockpick kit from his backpack. I shook my head and muttered, "My Welsh friend is some kind of delinquent, and he just hasn't told me yet."

He adopted a serious expression. "I've done some things in my past I'm not going to admit to, but this," he held up the kit, "was used more for learning secrets, than thievery."

What kind of people did he hang with, who kept secrets that needed to be locked away? I wondered, but kept my thoughts to myself. "It looks like the shift of people coming from work are getting into their routines on the equipment. Now is probably the best time for the locker room to be fairly empty. You'd better get going. It'll take you at least ten minutes to get down there."

An arrogant smirk tilted his lips. "See you in a few." Once he got out of my car, Drystan pulled his black hoodie up so it covered his blond-streaked hair, then slid his empty backpack over both shoulders and shot me a thumbs-up.

I copied his thumbs-up action, then shooed him on with the binoculars from my lap.

I followed his shadowy form down the hill, watching with

interest how quickly and efficiently he moved. There were stairs, but Drystan didn't take them. Instead, he vaulted from tier to tier down the cement structures edging them.

Once he crossed the highway, I lifted the binoculars to track his movements. I noticed that he stayed in the shadows, avoiding the lights in the parking lot. When he turned and pointed upward to one of the lights, I realized why when I shifted the zoom to the top of the light. Cameras were on a few of them. Smart. I wouldn't have thought of that.

When he reached the building in six minutes, I smiled. He'd had a reason to smirk at my "ten minute" comment. I expected him to go around the edge of the building and try to get into a loading dock or back door where delivery or laundry people entered. Instead, Drystan jumped onto the corner of the tall building's wall, grabbed onto a decorative ledge, then pushed off it to grip a higher ledge on the opposite wall. Pulling himself up, he grabbed onto a pipe that ran along the corner between the two buildings. He made efficient work of scaling the pipe to the roof of the lower building, then quickly ran along the wall across the rooftop to the door that connected the taller building to the shorter one.

I held my breath as he picked the lock, then exhaled in a gust of relief when he entered without sudden alarms blaring and roving spotlights scanning into the night.

As my heart hammered in wait mode, my gaze seesawed between the digital clock on my dash and the door Drystan had entered. Seven minutes had passed, and then another five. My neck tensed and my shoulders began to ache. Was twelve minutes long enough to get in and out? I wanted to ping his phone so bad, but was afraid he'd forgotten to turn it on vibrate mode, and my text would give his presence away. Instead, I bit my lip and waited, clenching and unclenching my fingers in a death grip around the binoculars.

CHAPTER 19

A blur streaked across the top of the three-story building. I quickly straightened and zoomed in. It was Drystan, wearing his backpack, but he wasn't alone. A taller guy in a ball cap and baseball-style jacket chased him at a speed that set my heart racing with worry.

I gasped as Drystan came closer and closer to the edge. God, he would be trapped! When he jumped, my heart lodged in my throat. I watched in shock as he landed in a tucked roll, then jumped right back up as if his legs were made of springs.

Unfortunately the guy chasing him followed, though he landed far less gracefully. He stood and stumbled for a second or two, then shot off in pursuit after Drystan, who was already scaling down the pipe like a ninja.

His pursuer didn't follow Drystan. Instead, he vaulted off the two-story building and landed on the ground below. I gaped. How was that humanly possible without breaking a leg? I called out in a hoarse voice, "Drystan, he's waiting for you!"

Drystan must've heard the other guy push his tall body through the three-foot hedge to get to him. Instead of jumping down, Drystan used the ledge to pull himself across the front of the building, while keeping his legs out of the guy's grasp.

When Drystan reached the end of the ledge, the guy was waiting for him at the corner. His arms were crossed, his stance confident, as if he knew Drystan wouldn't be able to hold himself up there forever. Drystan pulled his legs up a bit higher, then pushed off the wall in a powerful backward flip. Vaulting over the guy's head, he hit the ground on the other side of the bushes in a backward roll.

"Damn, that was impressive," I muttered.

Just as Drystan moved to stand, the guy wearing the ball cap burst through the hedge and landed a hard punch. The powerful hit knocked Drystan to his knees.

"Drystan!" I screamed and immediately started my car, yanking it into gear. Drystan held his hand outstretched in my direction. I paused, surprised when he staggered to a standing position, then quickly spun, drilling a powerful round-house kick into his attacker's chest. As the guy flew into the bushes, Drystan took off running toward the walled edge of the shopping center's parking lot.

When he was within a few feet of the wall, Drystan sprang into a flying jump, where he scaled the ten-foot wall with nothing more than springboard legs and one handhold on a covered light halfway up the wall. I watched in disbelief as he grabbed the wrought iron railing at the top, then pulled himself up to vault over the railing.

As he disappeared into the wooded area flanking the entire left side of the shopping center, I shook my head in amazement. Watching Drystan overcome obstacles in his way, while staying in constant motion, was like watching a monkey jump, twist, and swing his way through a jungle environment. Not a single action was wasted.

The moment the guy from the gym found a lower area of the wall he could scale, then jumped over it to follow after Drystan, my hands tensed on the steering wheel.

Drystan had told me to wait here. After witnessing what I just did, I had to trust he knew he could somehow find his way over to me without the guy pursuing him.

Fourteen agonizing minutes later, I received a text.

Drystan – 9:00 p.m. ~ Think I lost him. Meet me on the back side of the Furniture Place's parking lot. JIC, turn off your lights and roll down your back windows.

That was at least two miles away! I drove toward Furniture Place. It had closed down last year, so I understood why he'd chosen it as a meeting place. No one would be around and there weren't any parking lot lights. As soon as I turned into the lot, I flicked off my car lights, glad for the half moon to light my path back behind the warehouse.

My pulse thrummed in my ears as I pushed the buttons to roll down my back windows and steered my car toward the back side of the parking lot.

I'd barely turned the corner of the building when Drystan dove into my back seat. I let out a gasp of surprise, but quickly buzzed the windows closed.

He kept his head low and panted hard. "Take that...road." Sweat trickled down his temples as he pushed his hood back and pointed toward a narrow dirt road that led off the parking lot. "Came...this way earlier. Leads to a neighborhood. Steered the bloke in the opposite direction...then doubled back."

"Do you ever take stairs like a normal person?" I handed him an extra water bottle I'd brought, then followed his directions down the dirt road. "God, that was close, Drystan!"

"Stairs are boring." His lips crooked as he lifted the water bottle.

Five minutes later, Drystan finished off the last of the water just as my car emerged from the woods, entering an unfamiliar neighborhood. I turned on my lights, then plugged in the GPS so I wouldn't have to drive around aimlessly trying to find my way back to a main road.

As I followed the GPS's directions, I asked, "Did you recognize the guy who came after you? Was he someone from school?"

Drystan climbed into the front seat. "I'd turned off the lights in the locker room, since no one was in there when I entered. Once we were in the parking lot, I tried to catch a glimpse, but his baseball hat obscured his eyes. I think he had a buzz cut or something under that hat."

I wanted to punch my steering wheel that we still didn't know who this guy was. "Did you see him jump from that two-story building to the ground? That's impossible without breaking a leg."

He rubbed his jaw. "Not necessarily. I've seen a couple of blokes jump from that height while doing parkour moves."

"He didn't roll like you do to take the shock out of the impact. That seemed an inhuman leap for him to land on cement in an upright stance."

Drystan's eyes widened. "He landed without absorbing that jump?"

I nodded. "I cringed watching it."

Twenty minutes later, I pulled into the garage, closing the door behind my car. Drystan's swelling cheek made me wince. I was glad Mom had gone out with Mr. Dixon so I wouldn't have to explain *any* of tonight's events. "I can't thank you enough for your help, Drystan. Let's get some ice on your face."

Houdini let off a round of vicious defensive barks as Drystan entered with me through the kitchen door. "Hush, Houdini," I said, holding out my hand.

Houdini rushed to nuzzle my fingers. Shoving his big body between Drystan and me, he growled at Drystan, then pressed his nose into my palm.

Drystan took a step back. "He's a right big one, your dog."

When I saw the darker line of hair on Houdini's tan back fully raised in defensive mode, I took Drystan's hand and held it out palm-up so Houdini could sniff. "He's okay, Houdini. This is Drystan."

Houdini eyed Drystan warily. He sniffed hard, making sure to leave behind plenty of snot-drool. Eventually the raised fur on his back began to lie down, but he kept himself pressed firmly against my thigh.

"You can wash the drool off while I get some ice for you," I said, turning to pull out a clean dishtowel from a drawer in the island.

Drystan rubbed his wet hand on his jeans, eyeing Houdini with guarded respect. "I think I'll keep his scent on me while I'm here." He laid his backpack on the island, then moved around it to sit on one of the stools.

As I opened the freezer, Drystan said, "What's in that book

of yours, Nara?"

"Why?" I tensed, but forced my expression to relax before I set the flexible icepack on the clean dishtowel I'd laid on the island.

He shrugged and played with the zipper on his backpack. "I got the impression that the bloke chasing me thought I was trying to steal his 'prize' away from him. When he came around the corner and saw me shutting the locker, he yelled across the empty locker room, 'It's mine to present to him!' That's all he said."

"I don't know why it would be considered a prize." I frowned and skirted the island to press the towel-wrapped ice pack under his eye. "Here, hold this on the swelling for a little bit."

Drystan had inhaled a pained hiss when the cloth touched his face, but he put his hand over mine before I could release the towel. "You're not telling me everything. Don't you think I at least deserve an answer?"

His green gaze stared at me intently as his warm fingers clasped my hand tight. I couldn't pull away without hurting him, so I told him the truth. "Honestly, Drystan, I have no clue why this guy or anyone else would want my journal. It's just personal notes on a project I'm working on. Everything that's in there is stuff I've gotten off the Internet. In other words, nothing super secret or special. It's available to everyone."

"Well, some people think it has value." He sighed and released my hand. "What is your project about?"

I slid onto the stool next to him and started to speak, when Houdini moved close to rest his chin on my thigh. I rubbed his head as I gave Drystan an apologetic look. "I'm sorry, Drystan, but it's personal."

Grunting, he shook his head and unzipped his backpack, then pulled the green drawstring bag out by the strings. "I hope whatever's in here is worth the hassle it's taken to get it back."

I grabbed the top of the bag, guilt whipping through me. "When you saw yourself handing me this, did you know you'd be holding ice on your face?"

Drystan shrugged. "You said you needed to get it back, so I

helped. It seemed important to you."

My heart tugged that he'd gone after my journal knowing he'd get hurt. "I wished you'd told me everything."

"If you can hold stuff back, so can I," he shot back.

"I never would've let you do it, Dryst!"

A broad smile suddenly split his face and warmth reflected in his eyes. "Dryst. My first girlfriend used to call me that. It sounds very different in your American accent, though. Better, I think."

Gah! I couldn't believe I'd inadvertently used an old girl-friend's nickname for him. I'd used it like I did "Lane" for Lainey. "It was just my way of saying, 'Thanks, but you'd better spill your guts in the future,'" I said in a lighthearted tone as I tugged on the drawstring to open the bag. I just wanted to peek inside and make sure Ethan's book was still in good condition.

When my gaze landed on the smaller dark blue hardback book with brass corners lying on top of Ethan's leather book, my stomach twisted into a hard knot.

Oh God, no!

"What's wrong?" Drystan pulled the icepack away. "Is your journal not in there?"

"No, that's not it." I jumped up to grab my backpack lying against the couch.

As I frantically riffled through my bag, looking for the notepad I'd used for my interview notes with Freddie, Drystan touched my shoulder. "What's going on? You're very pale."

"I—I have to check something first." I flipped to the front page of the notepad where I'd jotted down Freddie's contact information, then grabbed my phone and dialed his number.

My hand tightened on my phone as Freddie's phone rang and rang and rang. I let it ring another ten times before looking at Drystan. "I know it's a lot to ask, but would you mind riding with me out to Afton?"

Drystan gripped my shoulders and turned me to face him. "Talk to me, Nara. What's in Afton?"

I bit my lip to stop it from trembling. "I'm worried about a friend. He's old and alone. I feel like I should check on him. Unfortunately, when I asked you to help get back my journal, none of that showed in my dream last night. But by taking back my book, I've also altered the rest of my day, which means none of this was in my dream either. I don't want to drive out there by myself at nine at night." Exhaling slowly, I skimmed my gaze past his shoulder to the drawstring bag. *I'm worried what I might find when I get there.*

~

DRYSTAN INSISTED ON DRIVING, and I was surprised he waited until we were on the road to say anything, but the moment we hit the highway, he glanced my way. "We have twenty minutes until we reach Afton. You freaked out when you looked in that bag. I think it's time to fill me in."

Even though he sounded calm, I saw the tension in his tight grip on my steering wheel. I freaked because I knew there was no way Freddie would have parted with his book willingly. All I could hope was that when this guy broke into Freddie's house, Freddie was in the sanctuary tending his ravens. My mind pinged to the fact that Freddie had an entire wall of interesting raven books. There was only *one* way the thief would have known this particular book was very special, and that was if he'd forced Freddie to tell him. Then again, maybe the thief had the ability to recognize the blue book's "specialness" in some other way, leaving Freddie unharmed. But if Freddie truly believed the book belonged to me, then why hadn't he called to tell me it was stolen? Could he have given it to the thief willingly? If so, why?

"Nara," Drystan called my name in a terse voice, drawing me out of my conflicted musings.

"Sorry. I was just thinking about Freddie." Before we left my house, I'd run upstairs to hide the drawstring bag under my mattress, then invited Houdini up on my bed. No way anyone was getting near those books again, not with my guard dog laying on them. I met Drystan's expectant gaze and I tried to think of the best way to explain without bringing Ethan into it. Focusing on the ravens would be closest to the truth. "The project I'm working on, the one in my journal, is the study of ravens."

Drystan shot me a skeptical look. "I'll admit you have a right odd obsession with these birds. I've even seen a couple on your car—which is also weird, by the way—but how is the study of ravens in any way personal? Why didn't you just tell me?"

I sprinkled the truth with embellishments from my research. "Based on your reaction to my 'odd obsession' and the fact some people are superstitious about ravens, seeing them as an omen of death/witches/the devil in bird form, et cetera, I preferred to avoid the judgment and keep my project private."

He shook his head, clearly confused. "What is your project specifically about?"

I spread my hands and shrugged. "Just the study of ravens. The man we're going to see, Freddie Holtzman, has studied ravens all his life. I interviewed him yesterday in order to learn some background information on ravens from someone who'd actually raised them."

Drystan rubbed his forehead. "I still don't get why you're so freaked out? You seem really worried for this Freddie person. Why?"

I took a steadying breath. "Because my journal wasn't the only one in the drawstring bag. A book Freddie showed me yesterday was in there too."

"How do you know it's not just another copy of the same book?"

I pressed shaky fingers to my temples, trying to prevent the headache looming. "I hope you're right and that I'm totally overreacting, but what are the chances of a *thief*, who stole a journal all about ravens from me, also having a copy of a book about ravens published almost three decades ago in the United Kingdom? A book that *I* just looked at yesterday? Maybe it's just a big coincidence, but Freddie's all alone out there. I have to make sure he's okay."

"You're right. That's all a little too coincidental." Drystan set his lips in a grim line and pressed harder on the gas pedal.

CHAPTER 20

a s soon as Drystan rolled to a stop in Freddie's driveway, I jumped out of the car, bolting toward the house.

"Nara, wait!" Drystan called after me, but I continued up the stairs to hammer on the front door with rapid knocks. My heart thumped so hard, my entire body jerked.

Drystan had just made it to the bottom stair when I pivoted and passed him, running down the few stairs.

"You haven't even given him a chance to answer the door." Drystan closed in on my heels as I headed toward the back of the small house.

"He could be working in the raven sanctuary back in the woods," I said over my shoulder when my gaze snagged on the jagged glass where the sliding glass door used to be. "God, no!" A pit formed in my stomach and I had to force myself to lower my gaze to the deck floor. When I only saw broken glass, I let out a breath of relief.

Drystan stepped in front of me, a muscle working in his jaw. "Call the police, Nara. There's a lot of blood here."

I dialed 9-1-1 and reported a break-in, letting them know we thought someone was injured. The operator tried to keep me on the line, but I told her I'd be waiting outside for the police to arrive.

As soon as I hung up, Drystan and I moved closer to peer

through the window into Freddie's living room. The built-in bookcases along the back wall had been decimated. Shelves and books were everywhere. The couch, end table, and kitchen table had also been overturned, as if someone had been dragged or thrown from the opposite side of the room through the living room and into the breakfast nook area where they crashed through the sliding glass door. My stomach turned at the sight of so much blood on the deck floor. I tore my gaze away and called through the broken window, "Freddie? Can you hear me? Freddie?"

Sudden frantic *raacck* sounds came from the trees in Freddie's backyard. A few ravens flew in a circle high above the sanctuary. Every so often one would break off and dive bomb some other big bird that was trying to venture into their group.

"Vultures," Drystan murmured.

I shook my head. "The birds in the circle are ravens."

"I meant the ones the ravens are attacking...they're vultures."

"We need to check the sanctuary!" I took off toward the footpath at the back of the yard. Just as I entered the woods, Drystan grabbed my hand and pulled back. "No, Nara. Let's wait for the police."

"Freddie could be hurt and need our help," I cried, yanking my hand away. I ran as if every second counted. I had to get to the sanctuary. I had a feeling it's where Freddie would have gone if he were hurt. He'd said he never felt alone when he was with his ravens.

I heard the alarm in Drystan's voice when he called my name, but I didn't stop. I had to be there for Freddie. Had to help him. I was so focused on getting to the aviary that I didn't look up until I'd passed through the entrance.

Horror shot through me at the image of Freddie's bruised and bloody face, his head twisted at an unnatural angle. His limp body dangled fifteen feet up in the main oak tree, held only by a broken tree branch poking through his chest.

"No!" I shrieked. "No, no, no. I'm so sorry," I continued, my voice breaking. I tried to step forward, but Drystan grabbed me and turned me away.

Pressing my face against his shoulder, he whispered in a shaken voice, "Every day, Nara. God, every damned day!"

As I cried against his shoulder, I realized hazily that he was talking about teaching me how to defend myself. After a couple of minutes, the ravens' shrieks in the sanctuary filtered into my consciousness. I wiped my eyes on my sleeve and glanced up. A group of ravens—Freddie's ravens—were taking turns fighting off scavenging vultures and smaller black birds, who were trying to get to the source of blood and smell of death floating through the woods.

"Look." I pointed to the defending birds. As Drystan's gaze followed my line of sight, I called over the loud din, "They're treating Freddie like their own kind. Protecting his body from the scavengers." Freddie would feel honored, I thought morbidly.

Drystan pulled me away from the carnage, his face a bit paler, strain creasing his mouth. "Let's go wait for the police by your car."

I let Drystan walk me to my car, my body numb. Just as we reached the driveway, we heard the police siren down on the main road turning onto the long drive.

My mind finally kicked into gear and I looked at Drystan. "Please don't mention the real reason I thought we should check on Freddie to the police. We'll just tell them that I forgot my notepad I left here the other day when I interviewed him and I came by to get it. That's when we discovered the break-in."

His brows drew down. "But if the stolen book is the reason Freddie was killed, the police should know that, Nara."

I spread my hands. "We don't know that for sure. We don't even know if the same guy who stole my journal did this or if there is any connection at all."

"But it would give the police something to go on," he shot back, gesturing toward the house.

"The police are going to ask us what this guy looks like. You said you didn't get a look at him. Whoever did this will hopefully have left some kind of evidence behind. If he didn't wear gloves, the investigative team should be able to get fingerprints from the torn down bookshelves or maybe even from..." I paused, then swallowed hard, continuing in a whisper, "Freddie's body."

Drystan blew out a harsh breath. "God, Nara. How'd he get that old man up in the tree like that?"

I closed my eyes for a second, the horrific image of Freddie burned in my eyelids. "I don't know. What I do know is...that if we tell the police about the book, they'll take it as evidence and I might never see it again."

"Why is it so important?" he asked, clearly perplexed.

The police car was almost upon us. My stomach knotted as its blue lights reflected off Drystan's hardened features. I grasped his arm tight. "Please, Drystan."

When he pressed his lips together and glanced up at the police officers talking on their radio in their car, I spoke quickly, "Lainey can keep me updated on how the investigation is going. She has a way of wiggling information out of her dad. If the police don't find any evidence that will lead them to a suspect, I promise I'll turn the book in. I want whoever did this to Freddie caught and punished!"

I could see in his eyes that he thought I was crazy not to turn the book in now, but he didn't know that Freddie had tried to give me the book because he'd truly believed I was the rightful owner. I owed it to Freddie to find out why the stranger, who'd entrusted him with the book all those years ago, believed it was so important.

As the police officers got out of their car, I squeezed his arm and lowered my voice, "That book was very special to Freddie. If I'm the reason that guy who stole my journal came after that sweet old man, because I somehow unknowingly led him here..." I paused and choked back a new round of guilty tears. I sniffed and finished, "The least I can do is keep the book safe and not let Freddie's death be in vain. God, why didn't I dream this part? I could've saved him!" *Why didn't I take the book? Maybe Freddie would still be alive if I had.*

Drystan wrapped his arm around my shoulders and spoke quietly next to my ear. "Don't blame yourself, Nara. You said that coming here wasn't in your dream last night. Tonight may be from 'ell, but there's one good thing; between my hoodie and the lack of lighting, I don't think the bloke I stole the books from got a good look at me either. Freddie's book should be safe with you, especially under Houdini's protective guard."

I only had time to whisper "thank you" when the two police officers walked past the back of my car and the lanky, blond-haired one stepped forward, saying, "Were you the young lady who called nine-one-one about a break-in?"

~

WHEN I WALKED into the house at midnight, Mom was waiting for me. Her posture was stiff as she stood up from one of the barstools, her lips set in a hard line. Houdini immediately woofed his greeting.

"Nara! Where have you been? I sent you a couple of texts, then left a voice mail—what's wrong? You've been crying." She immediately rushed to my side and gripped my shoulders. "Are you hurt?"

Even though the police had assured Drystan and me that our identities would be kept confidential, and the media would never know who reported the murder to the police, they still took down our names and addresses in case they needed to get into contact with us later, which meant, I couldn't keep this from my mom. I was exhausted from the grueling questions from the police, but I knew this couldn't wait until morning.

I shook my head and clasped my mom's hand as I led her back to the stools. "I was just interviewed by the police for over an hour."

"Whatever for? Did someone try to hurt you?" Mom asked in a higher pitch as she sat down beside me.

"It wasn't about me." My hands shook as I ran them down my face to help settle my nerves so I could tell her the same story I told the police. "An older man I interviewed this week for a project I'm working on for school was killed sometime last night. I'd forgotten my notebook at his house. Since he lived all the way out in Afton and it was nighttime when I realized it, I asked Drystan to go out there with me to retrieve it." I took a steadying breath. "That's when we discovered the break-in and Freddie's...I mean, Mr. Holtzman's body," my voice broke as I finished. "It was pretty awful, Mom."

"I'm so sorry! Thank God Drystan was with you." Mom wrapped her arms around me. "I understand if you don't want to rehash the horrible details." Pulling back a little, she brushed my hair away from my face. "I've never lost anyone to a violent death, so I can only imagine how you must be feeling. With everything that's happened recently—the scare with the shooting and now this—if you want to go to counseling to help you work through it, I'll get a referral from our doctor for the best counselor."

I shook my head. "I can handle it. It's just that...he was a very nice man, who didn't deserve what happened to him." Curling my hands into fists, I ground out, "I hope they catch the sick bastard who did this!"

Mom's eyes widened, but she didn't say anything. She probably figured my anger was good therapy.

I sighed and let my shoulders slump. "I'll be fine, Mom. I'm just exhausted and sad. Right now I just want to go to bed."

Mom walked me upstairs and once I'd climbed under the covers, she even patted the bed to encourage Houdini to keep me company. Rubbing the top of his head, she said in a soft voice, "Nara needs your special animal love, Houdini. Make sure you give her an extra dose tonight."

She studied me pensively, then turned and left the room. A couple of minutes later, she handed me a tablet and some water. "I can tell your head hurts. Take this and get some sleep. You'll feel better tomorrow."

I did as she asked, but as soon as mom left my room, I grabbed my phone and started to dial Ethan's number. I was just about to hit Send when I remembered he'd gone skiing with his dad. With a grunt of frustration, I pulled Ethan's journal and Freddie's book from under my mattress.

As I ran my fingers across the metal corners on the blue book, tears blurred my vision. I blinked them away and tried to focus, turning to page one. Maybe I missed something of importance while flipping through it at Freddie's house. I'd only read through the first ten pages when my eyes began to droop.

I jerked my head upright and blinked, trying to clear my head once more, but my eyes blurred. I rubbed them and yawned so loud that Houdini raised his head.

"Why can't I keep my eyes open?" I slurred right before I fell asleep with the book tucked against my chest.

~

MY EYES FLEW OPEN, my heart pumping as if I'd been dosed with adrenaline all night long. Slamming my fist on my covers, I jarred Houdini awake as I said to him, "She gave me that awful PM headache medicine!" Argh! No wonder I felt like I was having heart palpitations. Everything in my dreams flew by in supersonic speed. Useless, of course. Now that he was awake, Houdini wasn't about to be ignored. Once I returned to my room from taking him out, Patch was impatiently waiting at the window.

As soon as I let Patch in, he flew to the raven statue, even bypassing his regular paper shredding ritual. I laughed and handed him a piece of kibble, then did the same for Houdini. The dog settled at the end of my bed, chin on his paws, eyes watching the bird for any sudden aggressive movements.

I snorted that I was being completely ignored by both animals, but at least their distraction with each other let me focus on Freddie's book. I crawled back into bed and started reading where I'd left off last night. I was about a third of the way through the book when Patch squawked at something and Houdini gave a startled bark. I jumped at the sounds and one of the book's corners caught on my sheet.

"Settle boys," I said as I closed the book so I could gently untangle the sheet from the metal corner. The last thing I wanted was to inadvertently break it off. I turned the book cover and pulled at the sheet with a gentle tug. When the material slid free, I exhaled and started to flip the book back over into my hand when my gaze locked on the spine, specifically the gold symbol.

I gasped and ran my fingers along the intricate swirls. *It looked just like...*

I lifted the pendant from under my shirt and compared the silver charm my grandmother had given me to the symbol on the spine. They appeared to be the same design.

My heart accelerated in steadily increasing thumps as I pulled the long necklace over my head, then held the pendant between my fingers beside the spine to compare them. They were identical. *Were they the same size too?* I moved my silver pendant over the gold symbol. As soon as I lined them up, the pendant flew from my fingers, attaching itself to the symbol on the spine.

I let out a gasp and jerked upright in my bed. When I gently lifted my chain out of the way, that's when I noticed that the half moon brass plate at the base of the book's spine had flipped open. The moment I slid my pendant away from the symbol on the spine, the brass half moon slammed shut. "No way!" I whispered, glancing at Houdini. His only response was to tilt his head as if he were trying to understand what I was saying.

I placed the pendant back on the symbol. When the brass plate at the bottom popped open again, I peered into the dark space between the spine and the book's binding. "What are you hiding?" I tilted the book. Nothing. As I shook it gently, a thin roll of parchment paper slid into my lap.

"I'm so sorry, Freddie. I had no idea..." I said in a hushed, regretful tone. I picked up the paper, then gently began to unroll it with shaking fingers.

No taller than four inches high and six inches wide, the paper featured a drawing of a raven flying toward the sun, another raven standing with its wings folded on the ground, then yet another raven flying below the ground where the raven stood. They weren't drawn vertically, but diagonally from each other. I wasn't sure if the drawing was supposed to depict one raven in three different positions, standing, flying up, and then flying down, or if it was supposed to represent three different ravens. I scanned the picture, my greedy gaze memorizing every detail. *Was this what the thief wanted? Why was it worth killing for? What did the drawing mean?*

Maybe if I drew it myself, it might give me some idea behind its meaning. I leaned over and grabbed a pen and Ethan's journal. As soon as I flipped to an empty page, the stiff paper in my hand suddenly felt flimsy. I glanced at the unrolled paper and watched in disbelief as it began to grow thinner and thinner until it completely disintegrated in my hand, joining the dust flickering in the sunlight.

I gaped at my empty hand, then slid my gaze to Houdini's. "That was *real*! Not some crazy hallucination. You saw that, right?"

He just blinked. Patch wasn't paying us any attention. He was too busy playing with my necklace on the statue.

I set my pen to the page, intending to draw as fast as I could before the image faded from my mind, then I paused. That picture was hidden for a reason. A man died protecting it. Maybe it wasn't a good idea to recreate it. At least not until I could figure out what it meant. I stared at the blank page for several minutes, wracking my brain for answers to the meaning behind the picture. When a text beeped on my phone, I jumped. Holding my hand over my thudding heart, I grabbed my phone to check the text. Maybe Ethan had gotten back early.

Drystan – 8:30 a.m. ~ Don't forget. Nine a.m.

"Really, Drystan?" As if he heard me, another text came through.

Drystan – 8:31 a.m. ~ No excuses. You need the distraction.

I didn't want to sit around thinking about how if I'd only believed Freddie and taken the book, he might still be alive. I pulled my necklace away from the spine and watched the brass plate pop back into place. Once I'd put the necklace back on, I texted him.

Me – 8:32 a.m. ~ See you at nine, slave driver.

Drystan – 8:33 a.m. ~ Water.

Me – 8:33 a.m. ~ Yeah, yeah. You still owe me a latte.

It was after eight-thirty. No time for a shower. I'd be late again if I didn't hurry. I ripped off my sleep t-shirt, then removed the necklace, but I paused to stare at the pendant before I slid it into my jewelry box. *Did my grandmother know that her necklace was a key to unlocking a hidden picture people would kill for? Did she know what the picture meant or why it was so important?* When Drystan and I were done for the day, I'd call Gran and find out what she knew about the necklace.

CHAPTER 21

"**W**hy did I have to find out what happened to you last night from my dad, of all people?" Lainey literally pounced on me, hugging me tight, the moment I walked in from my workout with Drystan.

I glanced over her shoulder at my mom, who was skimming the paper while eating a late lunch at the island. She paused from taking a bite of her sandwich, brow raised as if to say, *Why haven't you told your* best friend *about last night yet?* Instead, she said, "Lainey's been here since noon, waiting for you."

"Are you okay?" Lainey searched my gaze.

I exhaled a slow breath. "It's not something I'll ever forget, but working out helps with the stress of it all."

When I caught Mom's nod of approval, I knew she felt better about letting me go this morning. She'd tried to stop me until I explained that I needed the exercise to work through things and to get rid of the grogginess from the PM medicine she'd given me. Before I left, I'd made her promise never to give me that medicine again.

Mom lifted the paper. "There's an article about Mr. Holtzman, Inara."

"What does it say?" I peered around Lainey's shoulder. *Did they have a suspect?*

She skimmed her gaze down the fine print. "It says he was

found in the sanctuary, and that the circumstances of his death are being investigated, but no arrests have been made at this time."

The image of the birds trying to defend him from other predators flashed through my mind, making my heart ache. *The ravens!* I tensed. "Does it say what will happen to his ravens?"

Mom skimmed some more. "The Wildlife Preserve has offered to take them since they've had experience fostering ravens."

My body slowly relaxed. The ravens were so loud last night, their pain and sadness echoing through the woods as the coroner drove away with Freddie's body. "I'm relieved to hear they'll have a new home and won't just be tossed into the wild. I've heard good things about the Wildlife Preserve."

"I would've freaked if I'd been the one to stumble upon a murder scene. I'm so glad you're okay." Lainey squeezed my shoulders. "First the library, now this—"

My grip on Lainey tightened, tension ebbing through me.

"What about the library?" Mom asked, alarmed.

Lainey glanced over her shoulder and said in a casual tone, "Oh, just Nara having to be tortured with library research recently."

Nice save, Lane.

Turning back to me, she continued, "If you had just answered my texts, I wouldn't have had to wait at your house for the last two hours. Though while I waited, I've learned all kinds of things I didn't know about you." She paused and glanced at Houdini now leaning against my leg. "Like the fact you have a dog, and that Drystan is teaching you self-defense." The last she said with narrowed eyes.

Both Mom's eyebrows were raised now. Great. I'd told her we were running together. Nothing more. With her back to my mom, Lainey whispered, "I texted him and asked what you guys were doing at the park."

I waved my hand, feeling the burn in my shoulder and stomach muscles. "It's only my second day. Drystan thought it would be a fun addition to the running. Did you know he does parkour?" I asked, changing the subject. The last thing I needed was my mom to freak out because I felt I *needed* lessons in how to defend myself.

"What's parkour?" Mom and Lainey said in unison.

"It's easier if I show you." I walked over to the laptop Mom used for bills, then sat down at the kitchen desk and opened the laptop. I typed in "parkour video" to pull up a couple for them to watch.

When the videos were over, Mom said, "Wow, that's pretty amazing. Reminds me of that opening chase scene in the remake of *Casino Royale*."

I nodded. "That's exactly what parkour is, just like in that scene...well, except there's usually not bad guys involved." *Oh, the irony of that comment...*

"Drystan can do all that stuff?" Lainey's eyes were wide. "No wonder he's one big muscle."

"Yep, he can do that. He says it's a state of mind, a way of living your life in a constant state of natural motion."

"Matt's going to want to do that crazy stuff once he learns Drystan can teach him how." Lainey shook her head and snorted. "He'll probably break his leg."

Did I detect a bit of worry in her tone? Like she cared if Matt got hurt? "Drystan will be glad to have someone to experiment with."

"Matt's *not* doing those insane acrobatics." Worry flitted across Lainey's features. When she saw me watching her with a sidelong look, she flipped her hair and continued in an airy tone, "I mean, it'll totally ruin the impact if he escorts me into the dance on crutches."

I raised an eyebrow. Lainey wasn't as unaffected by Matt as she let on.

"You're not doing dangerous stunts like that, are you?" Mom glanced at the screen once more, looking worried.

I shook my head in fast jerks. "No way. Drystan has shown me concepts, but I don't have the muscles to do extreme stunts. He's just teaching me some of the moves as another way to stay in shape, that's all."

Mom visibly relaxed. "Well, then. I'm suddenly less concerned."

I pinned Lainey with a knowing look. "So you came over here and waited for two hours just to yell at me for not answering your texts?"

Lainey gave a sheepish smile, then retrieved an oversized duffle bag she'd set by the front door. "Well, that and the fact we need to pick out masks."

"Masks?" Mom had returned to her stool and was crunching on a baby carrot.

Bag in hand, Lainey returned to my side, beaming at my mom. "Yes, for Saturday's winter dance."

"You have a dance coming up, Nara?" Mom's attention shot my way. "Why didn't you tell me? We need to get you a dress."

Thanks, Lainey. I kicked Lainey's foot before standing. "I didn't mention it because I'm not going."

Mom looked perplexed. "Why not?"

Really Mom? I frowned. "Because I'm not going without Ethan."

"Ah," Mom said, nodding.

"I told Nara we can all go as friends. She's just being stubborn. But she at least promised to help me pick out my outfit," Lainey beamed, then slid a 'you *did* promise' gaze my way. Without missing a beat, she tugged me toward the stairs. "Hurry up and get a shower, Nara, so we can start trying on all these masks."

I eyed the bag. "That's full of masks? What'd you do, buy one of everything?"

Lainey nodded. "I knew getting you to drive with me forty minutes to the specialty store would be near impossible." She shrugged and glanced down at the bag. "I'll just return them once you help me make a decision."

Ugh, I had promised I'd help her pick her outfit. As I jogged up the stairs, I was glad I'd already hidden Ethan's and Freddie's books back under the mattress before I left to meet Drystan. Lainey followed fast on my heels, dragging her bag of masks up the stairs behind her.

Trying on masks with Lainey meant I'd be busy the rest of the day. It wouldn't be just about the masks. She'd want to discuss hair and makeup and probably Jared. All I wanted to do was take a long shower to ease my sore muscles, then read my grandmother's journal from front to back. While I gathered a clean set of clothes from my drawers, the conversation I'd had with Gran after my practice with Drystan had left me itching to pull out the silver-paged journal. She'd said her sister only wore gold, but that hopefully Margaret mentioned the necklace in her journal since she'd asked Mom to give it to me when I was old enough.

Lainey bouncing excitedly on my bed drew me out of my musings. I headed for the shower with a sigh. I definitely wasn't going to get to read my grandmother's journal until after dinner.

Fifteen minutes later, I came out wearing a t-shirt and yoga pants while pulling my semi-dried hair into a ponytail. Lainey grabbed my hand and tugged me over to sit on my bed, her expression subdued. "I called my dad while you were in the shower to find out if he could get any information about that poor man who was killed."

Every fiber in my body froze. "What did your dad say about Freddie's case?" I whispered, almost afraid to hear.

She squeezed my hand. "I know it's little comfort, but the early findings from the autopsy is that Freddie died from the blow to his head when he was thrown through the glass door. Nara, he was already dead when he was impaled on that tree branch. My dad did say that they're scratching their heads over how his attacker got him up there. Other than Freddie's fingerprints and yours from your time there the day before, they only found one other set at the crime scene."

My breathing started up again. At least Freddie hadn't suffered through that kind of brutal, deliberately malicious torture, and thank God they'd found fingerprints. "Did they find a match to the prints?"

She shook her head, sympathy in her gaze. "Not yet. Remember the prints have to be in the database for them to find a match."

I was so thankful Freddie wasn't aware what his killer had done with his body. He'd be sickened if he knew his raven sanctuary had been defiled in such a way. I think

Freddie would have approved of the Wildlife Preserve taking his ravens in. I didn't know if the birds understood what had happened last night, but they did understand death. They needed to get away from the place where their caregiver had violently died. It was no longer their *sanctuary*.

I squeezed Lainey's hands. "Please thank your dad for finding out some of the details. It helps relieve a little of my anxiety. At least they have a lead of some kind."

Lainey smiled, then yanked me into a quick hug, whispering in my ear, "Now you need a distraction." With a quick flip of her wrist, she unzipped the big bag on my bed with a flourish and said, "Let's get incognito, baby!"

When it came to distraction from one's worries, spending time with Lainey was like getting a shot of not-a-care-in-the-world medicine. It wasn't that Lainey was the perkiest person in the world, it was more that she made you care about what she cared about. It was like her enthusiasm somehow rubbed off on you.

We tried on every single Mardi Gras style mask: some with swooping feathers, others with dangling pearls and silver beads, ones that you had to hold with a stick and the kind that strapped to your face with an elastic band. The masks' colors were various mixtures of white/ice blue, white/silver, and all white.

Then we moved on to hairstyles, figuring out which ones worked best with the masks we liked. Lainey stayed through dinner—Mom ordered pizza and made a salad—and by the time Lainey left, my heart still ached over Freddie, but it wasn't the same stabbing kind of pain. It was more of a dull, steady burn.

As I helped Mom put away the clean dishes from the dishwasher, she paused from wiping the water from the bottom of a coffee cup with the hand towel. "I know you said you aren't going to the dance, Inara, but maybe you should consider going just for fun. It would keep you from dwelling, and right now I think keeping your mind occupied with positive thoughts is a good thing."

I slid the stack of plates into the cabinet. "I had fun primping with Lainey, but I'm not going."

Mom frowned. "After what you've been through recently, I don't think Ethan would object to you going. You need to get out and have some fun."

If Ethan knew what had happened, he'd be on my doorstep in a matter of hours. A part of me wanted to call him, to tell him I needed him holding me close, to hear him promise me everything would be all right. I'd tell him everything that had happened, even down to the hidden picture that disintegrated as soon as I tried to draw it in his journal. I concentrated and tried to recall the details of the picture, but it had already faded. All I remembered was that it featured ravens.

"Inara?" Mom's hand touching my shoulder, drew me out of my reverie. "I was saying that I'm supposed to go out of town at the end of the week through the weekend, but I'm going to cancel my trip."

I shook my head. "Don't do that. I have Houdini." He lifted his head from his bed by the door when I said his name.

Mom pressed her lips together. "I think I should stay."

"Aunt Sage should be back by then, too," I said.

Her eyebrows shot up. "She will be? Why hasn't she texted me?"

I shrugged. "I know she was going to some gem show while she was on vacation, so she probably got caught up in it. You know how she can be about her jewelry business."

Mom nodded and smiled. "She really can immerse herself. When did she say she's getting back?"

"At the end of the week."

"I'll give her a call." Mom put away the coffee mug, then turned and squeezed my shoulder. "I won't make plans until I've spoken with Sage."

Once the dishes were done, I took Houdini out, then claimed loads of homework, bolting upstairs as fast as I could. I snuggled under my covers and checked my phone, hoping for a surprise text or voice mail from Ethan, but there wasn't one.

With a sigh of disappointment, I turned on my bedside lamp, then retrieved my grandmother's journal from my nightstand. Two hours later, I'd read up through my first birthday, and while I loved the insight into my grandmother's thoughts and observations about people, my stomach had knotted since I hadn't run across any journal entry related to the necklace she gave my mother...and there were only three pages to go.

I sighed and turned the page, then sat upright, my grip on the book tightening when I read the preface to her next journal entry...

Today was a very strange, yet memorable day. My emotions ran the full spectrum from shock to sorrow to confusion to bewilderment, then finally to hopefulness.

CHAPTER 22

My focus snapped to the date in the upper-right-hand corner of my grandmother's journal. It had been written when I was a little over a year old. I quickly turned to the next page to read her entry.

Richard had a morning meeting in Washington, D.C., and since it was going to be a lovely April day, I decided to go with him. While he presented his pitch to the corporate bigwigs, I thought Inara would enjoy going for a stroll along the Potomac. Elizabeth and Jonathan had finally taken a vacation, and I was determined my granddaughter would have a wonderful time without them.

It was around two in the afternoon by the time I parked and put Inara in her stroller. The place was packed with people laying out on blankets in the grass, kids flying kites, kicking soccer balls, and throwing Frisbees. Airplanes taking off from Reagan National zoomed over every so often. Inara spent her time pointing at the planes and craning her neck to watch people zip past on skateboards, rollerblades, and bikes. She giggled when they did extra tricks just for her. I pushed her stroller slowly along the wide sidewalk, enjoying the busy energy of the place. The flowers were in full bloom, and every so often I stopped and pointed out my favorites among the clusters we ran across, rambling about the best time of year to plant and how I couldn't wait to start a flower garden with her when she was old enough to help.

"What were your favorite flowers?" I whispered wistfully. Planting a flower garden with my grandmother sounded wonderful. My heart constricted that we never got to do that.

When Inara suddenly went quiet, I thought maybe she'd fallen asleep. I pulled the sun canopy back on her stroller to check and saw that she was staring with vivid fascination at the sky. I thought she was looking at the airplane that had just taken off, climbing high in the sky, but her gaze was locked on the one huge area of blue where no clouds covered the sky. "What are you looking at, sweetheart?" I asked.

She pointed up, speaking in baby words that made no sense to me, but made total sense to her. By her expression, I could tell she was asking me something, so I squatted next to her. "What do you see?"

As she pointed toward the sky once more, I had just looked upward when I saw the airplane suddenly lift and then tilt in the air. At the same time it rolled to the right, its left wing was completely torn away, ripping off as easily as tissue paper.

I was glad I was squatting because my legs gave out. I fell to my butt, watching in shocked horror as the plane plunged down and into the Potomac.

Screams echoed all around us as people reacted to the crash. Most began running toward the water's edge to see better, while others dialed 911 on their phones. There was even a couple who screamed they had family on that plane. Inara began to cry, reacting to the screams and fear on people's faces.

I stood on shaking legs and picked her up. Pressing her baby face close to mine, I cooed in a calming voice in her ear, "It's going to be okay, sweet baby." All I could think was...all those people, gone in an instant. A sickening feeling dropped in my stomach, spreading to my limbs, but I had to keep it together and be strong for Inara.

She arched her back and screamed, clearly terrified by the chaos. I started to pull her close once more, when a man's hand gently palmed the top of her head.

"Be calm, little one. All will be well," he said in a soothing, deep voice.

Inara instantly quieted, and as she stared at the man standing beside me with avid curiosity, the tears in her bright green eyes dried. I turned, my gaze traveling up his custom-made suit to his unusual golden gaze. He was Viking-tall with an arresting, sculpted face, framed in short blond hair that curled slightly on the ends. He looked to be in his late thirties, but his eyes held a Zen-like calm and wisdom. He was so beautiful, I was surprised no one else had spared him a glance, despite the pandemonium going on around us.

"Thank you for calming her," I said. Somehow, even as sirens blared and people continued to run around screaming for someone with a boat to help the survivors from the water, the reassuring tone in his voice had settled my nerves too. I still felt worry for the people in the plane, but the panic that had gripped my stomach disappeared.

Once he lifted his hand from her baby fine hair, Inara smiled and babbled something completely incoherent to the man. He returned her smile, then looked at me as if he'd forgotten I was there, when I said, "I think she likes you."

He withdrew his other hand from his pants pocket, then pushed his clasped fingers toward me, saying, "Take this and keep it safe. Once the age of maturity is reached, you'll know what to do."

The urgency of his words held a mesmerizing cadence. It was almost as if I didn't have a choice in accepting his strange request. No, that's not it. I wanted to honor his request. I'm finding this hard to accurately reflect my feelings about this surreal experience. Inara watched with rapt attention as I held out my hand, ready to accept whatever he planned to give me.

He lowered an unusual three-sided pendant and necklace onto my open palm in a cascade of silver, then folded my fingers around the keepsake with a curt nod before he strolled away with confident grace into the chaotic crowd.

I looked at Inara waving to the stranger's back, a happy smile on her face, and I knew exactly what I would do. When this sweet baby was old enough, this necklace would be hers.

Side Note: Later that day, I was shocked, but relieved when the news reported that no one died in that horrific plane crash. It was an absolute miracle!

That was the last entry my grandmother made. She'd died in a car accident just a couple of months later. I closed her journal with trembling hands. *Who was the tall, blond man who'd given my grandmother the necklace?* Freddie had also mentioned a tall, blond stranger had given him the book on ravens, but that had been in London. Could it possibly be the same man? Freddie hadn't been as descriptive about the stranger's appearance as my grandmother had been. Even though they were both tasked to hold onto something separately, the similarity of the requests and the fact that my necklace unlocked the hidden compartment on Freddie's raven book, convinced me that the tall stranger was one and the same.

I laid back and closed my eyes, trying to remember when Freddie said he'd gotten that book. He's said he held on to it for twenty-eight years. Since the stranger had given Freddie the book well before I was born, I couldn't assume that the book had definitely been meant for me. Yet based on my grandmother's odd experience that day she received the necklace, there was no denying that the key had been meant for me. Regardless, I had unlocked the book's secret. *What did that drawing I'd found in the book mean?* As I began to drift off to sleep, I wished Ethan were around so I could discuss all of this with him. Wednesday night couldn't get here fast enough. I could handle three more days. I hoped Ethan was finally at a good place with his family, because once I told him everything that had happened, he'd be on his way back to Virginia.

SCHOOL KEPT me distracted from agonizing about my planned Wednesday phone call with Ethan in a few days, as well as the sad part of last night's dream I didn't want to acknowledge. I'd stopped by study hall to let Lainey know I'd be in the library researching for a project for my history class. I'd gotten the idea for the subject, *Mysterious and Inexplicable Disasters in History,* after that car accident I'd seen on Highway 29 the other morning on the way to school. I still didn't believe it had been a hallucination, yet I couldn't explain it either.

My chest felt as if a heavy weight had been dropped on it when I walked up to our table. Harper took notes from her math book, while Lainey flipped through a hairstyle magazine.

I smirked to see them completely ignoring each other. "I thought you'd picked out the hairstyle you wanted already?" I commented to Lainey.

"Oh, I have." Lainey glanced up from the magazine with a grin. "Was just making sure I didn't find anything I liked better."

"Are you taking your man to the dance, Harper?" I asked.

Her head jerked up from the book, surprise flitting across her face. "How'd you know I had a boyfriend?"

"I have my ways," I said in my best sneaky voice, then smiled. "Actually, I saw him pick you up at CVAS."

"Oh." She flipped the page in her book. "We'll probably go. Are you going?" she asked, cutting a narrowed sideways glance at Lainey.

Oblivious to Harper's look, Lainey stopped thumbing through her magazine, her eyes locking on me. "Are you going, Nara? And *why* are you still standing?"

I sighed. "The answer's still no."

"Even your mom thinks you should go," Lainey cajoled. "I *will* convince you, you know."

I shook my head and thumbed back toward the classroom door. "I'm heading to the library to do some research."

"Research?" Lainey wrinkled her nose as if it were a dirty word.

I nodded. "I need to document four historical disasters that occurred under strange or inexplicable circumstances."

"You pick the oddest subjects for projects," Lainey tutted.

"Hey, Nara," Harper cut in, her face reflecting sympathy. "Did you see the paper this weekend about Mr. Holtzman's sad death? I was so surprised when I saw his name in that article, since you'd recently mentioned visiting him."

I swallowed my emotions and tried to ignore the knots snarling tighter and tighter in my stomach. "Yeah, I saw it. I still can't believe he's gone."

"I saw an article in the paper that they're having a memorial for him today," Lainey said, her tone softer. "Are you going?"

"I—I don't know," I stammered, trying for a normal response. This was the hardest thing about my gift. Having to experience things that upset me, twice. I could've just gone straight to the library and avoided the conversation, but in my dream I had gone to the memorial that evening, slipping into the back of the funeral home to keep a low profile. Then, when I went to pay my respects at Freddie's closed casket, all I could think about was *why* it was closed. I broke out in loud, sobbing tears, embarrassing myself. I'd hoped that hearing Lainey ask me about going to the funeral twice would be the reminder I needed to stay away. I was just too emotional about his death.

Lainey caught my hand and squeezed. "The only reason I saw the article was because it'd made the front page news. The paper said since Mr. Holtzman didn't have any living family, his colleagues at the University have taken responsibility for his funeral. It's at Bradford's Funeral Home from four thirty to six thirty. I'll go with you if you want me to."

I opened my mouth to speak, but nothing came. Finally, I croaked, "I'm good. You don't need to go."

Before Harper or Lainey could say another word, I bolted from study hall. Throwing myself into research would keep me from thinking about Freddie's funeral or my own guilt.

I typed in several search terms like "unexplainable disasters," "mysterious disasters," and "weird events in history" on the library computer until I found what seemed like four interesting subjects that spanned the globe as well as time. I wanted to go back as far as possible, but also pick subjects that had pictures, or even better, videos taken by observers who happened to witness the strange event taking place.

After a half hour of searching, I'd found four interesting subjects from all over the world and that dated from 1908 to 1945: The Great Molasses Disaster in Boston, Massachusetts: the elephant stampede in Chandaka Forest, India: the high-powered explosion near Tunguska River in Russia: and the B-52 bomber that crashed into the Empire State Building in New York.

Even though I'd met my quota of events, it bothered me that none of my events had any video footage. I'd only been able to find still photos. In my dream, I'd closed the computer and moved on, but with the guilt about Freddie's impending funeral weighing heavy on my mind, I needed something positive to help offset all the sad thoughts.

I decided to research the airplane crash my grandmother described in her journal. It met my "unusual" criteria, plus it was a fairly recent disaster that might actually have live footage. That way if I could find live video, I could end my oral presentation on a positive note by showing the class the impactful video of the crash, and then amaze them with the fact that everyone survived.

I found several online videos posted of the Washington airplane crash. It was kind of surreal watching live videos of the event my grandmother described, but I clicked through them all anyway, so I could see it all again with her notes about the event fresh in my mind. Finally, I clicked on the last one that happened to show the full event.

A mother had taken video of her kid flying his kite. He was making the kite do fancy dips and spins while she commented. When the airplane showed up in the background, my finger froze over the mouse button and I felt the blood drain from my face. The plane wasn't the only thing I saw; a huge bubble rippled across the bright blue sky like a building ocean wave.

"No way," I whispered as I watched the steadily increasing curve of the bubble move along the nose of the airplane. At first, it just slowly tilted the plane, then the curve vaulted in height, the spike slicing across the wing, shearing it off like a knife stripping a thorn from a rose stem.

Something had started to burst through the warped sky, a vein of bright light splintering along the blue, but the woman screamed, "Oh my God," then pulled the video camera's view away to follow the plane falling toward the river.

The bubble in the sky was exactly like what I'd seen that day I witnessed the car accident between the red and silver car on Highway 29. My hand shook as I saved the video clip to my flash drive, then emailed it to myself. *Proof!* I now had proof that I wasn't losing my mind.

∼

"LAINEY, CHECK THIS OUT!" I rushed up to Lainey, who was standing close to Matt as they leaned against his Jeep. His arm was slung over her shoulder, and he rubbed his hand up and down her arm to keep her warm.

"What are you so excited about?" she asked with a laugh as I pulled my phone out of my backpack and opened my email.

"Wait, let me get it queued up."

Lainey leaned over my left shoulder and Matt leaned around my right one as I played the video clip for them.

When it was over, Lainey cast a glance Matt's way, then spoke cautiously. "Um, is that for your history project? You seem a little too excited about a plane crash that probably killed everyone the moment they hit the water."

I shook my head. "No, everyone survived that awful plane crash, but that wasn't why I showed you the video, Lainey. I was showing you what *caused* the crash. I can't believe no one reported it." Pointing to my phone's screen, I continued, "This is exactly what happened the other day on Twenty-Nine. It's *what* caused that car accident we saw."

A crowd of cheerleaders and football players streamed past, including Jared and Tarra. Matt didn't even glance their way as he pulled Lainey in front of him and wrapped his arms around her waist. "Reported what, Nara? I just saw the plane dip, then lose one of its wings before falling out of the sky." He glanced down at Lainey looking up at him. "Is that what you saw?"

She nodded. "Me too. What are you seeing on that video, Nara?"

"Ugh!" I played it again for them, this time pointing to the sky in front of the plane. "Don't you see it…the sky warping, bubbling up? Then…here…the bubble spikes and tears off the wing."

Lainey and Matt exchanged a look. "Ummm, no, we don't see—" Lainey began when I glanced up and spotted Drystan walking with a blonde girl on one side and a brunette on his other. It was like his new black eye was an eye-patch, drawing girls like barmaids desperate for the dangerous pirate's attention. "Drystan!" I called, waving him over.

"That's my ride. Got to go, ladies."

As he veered in our direction, they said in dreamy voices, giving him little waves. "Bye, Drystan!"

Between that and passing him in the hall earlier while Sophia and Miranda hung on his every word today, I felt nauseous. Go figure the one time I spotted him at school, he'd be chatting it up with the only two girls from my soccer team I couldn't stand.

Drystan stopped beside me and said to Matt, "I'm working the crowd for you, Matt. You're closing in on Jared in votes. You'll have that crown this Saturday."

Matt laughed. "Thanks for the pimpage, Drystan."

"It's amazing how your 'Matt campaigning' gives you the perfect excuse to flirt with an entire group of girls at the same time," Lainey teased.

"Byyyyye Drystan," I mimicked the girls' voices with an eye roll.

Drystan smirked and tapped the tip of my nose. "You sound jealous."

"Jealous?" I snorted. "Seeing them act like that makes me think…'have more pride than that girls, puh-leeze!'"

Drystan laughed and shoved his hands in his pockets. "If I ever want the blunt truth, I'm glad you'll always be there for me, Nara. What's up?"

I started to tell him when Lainey snickered and talked over me. "Nara's seeing things."

I glared at her. "Quit trying to influence him before he has a chance to see for himself."

Drystan's eyebrows shot up. "See what?"

"Watch this." I turned my back to him and quickly said to Lainey and Matt, "Don't say a word," before I held up my phone.

Drystan set his chin on my shoulder and watched the video clip. When it was over, he glanced at me. "It's a video of a plane crash."

I spun my hand in a circle. "Annnnnd?"

"And?" Confusion flitted over his features. He glanced at Lainey and Matt for help.

They both shook their heads. "Not getting any hints from me, man," Matt said, amusement dancing in his eyes.

"And...tell them what caused the crash," I said, fully expecting him to back me up.

Drystan lifted his shoulders. "I can't tell from that video. The plane suddenly veered, tilted over, then lost its wing, which is what caused it to crash."

I pressed my lips together. "What caused it to tilt over?"

"When was this video taken?" Drystan asked, holding my gaze.

I could tell he was trying to figure out if this involved my ability. I sighed and closed the video. "It was taken over fifteen years ago."

"So, are you guys going to the park today?" Lainey cut in, her gaze darting between Drystan and me.

I shook my head. "No."

"Yes," Drystan said.

I frowned at him. "I'm sore." *And upset you couldn't back me up. Maybe I am losing my mind.*

He gave me a hard look. "You'll work your way through the soreness."

"I'll go with you, dude," Matt said, while rubbing his hands together. "I can't believe you held out on me. I'm totally ready to try some of that stuff."

"Drystan would love to teach you—"

"Not today." Drystan interrupted me, his determined gaze never leaving mine. "Nara should continue training."

"Fine," I snapped. "I'll meet you there at four."

ONE NICE THING about meeting at the park in December is that the only people we'd run across were joggers. We pretty much had the run of the place, which was great when it came to Drystan showing me some more of his parkour moves on the various stairs, cement handrails, brick walls and buildings throughout the park. He even encouraged me to try a couple of them, which resulted in laughable moments and bruises for my efforts.

After running for three miles throughout the paths in the woods, Drystan and I ended up in the clearing, where he sent me back up on the slackline.

As soon as I got my balance in the center of the line, he commanded, "Now jump off."

"Are you nuts?" I stared down at him from my precarious position. "I'll break something."

Drystan waved his hands toward his chest. "Come on. We've practiced on ground level plenty of times. You have the roll down now. You're never going to learn to land properly if you don't practice from some places of height."

"How about I jump from two rungs up on the ladder?"

"You're not that high up, Nara."

"Feels like it to me." When I shook my head, he ran up the ladder, then started to step on the line. "Wait!" I held one hand up and my feet jiggled. I adopted the posture to rebalance myself. "Get back down there."

He flashed a brief smile. "I will if you promise to try."

I flicked my wrist and gritted out, "Fine, but you need to get down there and make sure I don't crack my spine."

"Great!" He jumped off the top of the ladder, then landed into a tucked roll. Standing, he waved me on. "Remember to tuck your knees when you jump, then point your toes as you move toward the ground."

As I took a deep breath, he continued, "And don't forget to land on the balls of your feet, then use your bent knees to help you roll forward at a diagonal and back onto your feet."

"Easy for you to say, Rubber Man."

He laughed. "Jump or I'm coming back up there."

After I'd jumped from the slackline into a tucked roll ten times, my shoulders, spine, and hips were beat. On my eleventh jump, Drystan seemed satisfied that I'd finally gotten the concept of the correct roll technique. "One day you'll be able to do that on concrete."

I grimaced. "I seriously doubt I'll ever willingly jump from a seven-foot height onto concrete."

"That jump I made from that gym's rooftop to the other building's roof was higher, Nara."

Ugh, I'd forgotten about that. Guess we were moving to harder surfaces. I glanced at the leafy ground I'd been landing on. Right now my brain couldn't process the idea of jumping toward an unyielding surface like a rooftop or pavement on purpose. "Can we at least work our way up to concrete? Maybe move to the hard, clay-like ground near the playground equipment first?"

"Of course. That was the plan." He paused and glanced at the darkening sky. "It's probably time to call it a day."

"Let's spar for a few minutes." I winced as I stood, but set my feet on the ground in a ready stance.

"We've been at this for a couple of hours," Drystan began, then adopted the same position when I raised my hands in defensive mode.

We circled each other for a few seconds. "Aren't you exhausted?" he asked, right before he lunged and struck out, aiming for my shoulder.

I deflected his punch, knocking his hand to the side. I ached everywhere. My bruises had bruises, but I wasn't stopping. I struck back with a fast punch, which he deftly defended. While he was distracted, I slammed my foot into his thigh.

"Nice one," he gritted, hopping from foot to foot like a boxer shaking off pain. "What are you trying to avoid at home?" As soon as he spoke, he swept his leg out.

I hopped back just in time to avoid being knocked off my feet. "Not avoiding anything." I shifted my stalking stance and pivoted in the opposite direction to throw him off balance. "You insisted on training, so I'm training."

Drystan narrowed his gaze, then lunged for me with a ferocity I wasn't expecting. We landed on the bed of leaves and air whooshed out of my lungs. Before I could recover, he grabbed my wrists, holding me down.

"Truth, Nara, or I'll think you're sticking around longer than usual because you *want* to spend more time with me."

I struggled and my chest heaved, but he wasn't moving.

"Stop being such an ass and let me up."

He shook his head and sat down on my hips, his fingers tightening around my wrists. "Not until you tell me. Does it have something to do with that video? I could tell you were hoping I'd see something. As much as I wish I could've, I didn't see anything."

I couldn't tell Drystan how I felt like crap for intentionally working out until it would be too late for me to go to Freddie's memorial, but my guilt over Freddie's death and now my avoidance of his memorial had built to a near paralyzing ache in my stomach. Working out with Drystan helped me temporarily forget.

"I'm tired," I finally said. "You're right. Now's a good time to quit."

He pressed his mouth into a thin line. "You haven't been the same since we discovered Freddie's body. Talk to me."

The mention of Freddie's name brought my suppressed tears to the surface. I would never share the secret Freddie had lost his life to protect, but I could share a little of my guilt. Tears trickled down my temples and I whispered, "He tried to give me that book, Drystan. If I'd only taken it, he'd still be alive."

"It could've been you instead!" Drystan snapped. He heaved a sigh, then shifted off of me. I let him pull me to a sitting position, but he surprised me, tugging me close to throw an arm over my shoulder.

"You couldn't have known. Don't let this eat at you, Nara. If you need to use me to help you get over Freddie's death, to help you find closure," he lifted his free hand and dropped his voice to a husky tone, "I'm at your service."

I ignored the double meaning behind his comment and elbowed him, feeling a bit better that I'd shared some of my rollercoaster feelings with someone. Keeping it all bottled inside was exhausting. "I'll take you up on the sparring part. Kicking the crap out of you definitely helps."

He shook his head. "You're hard on a bloke's ego."

I cracked a smile and dried my eyes with the back of my sleeve. "Your ego got plenty of stroking this afternoon. The girls were hanging on your every accented word."

"And yet you seem immune to it," he said in a dry tone.

"Your voice has its charm," I said, dropping into a heavy Welsh accent.

"Hey, that was pretty good." Surprised pride reflected in his eyes.

I adopted a smug look. "And you said I wasn't paying attention."

"Lainey's right. You really need to get out and have a good time. Go to the dance with us." He grinned and pointed to his face. "Who else would be willing to go with me sporting this shiner?"

I punched him in the shoulder, then sprang to my feet. "That's low, playing on my guilt. You know I feel bad that happened to you."

He gave an unrepentant shrug and leaned back on his hands. "You're totally stressed. I'm just trying to help you have some fun."

I tilted my head, inspecting his shiner. "You know, that black eye is a beacon, drawing girls like lost ships to a light-house. I'll bet they're all hoping you'll ask them to the dance. You should take advantage of that."

"Girls always want more." He snorted. "Why bother when I'll be heading back over the pond in six months."

He had a point, but at the same time... "Haven't you ever heard of carpe diem?"

His hair shifted forward with his raised eyebrows. "Seize the day?"

"Exactly. Seize it, Dryst. You never know what tomorrow will bring."

"But you do!" he shot back, grinning at his own joke.

When I rolled my eyes, he laughed, then jumped to his feet. "I'll think about it," he said as he brushed leaves off his hands. "It's late. Let's head out."

CHAPTER 23

*A*fter three days of working out with Drystan, trying new moves, and eventually overcoming my paralyzing fear of concrete, I was able to test my ability to roll safely. My body was battered for my efforts, but Drystan seemed satisfied I wouldn't break my legs. Sparring with Drystan might've left me physically exhausted, but my brain never stopped thinking about Freddie's death. When I wasn't working out, the dull ache of guilt in my stomach quickly returned.

Wednesday night had finally arrived. I waited as late as I could to call Ethan. I didn't bother texting him to let him know I'd be calling. The way we'd left things, texting wasn't going to cut it. So much had happened since then, I needed to hear the reassurance in his deep voice, to know that he would be coming home soon.

Houdini snuggled close to me in bed, and I moaned as I petted him. "Easy boy, I'm so banged up, please don't bump me too hard." I eased into the softness of my pillow, glancing at my clock. Quarter 'til eleven. I was just getting ready to dial Ethan's number when Mom appeared in the doorway of my room.

"I didn't get to speak with Sage," she began, leaning against the doorjamb. "I just kept getting her voice mail. She did text me to let me know she'd be back on Friday afternoon."

I perked up with that tidbit of news. Hopefully that meant

my aunt had answers about my dad. "Great, I'll plan to go spend some time with her."

Mom gave an encouraging smile. "Why don't you pack a bag and stay with her this weekend while I'm gone."

I shook my head and rubbed Houdini's back. "I can't leave him overnight. And with three dogs, Aunt Sage's house is already crowded. I'll be staying here."

Mom sighed, then wagged her finger at Houdini. "Take good care of her, boy."

When he woofed his agreement, I laughed. "When are you getting back?"

"Late afternoon on Sunday, just in time to wish you an official 'Happy Birthday.'"

We shared a smile, and as soon as Mom shut my door, I dialed Ethan's number. When it rang and rang, then eventually went to voice mail, I hung up without leaving a message. I knew it was a long shot. Ethan had said it might be Thursday night before they got back, but the disappointment unraveled my tightly wound anticipation, splitting open all my carefully concealed wounds. I turned off my light and wrapped my arm around Houdini's rump, letting silent tears drip onto his soft fur.

As if he understood my sadness, Houdini shifted from his normal door-guarding position. When he began to lick away my tears, I cried harder, loving his doggie sympathy. I rubbed the top of his head and willed myself to buck up. "Tomorrow night, buddy. He'll be back tomorrow night."

Houdini finally settled, but he didn't turn back toward the door. Instead, he rested his chin on my arm and stayed that way all night long.

As SOON AS school let out the next day, I texted Drystan while standing at my locker.

Me – 3:45 p.m. ~ Bailing on training this afternoon. Have something I need to do.

Drystan – 3:47 p.m. ~ Need some company?

Through the windows that ran across the front of the school, I saw him standing right outside the entrance of school, holding court with six girls. They were multiplying. What'd he do, spray himself with pheromones?

Me – 3:47 p.m. ~ Thanks, but I need to do this on my own. See you tomorrow.

Patch and his buddies flew down to my car the moment I reached for the door handle. With a half smile, I set out enough kibble for each raven to have one piece. They gobbled up their food, then let out appreciative squawks. After they flew away, I typed a text to my aunt.

Me – 3:48 p.m. ~ Just checking on you. Mom said you'll be back tomorrow afternoon. Call me and I'll come over so you can fill me in.

If anyone could get answers out of people it was Sage. Hopefully she found a way to contact my dad while he was out of the country. I wanted to show him that video of the plane crash. I assumed I inherited my ability to see it from him. Hopefully he could tell me what it was.

Once I sent the text, I dialed Gran's number.

"Hello?"

"Hey, Gran. I finished Margaret's journal. Even though reading it made me a little sad that I didn't get to grow up with her in my life, I loved getting to know my grandmother on a much more personal level. Thank you for giving it to me. "

"You're welcome, dear. Did she mention the necklace?"

"She did. It was a gift from someone and she decided to give it to me."

"That sounds just like my sister. She was generous that way."

"I was hoping you could tell me something. She mentioned that she pointed out her favorite flowers to me during a trip we took to D.C. I was a little over a year old at the time, so I don't remember. Do you remember your sister's favorite flowers?"

"Margaret was a flower lover." I could hear the fond smile in Gran's voice as she continued, "She always had them blooming throughout the year at her house. Let's see. In the spring, she loved tulips and sunflowers: in the summer, zinnias were her favorites: in the fall asters: and in the winter, it was winter irises and roses."

"Thanks, Gran. That helps. How are the Westminster Storage Wars going?"

Gran snickered. "Clara's upset that I've been able to remember more than her just from looking at old photos. We had a contest where we pulled random photos out of a box and had to tell the story behind them. Ha! She might be quicker on the draw when it comes to bingo, but my visual synapses are working far better than hers. She's been holed up in her apartment pouting and poring over old photo albums trying to trigger her memories ever since. She'll come around by tomorrow."

I turned down the road that led to a local florist shop. "Wouldn't it be less stressful if you and Clara just enjoyed each other's company instead of competing all the time, Gran?"

"What's the fun in that? This competition between Clara and me helps keep us on our toes. Our bodies might be as reliable as a one-shot musket, but we'll do whatever we can to keep the old brain firing like a machine gun."

Gran comparing her brain function to stuttering, rapid-fire bursts of gunfire was oddly accurate. I chuckled. "Okay, I get it, but please, just don't try to climb anything. Remember, musket."

"Deal. Do me a favor and tell your mother I want to be invited over for dinner so I can meet this new man in her life. Has she cooked for him yet?"

"She's made spaghetti," I said in an upbeat tone.

"I meant something other than the *one thing* she knows how to cook."

My car rolled to a stop in front of the flower shop. "Not that I know of."

Gran snorted. "Then he must really like her if he's still sticking around. Yep, I need to meet this man and give my stamp of approval since your grandmother's not around to do it. Tell your mom I'll expect an invitation soon."

"I will, Gran. I'll talk to you later."

Once I hung up, I took a deep breath. Last night I'd

dreamed that I worked out with Drystan and then came home to see a blip on the evening news about Freddie's well-attended memorial earlier in the week. The newscaster went on to say that Freddie had been buried in Oak Lawn Cemetery.

I got out of my car and mumbled as I reached for the door to the florist shop. "Time for some closure."

~

THE CEMETERY CARETAKER was kind enough to point me to Freddie's grave, which sat in the far left corner of the beautifully manicured Oak Lawn grounds.

Freddie's newly dug grave of recently patted down earth tugged at my heart as I approached with a bouquet of winter roses and irises. I knelt beside the grave and welcomed the frigid, damp soil soaking into my jeans as I propped the flowers up against his gravestone.

"I think my grandmother would've brought these for you, Freddie," I said quietly, lightly brushing my fingers over the soft petals of the white and purple flowers. Cold wind whistled, forcing me to dig my hands into the leather coat's pockets and bury my nose in the soft red cashmere scarf to stay warm. Huge oak limbs swayed above, while dead leaves tumbled around other graves, catching on one headstone before whipping away to catch on another in the distance.

I stared at the epitaph carved onto Frederick Holtzman's grave and sadness pressed heavily on my chest.

He dedicated his life to his research, and upon his death the ravens honored him.

I traced the carved letters with my fingers. "Please forgive me. You were so sure, but I didn't know the book was meant for me." Flattening my palm against the cold stone, I blinked away the tears that threatened and drew on my inner resolve as I whispered, "I discovered the book's secret, Freddie. I wish you'd been there to see me unlock its hiding place, then watch it disintegrate in my hand. It was magical. But don't worry..." I paused and tapped my temple. "It's locked in here, hiding just under the surface." I straightened and conviction seeped into my voice, giving it strength. "I promise I'll fulfill my part and discover why that drawing was so important."

The wind picked up, howling and blowing around me in gusty swirls. A small cyclone of crunchy brown leaves formed on a grave a few feet away, drawing my attention. I watched in fascination as the cyclone drew closer. Once the whirl of leaves moved until they were only a foot away, the distinct smell of spicy chili and burning wood wafted toward me, growing stronger with each rotation. Goose bumps scattered across my skin.

Freddie had heard me.

When I closed my eyes in relief, I thought I felt the weight of invisible hands land on my shoulders. I might've imagined it, but I could've sworn the hands gave a gentle squeeze. All I knew was that a strong sense of comfort and support washed over me, slowly unknotting my stomach.

I opened my eyes and nodded. "Be at peace, Freddie. It's my turn now."

I FELT SO MUCH BETTER after my trip to the cemetery that instead of wanting to cry on Ethan's shoulder, I was looking forward to our conversation. If Ethan asked me details about what I'd found in Freddie's book, I still couldn't describe what was on the paper, but I'd been allowed to see it before it disintegrated for a reason. I hoped that when it mattered, it would come back to me.

This time I didn't wait so late to call Ethan. At ten, I leaned back on my pillow and dialed his number. Two rings later, the phone picked up.

"Hello?"

The last thing I'd expected was a female to answer Ethan's phone. And it didn't sound like an older woman, either. The voice sounded close to my age and tired...or sleepy, as if I'd woken her.

"Hello?" she repeated.

"May I speak to Ethan?" I said in a surprisingly calm voice, even though I wanted to scream, "Who are you, and why are you answering my boyfriend's phone late at night?" There had to be some rational explanation.

She yawned. "He's taking a shower right now."

I gritted my teeth and asked evenly, "Who is this?"

"Danielle," she breathed out.

"Danielle, would you please give Ethan a message?" I spoke in a polite tone, while I seethed inside. There'd better be a freaking great explanation for a girl answering his phone and casually speaking about him taking a shower as if it was no big deal. I couldn't *wait* to hear it. "Tell him Nara called and would like to talk with him as soon as he's available."

"Will do," she said in a perkier voice.

Before I could say another word, she hung up.

I stared at my phone in shock. I gripped the handset and resisted the overwhelming urge to chuck it across the room. Instead, I fell back on my pillow to wait.

When eleven rolled around without a call, I checked to make sure my ringer was turned up, then I checked to make sure he hadn't sent a text.

Nothing.

Anger shot through me, so fast and fierce, if I'd looked in the mirror right then my face would be steaming red.

With precise, measured movements, I opened my text window and typed out one word to Ethan.

Me – 11:05 p.m. ~ TTTWFO?

I hit Send, then waited for him to respond.

$\mathcal{A}$t the end of the next day, a text finally came through on my phone right after I'd closed my locker. I'd been so wound up waiting to hear back from Ethan—jealousy and anger simmered inside me all day—I grabbed my phone from my backpack and turned away from Lainey yammering about dance decorations.

When I saw the text wasn't from Ethan but from my aunt, despondent fury whipped through me, jacking the heat flowing through me from simmer to a rolling boil. I'd gone through an entire day at school on very little sleep. Not only had I fallen asleep waiting, but I'd woken up every hour last night to check my phone. When I woke up at four, I hadn't been able to fall back asleep.

Aunt Sage – 3:45 p.m. ~ Please come straight to my house after school.

"Nara!" Lainey huffed. "I was talking to you. Is that Ethan?"

"Not all of us care about the dance," I snapped. When a hurt look crossed her face, I realized I sounded like a jerk, so I softened my tone. "Sorry, Lainey. It's from my aunt. She just got back in town." I frowned at the screen. That was a very short text. I quickly typed one back.

Me – 3:46 p.m. ~ Glad you're back safe. Missed you! Did you find out anything?

Aunt Sage – 3:47 p.m. ~ Missed you too. Will tell you when you get here.

Again with the short answer. Maybe she was saving all the details for an in-person discussion.

Me – 3:47 p.m. ~ Can't wait to see you. FYI, I didn't sleep well last night, so I'm coming over blind.

"Want to stay and help us decorate the gym?" Lainey asked in a hopeful voice, then grimaced. "I had no idea when I volunteered just *how* much help they'd need."

It was good for Lainey to volunteer every once in a while. I couldn't help but inwardly smile at how inconvenienced she seemed by all the hard work. Maybe she'd come to appreciate what the rest of us do when we volunteer. "I can't. My aunt just invited me over. She's expecting me right after school."

"Fine, bail on your best friend."

I shrugged and pointed to my aunt's text. Lainey started to sigh her frustration, but then her eyes lit up when her gaze landed on Matt strolling down the hall. She walked off in his direction, calling, "Hey, Matt, guess what you're doing on a Friday night…"

I sent Drystan a text.

Me – 3:48 p.m. ~ My aunt just got back in town. She wants me to come over after school, so I can't go to the park today. Plus, I think you'll be stuck at school decorating. *snicker*

When I didn't get a text back right away, I put my phone in my backpack, reminding myself to charge it as soon as I got home. I'd forgotten to plug it in last night since I was waiting to hear back from Ethan.

A half hour later, I drove up my aunt's long, tree-lined driveway to her house. I walked slowly toward her porch, squeezing my hands around my keys so hard they dug into my skin. Since I woke so early, I hadn't dreamed this far into my day last night. I had no idea what I was about to hear.

Aunt Sage pulled me into a tight bear hug the moment I walked in her door. Bo, Luke, and Duke also took turns throwing themselves against my legs.

"Wow," I said as I kept one arm around Aunt Sage while trying to pet each of her dogs with my other hand. "I don't think I've ever received such a huge greeting. I've missed you guys too."

Once everyone settled, I expected my aunt to lead me straight into the kitchen and feed me one of her famous pies like she usually did, but this time she pulled me over to sit on the couch with her.

I could tell by her expression and the way she pushed her red curls behind her ear something was wrong. I clasped her wrists to calm her nervous movements. "What is it, Aunt Sage?"

Concerned hazel eyes met mine as she clasped my hands. "I didn't get in to see your dad's secretary until mid-week."

I clutched her fingers, my heart starting to speed up. "What did she say?"

"She said the same thing that she'd been saying on the phone, that your dad was out of the country on a business trip."

I shook my head. "I don't understand—"

"Let me finish, Inara," she interrupted, her tone sharper than I'd ever heard it.

I tensed and clamped my lips shut, nodding.

Sage ran a hand through her hair. "Like I said, she kept saying the same thing, so I came back the next day and offered to take her to lunch for taking such good care of my brother all these years. While we ate, I worked in the fact that I read Daily tarot and when I saw she was interested in having a reading done, I traded a reading for the truth."

My eyebrows shot up as worry gripped me. "The truth?"

Aunt Sage nodded solemnly. "After her reading, she told me that they don't know where he is. That your father just disappeared."

"Why—why didn't they call the police? Why would they try to keep something like this quiet?"

Sadness crept into my aunt's gaze. "I'm pretty sure I know why. Not long after he left, your dad sent me a package with a key and a note inside. The note said that if anything ever happened to him that I was to use the key and retrieve what he'd locked away in a safe deposit box."

My pulse pounded so hard I heard my own heartbeat. I pulled my hands away from hers and set them on my thighs in tight fists. "Do—do you think he's dead?"

She bit her lip and shook her head. "I don't know, sweetie, but just in case we never hear from him again—" Pausing, she turned and picked up the remote to the DVD player. "Your mom mentioned what happened this week. She's worried for you. I'm so sorry about Mr. Holtzman, Inara. I wish I could hold off on showing you this, but I knew you'd insist on learning what information I could gather the moment I got back." With a sigh, she handed me the remote. "Watch this and we'll talk—about your dad, Mr. Holtzman, whatever you want —when it's over."

When she got up and started to walk out of the room, I asked, "Have you seen it yet?"

She shook her head. "The note your father wrote on the DVD cover said, 'For Nari's eyes only,' I'm honoring his wishes."

After she disappeared into her jewelry studio, I stared at the remote in my hand for several seconds, biting my lip with indecision. All my questions about my powers might finally be answered with the click of a Play button, but the knowledge that these answers came at the cost of my father's disappearance—or worse—felt like a double-edged knife sawing through my heart.

Bo jumped on the couch and nuzzled my wrist with his wet nose. I stroked his white head until the Jack Russell settled beside my thigh. Then Duke, the Shepherd mix Ethan and I had rescued, lowered his solid frame on the other side of me, setting his chin on my thigh. When Luke circled his massive Rottweiler body and laid against my feet on the floor, the dogs' collective warmth and support gave me the courage to lift the remote and hit Play.

A picture popped up of a dark-haired man with dark green eyes wearing a light blue button-down shirt and gray slacks as he leaned against the corner of an office desk. By the décor and window in the background, I could tell he was in a home office.

"Hi, Nari," he began, then cleared his throat. Loosening his red tie, he unbuttoned the top button of his dress shirt. Tension ebbed from him as he folded his arms and gave a nervous half smile. "A part of me hopes you'll never have to watch this, but my selfish-half wishes I could've given it to you the day I left."

He looked so young and handsome, seeing the conflict on his face made all my locked away happy memories of him come flooding back in a swell of bittersweet sadness. "Why did you leave?" I asked the screen in a shaky voice.

He adopted an intense expression, his hands gripping his biceps. "I want you to know that leaving you and your mom was one of the hardest things I've ever had to do in my life, but I did it to protect you."

He jammed his hand through his hair, glanced away and sighed, then looked back at the camera. "God, I'm screwing this up. Let me start from the beginning. Maybe then all of this will make more sense, and one day you'll find it in your heart to understand."

Nothing you could say would ever help me understand how you could leave us. I set my jaw and folded my arms, waiting to hear what he had to say.

My dad stood and shoved his hands in his pockets, pacing in front of the camera. Stopping, he looked right at the lens. "I've had the ability to see my entire next day through my dreams the night before since I was a little boy. I learned to deal with it, living my life one day at a time." He gave an ironic crooked smile before continuing, "I met your mother in college and instantly fell in love. I graduated and got a great job working for the government. Once I had a stable job that I loved, one where I truly felt like I could make a difference in the world and that would also allow me to provide for my family, I asked your mom to marry me. Elizabeth meant every-thing to me, and when you came along, all seemed right in the world."

He smiled briefly, reflecting on happy memories. I pressed my lips together. *If you were happy, why did you leave? What changed?*

"I never told Elizabeth what my real job was at the DOD— that's Department of Defense. I didn't tell her because she didn't know about my ability. I wanted a normal life, Nari. You and your mother gave me that, a normalcy I hadn't had since before my abilities showed up as a child." His eyes pleaded for me to understand.

This part, I did get. Wholeheartedly. But after living with the ability to see my next day for almost a decade, I'd pretty much become accustomed to it. I thought about my mom and wondered how she would have reacted if she'd learned the truth about Dad's ability. She was such a black and white person, I wasn't sure she would have believed him even if he had told her the truth.

Dad blew out a breath, bringing me back to the present. "In my first job with the DOD, I was an analyst, poring over intel collected by agents in the field. When my boss figured out what I could do, he immediately set me up with my own covert division. Other than my boss and a couple of higher-ups, who had to approve the funding for the division, no one knew what I could do."

Excitement filled his gaze. "You know what it feels like to see your entire next day, Nari. Now imagine what you could do with that ability if the whole purpose of your job was to watch daily events?" He spread his arms wide. "You could help save the world! You could stop terrorist attacks before they ever happened. You could avert catastrophes like jumbo jet crashes or minimize lives lost from natural disasters like tsunamis or earthquakes that would've taken thousands of lives. *You* could be the early warning system."

Sudden sadness rolled across his features. "But then things started happening at home. Events that weren't in my dreams or that went totally against my dreams. I felt helpless. You and your mother were in a car wreck. Elizabeth broke her leg falling off a ladder, then later her arm in a fluke flyaway swinging door. I felt as if my family was being punished—worse —*targeted*. For the first time in my life, events were happening in my personal life that I couldn't predict."

When he shoved both hands through his hair and tortured guilt filtered through his expression, I pressed a trembling hand to my lips. He didn't know about Fate. He didn't know there'd be consequences...

Anguish filled his face as he glanced at the camera. "When that bookshelf almost fell on you, I realized it wasn't just my imagination. I'd bolted the damn thing, but it yanked out of the wall as if ripped out by an unseen force. I couldn't let you or your mother get seriously hurt because of me...because of my actions."

He shook his head, bafflement in his furrowed brow. "You'd think with all the lives I'd saved, *good* karma would come my way. Instead, danger stalked my family."

Lifting his gaze to the lens, his eyes begged me to understand. "I didn't know what was causing it. I didn't know if it would continue to go on forever, but I did know it was getting worse, and the 'accidents' seemed to coincide with my prevention of huge catastrophic events. What I *could* do was remove myself from your lives, and by doing so, I could take away the bad karma that seemed to be hurting my loved ones with every move I made."

"It was Fate, Dad!" I yelled at the screen. "He was making you pay for every single life you saved." No wonder Fate spoke about my father with such deep loathing. In his daily job, my dad constantly challenged Fate in huge, sweeping ways. Every. Single. Day. Fate must hate him with molten intensity.

Now it made sense why Fate had attacked me when he did. Fate hadn't bothered me until that day I stopped the bomb from going off at school. He didn't want me to follow in my father's footsteps, saving many lives at once with a simple phone call. Fate must absolutely despise how easily we'd derailed his plans for so many lives. I would never have figured out that Fate was behind the things happening to me without Ethan there questioning everything. Nor would I have been able to face Fate down without Ethan's ability to allow me to see the "unseen" via my dreams. My father didn't have an Ethan in his life when all that stuff was happening to our family.

"I'm sure you're probably wondering why I didn't leave this for you *and* your mother." Deep regret etched grooves around his mouth. "I will always love you both with all my heart, but it's best if your mom believes me to be a deadbeat dad and deserter husband. You're only watching this video because I asked Sage to show this to you *only* if you inherited my abilities."

He put his hands together and pressed them against his lips for a second, then pulled them away. "With your power comes a great responsibility. You'll feel compelled to get involved, to save lives. Please don't follow my path, Nari. Once I got a taste of how I could help the world, of all the good I could do with my abilities, my conscience wouldn't let me turn my back on it. How could I walk away from the thousands of lives I could save? How could I sacrifice them for my own personal happiness?"

"What about your family's happiness?" I choked out, tears trickling down my cheeks. I hated that he chose the world over his family, even as a part of me understood how torn he must've felt when he left us. He was right to keep this video from Mom. She would never understand. If she learned the truth, she would flip out that he'd left when he still loved her, loved us. But Mom didn't have to live with the conflicting emotions our powers left us with every morning when we woke up. She didn't have to decide to act or not act. Ever. She had no idea how crippling and guilt-inducing that could be.

My dad spread his hands toward the camera. "I don't want this life for you, Nari. Do *not* take a job that will exploit your powers and absorb you so completely. Even if it's for the greater good, don't open yourself up to the all-consuming guilt. Learn from my mistakes and *live* as normal a life as you can, *despite* your ability. That is what I hope you can accomplish for yourself. I love you, Nari, and now I hope you understand why I made the decision I did."

The video ended and I was about to turn it off, when my dad popped back up on the screen.

"Hey, Nari." He exhaled deeply and rolled his shoulders as if gearing up for what he was about to say. His hair had grayed at the temples and he had a few more wrinkles. He looked a little thinner too, but otherwise he'd aged well. My eyes widened when I realized that the date at the bottom of the video was a few days after I'd called in the school bombing.

"I recorded the first part of this video not long after I left when you were little. I hadn't intended to record any more, but when I saw that you'd called in the bombing—yes, we can tap into any camera in the country. Anytime. Anywhere. Always keep that in mind, sweetheart—I thought I should add this last bit."

Pride filled his gaze, a smile tilting his lips. "You've grown into a beautiful, confident young woman, Nari. I'm so proud of you." His smile slowly faded into a serious expression. "Please take my advice and don't get involved. And yes, I'm saying this with the full knowledge there will be lives you won't save." His lips twisted in an ironic smirk. "During my two decades with the government, I've saved hundreds of thousands of lives...on an epic scale. So as far as I'm concerned, in the gambling risk of life, I've more than covered my marker *and* yours. I want you to consider yourself absolved of the responsibility. Our family has sacrificed enough."

He gave a sad smile. "I love you, Nari. Live *your* life and only yours. Be happy. That's all I've ever wished for you."

I wasn't sure how long I sat there staring at the blank TV screen, but my aunt finally came back into the living room.

Bo jumped down when she sat beside me on the couch. "Are you okay, sweetie?" she asked, reaching up to brush my hair out of my eyes.

My earlier tears had long since dried, but I scrubbed my cheeks anyway. "Did you know about his job, Aunt Sage? Did you know why he left?"

She nodded. "Your father was so upset the day you got this. You were just a little thing." She brushed her fingers across the small scar on my brow I'd gotten when the bookshelf tilted and a bookend fell on me. My dad had rolled me out of the way just before the shelf crashed down. "He came to me and I helped as best I could." Tears filled her eyes. "It broke my heart that he had to leave, Inara, but he honestly didn't have a choice. Your mother had already been hurt a couple of times, and then your life had been threatened in a way he couldn't explain. He would've fallen apart if something happened to either of you. You and your mom meant everything to him."

My heart ached so much, it felt like it might implode. I pressed my lips together to keep from sobbing all over again. "I wish I'd known the truth."

She nodded, sadness in her gaze. "Now you know why it was hard for me to hear how much you resented him. He made me promise to never tell."

I tensed. "The truth doesn't change the fact he chose his job over us." My shoulders sagged as I continued, "But I do understand being torn between what's right and following my heart. Sometimes it's not always so black and white."

She cupped my cheek, sympathy in her eyes. "I don't think he expected your forgiveness, Inara. All he hoped for was your understanding."

I nodded, then straightened and spoke with fierce intensity, "He's not dead!" For my own self-preservation, I needed to believe that was true. To believe I would see him again.

My aunt exhaled a tired sigh. "The government division he works for has tried to find him. For obvious reasons, they don't want to give up on their most valuable—and one of their most covert—assets, but they've exhausted all their current leads."

I fisted my hands on my knees. "It can't end this way. Not now that I know the truth." *He needs to know about Fate. I can tell him. He could have a life, maybe even a semi-normal life with his family!*

"I'm right there with you, sweetie." My aunt pulled me close, her arms wrapping around me, enveloping me in her warmth. When I leaned into her, hugging her fiercely, she tightened her hold and kissed the top of my head. "Don't worry. I'm not giving up on my brother. Now that I've made a connection with his secretary, she's promised to keep me informed of any developments. I spent the week searching through his apartment and I've brought a box of paperwork and receipts home. I plan to go through them, looking for any clues as to where he might've gone."

I lifted my head. "Didn't his division already do that?"

"They have, but I still want to look for myself."

"Where is it? I can help."

My aunt shook her head. "Not today. I've already skimmed through the stack once. I need a day away to clear my head before I dig back in. You can help me then if you want to."

When I nodded my agreement, she leaned back and gave me an encouraging smile. "Would you like to help me make a few pies? I owe my neighbor a couple for taking care of the boys."

"Sounds good." I stood and forced a smile, welcoming the distraction. I didn't want to process everything about my dad right now.

Aunt Sage tugged me toward the kitchen. "While you help me roll out the dough, you can tell me what you've been up to while I was gone."

My aunt knew about my ability, but she didn't know about Ethan's or about Fate, so I wasn't going to discuss anything related to those subjects with her. If I told her everything that had happened recently, she'd probably lock me in her house until my mom got back. Drystan would be a safe subject and the fact that I got a dog. She'd love Houdini. I really hoped Mom let me keep him.

As she led me through the kitchen doorway, I asked, "Have you ever heard of parkour?"

CHAPTER 25

*J*t was late afternoon by the time I slid into my car to head home. My aunt had wanted me to stay, but she understood once I told her about Houdini. I glanced at my phone I'd purposefully left in my car—so I wouldn't obsess while at my aunt's—to see if Ethan had called. There was only a text from Drystan.

Drystan – 4:50 p.m. ~ Save me from this torturous dance decorating committee!

An amused smile briefly touched my lips as I started my car, but fifteen minutes into the thirty-minute drive home, thoughts about Ethan's silence began to gnaw deep gashes in my stomach. I shook my head to push away my worry he might've found someone else while he was in Michigan. My thoughts only boomeranged to other worries, cracking open the door I'd firmly shut on my dad's revelation.

As memories of my dad began flowing into my consciousness, an emotional rollercoaster of pain, sorrow, and regret followed the flood. By the time I pulled into my driveway, my back and shoulders hurt from all the tension building inside me. I parked my car and rolled my head from one shoulder to the other to ease some of the ache, then hurried through the garage to the kitchen door. I'd just passed by the leaf blower when the unfamiliar writing on the note attached to it snagged my attention.

Nara, your leaf blower is ready to go.

David.

Guilt drilled into my gut as if I'd run into the path of a baseball bat in a "homerun" swing. I had introduced Mom to Mr. Dixon. Even though it was perfectly normal for my mother to date, especially after waiting so long to finally meet someone, I couldn't stop the sick feeling flooding my stomach. Mom had never stopped loving my dad. If she knew he still loved her...

Oh, God! Too much. It was just too freaking much to deal with. I couldn't get inside fast enough. When I ran into my room and quickly began to change into workout pants and a sweatshirt, Houdini started jumping all over me, wanting attention.

I pushed him down and patted his head. While I pulled my hair up into a ponytail, I said, "Don't worry, boy. After you do your business, we're going running."

Ten minutes later, Houdini and I took off running. I headed for the woods at the end of the cul-de-sac. Once I saw Houdini had no plans to leave my side after he kept slipping the leash, I folded the leather length in my tight fist.

Ten minutes later, I entered Ethan's neighborhood. As soon as I saw his house, my stomach knotted. I veered off to the right and into another set of woods on the opposite side.

I ran and ran, crossing around another neighborhood, through a trailer park where I eventually ended up on a quiet tree-lined road that climbed and climbed before it turned into a dirt road.

My leg muscles strained and my lungs felt as if someone had lit a slow-burning match inside them, but I kept going until I couldn't run any more.

Houdini panted hard, his tongue hanging, drool dripping in

fat drops on the dirt road under him. My muscles had finally given out, turning my legs to jelly, and I slithered to my butt.

I scooted to the side of the dirt road and hooked my arm around Houdini's back so we could stare across the gorgeous horizon and watch the last of the sun fade away. Up here, I didn't have to think about the things that bothered me. I could just enjoy the mountain view.

I must've zoned out because a sudden blaring horn and bright lights came barreling toward me. "Go, Houdini!" I ordered and pushed him down the steep embankment. All I had time to do was jump the six-foot distance to the parallel paved road below. As I hurled toward the road, everything Drystan had drilled into my head came flooding back. I managed to hit in a perfect roll. Houdini ran to my side as I rolled onto the balls of my feet.

I took a shaky breath and glanced left and right, thankful a car wasn't coming on the road I'd landed on. "You crazy idiot," I yelled, waving my arms at the taillights of the car to let the driver know he'd almost hit me. He didn't bother putting on his brakes, but instead rolled down his window and gave me the one-finger salute.

I patted Houdini's back with a trembling hand and said, "I really don't want to admit to Drystan that he was right. Let's keep this between us…okay boy?"

As my panicked breathing settled, I saw that Houdini's and my breath came out in frosty plumes. Actually cold weather wasn't my current problem. I had no idea where I was, or how to backtrack.

I'd run blindly as if distance could take care of my worries. Exhaustion had dulled the screaming thoughts in my head to hoarse whispers—which I would take for now. At least my stomach didn't hurt any more. "Thank goodness for GPS, buddy," I murmured to Houdini and pulled my phone out of the hidden pocket in my sweatpants.

"No signal" blinked in bold letters on the screen.

"You've got to be kidding me!" I scrambled to a standing position, held the phone up and spun in a circle, hoping to capture a signal.

Nothing.

If I couldn't call, could I at least send a text? I quickly typed one to Lainey.

Me – 6:00 p.m. ~ Come get me, please! Went running. Need a ride.

Lainey – 6:05 p.m. ~ Still stuck at school with these stupid decorations. Drystan is jumping for joy to leave. Where are you?

Me – 6:06 p.m. ~ I don't know. I went running blindly and now I'm not sure where I am. No signal here, so no GPS. Stupid. I know. At least texting works.

My phone screen blinked on and off for a second, then a warning came through, *Charge your phone. Battery almost dead.*

"Argh!" I ground my teeth at my own stupidity, then sent another text.

Me – 6:07 p.m. ~ Great! Battery almost dead.

Drystan – 6:08 p.m. ~ Do you have GPS tracking on your phone in case you lose it?

Me – 6:09 p.m. ~ Yes!

Drystan – 6:10 p.m. ~ What's the website link and password to get to it?

I quickly sent the info and password.

Drystan – 6:14 p.m. ~ Okay, I see you. Where the hell'd you go? Put your phone on battery save mode. Don't want to lose the signal. Be there as soon as possible.

Me – 6:14 p.m. ~ Thanks, Dryst!

Drystan – 6:15 p.m. ~ STOP texting. Battery save mode now!

"Okay!" After I clicked on the battery save feature, I wrapped my arms around myself to stay warm and waited.

Twenty minutes later Drystan drove up in Matt's Jeep. Once Houdini climbed in the back seat, I hopped into the front and closed the door, welcoming the warmth inside.

"What were you thinking?" Drystan grabbed the stick and shifted into Drive.

"That was the whole point. I wasn't." I rubbed my hands together, then moved my cold fingers in front of the vent.

"Nara…" he began, then paused and pushed the heat button up a notch. "What's going on?"

"Thanks," I muttered, then pressed my hands flat against the blast of heat blowing out of the vent.

Once Drystan turned onto a main road, he shot a look my way.

"There's just a lot going on in my life right now." I rolled my head from one shoulder to the other. "I went running to forget for a while. Exercising always helps."

"You should never have gone alone," he snapped. "You should've rang me to go running with you."

I was surprised by his admonishment. "You're not responsible for me, Drystan." I reached back and patted Houdini's head. "Plus, I wasn't alone."

He cut his gaze to Houdini in the rearview mirror. "You know what I mean." Exhaling, he asked in a calmer tone, "Do you want to talk about it?"

When I shook my head, he scrubbed his fingers through his hair. "You are the most frustrating, confusing person I've ever met." He grabbed the stick shift in a tight hold. "Just when I think I've earned your trust, you shut me out."

I gripped his hand on the gearshift. "It's not you, Drystan. Things are just...piling on at home and I'm a bit stressed. That's all."

Drystan turned his hand over and grabbed mine. "Then we need to 'unstress' you. You're going with us to the dance tomorrow. I'm not taking no for an answer."

His insistence actually brought a sense of relief. He was right. I needed to get out and have some fun. We'd have a great time. Once the dance was over, I'd think about why I hadn't heard from Ethan, my worry for my dad, the mystery behind the secret of Freddie's book, the fact people thought Ethan's book was worth killing for...all of it.

I squeezed his hand. "Okay, I'll go."

Drystan's gaze jerked to mine. "Really?"

I laughed, nodding. "I'll be your good luck charm. While you're star-struck by the girls' fake eyelashes, spiked heels and slinky gowns, I'll help you see past their glamour. That way you'll know who's worth asking out. First heads-up, steer clear of Sophia and Miranda. They're vicious."

Drystan grinned and released my hand to shift the gear while he turned a corner. "We're going to have a brilliant time."

"Well, there is the problem of a suit. You'll have to get one, and you can't wear black since the theme is 'ice.' It might be too late to find a tux in the right color."

"Matt will help me find something," he said. "What about you? Do you have a dress?"

I shrugged. "I won't be dressed as formal as most of the girls, but I'm sure I can borrow something of Lainey's. Speaking of Lainey," I paused and pulled out my phone to send her a text.

Me – 6:45 p.m. ~ I'm going to the dance with you. Aren't you happy? Um, can I borrow something to wear?"

Once I sent the text, I saw my mom had sent me one asking how I was doing. I replied back, letting her know I was fine.

Lainey – 6:48 p.m. ~ SQUEEEE! I'm so HAPPY you're going. We're going to have a fabulous time. I'll be over in an hour.

Me – 6:49 p.m. ~ Okay. See you soon.

I still hadn't received a call or text from Ethan. *Later. I'd deal with it later.* I chanted the calming thought in my head over and over. When we were almost to my house, I checked my phone again. Nothing. The chant wasn't working. Frustrated with myself, I turned my phone off completely.

Drystan pulled into my driveway and put the Jeep in Park. "Delivering you safe and sound."

"Thank you for rescuing me from myself." I gave a wry smile, then opened the door. Houdini jumped out and immediately ran to the grass. Looked like pooper-scooping duty had been added to my duties in addition to leaf-blowing.

I noticed that Drystan hadn't replied with a funny quip or even a teasing dig. When I glanced his way, he appeared to be mulling something over.

"What's wrong, Drystan? I can tell you've got something on your mind."

He looked at me pensively. "Would you be willing to help me with something?"

I shut the car door and turned to him. "Of course! Anything.

You've been there for me many times. I'll be happy to return the favor if I can."

He exhaled a relieved breath and reached in his back pocket, then carefully unfolded a white card with black lettering. "I've had this invitation from my uncle for weeks. I planned to ignore it."

"Why?"

Drystan shrugged. "Because I don't know if he's just going to drill me about my ability."

I rubbed my forehead. "Hold on. You were upset with your father for *not* acknowledging you or your ability, but your uncle *wants* to, not only acknowledge you as his nephew, but to discuss your ability, and you don't like that?"

He lowered his hand to his lap, a grim look on his face. "I've pretty much lied to him, telling him my powers had faded as I grew older."

The things he'd said to me in the past about his uncle made sense now. "Is that why your uncle says you're in 'denial'?"

He nodded. "I don't trust his motives. Why'd he only contact me after my father was dead? Why didn't my father mention he had a brother?"

"You said your father never married your mother. Is it possible that, just like you didn't know about your uncle, he didn't know about you or your mother either?" I glanced at his tight grip on the cardstock paper. Clearly he was torn about going. "How can I help you?"

"The event is tonight." Drystan rubbed his finger along the black lettering. "I want to know my uncle's not going to spend the whole time grilling me about my ability," he said in a derisive tone, then shrugged. "I guess I want to know he wants to get to know me for *me*, regardless of what I can do."

When he found out about my power, Drystan had commented that if he'd had my power, he'd use the heck out of it. Was he thinking about this invitation when he said that? "Are you asking me to help you see yourself talking with your uncle?"

As he slowly nodded, I smiled and reached for his fist

clasping the half-crushed invitation. I wrapped both of my hands around his and said, "Then have a look."

Drystan's eyes floated closed. It was a whole minute before his gaze snapped open again.

I released his hand. "Well?"

"My uncle's ten years older than my dad—who was forty-nine when he died. He's stockier, but I can see the resemblance. He talked about school starting up, footba—er, soccer, and asked if I'd made friends here yet." Drystan smiled, relief reflected in his green eyes.

I smiled back. "Have a good time with your uncle tonight."

I CAME out of the bathroom after my shower to find Lainey sitting on my bed, Houdini snuggled against her leg.

"Ohmygod!" I sucked in a gulp of air and gripped the towel around my chest. "You scared the crap out of me!" I shot my dog an accusing look. "Some watchdog you are!"

"He knew I didn't have evil intentions," Lainey said, snickering while she ran a hand down Houdini's back.

I narrowed my gaze. "How'd you get in here?"

She grinned and flicked her hand, her chunky, multicolored bracelets clinking on her arm. "I remembered the code on your garage door. You know, you really should lock the inside door, Nara. My dad drills that into my head all the time," she said, pursing her lips.

I rolled my eyes and used the edge of the towel to dry the ends of my hair as I walked over to my dresser to pull out some clean clothes.

"Just get your underwear for now." Lainey clapped her hands in a chop-chop manner.

I scooped up a bra and underwear, then glanced around my room, looking for the dresses Lainey brought for me to try on. Only her oversized purse lay on my desk. "I thought you were going to bring a couple of dresses?"

Lainey shooed me into the bathroom, her eyes alight with excitement. "Put on your underwear and dry your hair."

As soon as I walked back out of my bathroom, Lainey grabbed my hand and tugged me over to my bed, where a coat-sized silver box with a gold lid sat at the foot. "Open it, open it. I can't wait to see your face!" She bounced from one booted foot to the other, her eyes alight.

I eyed the fancy box. Maybe that gorgeous black coat she got for Christmas came in it. Smiling that she wanted to make me feel special by wrapping one of her dresses in special packaging, I lifted the lid and began, "I love how goofy you are, Lane—ohmygod, Lainey! What—what is this?" I dropped the lid and stared at the white and silver Grecian-style dress she'd insisted that I try on at the formalwear store.

"You should see your face," Lainey squeezed my arm and squealed in my ear. "That was SO worth it!"

I gaped at her. "I can't afford this dress."

She shook her head and pulled the dress from the baby-pink tissue paper, holding it up to my chest. "This is my gift to you, Nara. You were too gorgeous in it. Even if you're not going with Ethan, you deserve to look your very best at the dance."

My hands shook as I clasped the soft fabric. "When did you get it? You didn't have time to go to the store before you came over."

Lainey adopted a smug look. "I bought it while you were changing back into your clothes. You were so oblivious, you didn't see them zip two dresses into the black plastic garment bag."

"But I told you I wasn't going," I said, surprised by her sneakiness.

Lainey nodded. "I bought it just in case you changed your mind. If you didn't end up going, I would've returned it. No big deal."

But it was a big deal. My fingers dug into the dress. "This was the most expensive gown in the store, Lainey. It costs more than yours. It's too much!"

Lainey gripped my shoulders and hugged me close, whispering in my ear, "You've been through a lot and need some fun in your life. I love you like a sister, Nara." She pulled back and finished in a stern voice, "So shut up and put on the dress."

While Lainey dabbed on my makeup, then pinned up my hair, she babbled about the plans she and Matt had made. When she slid the last bobby pin in my hair, she commented casually, "By the way, my dad told me that they have a new lead on the guy they suspect killed Mr. Holtzman. They went through his P.O. box and found a gym membership. They'll be staking out the gym this weekend, hoping he'll show."

My heart leapt a little. I felt a bit lighter, knowing the police were on the right track. There would be justice for Freddie! "Thank you for keeping me up-to-date," I said quietly.

Lainey nodded, then switched back to dance plans. "As far as transportation for tomorrow night, now that there's four of us going, I'm thinking of calling a driver to pick us up. It won't be a limousine, but probably a town car. I've checked and it'll be a tight squeeze, but four can fit in the back."

Before I could answer, she turned me toward the stand-up, full-length mirror beside my dresser and squeezed my shoulders. "You're so freaking gorgeous!"

I blinked at the girl staring back. She looked beautiful, almost perfect. Like a Barbie doll. Only this doll's smile didn't quite reach her kohl-smudged green eyes. It was fun getting dressed up, but the one person I wanted to see me looking so elegant wasn't going to be there. The sad thought eclipsed my brief excitement.

Lainey pouted at my reflection in the mirror. "Smile, Nara. Do you have any idea how many guys' jaws are going to drop when you walk in the dance?" She smiled and gave an evil chuckle. "Or how many girls are going to want to claw your eyes out."

When I pursed my lips in the mirror, she suddenly snapped her fingers. "Oh, I almost forgot." She reached inside her purse, then caught my gaze. "Close your eyes and don't open them until I tell you to."

I snapped my eyes shut and waited for her cue. When I felt something cover my eyes, then her fiddling with my hair and tucking edges in, a mischievous smile tilted my lips. A mask.

I'd forgotten we had to wear one. I could be totally anonymous, someone else for the night. Someone without any worries.

"Open your eyes, vixen!" Lainey said.

The secret smile was still on my face when I opened my eyes. The mask seemed to emphasize my smoky eyes and full, pouty lips, making me look much older. Now I *really* didn't recognize myself.

A sudden flash of light blinded me. I glanced in Lainey's direction to see her lowering her phone and grinning like a proud pageant mom. "You're going to knock the wind out of everyone, Nara Collins!"

"Thank you for the dress, for trying to cheer me up…" Emotion made my voice crack. "And…for everything."

Lainey adopted a stern look and wagged her finger. "Don't you dare cry. You'll ruin all my hard work." She swept her hand up and down to cover my entire outfit. "Do you think you can duplicate this look tomorrow night?"

CHAPTER 26

" *H*urry *up, Nara!" Lainey fusses and pulls me out of my bedroom into the hall. My thigh muscles protest the sudden, jerky movements, but I grit my teeth and let her take the lead.*

When she starts to tug me down the stairs, I almost trip on my dress. "Lainey," I squeal and yank my hand from hers to grab the handrail. "I'd like to make it down the stairs without breaking my neck."

"Fine," Lainey huffs, then hikes up her pale blue gown's skirt to quickly skip down the stairs.

I follow at a slower pace, one hand on the rail, the other holding the hem of my gown away from my shoes. Each step tightens my calf muscles, so I stop for a second to flex my right calf to keep it from cramping. I'll never go running endlessly again!

As I reach the midway point, whistles pierce my ears. Matt, Lainey, and Drystan stand at the bottom of the stairs, looking up.

"Wow, Nara. You look fantastic!" Matt grins and wraps his arm around Lainey.

Lainey's red curls cascade down her back as she presses her hand to his white tux's lapel, then tweaks his pale blue tie. Straightening it, she grins at him. "I know, right?"

Dressed in a steel gray tux, Drystan's blond-streaked hair stands in messy abandon behind a gray mask with black edging. I continue down the stairs and self-consciously touch my hair. Has one of Lainey's carefully pinned, dangling curls come loose? *Nope. I glance down at my strapless dress to make sure it hasn't slid down.* Still in place. *Drystan's green gaze is impossible to decipher behind that mask.* Why is he being so quiet? Why hasn't he uttered his usual quips, like, "You clean up well." Or "Glad to see you own a dress." *Not that I expect him to load me with compliments, but the lack of comment is deafening.*

"I think you've struck Drystan dumb." *Lainey giggles as I reach the last stair.*

Her words seem to jar Drystan into action. "For once, I'm speechless," *he says, his accent heavy as he takes my hand to help me down the last stair.* "Bravo, Inara."

I grin, brave behind my mask. "Back at you. Ready to show me how Welsh boys dance?"

Lainey insists that Matt slide across the town car's back seat first, then she follows. Once she's inside, she beckons to Drystan, "You next, Drystan, then Nara."

Lainey wasn't kidding about the tight fit in the back. Before the stern-looking driver closes the door, he suggests both Drystan and Matt put their arms around our shoulders. They do as he asks, which gives him just enough room to close the door without pinching my shoulder.

"Cozy." *Matt chuckles as the driver pulls away from my house.*

As music begins to float through the speakers, Lainey snickers and whispers something in Matt's ear. He leans close and whispers something back, but the music drowns out their words. I shake my head as I realize they're hatching their plan for the evening.

The weight of Drystan's arm on my shoulders reminds my body just how hard a workout it has had this past week. "I'm so sore," *I moan.*

Drystan flashes a mocking smile. "You're the one who went running for the hills yesterday."

"I was referring to your insistence I learn how to do a landing roll on a hard surface." *I close my eyes and lean my head back on his arm, heaving a sigh.* "That soreness is all your fault."

He taps the tip of my nose. "One day, you'll thank me."

"Thank you for your help, Drystan," *I begin in a sincere tone, slit-*

ting one eye open. Shutting my eye once more, I smirk. "And for making me one big walking bruise."

"Every bruise is a step toward constant motion."

Lulled by the music and the car's smooth drone, I smile my agreement. "Being still isn't so bad."

"I can think of one benefit. Carpe diem, Nara," *Drystan says in a low voice, right before his lips press against mine.*

His kiss shocks me into immobility, but when Drystan's hand slides along my jaw, and his thumb tilts my chin toward him so he can deepen our kiss, my heart jerks. I grip his hand and pull my mouth from his, whispering desperately, "No, Drystan!" I love Ethan. Only Ethan.

As I stare into Drystan's eyes, time seems to stand still.

This can't be happening! No, no, no. This didn't happen. I didn't kiss him. I didn't betray Ethan. *I tell myself the same thing over and over, my breathing turning rampant. As my heart pounds in time to the freak-out going on inside my head, suddenly everything begins to blur.*

The spinning of lights and colors is so dizzying, I close my eyes and curl my hands into fists in an effort to settle the nauseous sensation swirling in my stomach.

Finally the spinning stops, and I open my eyes.

I'm standing in my bedroom while Lainey slides a bobby pin into my hair. "By the way, my dad told me that they have a new lead on the guy they suspect killed Mr. Holtzman. They went through his P.O. box and found a gym membership. They'll be staking out the gym this weekend, hoping he'll show."

I blink at Lainey, speechless to be experiencing yesterday all over again. My heart races so fast, I sway a little. I feel as if I might pass out, but I catch myself and straighten, then manage to speak. "Thank you for keeping me up-to-date."

Lainey nods, then switches back to plans for the dance, "As far as transportation for tomorrow night, now that there's four of us going, I'm thinking of calling a driver to pick us up. It won't be a limousine, but probably a town car. I've checked and it'll be a tight squeeze, but four can fit in the back."

You can't get in that car! "*I—I'm going to run a little late for the dance. My aunt asked me to do something for her. I'll meet you guys there."*

Disappointment flits across Lainey's face, but she nods and turns me toward the stand-up, full-length mirror beside my dresser. She squeezes my shoulders and grins. "You're so freaking gorgeous!"

My lips tremble as I smile at her in the mirror. I exhale an inward sigh of relief, and my head reels with what has happened. Ohmygod, I've gone back in time. Freaking back in time!

Woof, woof, woof, woof, woof, woof!

I sat straight up in bed as Houdini threw himself toward Patch behind the window's glass. Oblivious to the fact his back leg had entangled in my backpack strap, my dog continued his frantic lunge-and-growl movements until I got out of bed.

A loud, crackling jolt of electricity zapped from my hand to his head when I moved to pat him, making us both yelp in pain. His brown eyes snapped to me, a mixture of confusion and contriteness. "Sorry, boy." But at least I had his attention. "Settle, Houdini."

Did that really happen? Did I change the conversation I'd had with Lainey? I glanced at the clock on my nightstand. Eight. Lainey usually didn't get up until at least ten, but I couldn't wait. I had to know.

Electricity hung in the air, raising the tiny hairs on my arms. When my hand moved within a few inches of the cordless phone on my desk, a long, white-hot arc zinged from the phone, hitting my fingers and throwing me back. I landed hard on my butt. I couldn't feel my lips or my teeth, and my arms and legs tingled as if they were full of crawling bugs.

"Stop it!" I growled into the air and retrieved a dirty sock from my floor. Fate was beyond pissed, but I didn't care.

I hadn't consciously controlled what just happened in my dream, but this extreme reaction from him told me I had done something. Once I'd shoved my hand inside the sock, I grabbed the phone, dialed Lainey's, then changed it to speaker. My face wasn't going anywhere near the phone. Why give Fate another target?

"Hello?" she said in a sleepy voice.

"What time did I tell you I'd meet you at the dance?" I asked, breathless.

"Huh?"

Maybe my odd dream was just me *wishing* I could change it. My heart thumped as I repeated my question.

Lainey yawned. "You never did say. I'm still bummed you're not riding with us. What time should I tell Drystan to walk outside to meet you?"

My legs gave out and I fell toward my bed, hanging halfway off. "About a half hour after you arrive."

"So, seven thirty?"

"Yeah," I croaked. "See you there."

"You've got to break this habit of getting up so early," Lainey said in a tired voice. "See you at seven thirty, not a minute later."

I punched the Off button with my sock-covered finger, then stared at the phone. I'd changed my future...inside my dream. What was that called when a person manipulated events in a dream while they're dreaming it? Lucid dreaming...that was the term. Except my lucid dream changed my future before it ever happened.

And I had no idea how I'd done it.

Drystan stood outside the school as I walked up the sidewalk. My breath frosted in the air and my toes in the silver-heeled sandals had started to tingle from the cold. I picked up my pace and shifted the silver shawl I'd borrowed from my mom's closet to cover my exposed cleavage. I felt better...and warmer for wearing it.

Drystan looked just like he did in my dream—handsome and confident with his blond-streaked hair standing up in defiant haphazardness behind his gray mask. I'd bet money the girls I'd seen hanging around him at school this week had been all over him ever since the dance began. When I stopped in front of him, I smirked and wiped at least three shades of lipstick smudges from his jaw with my thumb. "Looks like you're doing just fine without a good luck charm."

He bowed and smiled, saying in a formal tone, "My beautiful rescuer has arrived. I'm now the luckiest bloke here."

His compliment surprised me, and even though I knew he was teasing, I couldn't help the blush that shot across my cheeks. I'd never been more thankful for a mask than I was at that moment. Seeking a distraction, I held my keys out and rambled, "Would you mind holding onto my keys? Keeping up with a purse will be impossible in there."

Drystan tucked my keys in his pocket, then stepped close to touch my jaw, a knowing smile tugging on his lips. "Did you know you blush all the way down your throat?"

His mask's black edging only enhanced the sparkle of amusement in his eyes. I swatted his hand away and tried to ignore the heat suffusing my face. "Stop teasing me, Drystan. How'd it go with your uncle last night?"

"It's a start, at least. Thank you for your help." He gave a sincere smile, then tucked my hand in the crook of his arm. "Let's go have some fun."

After we'd handed our invitations to the teachers manning the entrance of the gym, Drystan chuckled in my ear as he escorted me under the dangling silver icicles hanging across the arched entry. "It's a good thing I know how to kick some arse. I have a feeling I'll be the one knocking blokes away from you all night."

The thumping music and amazing decorations inside the dimly lit gym distracted me from responding. I couldn't believe the complete transformation from domed building into a winter-themed fantasy world. Pale blue, white, and silver swirled swaths of fabric had been artfully hung to not only cover the dome structure's ceiling beams, but with its iridescent glittery coating and the main door opening and closing, the constant push and pull of air created an overall effect like waves of icy water floating above us.

On the far side of the gym, a popular local band, dressed in white tuxes, played the latest pop song on a huge stage that had been decorated with jagged blue and silver edging made to look like shards of icy stalagmites. Food tables stood on opposite sides of the gym, flanked on either end by sculptured fountains dribbling punch over the fountains' iced edges.

Special lights hung from the ceiling projecting snowflakes on every wall surface, while blue and white lights strobed the dance floor packed with guys and girls gyrating in a sea of silver, white and pale gray formal outfits to an upbeat, fast-paced song. As we moved farther into the room, heavy fog hung at knee level, puffing away from our legs with each movement we made.

The masks made it near impossible to recognize anyone right away, but we hadn't stepped too far into the room before Lainey came running up, one hand holding her skirt's hem off the floor, the other latched on to Matt's hand, tugging him behind her.

"You made it!" Releasing her dress, she swept her arm wide. "What do you think about the decorations?"

I grinned and glanced around the room once more. "It's truly amazing, Lainey. You should be involved in all the dance decorations from now on."

She made a slight choking sound. "Oh no! Never again. This about killed me."

"Us!" Matt grunted and wrapped his arm around her waist. "You look great. I'm glad you could come, Nara."

The fast-paced song had come to an end, and the lead singer announced a newly requested song right before the guy on keyboards started up with slow, melodious notes.

"Come on, Lainey," Matt grinned. "They're playing our song."

Gingerly touching her pile of auburn pinned-up curls to make sure none had fallen, Lainey surreptitiously glanced around the room until her gaze landed on Jared and Tarra snuggling close on the dance floor to the slow song. "Yes, they are!" She waved to us and allowed Matt to lead her into the throng of people, where they began to dance up-close and personal just a few feet away from Jared and Tarra.

I sighed. "Why do I have a feeling that isn't going to end well?"

Drystan glanced at me, surprise in his eyes. "Wait? You don't know what happens tonight?"

Crap, I was so used to others *not* knowing about my ability. "Uh, I um...didn't sleep well last night. Most of tonight is a blur."

A secretive smile lit his face, sending road flares of panic shooting straight through me. "Let's dance—"

"Drystan," A thin, blonde girl, who always sat at the front of my Spanish class interrupted and stepped close to grab his free hand. She tilted her chin toward her chest and looked at him through her mask with flirty doe eyes. "You promised me a dance earlier, and then you disappeared."

"Hi, Shell." Drystan's grin turned to an apologetic smile. "Nara's here now, so—"

"You promised before I arrived." I smiled and nudged my shoulder against his. "You should keep your promise."

"Thanks for understanding, Nara," Shelley said at the same time she started to tug Drystan away.

He stayed rooted beside me, looking skeptical. "Are you sure?"

"Remember, luck is on your side," I reminded him. "Go on, I'll be right here."

His eyes lit up and I could tell he remembered my promise to give him the scoop on the girls at the dance. "Okay, be right back."

As I watched Shelley practically wrap herself around Drystan on the dance floor, I realized that encouraging him to dance with other girls might be the answer to avoiding what happened in the car on the way to the dance in my dream. Maybe I'd misread it, and he hadn't developed feelings for me. Maybe he was just reacting to our close proximity in the car and he really was just "seizing the day." I breathed a little easier once I'd reasoned it all out in my head. I could work with that.

"Hey, Nara!" A beautiful dark-haired girl wearing a white one-shoulder dress approached. Tiny pale blue hand-stitched flowers decorated the thin shoulder strap that wound across her chest and then down the front of her flowing skirt in an intricate vine pattern. She was stunning with her dark kohl-rimmed eyes blinking at me behind a pale blue mask. Even though her voice had sounded familiar, it took me a second to recognize her. I'd never seen Harper with makeup, let alone her stick-straight hair curled and piled high on her head. "Hi, Harper. Wow, you look fantastic!"

"Thanks!" Harper beamed and turned to the guy, whose arm she held in a firm grip. "Nara, I'd like you to meet my boyfriend, Drake."

Dressed in a fitted white tux with tails, Drake's bald head gleamed in the dimly lit room. "Nice to finally meet you, Nara. Harper has talked about you non-stop since you two met."

"Nice to meet you too, Drake." His deep voice made him appear older, but then so did his rangy build and sharp jawline. I couldn't help but fidget under the steady regard behind his fitted pale blue mask. His dark eyes appeared to be assessing me, as if he were weighing whether or not I was worthy of being Harper's friend.

When he didn't say anything else, other than to smirk slightly, I glanced at Harper for help. She was too busy staring at him in adoration, like her world totally revolved around him. He obviously wasn't much of a talker. What did she see in him? Was it because he seemed edgy, which was so different from her buttoned-up life? I couldn't take his assessing stare any longer. "Well, I hope you all have a great time tonight," I said, edging away.

Harper tore her gaze from Drake long enough to wave. "You too."

I moved to the other side of the room and stood along the edge of the dance floor. My gaze settled on the blonde girl snuggling close and personal with Drystan, which made me think of Ethan. I really wished he could've come.

A second slow song started up and another girl, this time a brunette, snagged Drystan from the blonde. He scanned the crowd, looking for me. I started to wave, but someone gripped my elbow and spoke in my ear.

"Dance with me, Nara."

I tugged against Jared's grip, but he whispered, "Please, I want to talk."

What could he possibly want to talk to me about? When his gaze skipped through the crowd to land on Lainey and Matt, I pursed my lips. "Where's your date?"

"She's in the bathroom with her girlfriends." He tugged me forward, pulling me deep into the dance crowd.

He tried to wrap his arms around me, but I pushed on his shoulders to keep some distance between us. "What do you want, Jared?"

He narrowed his gaze over my shoulder, then spun me around so his back was to Lainey and Matt dancing. "What's the deal with Lane and that guy? Does she really like him or is she just trying to get back at me?"

I stiffened, offended for my friend. Even if he was right, the fact he was asking about Lainey spoke volumes. "What's *your* deal? Do you really like Tarra? Or are you just trying to win the crown tonight?"

Confusion filtered through is gaze. "I—I don't know." He actually seemed genuinely conflicted.

At that moment, Lainey's gaze snagged mine across the room. Eyes wide, she yanked Matt closer and mouthed over his shoulder, "What are you *doing*?"

I stepped closer to Jared and whispered in his ear, "You threw her away, but now that someone else wants her, you're all interested again?" I met Lainey's curious gaze and mouthed, "I don't know!" Taking a step back from Jared, I locked gazes with him and continued, "Grow up, Jared," then turned and walked off with brisk movements, ignoring my protesting muscles.

a s I reached for a cup to pour myself some punch, a girl spoke in my ear in a low hiss, "Bet you couldn't wait for me to go to the bathroom so you could move in on Jared! Don't think I don't know you used to have a crush on him."

I poured my drink, then cast my gaze over Tarra's bright blonde hair to her perfect, tanned body wrapped in a silver-sequined dress displaying every curve. The crush I'd had on Jared seemed like a lifetime ago. Ethan eclipsed everyone in my mind.

"Old news," I said, shrugging. "For the record, Jared asked me to dance."

Silver glitter-coated eyelids narrowed behind her silver mask, creating a creepy eyeless effect, instead of the sultry one I was sure she was going for. "I don't believe you."

I took a sip. "I really don't care if you believe me or not. It's the truth," I snapped. As Tarra walked off in a snotty huff to look for Jared, annoyance rippled through me. Her rocky relationship with Jared had unleashed the questions I'd tucked into the back of my mind about Ethan. Why hadn't he called me back? Who was the girl who'd answered his phone? My stomach churned as another worrisome thought occurred. When Ethan did finally call me, would I like the answers he gave?

An upbeat reggae song started at the same time Drystan whispered in my ear, "Ready to find out if this Welsh bloke knows how to dance?"

I grinned and set my cup on the table, putting my hand in his outstretched one. "Absolutely!"

Drystan really did know how to move, and while we danced to a long set of nonstop, fast-paced songs, I was able to forget about everything and lose myself in the rhythm of the beat. After a while, Lainey and Matt made their way over to hang with us, which made dancing to popular songs even more fun. This is what I came for...giving myself up to the fun and enjoying time with friends.

"You're really a lot of fun when you let your hair down, er... pull your hair up, Nara," Drystan spoke over the music.

Lainey heard him and shoulder-bumped me, making me bump Drystan in turn. "She says, 'right back at you.'"

I snickered at her silliness, then raised my arms in the air to snap my fingers, swiveling my hips to the beat. "I guess you Welsh know a thing or two about rhythm."

With a bark of laughter, Drystan gripped my waist right over the diamond cutouts, his hands warm against my exposed skin. Lifting me off the ground, he swung me around in a circle. "You have no idea," he said, eyes twinkling behind his mask while his mouth tilted in a lopsided, sexy grin.

Just as my feet touched the ground, the lead singer announced, "The mask unveiling will be coming up soon, and after that, we'll reveal the Ice King and Queen. Stay tuned!"

When the band began playing a slow, sultry song, I said in a lighthearted tone, "That's our cue to get something to drink." I started to walk off, but Drystan grabbed my hand and pulled me back.

"Uh-uh..." Stepping into my personal space, he wrapped his arm around my waist and pulled me close. "I've waited all night to dance with you. The drinks can wait."

I shook my head and smirked as my hands settled on his shoulders. "But we've been dancing for at least forty minutes."

"Not like this, Nara." He began to slow dance to the lulling melody, his hand sliding up my lower back. He'd moved close enough that I felt his heart pounding against mine.

I gave a nervous laugh. "See, we've both just had a workout. We need hydration—" I trailed off, my gaze snagging on Lainey and Matt. I hoped to flag her attention so she'd go to the refreshment table with me, but she was staring at Matt. He said something, and then...he kissed her. Lainey seemed surprised by his kiss, but I blinked in shock when she began to kiss him back with equal enthusiasm.

"And just like that, it all worked out brilliantly." Drystan chuckled in my ear, drawing my attention back to him.

"I—I'm happy for them. Surprised, but happy."

Drystan's hand slid under my shawl, his fingers pressing against my exposed skin on my upper back, drawing me so close I was forced to look up at him. "I'm glad you're here," he said in a husky voice. As soon as he finished speaking, Drystan lowered his head toward mine.

Tension had been building inside me ever since he pulled me into his arms for the slow dance. I slid my hands from his shoulders to his chest, creating some distance. "Drystan," I began, just as a hand landed heavily on my shoulder.

"I believe you promised to dance with me tonight, Nara," a familiar deep voice rumbled in my ear.

Drystan's hold tightened around my waist and he snarled, "Not on your life!"

Ethan's tense stance radiated fury. His fingers dug into my shoulder ever so slightly. "Do you want to bet yours on it?"

The menace in his voice matched the deadly shine of his dark eyes behind his black mask.

"Hi!" I said with a surprised smile, my voice pitching higher as I gripped Ethan's hand on my shoulder with an I'm-so-glad-you're-here squeeze. My heart thumped harder than it had all night as I pulled out of Drystan's grasp. "It's okay, Drystan. This is Ethan."

As I met Ethan's gaze, I couldn't believe how much broader his shoulders appeared or how incredibly drool-worthy he looked in an all black tux. But his unique mask had snagged and held my attention. Below the eyeholes, the black mask sported a slight beak, reminding me of a raven. I smirked, acknowledging his appropriate mask, before I nodded to my dance partner, "Ethan, meet Drystan."

Without another look at Drystan, Ethan tugged me away. Once we'd moved deep into the throng of people, he wrapped his arm around my waist and pulled me close.

"That was rude, Ethan!" I gasped for breath at the same time I gripped his shoulders. Shock couldn't begin to describe my feelings. When I had to tilt my head back to see his eyes, I realized he'd also grown taller since I'd seen him last, by at least an inch and a half. Holy cow, what'd his parents fed him in Michigan? Miracle-Gro?

Ethan's narrowed gaze followed Drystan until he left the dance floor. "If I'd stayed near him a second longer, I would've pounded him into the floor for touching you," he said in a barely controlled tone.

"We were just dancing. He's a friend. What has gotten into you?" I said, completely taken aback by his anger.

When his gaze returned to mine, Ethan's fury simmered to a steady burn. "He wants you, Nara! Is that all it took? A month for you to forget about me? About us?"

It was hard to read Ethan's face behind his mask, but his shoulder muscles under my hand had turned hard as a rock as his arm tightened around me. *All* I'd done since he left was focus on him. My own anger rushed to match his. I jerked my chin up a notch. "Who's Danielle? And why didn't you call me back?"

Ethan started to speak when the lead singer called out over the song, "Okay everyone, time to take off your masks!"

In fluid movements, Ethan removed my mask, then pulled his own off, saying in a low grumble, "I don't like not seeing your face."

A collective murmur rippled through the people around us, drawing my attention. Everyone must've noticed the lone guy who'd showed up at the dance wearing all black in complete defiance of the dress code. But apparently, they didn't recognize him until he pulled off his mask.

I was a bit shocked too. The mask hid the fact he'd cut his

hair. Now it was super short on the sides and a mess of spiked bangs. The new cut allowed full access to his deep blue eyes, which were currently sweeping the crowd of people around us. He met every single pair of eyes looking at him with his own bold, assessing "yes, I'm looking at you" stare.

"Well?" I asked, wanting…no, *needing* to hear his answer.

He clasped my hand on his shoulder. "Not here, Nara. Let's go."

As he purposefully cut through the thickest group of people, aggressively shouldering his way past everyone, my brain screamed, *What had happened in Michigan?* This wasn't the same Ethan who left. That guy preferred to avoid physical contact with others. Now Ethan appeared to be going out of his way to brush against as many people as possible on his way off the dance floor.

I didn't know what to think, but I was done being kept in the dark. Just as we stepped off the dance floor, I tugged hard and dug in my heels, yanking him to a halt. "I want answers now, Ethan. Not later!"

When he cut his gaze back to me, volatile emotions churned in the dark blue depths, making his eyes appear almost black.

Drystan stepped to my side and clasped my free hand. "You don't have to go if you don't want to, Nara." His gaze openly challenged Ethan.

Ethan's jaw muscle flexed as he looked down at Drystan holding my hand. When his gaze flicked to mine, his eyes swirled, turning black as obsidian. I hadn't imagined the darkness earlier. Ethan's hand tightened around mine, and a vibration began to tingle between us, rippling up my arm. He was on the verge of exploding, and he was asking me to take care of Drystan, or he would.

I slid my hand from Drystan's and adopted a reassuring smile. "I'm fine, Drystan. I'll be back."

Drystan set his mouth in a grim line, then nodded, shoving his hands into his pants pockets.

The moment we stepped outside into the cold, Ethan asked, "Did you drive?"

I nodded and he started in the direction of the parking lot, but I tugged on his hand much harder this time. "I'm *not* bailing on Lainey, Ethan."

His shoulders flexed, but he didn't say a word. Instead, he shifted direction, moving toward the field house building next to the gym. Thankfully the custodial staff had turned all the outside floodlights on for the dance, which made it easier to wind our way down the sidewalk that skirted the back side of the gym. The field building housed the physical therapy equipment, including soaking hot tubs, first aid rooms, and the coaches' offices.

"Who is Danielle?" I repeated. Ethan never relinquished his hold on my hand, and with his brisk pace, my shawl kept falling down my shoulders. I resorted to carrying it while working hard to keep up with his long stride. I wasn't cold at all, because each step I took worked up my own angry, jealous lather.

"She's a cousin," he finally said over his shoulder right before he yanked open the field house main door.

A cousin I could deal with. Would've been nice if he'd mentioned her before now though! I straightened my shoulders and allowed him to tug me into the building. I was surprised the building was unlocked, but then I remembered the back of the building had tons of storage space. That's probably where most of the decorations, tables, and other paraphernalia for the dance had been stored.

A myriad of smells of menthol, camphor, rubbing alcohol, bleach, chlorine, and faint sweat wafted our way as we passed the various rooms in the building. Once we reached the office area, Ethan tried one door and found it locked. Moving to the next office, he turned the knob. I thought it was locked too, but then suddenly he was tugging me inside.

Outside floodlights streaming through the office blinds provided enough light for us to see each other. "Why didn't you text me back? Call me…anything?"

Ethan quickly shut the door and before I could pull away, he set my back against it, his hands caging me in. His face, full of hard lines, moved close to mine. "Do you still love me, Nara?" he ground out.

I stiffened, offended. "What kind of question is that?"

He closed his eyes for a second, then locked gazes with me once more. "All the other bullshit, texts that never made it, guys who think they can have you, stuff happening out of my control, a life I didn't choose, none of it matters," he growled. "But the way you feel about me does."

A life he didn't choose? Was he referring to his powers? I searched his angry gaze. For a brief second, vulnerable pain reflected in the dark depths, cracking through my anger. "I've done nothing *but* love you—"

Ethan's mouth cut me off, his lips pressing hard against mine. The fierceness of his kiss rocked me to my toes. I couldn't help but respond to it. Wrapping my arms around his shoulders, I kissed him back with all the longing and worry and fear I'd felt during his absence. God, I'd missed him...missed our connection so very much.

He must've felt it too, because Ethan pulled me close and deepened our kiss, his mouth moving over mine in a sensual, bone-melting glide. Full of heat and intensity, our attraction had built to fiercer heights since the last time we were together.

I felt smaller enveloped in his thicker arms and taller height, but at the same time more cherished. As we fell against the door, his hands slid down my sides, past my waist to cup the back of my thighs through my dress. He pulled me tighter against him, as if he couldn't get close enough, then kissed my jaw and spoke in a low, rough voice, "When I saw his hands on you, touching your skin, all I could think about was snapping him in half." His warm mouth moved to my throat and he nipped lightly, his grip tightening. "You're *part* of me, Nara. Always and forever."

"Together 'til the wheels fall off," I agreed, panting as I yanked at his shirttail, then tugged it out of his belt and pants. I needed to feel the warmth of his skin against my palms, wanted to press him even closer, to imprint his hard frame all over me, everywhere at once. He wasn't the only one who craved the physical connection. Sliding my hands along his back, I reveled in the new sharply defined muscles and pressed him against me. I couldn't get close enough. I didn't care that we were in some coach's office.

Ethan claimed my mouth once more, pressing his upper body against mine. Sandwiched between the door and his rock hard chest, I felt every thump of his heart knocking on my own, as if his body wholeheartedly agreed with his "you're a part of me" declaration.

High on the intimate thought, I smiled against his mouth and cupped the back of his neck, threading my fingers through his shorter locks. I missed the longer hair, but this haircut enhanced his defined cheekbones, instead of hiding them. Cool air hit my calf as he gripped my skirt and started to slide the soft material up my leg, raising the hem.

Just as his warm fingers grasped the back of my thigh, Ethan raised his head and narrowed his gaze, rumbling, "People are coming."

"What?" I listened. "I don't hear anything," I whispered as he released my leg and glanced around the dimly lit room.

As soon as he tugged me away from the door, the building's main doors clanged open and several guys' amped-up voices floated down the hall.

Footfalls clomped into the hall, and one person said, "The offices are down this way."

Ethan pulled me into the office's small storage closet, then shut the door behind us, dousing the room in darkness.

Now that he wasn't distracting me with bone-melting kisses, I asked in a low voice, "You really didn't get my TTTWFO text? Why didn't you call me when you got back from skiing like you said you would?"

Ethan's chest brushed against my arm. "No, I didn't get that text, but I think you liked my answer to that one better in person," he said in a low husky voice. "I was wondering why you were so quiet this week, but instead of calling, I decided to surprise you."

I smiled and murmured, "You accomplished your goal. Oh, by the way, your cousin sucks at giving messages."

"You talked to Danielle?"

He sounded surprised. So he really didn't know. "She

answered your phone when I called one night. She told me you were in the shower," I said in a sour tone. "I asked her to have you call me."

"She should've told me…" he began in an annoyed tone when footfalls came closer to the office.

Another male voice called out, "I'm pretty sure I saw something that'll work in Coach K's office."

Ethan slid me in front of him and whispered, "Shhhh" then rested his hands on my shoulders. I relaxed a little, glad he sounded upset with his cousin. She deserved his anger for not giving him my message.

"We'll find something to crown the rightful king!" another voice said right before a light suddenly flooded under the closet door, giving off a dim glow inside the small space.

In his excited state, Drystan's Welsh accent sounded even stronger outside the closet door. Ethan's fingers tightened on my shoulders, and he moved closer until I could feel his heart thump hard against my back.

A rattling echoed from across the room and one of the guys said, "Damn, this cabinet's locked."

"No problem." Drystan said, then a drawer slid open and someone rummaged through it.

While Ethan ran his thumbs along the back of my shoulders, warm breath rushed against my ear, sending tingles along my neck and scattering down my limbs.

He surprised me when he bent to press a kiss on the back of my left shoulder in the same place he'd just rubbed his thumb. The sounds in the office faded away as a jolt of scorching heat flooded into my skin where his lips connected. I gasped as a cool sensation quickly followed the searing intensity. Goose bumps skittered along my body and the tips of my fingers and toes tingled. Though Ethan hadn't said a word, I'd felt his emotions. His kiss had been intimate and boldly possessive, as if he'd just branded me, and an overwhelming, tender, "I claim you" message settled in my heart.

You're mine too, Ethan.

As he straightened, I glanced over my shoulder into his hooded gaze, hoping he could see how I felt.

Ethan slowly turned me around in the confined space. When he gripped my waist, then effortlessly lifted me to his towering height as if I weighed nothing, I grasped his shoulders and mouthed, "What are you doing?"

His smile oozed devilish intent, making every nerve in my body stand at attention. "Fulfilling a promise, Sunshine," he whispered right before he pulled me close and planted a warm kiss along the plump curve of skin peeking above my bodice. When he moved to give the same attention to the other side, I dug my fingers into his shoulders and bit my lip to keep from making any noise. The raven feather I'd kept from our picnic, the one he'd tucked in my bra as a promise, had fallen out of his journal. I'd been sad when I realized it was gone, but the real deal was far more seductive and intensely emotional. Whenever he touched me, Ethan made me feel so much, it was hard to contain my response.

When he lowered me to my feet, the guys had finally freed whatever trophy they planned to take back to the dance. After they exited the office, I inhaled and exhaled slowly in order to get-a-grip, then straightened my shaky legs and met his gaze. "I can't believe you expect me to go back to the dance after that."

The seductive look he gave me sent puffs of steam shooting straight to my belly. "Who says I want you to go back to the dance?"

CHAPTER 28

*E*than and I had just made our way to the food table when Lainey waved to me from across the room and mouthed, "Bathroom." then pointed to the gym entrance.

While Lainey skirted the crowd, heading toward the entrance, I looked at Ethan. "Lainey wants to talk to me about something. I'll be right back."

Before I could walk away, he glanced at the locker room doorway on the far side of the gym. "The bathrooms are that way."

"They're crappy and smelly. The dance committee got the school to agree to let us use the school bathrooms in the main building for tonight."

"I'll go with you then."

I put my hand on his arm. "There's always people coming and going to the bathrooms, so I won't be alone. I'll be right back."

As I headed toward the door, I heard Matt yelling above the crowd, "Hurry back for our dance, Lainey!" He spun to the revved-up hip-hop beat while holding something gold—was that a trophy?—above his head. Drystan danced in the center of the crowd, surrounded by a pack of girls, trying to gain his undivided attention. Off to the left, Tarra and Jared sported their Ice Queen and King crowns, while holding court to the entire cheerleading squad and football players' cheers.

Everyone seemed to be having a blast. I smiled that it had all worked out as I followed a group of girls out of the gym and then through the main building's double doors.

Packed with groups of girls crowded in front of the mirrors, giggling and applying lipstick and in some cases even more makeup, the bathroom smelled of perfume and hairspray.

I shook my head at the girly chaos, then peered under the stall doors for Lainey's dress and shoes. When I didn't see her, I frowned and walked back into the somewhat quieter hall.

Where'd she go? I glanced into the darkened atrium—the custodians had only left on the lights at the front of the school for us—and tried to think like Lainey. She wanted to talk, but she had to know the bathrooms would be packed. Which meant…she'd gone to the other girls' bathroom close to our study hall classroom.

Mrs. Meacham had been outside talking to a parent chaperone most of the dance. At least I wouldn't have to sneak past her. My heels echoed in the open, two-story atrium, so I moved to my toes and quickly crossed it, then pushed open the door that led to the sophomore locker halls. Cutting through the locker hall wasn't the fastest way to the bathroom, but at least that hall had skylights. The rest of the halls were full of shadows.

I'd just turned down the locker hall when someone grabbed my neck and yanked me around, slamming me against the lockers.

"I want my books back, little tweet," my attacker hissed in a deadly voice.

My shoulders throbbed, but I bit back the gasp of pain from his manhandling and glared at the bald guy towering over me.

Drake!

Before I could speak, he grabbed my throat and slammed me against the locker once more. "I went to all that trouble collecting those books, only to have that little monkey-climbing shit steal them away. When I saw you dancing with that foreign kid, I realized who'd stolen my books."

"They weren't *your* books!" I snapped, while trying to decide which way to run as soon as I got free.

He sneered and dug his fingers into my throat. "I want them back!"

"You won't get them!" I croaked and grasped his wrist. A sharp-edged cufflink dug into my palm as I tried to jerk his hand from my throat. He was so strong. When he laughed at my failure, I gritted my teeth and tried to lash out with my foot, but my shoe caught in my dress.

Just as I freed my foot and swung it toward his knee, he straightened his arm and snickered. "I have a much longer reach now, little bird."

I frowned in confusion. He talked as if we'd interacted before. His "tweet" reference sounded just like the guy who'd attacked me in the library. Had that guy told him what happened between us? They obviously worked for someone. "Who were you stealing my books for?"

His lips curved in an arrogant, evil grin. "He'll be your worst nightmare."

"Why does he want my books?" I dropped my voice to a whisper and let a hand slip from his wrist.

When he leaned in to ask, "What did you say?" I swung my free arm, slamming my fist into the side of his head.

He grabbed his head and stumbled to the side. "You conniving bitch!"

I hiked my hem and took off in the direction of the bathroom. If I could get there, I'd bolt the door from the inside. I prayed Lainey was there, so we could use her phone to call the police.

Hard-soled shoes hammered the floor directly behind me right before he grabbed a handful of hair and pulled me back against his chest in an excruciating, painful yank.

"I'm really going to enjoy torturing you," he hissed in my ear, then let out a low chuckle. "I'm glad you're young enough to handle some bumps. I hated that old man going down for the count so quickly. It pissed me off that he hadn't felt me pin his puny body to that damned raven tree."

His admission to Freddie's murder ignited the burning in

my stomach, snapping something inside. With a growl of fury, I ground my spiked heel into his shoe and slammed my fist backward, pegging him in the groin.

The second he released my hair, I started to run when I realized I didn't hear his howl of pain right behind me anymore. I turned just in time to see his arms and legs flailing as he flew through the air down the hall in a blur of white. His body slammed into a set of lockers, denting them before he fell to the floor, heaving an audible grunt. Ethan stood where Drake had been just a second before. He stared down at me with eyes as dark as night. "Get out of here, Nara!"

Hard lines creased his face, making him look much older. I'd never heard such fury in his voice, nor had I seen the kind of vicious look he turned toward Drake when the guy crawled to his knees and sucked in a lungful of air.

"He killed Freddie—a sweet old man who tried to help me. Let's get out of here!" I grabbed his arm and tried to tug him along, but he effortlessly uncurled my death grip from his arm. His jaw worked for a second, the reproach in his black eyes flickering over my face. He was angry I hadn't told him.

He turned away from me and said over his shoulder, "I mean it. Get out now!"

His fierce tone spurred me into action. I ran and tried not to wince at the punching sounds or the distinct reverberation of bodies slamming against lockers. Once I turned the next corner, I veered down the hall that led to the girls' bathroom. I wasn't leaving Lainey behind.

Swinging open the bathroom door, I called in a breathless, frantic voice, "Lainey, we have to get out—"

I froze. Harper leaned over Lainey, squeezing my best friend's neck with a gleeful look of vengeance on her face.

Even though red scratches welted Harper's arms, Lainey was in serious trouble.

"Let her go!" I screamed, rushing forward.

Just as Lainey fell to her knees, her face straining with the need to breathe, I slammed my fists down on Harper's arm, dislodging her hold.

"Stupid bitch!" Harper turned her fury on me with a vicious

backhand. She took advantage of my head whipping to the side to grab my shoulders and jam me against a locked stall door.

I blinked past the pain searing across my face and grabbed a fistful of her pinned hair. Yanking hard, I hissed, "Get off me, you crazy psycho!"

I tried to hit her in the stomach, but Harper turned at the last second and my fist caught her hip instead. She gritted her teeth and grabbed my throat with gleeful, wild-eyed excitement, grating out, "You're not worth the effort."

She squeezed and I knew I had very little time to save myself and Lainey. I gripped the top of the stall above my head, then yanked my knees up between us, breaking Harper's chokehold.

Harper flew at me with payback raging in her eyes, but I shoved my bent knees forward, slamming her in the chest with everything I had.

Harper stumbled a few steps, then caught herself on the sink behind her. Recovering quickly, she lunged for me once more.

"Get away from her!" Lainey yelled at the same time she swung her fisted hands into Harper's jaw.

When Harper crumpled to the ground, then slithered to her side on the floor, Lainey unclenched her hands and threw herself in my arms, babbling, "God, I was so scared, Nara. I *told* you she was a lunatic!"

I hugged Lainey for a second, then pulled back to stare at Harper. She looked so innocent and peaceful lying on the floor, her chest rising and falling in steady breaths. "We need to call the police," I said in a shaky voice. "Do you have your phone?"

Lainey rubbed trembling fingers under her wet eyes to wipe away mascara smears. "There's an officer patrolling the parking lot tonight, remember? We'll go get him."

I nodded. "Did Harper say anything to you before she attacked you?"

"All she said was, 'I'm tired of you getting in my way, taking up all Nara's time." Lainey rolled her eyes. "Crazy, jealous stalker psycho!"

Lainey thought Harper was jealous, but with Harper's

connection to Drake, I was pretty sure her desire to spend time with me had more to do with hoping to get access to my house and stuff, than developing a friendship. She'd attacked me too.

"You go find the officer. I'll meet you outside." I worked hard to calm my voice for Lainey's sake. I wanted to check on Ethan.

Lainey's hands shook as she pinned a curl that had come loose from my hair. "I'm not leaving you here alone with her."

I gestured to Harper's prone body. "She's knocked out, but just in case, I'm going to grab a chair or something to block her in the bathroom."

"Good call." Lainey glanced down at Harper once more and squeezed my hand. "This is crazy!"

I gave her a gentle push toward the door. "Go! I know it's darker that way, but take the senior hall back. It's shorter."

Lainey started toward the senior hall, but she paused at the sounds of fighting going on down the locker hall. I shooed her, mouthing, "Hurry!" Once she was out of sight, I moved fast, grabbing a chair from our study hall classroom to block the bathroom door, but since the door swung inward, I was pretty much out of luck.

When a loud, crashing boom echoed, I dropped the chair and left Harper in the bathroom to backtrack to Ethan.

The screeching and fury reverberating in the sophomore locker hall as I drew closer turned my legs to jelly. I wanted to run in the opposite direction, but I had to know Ethan was okay.

I peered around the corner and covered my mouth to keep from making a sound. Dark marks marred several areas on the floor, a few of the lockers and parts of the ceiling. Claw-like rips gouged through the metal on an entire wall of lockers. At the end of the hall closest to me the floor had a huge hole of crumpled and smashed tile as if something or someone had been slammed into it with terrific force.

Drake stood on the far end of the hall and Ethan stood close to my end, facing each other with murderous looks. They panted and bolted for each other at full speed. Drake snarled and leapt in the air toward Ethan first, but Ethan veered to his left and ran up the side of the lockers, before springing off them in Drake's path.

Unlike Drystan, who'd used at least one handhold to climb, I didn't see Ethan use anything but sheer momentum to run up the side of the lockers. He let out a fierce roar and clotheslined Drake, sending the guy flying back into the lockers once more.

Before Drake could recover, Ethan stood in front of him, grabbing him by the throat. He lifted Drake high against the dented lockers until his dress shoes dangled off the ground. The look on Drake's face was sheer evil as he hammered a hard fist into Ethan's shoulder. The horrific, guttural sounds that came out of him didn't sound human.

When Drake released a grunt of laughter, my insides tensed. "That little bitch of yours actually taught me something. Want to see?" Suddenly Drake curled his legs upward, and guilt rushed through me when he used the same move on Ethan I'd used on the guy in the library. Ethan slammed to the floor, a sickening sound that knocked me in the gut. I bit back a cry as the force of the impact cracked the floor all the way down the hall. Ethan slid several feet, his body spinning like a top, scattering broken floor and ceiling pieces in his wake.

Drake didn't wait for Ethan to recover. He vaulted into a run and took a flying leap after Ethan. I pulled my hand from my mouth, intending to warn Ethan, but he blurred into action. He curled into a roll, then pushed up on the balls of his feet, his head down, hands on the floor...and his *back* to Drake.

While Drake arced in the air toward him, I screamed, but only a wheeze came out. Ethan grasped something lying among the floor rubble and calmly stood. Fisting his hand around a silver-handled weapon—was it a knife?—he looked up, his face a study of focused concentration.

Gravity and momentum pulled Drake toward him, but Ethan didn't move. He took a step back, bent his knees slightly, then jammed his right arm in a backward motion at the very moment Drake landed on him.

Drake's body arched off Ethan's back as if he'd been wounded, yet he didn't pull away. Something held him in place, keeping him from sliding off. That's when I saw the silver tip of something sharp poking through his back. Yellow smoke exploded out of Drake's body like a detonated airbag. The horrific screech that accompanied it made me shudder. Just as quickly as the smoke appeared, it disappeared. In a blink it had vanished.

"For Nara...and Freddie," Ethan gritted out in a tone of finality, then twisted his hand to the left.

As Drake's body exploded into a fog of thick dust, I gaped while the famous saying about death, ashes, and dust popped morbidly into my mind. I blinked, trying to see past the hazy cloud of Drake's ashes. *What had Ethan used to obliterate him?* Just as Ethan straightened, I caught a brief glimpse of a sword in his hand with a black feather decorating the blade and a raven symbol near the hilt.

Ethan tilted his head up, but I jerked out of sight, throwing my back against the cool wall. I wasn't ready for Ethan to know I'd seen him. I needed to process everything first. I took a deep breath and pulled off my heels, then ran toward the senior hall.

Once I ran outside, I leaned against the building to gulp in the cool night air.

I'd just slipped back into my shoes when Mrs. Meacham touched my shoulder, her forehead creased in concern. "Are you all right, Nara?"

Lainey came running up with the police officer, an expectant look on her face. I waved Mrs. Meacham off, saying, "I'm fine," and then let Lainey drag me in to the school alongside the police officer.

When we reached the bathroom we'd left Harper in, Lainey and I were shocked to find it empty.

While Lainey followed the officer back outside to give him all the information she could about Harper, I started toward the gym to find Matt for Lainey when he came walking out. "Where's Lainey?" he asked, frowning. "I thought she was with you."

After I'd explained what had happened, Matt's expression turned fierce. He started to go after Lainey, but I grabbed his hand. "Please just be there for her tonight, Matt. She's been through a lot."

He set his lips in a grim line. "You don't have to worry about Lainey, Nara. I'll take good care of her."

The look on his face said so much more. He'd really fallen for Lainey. "Tell her I'll call her tomorrow," I said, smiling my appreciation. I turned to head back inside the gym, but paused when my gaze landed on Ethan standing to the left of the gym entrance.

He had a baseball-sized hole in his jacket sleeve, disheveled hair, a bruise on his jaw, and a couple of splotches of white ceiling and floor tile on his pants that he hadn't been able to wipe away, but otherwise he looked unharmed. Regardless how I felt about what I'd just witnessed, I was glad he was safe. I stepped close and wrapped my arms around his waist. "Where'd that insane guy go?" I asked, hoping he'd share.

Ethan settled his arms around me, then jerked his chin toward Lainey talking to the police officer. "What's going on?"

I was disappointed he'd avoided answering my question, but maybe he wanted to talk to me about it in private. Where had he learned to fight like that? What *was* Drake? And should I feel any sympathy for someone who'd bragged about killing Freddie and had every intent to kill me in an equally brutal way? Did Ethan know why Drake was after me? Where'd he get a sword that looked just like the one on his back? And he was upset with *me* for holding back? Question after question popped in my mind, making me dizzy, so I focused on answering his question instead.

While I told him what happened in the bathroom, and then explained that Harper was Drake's girlfriend, he ran his hands over my shoulders and arms as if proving to himself that I was okay. He gently cupped my face where Harper had slapped me and stared at me with a combination of worry, guilt, and frustration as he murmured, "But I only saw the one."

I frowned. "What do you mean?"

Ethan shook his head. "Never mind. So she got away?"

I snorted my disgust. "Yes. What happened with her boyfriend?" I looked him straight in the eyes, my gaze pleading, *Please tell me what happened in the hall, Ethan. Tell me the truth!*

Ethan stiffened, his jaw hardening. "He'll never bother you again. Don't worry."

He'd told the partial truth at least. I sighed and laid my head against his chest, seeking his warmth and strong, protective embrace. "Unfortunately, I have something he wants, something he's already killed for once. I don't think he'll stop until he gets it. And even if he really is gone, I have a feeling Harper will eventually come looking for it."

Ethan tilted my chin, his stunned gaze boring into me. "Something he wanted? What are you talking about? What did he want?"

His confusion was sincere. Ethan didn't know what Drake was after. "It's a long story that started with me researching ravens as a way to stay connected to you while you were gone, and it ended with me finding out that we're *both* connected to ravens. In different ways, but definitely connected."

Ethan clasped my shoulders. "We're *both* connected? How?" As soon as he asked, his face set in determined lines. "I need to know everything that's happened. This can't wait, Nara. Are you ready to leave now?"

My questions can't wait either. I nodded. "I just have to run inside and get my keys."

Lainey and Matt walked inside the gym with me. While Matt went to tell Drystan that he and Lainey were heading out and to ask him to bring me my keys, Lainey hooked her arm in mine.

I gave her arm a gentle squeeze and frowned at the slight red marks marring her pale neck. "You'll probably bruise pretty bad, which will freak your dad out. If you don't want him putting you under lock and key, I suggest scarves until they're gone. Until they find Harper, we're going to have to keep an extra eye open."

"You sound like you've been through this before," she rasped, respect reflecting in her tone. "I had no idea you knew all those moves. Thank you for saving my life."

Sadly, there seems to be a glut of people trying to strangle me lately. I forced a confident smile. "We both have Drystan to thank. He's taught me a lot about self-defense. And you wield a mighty two-fisted hook yourself."

When she snorted and glanced down at her swollen knuckles, I asked, "What did you want to talk to me about in the bathroom, anyway?"

"I was going to ask what Jared wanted, but—" She broke off, then shrugged. "After what just happened, I really don't care. Matt and me…" Her gaze ate up every inch of Matt as he talked to Drystan on the dance floor.

Her happy sigh made me laugh. "I told you he liked you! Who'd have thought that with all the scheming you two did, you'd end up falling for each other? Ha, I love the irony. I'm so happy for you both."

She gave me a knowing grin. "I'm glad to see Ethan showed. Though he had to have already been on his way when I sent him the picture."

"What picture?"

She clicked on her photo button on her phone and showed me. She'd sent the picture she'd taken while she helped me get dressed yesterday, the one of me with the sexy pout. She'd also added the text underneath…*This is what you're missing!*

No wonder Ethan came in blazing. I was just shaking my head at her when Matt strolled up and wrapped his arm around her waist. "Ready to go, Lainey?"

As she nodded, he looked at me. "Drystan said he'd bring your keys in a sec."

After Lainey and Matt left, it wasn't long before Drystan came off the dance floor. Sweat glistened in his hair and he had a girl hanging on each arm.

He nodded to the girls and said, "I'll meet you ladies at the food table in a minute."

I watched them walk off and giggle to each other with an amused smirk. "You *so* didn't need a good luck charm tonight."

"Come with me," Drystan said in a serious tone. All sense of the happy-go-lucky Drystan he'd projected to his dance partners completely disappeared as he clasped my hand and pulled me over to a café table off to the right of the band's stage. After he handed me my keys, he slid a chair out, then grabbed what he'd hidden under the table. "You left this behind."

I stared at the bundle of silver silk in his hand, and my face flamed when I remembered where I'd left my mother's shawl. I'd been so distracted by Ethan's heart-stopping kiss that I'd completely forgotten I'd dropped it in the coach's office. Drystan must've found it when he was there with his buddies.

"Thanks," I said past my gulp of embarrassment, pulling the material out of his hand.

I lifted the shawl and two items unrolled from the silky material, falling to the floor. I bent to grab my mask, while Drystan retrieved Ethan's.

When I reached for Ethan's mask, he didn't release it. My gaze locked with his worried green one as he spoke in a hushed voice, "I don't see him. At all."

Welcome to my world. I don't see Ethan either. I nodded my understanding, my mind far away. I was ready to be alone with Ethan. "I know."

Drystan frowned and shook his head, refusing to release the black mask. "No, Nara, what I'm saying is…I see darkness. Total 'effing blackness!"

Ethan definitely had an on-the-verge-of-eruption vibe I'd never seen before tonight. From the way he acted when he saw me with Drystan, to the fight in the hall with Drake. That fight was beyond frightening—the violence, the powerful strength, the focused detachment as he rammed him with a sword!—but even though I couldn't explain any of that yet, through it all, Ethan had still thought of defending me and another innocent person. He was *still* Ethan. Drake was pure evil. Of that I was certain.

I laid my hand on Drystan's jacket sleeve and nodded. "I'm the light, Drystan. I'll be fine."

I started to turn, but Drystan clasped my wrist. "If there's enough darkness, even light can be completely consumed by it, Nara."

"Not if it's the brightest kind of darkness." I smiled at his baffled look and squeezed his hand, then walked away.

CHAPTER 29

*E*than stood just inside the entrance of the gym with his arms folded. A sour look creased his face as I approached.

"I don't like him touching you, Nara."

"I know." I sighed and breezed past, leaving him with nothing to do but follow me out of the entrance and into the cool night air.

Before I'd taken more than ten steps, he grasped my elbow and pulled me to the side. Taking the shawl out of my hands, he said, "It's freezing out here," then wrapped it around my shoulders the way I'd worn it earlier.

Once he finished tying it, he said, "What'd he say to you?"

I tilted my head and decided to tell him the truth. "He thinks you're bad for me. That you'll consume me."

Ethan's gaze narrowed and his jaw muscle jumped as he gazed back toward the gym with sheer dislike.

I ran my finger along the twitching muscle. "Do you plan to consume me, Ethan?"

His gaze snapped back to mine and he clasped my shoulders, pulling me so close I had to crane my neck to meet his darkened gaze. "Not in the way he meant."

Every bone in my body melted at the heated look in his gaze as he stared at my lips with hungry intent. But instead of kissing me, he pressed his lips tenderly to my forehead and spoke in a desperate whisper, "You totally break me apart, Nara. You're the only one who has the power to do that. *You* consume me."

I wrapped my arms around his waist and met his tortured gaze, hoping he saw all the love I felt for him reflected in my eyes. "Take me home and then we can talk."

～

"WHAT ABOUT YOUR CAR?" I asked Ethan as he pulled mine into the garage.

He cut the engine. "I'll get it later."

The moment we walked inside, Houdini came charging at Ethan in a full-on attack mode. I screamed out, "No, Houdini!" at the same time Ethan grabbed either side of Houdini's jowls and pulled him down to the floor.

"Settle, boy!" he said in a fierce, commanding tone.

While Houdini alternately squirmed and growled as if he were confused as to what to do, Ethan glanced over his shoulder. "Hold him for a second while I take my jacket off."

I grabbed Houdini's collar. "I'm so sorry! He's never done this before." It wasn't easy holding a hundred-pound straining ball of muscle at bay while Ethan shrugged out of his coat. "Help!" I said when my heels began to skid across the floor. Houdini was growling less, but he was sniffing the air like crazy.

Ethan tossed his jacket on the floor and Houdini yanked out of my hold to dive onto the coat with vicious ferocity.

"That should keep him busy for a while." Ethan smirked, then clasped my hand and pulled me upstairs as Houdini began to shred the jacket.

"But your coat?" I resisted, freaked out by Houdini's behavior and the sound of tearing fabric.

Ethan snorted and tugged me along. "He recognized evil's scent all over me. He's the perfect guard dog. You'll have to tell me how you convinced your mom to let you have him."

Was that an indirect reference to Drake? With one last look at Houdini downstairs, I let Ethan pull me down the hall and into my room.

After he shut my door, I said, "Mom let me get Houdini after I almost got shot."

Ethan whipped around. "What! Someone tried to shoot you? Why are you just now telling me?"

"I'm not even sure if it was an accident or intended," I replied, holding my hands up in a calming manner. I shrugged. "Well, at least that's why Mom agreed. I've always wanted a dog, but after someone broke into my room and Gran got hurt, I was determined to protect myself and my stuff, hence...Houdini."

"Hold on...slow down. Tell me everything from the beginning," Ethan said just as Houdini began scratching at the door to be let in.

Ethan opened the door and grabbed Houdini's collar when he tried to bound into my room. "Not tonight, buddy. I'm taking care of Nara." He pointed to the doorway. "You can guard the door."

With a quick bark and a look to me, and then Ethan as if to say, "But, this is what I always do," Houdini held his ground.

Ethan patted his head. "She's safe." Houdini looked at me once more, then trotted back out and pivoted in a quick circle before laying down right in front of the door.

Once Ethan shut my door again, I shook my head in amazement and pulled off my heels. "You're going to have to teach me how you do that. He listens to me really well, but not *that* well."

Ethan clasped my hand and tugged me over to sit on my bed, then he grabbed the chair from my desk and set it across from me. As soon as he was seated, he grasped my hands. "Tell me everything that's happened."

"Before I tell you anything, I need to know...are things better with your parents now?"

Frustration flashed through his eyes, but he gave a quick nod. "It's as good as it'll get."

That was something at least. I took a deep breath, then said,

"You should always trust your instincts when it comes to me. If you get a vibe something's wrong, it probably is."

Ethan released one of my hands and jammed his through his hair, frustration written on his face. "Why, Nara? Why didn't you tell me the truth?"

I clasped his free hand in both of mine. "I didn't want to pull you away from your family. I wanted you to have the time you needed to heal, not just for you, but for us. It's what you said you needed, remember?"

Ethan went pale and I thought I saw remorse flicker across his face before he closed his eyes tight. Then his fierce blue eyes drilled into me. "You always come first, Nara. Keeping you safe is most important to me. Above all else. Do you understand?"

When I looked down and nodded, he clasped my chin and lifted my head so I had to look at him. Running his thumb across my bottom lip, he pulled it from my teeth. "Now tell me everything."

And so I did. I told him about Fate's new scare tactics and the guy who attacked me in the library. When I got to the part about my library attacker wanting me to give him my journal and how I flat-out refused to give it up, Ethan looked confused. "What journal?"

"Oh!" I jumped up and retrieved both his leather journal and Freddie's blue book from under my mattress. Ethan turned the chair sideways as I handed him the journal. "This was supposed to be a surprise for you when you returned, but under the circumstances, I may as well give it to you now."

Ethan thumbed through my raven journal, while I paced and told him the rest. Well, most of it. Just like I protected Ethan's secret, I protected Drystan's as well, making up another reason as to how Drystan and I recovered the books from Drake's locker. I also left out my training and my lucid dream concerning Drystan—Ethan was jealous enough.

I refused to discuss the news about my dad. I wasn't ready to pick open that fresh wound on top of the others I was tearing apart. When I was done, I stopped pacing and cracked open the window for some much-needed air. I was flushed with anger and exhausted from reliving the emotional memories. Telling him brought it all back in its crushing, heartrending glory.

Ethan stood and cupped my face, his expression shattered. "Don't you *ever* put yourself at risk like this for me again, Nara. I'm not worth it!"

I clasped his hands, pulling them down. "Didn't you hear me? Yes, this started out about you, but we're connected, Ethan. Somehow, all this raven stuff…I was *supposed* to find that book, my necklace unlocked its secret. Freddie knew I was the one, knew it in his heart." Tears surfaced when I thought of Freddie. "And now he's gone because I thought the book wasn't meant for me."

Ethan pulled me close and his hand trembled as he pressed my head to his shoulder. "That Drake bastard could've done to you what he did to Freddie, Nara!"

I snorted a half laugh. "That's what Drystan said."

Ethan stiffened. "I'll give the guy that. He's right. As much as I hate to admit it, I owe him for being there for you."

I pulled back slightly and mimicked Drystan's accent. "He's actually a right nice bloke once you get to know him."

"I hate his accent!" Ethan bit out, his face darkening.

I'd tried to lighten the mood, but my comment about Drystan was probably pushing it. I laid my hands on his chest and had to stand on my toes to press a light kiss to his lips. "You must've grown a couple of inches while you were gone," I teased, trying to distract his thoughts from Drystan. Touching his hair, I continued, "I like your haircut. Now I can always see what you're thinking."

With a grim look, Ethan stepped back and sat down in the chair. He rested his forearms on his thighs, then hung his head, saying in a low voice, "What I'm thinking is that I'm not worth your love, Nara. I'm not worth all the effort you went to, the danger you put yourself in for this journal." He paused, flicking his hand to indicate the leather book on my bed. "I don't deserve this."

"Why aren't you worth the effort?" *Had things gone south with his parents?*

"I *am* dark, Nara. I live in the darkness."

"Is this about Drake? About what you did to him?"

Ethan stilled and jerked his gaze to mine, worry swirling in the blue depths. "What did you see?"

"What didn't I see?" I spread my hands wide. "Tonight I saw your eyes turn black as coal, more than once. I witnessed you throw an evil guy across the room like a rag doll, then jam a sword into him that expelled a yellow smoky mist out of his body before disintegrating him into nothing but dust. I saw it all, Ethan, and..." I paused and thought of how Drake had viciously defiled Freddie. I raised my chin a notch. "I'm not sad he's gone."

Ethan blinked a couple of times. "You saw the yellow smoke leave him?"

He sounded shocked. When I slowly nodded, he whispered, "But no one else can see it."

As much as I wanted to drill him with my own questions, his comment reminded me that I had something I wanted to show him. "Hold that thought," I said, then walked over to my desk to turn on my laptop. I sat on my bed and set the laptop on my knees, facing it toward him. "Watch this."

Ethan watched the video I played with a steady gaze. His expression was so hard to read, I couldn't tell if he saw what I had. When it was over, I shut my laptop, then returned it to my desk. Turning to face him across the room, I asked, "What did you see? What caused the airplane to crash?"

He looked at me for a couple of seconds, then simply said, "A ripple rolled across the sky. When the wave shot up right in front of the plane, the disturbance tore its wing off. That's what caused the plane crash."

I waved my arms in relief. "Thank God someone else sees it!"

Ethan's brow furrowed. "No one else could see that?"

I shook my head. "Not that I know of. That video was taken when I was a little girl. Remember that necklace my grandmother gave me, the one that opened the secret closure on Freddie's raven book?" When he nodded, I continued. "That was the day I'd looked up and pointed to empty blue sky *before* the plane crashed. Right after the plane hit the water, a stranger walked up, spoke to me, and then gave my grandmother that necklace."

Ethan shook his head, intrigued. "You must've seen the ripple back then."

I nodded. "That's my guess, yes. Realizing that made me feel better, because I'd seen something similar happen not that long ago on Highway 29. The sky split open, and this whirling dervish of hands, claws, feathers and scales came barreling through, surrounded by a cloud of smoke. The rift caused a car to wreck but when the 'ball of beings' landed on the car, they vanished. Poof. Just like that, as if they were never there in the first place." I squinted, then asked with a hopeful voice, "Have you seen anything like this?"

Ethan set his mouth in a thin line. "No, I haven't. Do you think the stranger your grandmother mentioned in her journal saw it? Did she ever figure out who he was?"

I shook my head. "I don't know. I just know that he gave her the necklace and then just walked away. A tall blond man did the same thing to Freddie. He approached and handed him that book about ravens." I pointed to the blue book on my bed. "He told Freddie to keep it safe and he'd know what to do with it when the time came."

I shifted my gaze back to Ethan. "The point to all of this is... you and I can see things other people can't."

"That doesn't make sense." He shook his head. "We're not the same. Our powers are different."

"But we *are* connected, not just by what we can see, but through the ravens."

"There's so much more going on here," he murmured, his brow creasing in bewilderment as he squeezed his hand in a fist on his knee.

I stepped closer. "Where did you get a sword that looks just like the one on your back? How did you know it would turn Drake to dust? And where did you learn to fight like that?"

He started to speak, then tension edged his face and he bent his head once more. His shoulders slumped as he slid shaky hands through his hair. "I don't deserve you, Nara. God knows I don't." Grasping his hair in tight fists, he continued, "The best thing for you would be for me to walk away…"

No, Ethan! My heart stopped and I took another step, ready to reach for him.

"But I can't let you go. I love you too much," he finished, totally wrecked.

He was torturing himself for no reason. He seemed reluctant to tell me more, as if he thought I'd push him away. Yes, I had questions, tons of questions, but I loved him. I would always love him. "Oh Ethan…" As I reached for his hand, something in alternating colors of red and black slipped out of his black shirt's cuff with his movements, drawing my attention.

He'd twisted the red ribbon and black rubber band that he'd taken from my hair that day we'd spent at the lake and wrapped them around each other, creating a bracelet. The red satin ribbon no longer shined. It looked worn and faded, as if he'd never taken it off. This whole time, he'd kept something of me with him while he was away. The knowledge melted my heart and was exactly what I needed to stave off my questions until later.

I slid my hand on top of the fist in his hair and laced our fingers together. "Why can't you believe that you're worthy of love? You are, you know. Worthy. In so many ways. I love you, Ethan. I'll always love you…'til the wheels fall off."

Ethan exhaled a ragged breath, then wrapped his arms around the back of my thighs and pressed his forehead to my belly.

As soon as I slid my fingers into his thick locks, he looked up and slowly stood until he towered above me. Cupping my jaw, he slid his thumb along it, then pressed a tender kiss to my lips, murmuring against my mouth, "You'll always be my Sunshine."

My heart full of love, I turned my back to him and glanced over my shoulder to my zipper, saying, "This is my choice, Ethan. Real and in person."

CHAPTER 30

*E*than rested his hands on my shoulders, his thumbs sliding along the back of my neck as love and desire reflected in his hooded gaze. Leaning close, he whispered in my ear, "Imagining can't touch real. Ever."

I learned *that* lesson in the basketball coach's closet, I thought, shivering. Ethan had made me feel a hundred different emotions at once with his intimate kisses, and he was doing it again now. "I know."

I was surprised when he didn't move to unzip my dress. Instead a gentle tug tickled my scalp as he pulled a hairpin out. I bit my lip as the pin dropped to the floor. He reached for the one curl that had fallen, then slowly wound the end around his finger and lifted it to his nose. "Sunshine and floral shampoo. I've missed your sweet smell."

I smiled and fell in love with him just a little bit more.

One by one, he pulled my hairpins out until my hair flowed around my shoulders in a cascade of blonde ringlets. When he brushed my hair over my left shoulder, I closed my eyes in anticipation. I was so wound up, my heart thrumming at a humming bird's pace, I couldn't think straight.

The sensation of his fingers brushing against the side of my face surprised me even more. I swallowed an intake of breath as he slid my earring out of my right ear. After he'd done the same with the other earring, I'd held back my rampant breathing so long, I thought for sure I was going to pass out.

It took me a second to register that his fingers were touching my zipper. "Are you sure, Nara?" he asked in a rough rasp, sounding just as tortured and revved as I felt.

I held the front of my dress and waited. "More than anything."

He started to slowly unzip the material, but then he pulled the zipper down in a fast rip, gritting out, "Where the hell did all these bruises and scrapes come from?"

Crap! I'd completely forgotten about the intense training I'd done with Drystan this week. My spine and lower back were pretty beat up. "It's not what you think..." I began and started to turn, but he grabbed my shoulders in a tight grip and held me in place as his fierce gaze swept over my back. "I've just been training with Drystan."

His fingers dug into my shoulders. "What kind of training?"

I shrugged. "After everything that's happened, he thought it was a good idea if I learned self-defense."

Ethan skimmed his fingers along my spine, then snapped his angry gaze back to my face. "And he did this by beating the hell out of you?" With a hissing intake of breath, his eyes swirled bluish black. "I'm going to kick that bastard's ass for hurting you like this."

I covered his hand on my shoulder with one of mine. "Ethan, Drystan didn't do this. The ground and pavement did. I was learning to jump from high places onto hard surfaces by doing safe landing rolls."

Ethan gave a fierce scowl. "How is *that* self-defense?"

"It's not. It's a parkour move, but in learning the moves, it'll give me the advantage and a much greater chance of getting away safely, hence needing to 'perfect' a good landing roll."

Ethan cupped his other hand on my shoulder too, anger and guilt dueling in his gaze. "If I'd been around, you wouldn't have had to worry about defending yourself, Nara."

I smiled and squeezed his hand. "You can't be everywhere at once. Learning self-defense is good for me."

His dark gaze drilled into me. "Then I'll teach you."

I was only a week into my "month of training" promise to Drystan. I didn't want to discuss self-defense any more. I turned around and I let my dress slither down my legs. Once it reached my ankles, I put a shaky hand on Ethan's shoulder so I could step out of it.

Ethan had grasped my other hand to hold me steady, but the heated look in his gaze as it slid over my strapless lacy white bra and matching underwear only jacked my nerves higher. A hot flush of embarrassed heat, mixed with raging longing for him, spread across my skin.

As I kicked my dress away, the anger slipped from his face and he wrapped his hands around my waist to slowly pull me close. "You're so beautiful," he whispered, his voice husky with want. "I wish I could draw you like this."

I grasped his shoulders and gasped. "Don't you ever!" All I could think about was how that guy at school had grabbed Ethan's notebook full of drawings and flipped through it while Ethan was in the bathroom.

Ethan let out a low chuckle, his fingers tightening on my skin as he bent to nuzzle my neck. "This would be for my eyes only, Sunshine." He lifted his head and continued in a rough, dangerous rumble, "But you're right, I don't want anyone but me to see you like this. Ever."

I smiled shyly up at him as I unbuttoned his black shirt with trembling fingers all the way to his belt. Once I'd tugged it from his pants, I pushed the shirt past his thick shoulders, and the soft material slid out of my fingers to the floor, revealing his broader chest.

I trailed my hands along his skin. "I know you and your dad were doing a lot of sports stuff, but God, Ethan...you're beyond ripped!" He'd been fit before he left, but he no longer had an ounce of body fat left on him. As my fingers moved down his six-pack abs, I smiled when I heard his sharp intake of breath. He was just as affected by my touch.

When I reached for the button on his pants, Ethan swept me up in his arms and stepped toward my bed. I wrapped my arms around his shoulders and pouted. "Not fair, Ethan!"

But his lips landed on mine, cutting off my protest. As he

laid me back against my comforter and staked his claim on my heart all over again, I sighed blissfully against his mouth. I gripped his warm, hard shoulders and pulled him against me, claiming him back with equal intensity.

Sliding his hands along my waist, Ethan surprised me when he broke our kiss to roll me over on my belly.

"What are you doing?" I began, then gasped in excitement when he pressed a kiss to my shoulder.

"Saying I'm sorry I wasn't here," he rasped right before he moved to kiss the center of my back.

As he slid lower, I squirmed with anticipation under his hold, while my heart constricted at the realization he planned to kiss every last one of my bruises and scrapes.

Ethan cupped my hipbone in a firm grip, then slid his thumb gingerly over a scrape curving along it. Warm breath hovered over the wound and he murmured, "You're mine to protect, from Fate and everything else."

He pressed his mouth to my wound with such heart-wrenching tenderness, strong emotions rushed hard and fast, capturing my breath and then whooshing it out of me in shallow gusts. I loved him so much. "I like your kind of apology." I sounded breathless, but I didn't care. I moved so he could easily find the next bruise. "I think you missed a few."

My heart pounds as I run through the endless forest, full of dark shadows and looming trees. I zip my leather coat closed to stave off the cold, scanning the trees for shadows left and right, then spin in a circle. Where's the black amorphous figure? How long will it take for him to appear and form into the semblance of a human shape, even though he's far from human? He has no conscience, no feelings...only vast power, which he wields with Machiavellian viciousness.

Even though I'm asleep beside Ethan, I hadn't slipped on my crystal necklace to purposely seek Fate out in my dreams the way I'd done in the past. Yet Fate has somehow managed to zap me into the woods anyway. Did he bring me here so he can fulfill his promise of retribution?

Anger ripples through me and I stop running. I'm done looking over my shoulder, working myself into a freaked-out frenzy. I pant and turn in a full circle, screaming out, "Show yourself. I know you're here!"

"Welcome back!" Fate says from behind me in a gleeful voice.

I whip around, arms raised, fists in full-on defense mode.

"Puh-leeze!" Fate snorts in arrogant derision. He crosses his shadowy arms in a relaxed stance, then pretends to lean his nebulous body against a tree, his bottomless eye sockets staring at me with dark intensity. "I see you solicited your Corvus friend's help once more." A pleased smile replaces the downturned slit of a mouth on his dark face. "Didn't I tell you that you'd seek me out again?"

"I didn't—" I pause and lower my fists slightly. "You called him Corvus. What do you know about him?"

Fate shrugs. "He's none of my concern."

I frown. "Is that what you meant when you said you don't know his fate? How can you not know it?" I curl my lip, annoyed to admit it. "Everyone has a fate."

"Now you acknowledge me?" Fate snorts, then waves his hand dismissively. "Correction, every being has a destiny, a purpose, if you will." He points to his chest, puffing it up. "Consider me the journeyman, helping those in your realm along their path, keeping them on the straight and narrow. Fate—which you ignore ad nauseam—leads them to their ultimate destiny. Your friend doesn't fall under my purview. He exists outside my realm."

Ethan was right. Fate can't see him. Is that why Ethan has never been in my dreams? How can he exist outside of my realm? That didn't make sense. Ethan is a person, just like me. *"What is Corvus?"*

Fate's brow puckers in an are-you-really-that-stupid look. "It's a raven. Technically, the term is Corvus corax."

I glare at him. "I know that! I'm asking about the Corvus that exists outside of your realm."

He exhales heavily, his patience growing thin. "The Corvus maintain balance in your realm. Think of them as 'equalizer' enforcers."

Them? Enforcers? Equalizer? Is that what the yin-yang

raven symbol on the tattoo sword on Ethan's back represents, balance? What does he enforce?

I open my mouth to ask the questions pinging in my head, but Fate yawns and holds up his hand. "Ask the Order if you want to know more. This subject bores me."

Order? Another term I don't know. He might as well be speaking a different language. *"Who's the Order?"*

Fate snaps his fingers and makes an annoyed whilst sound. "Why did you seek me?"

He hadn't attacked me yet, which means he's either toying with me or he's waiting for me to ask him something. I shake my head. "You pulled me here somehow. I'm not here of my own free will."

When Fate's bottomless, empty eye sockets move in an impression of a human eye roll, an eerie shiver slides through me.

He leans forward and lets out a slow, teeth-grinding chuckle. "You changed the rules, Nara, which means your 'free will' won't save you this time."

Dread knots my stomach. Fate hadn't attacked me, because he knows that I can't use the same tactic I had before to protect myself from him. He knows he has all the time in the world.

Knowing about my dad's life, about his role in constantly changing people's fate on a massive scale, my fear of Fate intensifies tenfold. When I'd faced Fate before, I'd naively believed I could beat him because I had "fair and right" on my side. After all, Fate had bent the rules of nature by trying to eliminate me before it was my fated time to die. But now that I'd learned how my father's actions had fueled Fate's fury for over two decades, in a perverse sort of way, I understand Fate's need to exact justice. But that doesn't mean I'll let him take his pound of flesh without a fight.

"Well?" he says, sounding impatient.

Why is Fate engaging me? *"Why am I here? What do you want?"*

Fate straightens against the tree. "Did you really think you could change the past without consequences?" Folding his arms, he crosses his shadowy legs at the ankles, then shoots the full impact of his icy disapproval in my direction. The force sends a shiver all the way down my spine. "I thought your father was a menace, but your actions, even on such a small scale, are far more dangerous. You will cease immediately!"

When he mentioned my father with that sneer of malice lacing his tone, all the justified rage that I'd buried under the pile of "stuff I don't want to think about right now" after I'd learned the truth about my father, rushes to the front of my mind.

"How does it feel to have your house, your whole world, turned upside down by an outside force, Fate?" I goad, folding my arms over my chest to cover my false bravado. I didn't initiate that lucid dream on purpose. I didn't even know how I'd changed the past, but since Fate doesn't seem to know that I'll use it to my advantage. "That's what you did to my home, you twisted bastard! You stole my father from me and tore my family apart. We could've been happy!"

Fate doesn't lash out, but instead answers in a calm, cajoling tone, "And you still can be."

I blink at him and my quivering insides suddenly still. "What are you talking about?"

He lifts his hand toward his face and pretends to inspect nonexistent fingernails. With a sigh, he uncurls his fingers one at a time, flicking them in a puff of swirling smoke as if he has all the time in the world.

"Tell me!"

Fate looks up and narrows his hollowed eye sockets in devious slits. "Not until you promise to never change the past again."

I have to know what he knows about my father. Please let him be okay. Let him be alive. "Fine!" I snap. "I promise to never consciously change the past again."

Fate pushes off the tree, then steps close, bending toward me with a pleased smile. His coldness seeps all the way into my bones. "Now that you've given your oath, if you break your promise, little Nara, I can strip you of your power."

I gape and drop my fists to my sides. "You can't do that!"

He straightens to his full, towering height, an arrogant smile on his face. "Try me."

I clench my closed fists so tight my nails dig into my palms. I can't believe he's tricked me into agreeing without disclosing all the facts. Fury, justice, and payback slither through my veins like baby snakes full of concentrated venom.

Before I can speak, Fate sighs dramatically. "He's alive."

As all my tense muscles relax and I mumble, "Thank God!"

Fate snickers. "Well, you could *be a happy family if that's what he still wants. He didn't mention your mom in that last video—the recent one—now did he?"*

Fate pointed something out I hadn't realized while watching the videos. With purposeful intent, he'd dangled the carrot, given me false hope, then gleefully planted the seed of doubt, hoping it would rot me from the inside.

I grit my teeth and narrow my gaze. "I didn't change that dream on purpose. No conscious *effort was used." I shrug my innocence. "Guess it was just pure self-preservation kicking in, like when I made my promise to you," I finish with a smirk.*

Fate let out a furious roar and before I can move, he attacks me with lightning speed, slamming his body against mine.

I sail through the air, my arms and legs flailing. He hit me with such force, I can't even scream as I glance back and see a tree in my path. I try to turn to avoid hitting it, but my shoulder clips the trunk. Bone-jarring pain rips through my body as it spins straight toward the ground.

I land on my side with a loud ooumph, *skidding along damp leaves and bumpy forest underbrush. Once I finally stop moving, my hip and shoulder throb and a handful of leaves are jammed inside my coat.*

I twist around, looking for Fate. He's taking his time making his way in my direction. The fact he isn't rushing terrifies me more than anything. He's going to drag this out as long as he possibly can. My dad might believe he's covered my marker in life, but in Fate's world I'll be covering his.

I push to my feet and ignore the pain radiating along the right side of my body as I shake the leaves out of my coat.

I don't want to die here! I jerk my gaze around to see if there's a place I can hide. There's nothing but rows and rows of endless trees that are too thin to hide behind.

But I am asleep, so why can't I run much longer than in real life?

And so I do. I run from Fate. For a while, I evade his physical assaults, but he ups his speed, which forces me to change tactics. The next time he gets close, I wait until he's almost on me, then dodge around a tree, since I'd seen him avoid them earlier. As he bounces off the tree, I raise my fist in silent victory.

But my victory's brief and he comes after me with hypersonic speed. I can only dodge around so many trees for so long. When Fate suddenly disappears behind me, I glance back to see where he's gone even as I keep running. I don't believe for one second he's given up. Just as I shift my gaze forward, he reappears right in front of me. I bounce off his cold body and hit the ground with a powerful force.

As I look up at Fate staring down at me with a cold smile, my stomach churns. This isn't a battle I'll win. Leaves fall around him, hitting his head and shoulders before bouncing off.

"You're not giving up that easily, are you?" He spreads his arms wide. "I really thought Jonathan's little girl was made of much stronger stuff."

Another leaf falls and instead of sliding off, it sticks to his head. Before the cool wind can whip it away, Fate smacks it off, grunting his annoyance. "Well?"

"It's sad that you're wasting your time on one girl," I say even as I stare at the trees beyond his head and wonder, Why can't I use the leaves? *In this dream world, the trees were still full of leaves in colors of red, yellow, orange, and shades of purple.*

"Your dad keeps re-stitching new paths in my painstakingly balanced web, but you..." he points to me, "you put your hand inside and spin it around, ripping my web to shreds."

When a clump of leaves falls from the canopy of trees above, I wish more would quickly follow. Just as the thought enters my head, more leaves begin to fall in huge colorful sets. My heart pumps faster. Had I done that? *I sit up, then stand, brushing the leaves off my hands. "Do you really think I sit around trying to come up with ways to beat you?" I say, while thinking,* Form a whirlwind. *As the leaves begin to spin, my heart beats harder.* Amazing!

"Yes, I do!" he hisses.

Engulf him, *I order the leaf funnel, then say, "Well, maybe in this one instance."*

The whirlwind of leaves spin into him with hurricane force, quickly dispersing his form. As fast as Fate disintegrates, he reforms a few feet outside of the funnel of leaves.

Instead of displaying anger, he's clapping his shadowy hands.

"You've consciously manipulated your dream environment. Your power is mine!"

I tense for a second, then exhale and smile. *"You might want to recall the vow I made. This world isn't my past. That was my promise...that I wouldn't consciously change my past."*

Fate fists his hands by his sides, then begins to vibrate so fast I can't see him. Now that's *anger and he's about to blow. I need time to get away.*

Hit a home run! *I tell the funnel. It turns sideways, then smacks into Fate, hitting him so hard he flies through three trees, cutting them in half as he drills through them.*

I take off running and Fate comes after me in fast pursuit, but this time I use the environment around me. Move in his way. Don't let him past, *I tell the trees. Loud, resounding thumps sound behind me again and again, followed by Fate's bellowing roar, "Enough!"*

Suddenly everything disappears. I can't even see a floor under my feet. No forest. No trees. Nothing to manipulate.

I stop running and turn.

Fate approaches, a victorious smile on his smoky face. "Now it's just you and me."

And me, *I hear a voice in my head, yet it spoke in Latin.* Open your hand.

It's Ethan, but different. I realize it's the same Ethan from my dream before, the one who sounds older, wiser, like several voices at once.

I glance down and both my hands are curled into fists by my side. I uncurl my right hand.

Your other hand, Nara.

I lift my left hand and slowly uncurl it. Even though nothing's there, something brushes across my palm at the same time Fate yells, "No!"

CHAPTER 31

*J*jerked awake, my heart running full speed as something slid off my palm and along my fingers. Patch stood on the bed beside my hand. With a quiet *raaack*, he lifted his head and pulled at the chain, slipping the crystal completely away from my fingers and onto the comforter.

"Thank you, Patch!" I whispered shakily and pulled the sheet up higher as I laid my head back on the pillow to catch my breath.

"What is it?" Ethan sat up in the dim light, blinking to wake up. When he saw Patch, he frowned. "We shouldn't have left that window cracked." He shooed at the bird. "Go on! I can't believe you followed me here."

I sat up on my elbow. "Followed you? Patch has been here with me the whole time you were gone."

Ethan shook his head, but then paused when he noticed what Patch held in his beak. "What's he doing with your necklace?"

I pushed my hair out of my face. "Saving my life. I let him play with the necklace on my nightstand, and I guess he dropped it in my bed. I must've touched it in my sleep, and since you and I were sleeping, it was the perfect combination. Fate zapped me to his world for a battle of wills."

Ethan glared at the necklace Patch toyed with. "We need to destroy that crystal."

"It was a gift from my aunt. I'm not destroying it. I'll just lock it away." At the moment, I was more interested in what Fate had told me about him. I tilted my head and held his gaze. "What's Corvus, Ethan?"

Ethan had started to run his fingers through his mussed hair, but his hand stilled. He glanced at Patch, then shooed at the bird once more. "It's a raven."

"I'm talking about Corvus from another realm," I said in a calm tone.

"Another realm?" His brows drew down, confusion flitting across his face. "Where did you hear that?"

I shrugged. "The last time I faced Fate, he said he didn't know your fate. While I was there with him, I asked him why he couldn't see your fate."

Ethan stared at me intently. "What did he say?"

"He called you Corvus and said you have a destiny—a purpose—but he couldn't see your fate because you exist outside of this realm."

Ethan shook his head. "That doesn't make any sense. I exist." He hit his chest. "I'm here!"

Patch squawked at his raised voice, then hopped to my nightstand to play with the paper cube. I could tell Ethan recognized the term Corvus, but the rest was new and it freaked him out. I laid my hand on his shoulder. "It makes sense why you're the only one I can't see in my dreams."

Ethan cupped my face, his troubled gaze locking with mine. "I'm here, Nara! I'm right here."

I touched his jaw. "What *aren't* you telling me?"

Ethan's gaze shuttered, then he pushed the covers back and slipped his hand in his pants pocket. I sighed at the reminder he'd refused to take his pants off last night, and he wouldn't let me take anything else off either.

He pulled out a long chain with a flat silver inch-and-a-half wide disk dangling from it, then slipped the necklace over my head, saying solemnly, "Never take this off. Not even when you take a shower. Don't let anyone see it. Keep it hidden under your clothes. It'll keep you safe. When I get back, I'll tell you what I know."

I'd started to glance down at the disk on the necklace when his comment registered. I pulled my eyes back to his. "Back? You're leaving again?"

He shook his head. "I'm just going to get the rest of my stuff. I'll be back on Monday at the latest."

"Oh." Relief flitted through me as my gaze slipped back to the silver disk. It was the same yin-yang raven symbol as the one on his sword tattoo. "Where'd you get this? I've searched everywhere on the Internet for any mention of this symbol and found nothing."

Ethan lifted my chin. "Thank you for spending all that time on my journal, Nara, but I was serious when I asked you to let me do this on my own."

To hear him say that in person hurt even more. He must've seen in it my eyes because his gaze softened. "I'm trying to protect you. I think your Internet searches have attracted attention. And that's why Drake and that guy from the library wanted your journal."

"I got the impression they were working for the same boss." I paused, then frowned. "What's weird is that it was almost like they shared the same brain too, based on the things Drake knew that had taken place between me and the guy in the library."

Ethan stiffened. "I doubt you'll have to worry about that guy from the library."

I shrugged, since I didn't plan to go back there. "Regardless, there's nothing in that journal that anyone couldn't find on the Internet." As soon as I spoke, I realized that the raven symbol on the necklace was unique.

"What is it?" Ethan asked.

I pointed to the necklace. "I drew this symbol in your journal from memory. The guy in the library saw it when I dropped the book and it fell open." I touched the necklace once more. "Where did you get this?"

"I found it." He shook his head and snorted. "I wasn't even looking for it, but I was drawn right to it."

"You found it in Michigan?"

He wrapped his arm around my shoulder and kissed my temple. "I was taking a tour through a turn-of-the-century house and I discovered it hidden in a drawer."

"You took it?" I couldn't believe he'd remove something from private property.

Ethan shook his head. "I told you, I was drawn to it. Watch this." He lifted the medallion in his hand, held it for a second, then set the disk in my palm.

It felt like an oven-warmed stone. Awed, I met his gaze. "How'd you do that?"

He shrugged. "I don't know. It warms to my touch, so I didn't feel guilty taking it. I was led to it for a reason." Letting the necklace fall, he gripped my shoulders. "I mean it, Nara. Don't take it off. Understand?"

"Why?"

"It'll protect you," he said, his brow creasing with worry.

My eyes widened. "Protect me from what?"

"From guys like Drake."

"Where'd you find that sword you used on him? And don't tell me it was one of the swords from Mr. Martin's Civil War shadow box," I said, giving him a stern look.

Without a word, Ethan grasped my waist and settled me on his lap, facing him. Taking my left hand, he placed it on his right shoulder, then closed his eyes.

A few seconds later, a cold hardness began to form under my fingers. I jerked my hand back and gasped.

Ethan's grip around my waist tightened and his lips set in a grim line. "My tattoo is definitely permanent."

"Was that the hilt? It's...real?" My hand shook as I tentatively slid my palm across his shoulder once more. This time I only felt firm muscles bunch under my fingers. "How'd you make it do that?"

"I pictured Drake attacking you."

That must've been the hardness I felt along his back when we were dancing. He was pretty riled about Drystan. "When did your tattoo change again?"

"While I've been gone."

Fate had said he was an enforcer. Is that what the sword was for? But what did Corvus equalize?

"What was Drake?" I asked in a hushed voice.

Ethan's dark gaze glittered with anger. "Pure evil."

I wanted to demand that he tell me everything, but Ethan's expression suddenly shuttered. I had a feeling if I pushed him for more now, he'd shut down. "When you get back, you'll tell me everything?" I prompted.

He nodded, his fingers flexing on my skin. "Everything I know."

I looked down at the dragon tattoo on his forearm and slid my fingers along the flames edging it. Various religious symbols graced each leaping flame that licked around the dragon. Ethan had gotten the tattoo as a way to help him overcome the evil images that pervaded his dreams, since the images were projections of negative energy he'd absorbed from people he came in contact with. I touched each symbol one at a time. "Is it still helping you?"

"It does some, but not as much as being with you does. He trailed his fingers down my cheek, his gaze following the path. "You settle me, Nara. More so now than ever."

I smiled and grasped his hand, kissing his palm. Now that we'd spent time together, Ethan would absorb my dreams. At least for a few days, he'd see my entire day along with his nightmares each night. I liked being the bright light spearing through the darkness of his dreams, slaying his night demons.

Patch began to make annoyed *tok, tok, tok* sounds. He was ready to leave. I shook my head at the temperamental bird and climbed off Ethan, then pulled a quarter out of my nightstand drawer to set it spinning.

Patch grabbed it, then hopped/flew to the window, where he squeezed underneath the small opening and took flight.

"I don't believe it." Ethan sounded dumbfounded.

"What?"

He held up his finger. "Just wait."

I crawled back into bed, and a few minutes later, Patch flew back to the window, landing on the ledge outside. When he pushed his beak through and dropped the quarter on the floor, then flew away, I looked at Ethan. "That's never happened before."

He ran both hands through his hair and laughed. "Yes, it has. I wondered where that raven with the white patch got all those quarters he brought to me every day. Sometimes he'd just drop them on my head."

"But..." I looked at the quarter on the carpet, then back to Ethan. "That's impossible for him to be in two places at once. He couldn't fly that many miles every day."

He shook his head. "I have no idea how he's doing it."

"Aww, he was making sure we stayed connected," I said, comforted by the idea.

"You've never left my thoughts." Ethan touched my chin, then glanced outside at the dawn getting ready to break the sky. "Happy birthday, Sunshine."

He remembered! The changes in Ethan might have tinged him with dark edges, but he was *good* inside and he was still *my Ethan*. I didn't care if he existed outside of my realm. My love for him swelled with the blush of the sun sliding sleepily over the horizon. The rays hadn't made their way to my room yet, but I already felt their warmth radiating through me.

I smiled at him and slid the sheet down. "About that promise you made before you left..." As I started to pull at the thin baby-pink ribbon bow that held my strapless bra together, Ethan grasped my hand.

"Ethan..." I let out a confused sigh.

When he shook his head, I thought my heart might break from disappointment. "I've been waiting for just the right light," he said and then slowly pulled one of the ribbon's tails.

He'd made me wait for the right light? I wanted to punch his arm and kiss him at the same time. As I stared into his deep blue gaze full of love, intensity, and absorbed focus on his task, my insides churned with excitement and anticipation. *This* was why I loved him so much. He surprised me in beautiful, heart-stopping ways.

Just as the first tendrils of sunlight reached my room, the bow unraveled. Ethan took his time tracing a finger past the hollow in my throat, then down the center of my chest. When his knuckles brushed the top curve of my cleavage, I sucked in a breath and goose bumps scattered across my skin.

Ethan's eyes snapped to mine, a dark, sexy smile tilting the left corner of his mouth. My heart stuttered as he grasped my waist, then slowly pulled me close. Kissing his jaw, I slid my hands along his shoulders and welcomed his warmth as everything inside me bloomed to life.

～

I'M FLOATING on a plane of blissful, skin-buzzing happiness. Ethan touches my hair. A curl lifts and he inhales, drawing in my smell. Then his fingers slowly slide along my jaw and down my throat. Everywhere he touches, I tingle.

It bothers me that I can't see him, so I pull my sleepy eyes open long enough to catch a glimpse of him. He's shirtless and still wearing his black dress pants as he sits in the chair by my bed. Those pants are coming off, even if I have to undress you myself. *As soon as the wicked thought flashes through my mind, another thought occurs.* Why is he sitting? *My eyes flutter and as my body starts to stir, he lays his hand on my shoulder and whispers, "Shhh." As lethargic warmth flows through me, he lightly trails his fingers across my arm.*

"I love you, Sunshine," he murmurs in that deep baritone that sends chills down my spine as he continues to trace along my belly and then down my leg to my toes.

I mumble it back. I think. At least, I thought the words, "I love you too."

He chuckles and I smile before I lose myself again in sleep's blissful arms.

～

HOUDINI'S wet nose nudged me awake from a deep sleep. "Houdini!" I fussed, pushing him away as I tugged the covers to cover me. *Wait?* "How'd you get in here?"

My eyes flew open and I turned to ask Ethan when he'd let

Houdini back in. Only a folded piece of paper lay on the pillow next to me. *I didn't get to say goodbye.* Sadness flickered through me as I slowly unfolded his note.

Nara,

I'll be back by Monday night. Don't take off the necklace I gave you. It will keep you safe. I might not know how I know that, but I just do. Please trust me on this. Stay safe, and...no more Internet searches, library research or interviewing people about ravens, swords or tattoos. I promise to share what little I know when I get back. I have more questions about your connection to ravens too.

Happy birthday, Sunshine! I hope you enjoy your present.

TTTWFO,

Ethan

Present? I glanced around my room and my attention snagged on a six-inch square box wrapped in comics news-paper and a manila envelope leaning against it on my nightstand.

As I moved to sit up, something sharp poked my hip and then tickled my right side. *What's in my covers?* I yelped and leaned back to quickly push away the covers. There'd better not be a spider under there.

When my gaze landed on the lone black raven feather tucked along my hip inside my lacy underwear, tears prickled my eyes. "Oh, Ethan..." I said, swallowing my emotion as I slid the feather out. "I love the way you make promises." He'd insisted that we wait to go all the way until he got back, saying, "It'll be too hard not seeing you everyday afterward, Nara. I never want to leave you again." I smiled and ran the soft vane along my fingers. This feather was softer than the feather I'd lost, but the quill felt stronger. *Where did he get it?*

I tucked the feather in my hair, then found my bra in the covers and quickly tied it back on.

The manila envelope read *Open First,* so I gently lifted the sealed back. My heart jerked when I started to pull it out and saw it was a sketch of me. Had he drawn me like he'd said he wanted to? Pausing, I took a breath and slid the drawing the rest of the way out.

It was a gorgeous drawing of me laughing as I leaned over to throw a piece of bread to geese in a pond. As always, Ethan had dated the drawing in the right-hand corner. He'd drawn it the same day we'd gone on our picnic.

I smiled as I set the drawing on my bed. When I pulled the box closer, I read the note taped to the top of the box.

For those special moments you never want to forget. When it comes to you, all I need is a pencil.

Ethan

Touched by his sweet note, I picked up the box and tore through the comics. When all the paper fell away, I smiled through the emotion clogging my throat. Ethan had bought me a camera.

Houdini started whining, reminding me that he needed to go outside. "Okay, boy," I said, setting the gifts and feather back on my nightstand.

I hurried over to my dresser, grabbing a sweatshirt and jeans from the drawers. Once I'd slipped on my pants, I pulled on my sweatshirt as I walked back across the room. My shoulder twinged with a slight burning sensation from my movements, so I tugged the neck of my sweatshirt over my shoulder and glanced in the full-length mirror as I started to pass it.

I froze, my fingers digging into the collar. Tearing the sweatshirt off, I dropped it on the floor and turned my back toward the glass.

"Holy mother!" I slid trembling fingers over my shoulder to touch the tip of the stark white feather, then moved closer to inspect the tattoo on the back of my left shoulder blade. The vane looked just like a normal white feather, but the end of the quill didn't resemble a traditional feather. It was smooth on one side, but the other side had a jagged, tooth-like edge.

As I ran my fingers along the bottom of the quill, trying to see the uneven edge better, I remembered when I'd felt a burning sensation along my shoulder blade. I was in the coach's closet with Ethan when he kissed me on the shoulder. The moment wasn't just a physical sensation, but it had felt emotional and connected. Special. I'd felt...special!

Had he done this to me? Anger flared, quickly followed by disbelief. I chewed my lip for a few seconds as I reasoned through it. Whatever it meant, Ethan would never mark me with a tattoo, magically or otherwise, without asking me first. I *had* felt something shift between us when he kissed me in that same spot.

Could it have happened like my lucid dream? Triggered subconsciously? Intentional or not, it came from Ethan, so why was my feather white and not black like his? *Like his!* Things clicked into place that hadn't made sense to me before now. As I shrugged back into my sweatshirt, I thought about how the guy from the library and Drake had called me names like tweet, fledgling, and little bird. Both had also been raring for a good fight. And after everything that'd happened, I was pretty sure Harper wasn't trying to save me from being hit by that swinging door at CVAS like she'd said. Ha, she'd probably kicked the wedge away, sending the door flying. I'd felt her warm breath on my neck, because she'd been looking down the back of my shirt. She was trying to see if I had a tattoo on my back. They all thought I was Corvus like Ethan!

I moved on shaky legs to close my window and saw snowflakes starting to float down. Instead of closing it, I opened it fully and stuck my hand out. Several flakes landed on my palm, melting the instant they hit my skin. *Who or what were Drake, Harper, and the guy from the library? And why did they want to fight Corvus? Did Ethan know what they were? Had he heard of the Order?*

Tension tightened my shoulders, and I fisted my hand around the melting snowflakes as I looked up to see a snowstorm had started. *God, I had a feather on my shoulder!* My mom would freak if I ended up with a sword tattoo across my entire back. It wasn't like she'd believe me if I said, "It looks real for a reason."

I took a calming breath and closed my eyes tight against the frigid wind, whispering, "Hurry home, Ethan. We have a lot to talk about."

Thank you for following Ethan and Nara's journey!

IF YOU FOUND *Lucid* an entertaining and enjoyable read, I hope you'll take the time to leave a review and share your thoughts with others.

The next book in the series, **DESTINY**, is now available. Check out the **Other Books by P.T. Michelle** page for store links to the rest of the books in the BRIGHTEST KIND OF DARKNESS series. To keep up to date on when the next P.T. Michelle book will release, join my free newsletter http://eepurl.com/jriS9

OTHER BOOKS BY P.T. MICHELLE

In the Shadows
(Contemporary Romance, 18+)
Mister Black (Book 1 - Talia & Sebastian, novella, Part 1)
Scarlett Red (Book 2 - Talia & Sebastian, novel, Part 2)
Blackest Red (Book 3 - Talia & Sebastian, novel Part 3)
Gold Shimmer (Book 4 - Cass & Calder, novel, Part 1)
Steel Rush (Book 5 - Cass & Calder, novel, Part 2)
Black Platinum (Book 6 - Talia & Sebastian, stand alone)
Reddest Black (Book 7 - Talia & Sebastian, stand alone)
Blood Rose (Book 8 - Cass & Calder, stand alone) - Coming
June 2018

Brightest Kind of Darkness Series
(YA/New Adult Paranormal Romance, 16+)
Ethan (Prequel)
Brightest Kind of Darkness (Book 1)
Lucid (Book 2)
Destiny (Book 3)
Desire (Book 4)
Awaken (Book 5)

Other works by P.T. Michelle writing as Patrice Michelle

Bad in Boots series
(Contemporary Romance, 18+)
Harm's Hunger
Ty's Temptation

Colt's Choice
Josh's Justice

**Kendrian Vampires series
(Paranormal Romance, 18+)**
A Taste for Passion
A Taste for Revenge
A Taste for Control

Stay up-to-date on her latest releases:

Join P.T's Newsletter:
http://bit.ly/11tqAQN

Visit P.T. :
Website: http://www.ptmichelle.com
Twitter: https://twitter.com/PT_Michelle
Facebook: https://www.facebook.com/PTMichelleAuthor
Instagram: http://instagram.com/p.t.michelle
Goodreads:
http://www.goodreads.com/author/show/4862274.P_T_Mich
elle

P.T. Michelle's Facebook Readers' Group:
https://www.facebook.com/groups/PTMichelleReadersGroup
/

ACKNOWLEDGEMENTS

To my critique partners, J.A. Templeton and Trisha Wolfe, this book wouldn't be as polished without you. Thank you for helping make it shine.

To my husband and children, who're always willing to give their opinions on covers and such. Thank you for your patience and support...and for not being afraid to pick up a spatula.

And to my fans, thank you for loving the BRIGHTEST KIND OF DARKNESS series so much and for spreading the love by posting reviews and telling your reader friends to check it out. I appreciate you so much!

ABOUT THE AUTHOR

P.T. Michelle is the *NEW YORK TIMES, USA TODAY,* and international bestselling author of the New Adult contemporary romance series IN THE SHADOWS, the YA/New Adult crossover series BRIGHTEST KIND OF DARKNESS, and the romance series: BAD IN BOOTS, KENDRIAN VAMPIRES and SCIONS (listed under Patrice Michelle). She keeps a spiral notepad with her at all times, even on her nightstand. When P.T. isn't writing, she can usually be found reading or taking pictures of landscapes, sunsets and anything beautiful or odd in nature.

To learn when the next P.T. Michelle book will release, join her free newsletter http://bit.ly/11tqAQN

Follow P.T. Michelle
www.ptmichelle.com

f facebook.com/PTMichelleAuthor

▼ twitter.com/PT_Michelle

⊙ instagram.com/p.t.michelle

▶ youtube.com/PTMichelleAuthor